# Grief in a Sunny Climate

# DIANE SHALET

# *Grief in a*
# *Sunny Climate*

ST. MARTIN'S PRESS · NEW YORK

SHA

Grateful acknowledgment is made for permission to reprint the following:

"Send in the Clowns" by Stephen Sondheim. © 1973–1978.
Revelation Music Publishing Corp. & Rilting Music Inc.
A Tommy Valando Publication.

*Magic, Faith and Healing* by Ari Kiev copyright © 1974 The Free Press

*Design by Judith A. Stagnitto*

Library of Congress Cataloging-in-Publication Data

Shalet, Diane.
    Grief in a sunny climate / Diane Shalet.
      p.  cm.
    "A Thomas Dunne book."
    ISBN 0-312-11054-5
    1. Widows—California—Fiction.  2. Women—California—Fiction.
  3. Grief—Fiction.  I. Title.
PS3569.H323507   1994
813'.54—dc20
                                     94-2045
                                       CIP

First Edition: June 1994
10 9 8 7 6 5 4 3 2 1

*For Cecil, Ellen, and my parents*

........................................................................

# A C K N O W L E D G M E N T S

*and gratitude to:*

Ruth Cavin, my editor, who guided me through this book with grace, humor, and expertise.

Sasha Goodman and David Andrew, agents and friends, whose energy and faith astound and sustain me.

The talented members and leaders (Phyllis Gebauer, Rebecca Newman, and Sid Stebel) of my Writers' Group. You made every Wednesday night the highlight of my week. Thank you for allowing me to risk and teaching me to rewrite.

Phyllis Gebauer, who between the Wednesdays, continued to provide inspiration and clarity with enduring and endearing patience.

Diane Hailey for her artful suggestions and steadfast support.

Kathy Jones for her valuable assistance, enthusiasm, and friendship.

John Leggett for his wisdom and wit.

The Santa Barbara Writers' Conference for their encouragement.

My friends, who insisted I go the distance.

*"Life does not cease to be funny
when people die, any more than
it ceases to be serious
when people laugh."*

—GEORGE BERNARD SHAW

# Grief in a Sunny Climate

# O N E

*I sat at Michael's desk,* buried under a mountain of third-class mail. October 17, 1983. The second plea from *Newsweek:* YOU HAVE NOT RENEWED. PLEASE TELL US WHY. I answered for him: Because I died. Then signed his name.

My left arm felt stiff. I picked at the edge of the Band-Aid on the inside of my elbow. "Drink orange juice," the nurse had instructed. When I got home, I plopped some frozen pulp into half a glass of vodka. Now, mixing it again with my index finger and rattling the cubes, I stared out the window.

Four and a half years ago, when Michael was operated on, I made a covenant with God: "If he lives, I'll pay back every drop." Nine units of blood. Mine wasn't compatible. After my first visit to I.C.U. (they allowed me to see Michael five minutes each hour), I went down to the blood bank. I thought I could reimburse them every fifty-five minutes, but you can only donate fifty-six days apart.

1

Michael was discharged from the hospital in less than three weeks. And I kept my end of the bargain. Sixteen months later, God and I were square.

The room was warm. I sipped my drink.

A year ago, Michael had another operation . . . ten units. He died last month. Today, I made my sixth payment. What happened, God? A deal's a deal.

People tell me to keep on living but they're not specific about the process. Someone must know.

I got up, holding my glass, and opened the window.

We live—I mean, *I* live on a narrow street. Across the way, an elderly couple, severe and lean as woodcuts, stand in front of the Gaffney's door and ring the bell. Gray suited, they set their briefcases down on the porch. The man takes out a copy of what looks like *The Watchtower* and holds it against his chest. Jehovah's Witnesses. I don't know much about them except they give you free copies and worship the doorbell. . . . Mr. Gaffney yelled that he was in the middle of a nap and slammed the door.

Now they're headed toward Mrs. Schneider's and Felix the Doberman is going to plaster himself against the window, howling and frothing from his fangs, and put them into cardiac arrest.

What should I do? They'll get to the end of the block, cross the street, make their way to our house and ring the bell. Michael always said, "I'll get it!" because whenever I open a door something happens. One day, I bought ten two-pound boxes of Girl Scout cookies, more brooms than we have rooms to sweep, and earthquake insurance. Michael had been out of town. When he came home, I told him. He sighed. "No is one sentence," he said. "You can do it."

With two fingers I pressed the place on my forehead where he had kissed me. I can re-create the pressure of his hand. I can imitate his mannerisms. Each morning, I splash Lilac Vegetal, plumping my cheeks, patting my face, briskly. And, if I concentrate at a point nine inches below the top of the doorsill, I can visualize his shape—before he became ill—standing there in gray slacks, herringbone jacket. I see the broad shoulders that he flexed backwards to remind himself of good posture, long legs, a slight paunch that pulsed as he spoke. His voice was deep, resonant, a slow rumbling purr. I can hear that.

But I can't see his face. Perhaps I have seen it in so many lights, so chameleon in its expression that I cannot commit myself to one image. Gruff sometimes, but as sweet as a toy bear. Women at parties would say, "I'm in love with your husband. He's an adorable man." "Why don't they tell *me*?" Michael grumbled.

The phone rang. I jumped and turned away from the widow—I mean window.

"Hello."

In a breathy, one-note monody, I heard: "Good morning. This is Ms. Gaviota of the Social Security Administration office. We understand your husband has passed away, Social Security number 067-56-7890, and on behalf of the department, I would like to extend condolences during this difficult time. I assume I am speaking to the widow of the recently deceased."

I said, "You can tell all that from one hello?"

It just popped out of my mouth, followed by a dithering laugh. I was light-headed from giving blood and drinking orange juice.

My caller tried to comfort me, mistaking my strange sounds for hysteria, which it probably was.

"Forgive me," I kept saying through my laughter.

That's the way I am, lately. Labile. Swinging from morbid contrition to inappropriate hilarity.

Someone gave me a book that defines the stages of grief, but I don't know where I put it. This morning I found a pair of socks in the refrigerator. Now, I tried to focus on what the woman was saying, but the universe and I are out of sync. Michael is gone and the sweet reasonableness of my life went with him.

It seemed I was entitled to a lump-sum death benefit of $255.

"Huh?" I said. "For what?"

"Burial."

"Thank you, but that's been taken care of."

"We're required to send it to you. All I need are the answers to a few missing pieces."

Is this like "Wheel of Fortune"? I didn't say that because it would have been rude and I felt sorry for her. She has a terrible job—talking to bitter widows all day long. Besides, she was the first one to give me something. Everyone else took it away . . . Visa,

American Express. Even Union Gas and Oil down the street. And they know me! My friend Seymour said if I quit saying I was a poet I could be reinstated under my own name. That was after I took money from Michael's and my joint account and put it in my name to establish credit.

"What was your husband's occupation?" the woman asked.

"Actor." And then I did what I always do. Listed chronologically all the parts in all the Broadway plays, movies, and TV shows Michael appeared in. She couldn't place him.

I could hear Michael say, "Did she ask you for my credits?"

"But I want to tell her about 'Star Trek.' Everyone saw you on that."

*Ding dong.*

"Excuse me, Ms. Gavotta—"

"Gaviota!"

"I'm sorry . . . Gaviota. Could you hold on? I have to answer the door."

"Great!" Michael groaned. "Thirty years in the theater and I'll be remembered as an android."

I started down the hall, rubbing my hand along the stucco wall. "You said that before—the day you came home from the set and walked into the kitchen holding your arm straight out and I almost fainted because there was a jagged flap of skin hanging from the side of your hand.

" 'It's latex,' you explained, peeling the flap from the wrist to the knuckles, exposing wires and coils like the inside of a transistor radio.

"The special effects man said you could wear it home to show me. In bed that night, we took turns watching your hand, propped on two pillows. If you rolled over in your sleep, you'd ruin it. At four in the morning you whispered, 'Want to make love to a one-armed android?'

" 'How do we do that?'

" 'Verrry carefully. . . . If we generate too much heat, I'll crisp out.'

"I snuggled closer. 'So maybe we shouldn't.'

4

" 'Last chance. Tomorrow, Captain Kirk zaps me with a phaser gun and I disintegrate.' "

*Ding dong.*

I ran down the last of the hall and looked through the peephole. Jehovah! I flexed my shoulders, summoning a transfer of Michael's strength, and cracked open the door.

"Good morning." The couple greeted me in unison and introduced themselves.

Simon. Wire-framed glasses on a mournful face.

Margaret. Hair, center parted, slicked back into a bun.

And *The Watchtower*, upright like a pitchfork against Simon's chest.

"May we speak with you about the Kingdom of God?" Simon said. He pronounced it "Gad."

"Certainly. Come in."

They nearly perished on the spot. Simon sucked in his breath at the invitation and Margaret, who had pronounced herself *"Ma*garet" through New-England-winter lips, held on to Simon's arm.

I decided that before they retired to spread the Word they'd had a dry goods store in Boothbay.

"Please sit down," I said, pointing to the living room. "I'm on the phone with the Social Security office. When your husband dies, they let you know."

Michael slapped his forehead. "God dammit!" and strode out of the room.

Simon stood next to the couch. "Aye-up. . . . We are ringing down the curtain of this living generation. Armageddon is upon us."

"Huh?"

Margaret sat, folded her hands in her lap, looked up at Simon and then at me: "For the living know that they shall die; but the dead know not anything, neither have they any more a reward; for the memory of them is forgotten."

I had been hoping for something—I don't know—more in the nature of a spirit lifter.

Excusing myself, I started back to the den, mumbling, "I had to. I had to"—looking for Michael, wanting to explain.

In the past month, I'd gone from Chen Yeng Buddhism to Conservative Judaism. Quaker to Shaker. Theosophist. Calvinist. One week of Wahaabism and a drive-in church with a televised Baptist. I had to pledge an allegiance because without a tenet I was damned and exiled and would never find solace. I also had the notion that to live in the present was to betray Michael. The hereafter was safer. And so I went, a suffering Agnostic, petitioning for entry. . . . That's why I asked Simon and Margaret in. How could I say now, Jehovah move over? I was running out of religions. . . . Seymour said, "God is man's way of explaining the inexplicable" and I'd be better off in the hot tub. Seymour lives in Palm Springs. He's an Atheist. He's been calling every week since Michael died and warning me that if I didn't come to visit him, I'd fly into space. "I'm concerned about you." . . . There is no me.

I walked over to the desk and picked up the receiver. Maybe when I get off the phone, Simon and Margaret will come up with something paradisiacal.

"I'm sorry to keep you waiting, Ms. Gaviota, I have witnesses in the living room."

"They won't be necessary. The two of us can complete the process. It will just take a few minutes."

Ms. Gaviota lied. There were about 138 historical questions dating back to the Boer War. I dumped a milk crate jammed with papers on the floor, searching for the answers . . . mothers and mothers of maiden names . . .

"Your occupation?" Ms. Gaviota asked.

"I'm a po— po—" What was I going to do? I'd forgotten the last thing I told someone I was. "I'm a polemicist," I improvised.

"That sounds like interesting work."

"It certainly is." I hooked the receiver on my shoulder, picked up the phone and tugged on the extra-long cord, trying to walk and talk at the same time. The cord sprang back into angry spirals. Michael used to say, "They can send a man to the moon but they can't invent a cord that doesn't knurl!"

I made it to the living room doorway, cupped the mouthpiece and shrugged apologetically to Simon and Margaret, who were reading their Bibles. "This is taking longer than I thought. Would you like some orange juice?" I took a step toward the kitchen and the phone line popped out of the jack, obliterating Ms. Gaviota, who had just asked, "Have you ever been married before?"

I ran to the kitchen, inviting Simon and Margaret to follow me, and plugged the phone into the outlet above the counter.

The vodka bottle was next to the mini Minute Maid. "Excuse me," I said, pointing to the Smirnoff, "are you like Seventh-Day Adventists? I mean, can you have screwdrivers?"

"Wine, occasionally." Margaret looked up at Simon.

"*Mag*aret!" he cautioned.

"Yes . . . well . . . but not when we're doing God's work." And her eyes counted the tiles on the kitchen floor.

"I understand," I said as the phone rang. "I have to because I just gave blood."

They surged backwards and Simon gave another "Aye-up."

"Hello, Ms. Gaviota. I'm sorry we were cut off."

Crooking the phone in my neck, I made some straight orange juice but they didn't even look at me when I handed it to them. Just sat at the kitchen table, staring at their Bibles. . . . It was my fault. I upset them . . . so dumb of me, offering screwdrivers early in the day!

"Have you ever been married before?" Ms. Gaviota repeated.

"Yes. When I was twenty."

More questions, including Bernie's mother's maiden name.

"Place of divorce?"

"Chihuahua, Mexico."

"Were either you or your husband residents of Mexico?"

She asked it as though I were Benedict Arnold, so I hurried to reassure her: "No! I went down by bus. . . . I didn't even have lunch!"

Silence. Then a series of tsk-tsk-tsks.

The silence was worse than the tsks. "Did I get that one wrong?"

"I'm sorry. A divorce granted in a jurisdiction in which neither party is legally domiciled is invalid."

"But—but that's not possible! Bernie was an attorney. He sent all his clients there! . . . Hold on. Could you hold on?"

I dropped the phone and ran back to the den. Michael was

lying on the couch, a newspaper tented over his face. I could tell he was furious because the crease of the paper lifted and fell as he blew into it. . . . Michael was the one who wanted to get married. I'd already tried it and would have been happy just living together.

"Well, you got your wish," he muttered.

"I'm so sorry."

On my hands and knees, I searched for the divorce papers. "I'll take care of it. I'll fix it." . . . How could Bernie have done that to me? . . . That turkey! . . . There it was! Crumbling gold seal. Faded purple ribbon. . . . Racing back to the kitchen, I waved the document in front of the Witnesses and my sweating face.

"Ms. Gaviota, listen to this: *Poder Judicial del Estado de Chihuahua. Certificada de Sentencia de Divorcio.*"

I cupped the mouthpiece and sputtered to Simon and Margaret: "You'd think with a name like Gaviota, she'd speak Spanish!"

I kept reading and translating, searching for a reference to residency.

But she kept saying it wasn't valid.

"Jorge Cisneros put a stamp on it! If it wasn't legal, why would he sign his name?"

I would have lost it if Simon hadn't made a smoothing-the-waters gesture with his hands.

"It has to be valid!" I tried to lower my voice. "Both of us got married again!"

"Perhaps you should notify him?"

"Who? Bernie? I can't. He's dead!"

"Please hold on." And Montovani played "Dancing in the Dark."

"Oh my God!" I collapsed in the chair at the kitchen table between Simon and Margaret.

Margaret's hand, veined as a maple leaf, touched mine. It was comforting . . . like a grandma saying: Now don't you worry.

"May we know what religion your husband was?" she asked.

"Which one?"

Simon indicated to Margaret that he would take over. "Both of them."

"Jewish," I said.

They sighed. I know that sigh. I've heard that sigh before. It precedes the sentence Jesus was Jewish. Then, four hours later, you're eating a wafer or facing Mecca.

There was hope for me. I'm half Jewish. They smiled for the first time. It would only take two hours. When I told them my knowledge of the Bible was desultory but, as a poet, I found it to be a rich source of metaphor, the smiles vanished.

Ms. Gaviota came back on the line: "Well, I've talked to my supervisor. . . ." She sounded cheerier.

The ruling stood. My Chihuahua divorce was not valid, but death is. Therefore, the legality of the divorce is a moot point, since the record would show that I was lawfully married to Michael from the date of Bernie's death. . . .

"About six years ago," I said.

She offered her condolences but I told her it wasn't necessary. I had heard Bernie died quietly in his sleep. He was twenty-four years older than I was.

Ms. Gaviota also informed me that when I'm sixty-five, I can collect Michael's Social Security, but not Bernie's because we had been married less than nine months. And now that the preliminary phone interview was concluded, as soon as I brought in the necessary documentation, they would expedite my claim.

On either side of me, Bibles. Pillars of strength in small print. Maybe, that's why I was able to say, "Ms. Gaviota, did I call you? Did I ask for two hundred and fifty-five dollars?"

She explained that my lawyer had notified the office and that the department had instituted a new system of initiating calls to make it easier on the bereaved.

I took a deep breath. "Ms. Gaviota. Put me down for two husbands. Go ahead. I don't want anything moot, here. . . . But Bernie doesn't count. I haven't thought of him for twenty-two years, until you brought him up. . . . You see, if I take your money, I'm declaring Michael and I were married only six years and I'll have . . . fewer memories. We were married for twelve and that wasn't enough. Not when you love someone. . . . And another thing. If you wanted to make it easier on me, you should have waited until I was ready to come down to your office, in person, and stand on line for fifteen hours, like I'm supposed to. This has not been helpful."

I hung up the phone very slowly, because I knew when it hit the cradle, I would sob. And I buried my head between flattened arms, reaching towards Margaret's hands. I wanted her to touch me, praise me. But Simon placed a small leatherette book at my fingertips. *You Can Live Forever in Paradise on Earth.*

"Our Bible study meets Wednesday night," he said.

And Margaret added, "You see, my dear, we feel you are a spiritual babe who has come into our midst."

I picked up my orange juice and held it in two hands, taking a sip, and this little girl's voice came out of me: "I want to go to heaven. Michael's there."

But Simon told me there was room for only 144,000 people.

"I don't believe it! Where does it say that?"

The Bible pages crackled like candy wrappers and Simon pointed. There it was. Revelation. Chapter 14.

Margaret reached for my hand. I was shaking, but I didn't want her to touch me. Not after that. . . . Why weren't they leaving so I could lie down?

Because . . . because they were telling me

> *"My dear, you have committed a*
> *transgression . . .*

"A transgression?"

> *according to the Bible."*

Genesis, Exodus were thumbed and rustled, then snapped open at Leviticus:

> *"Chapter seventeen, verse ten," they*
> *read in unison: "And whatsoever*
> *man there be of the strangers that*
> *sojourn among you, that eateth any*
> *manner of blood . . .*

And I remembered. Of course! Jehovah's Witnesses . . . They don't believe in transfusions.

> *I will even set my face against that*
> *soul . . .*

"Why is that a sin?" I showed them my Band-Aid. "He would have died without it! I wouldn't have had him for four and a half more years!"

*that eateth blood . . .*

I ripped off the pink strip, poking at my vein:

*and will cut him off from my people."*

"Is *giving* blood a sin, too?"

*They nodded. Incontestable.*
*Apparently, it doesn't matter which*
*way it's going.*

"I would have drained every part of me to keep him alive!"

*They didn't answer. Just closed their*
*books and Margaret folded her hands*
*on top of the Bible.*

Slowly, I pushed *Paradise on Earth* toward Simon, stood up, moved to the counter and blew my nose in a paper towel. "I want to thank you for coming. . . . I don't think I'm a good customer for your religion. Or anyone else's."

"Hallelujah!" Michael hollered from the den.

They asked if they could leave the literature but I handed it back, then walked them to the door. Nothing was said after that. It was clear to the three of us. And corroborated by civil and religious authority. I was a bigamist and a bloodletter and could never enter the Kingdom of Heaven.

I didn't lie down. I called Seymour—told him everything, then announced that I was no longer a spiritual seeker.

"Good," he said. "Now you're ready for Palm Springs."

## T W O

**D**r. *Seymour Kahn opened* the door.

"Hi, Babe." He grinned and gave me an exuberant hug. "Let me look at you." As he held me at arm's length, his hands brushed the outsides of my breasts. It happened fast. But it happened.

Dr. Seymour Kahn, shrink to the stars, retired seven years ago and lives in Palm Springs. He will be sixty-seven on his Capricorn birthday. You never have to ask Seymour "What's your sign?" He's knobby, five feet seven inches tall, gray spade beard and (his hands were braced again on my breasts) goatish.

I disengaged myself. "Seymour, you have satyriasis."

He thought I said psoriasis. He's also hard of hearing.

"Since you've seen me"—he laughed, pointing to the offender and raising his voice in mock exaggeration—"I'M HARD OF HEARING IN ONE EAR."

He took my small suitcase and I followed him down the cool hall. "How're you doing?" he asked.

"Fine," I lied.

Turning his head as he walked, he nodded several times, as though he understood the hurt behind my terse response.

"Make yourself at home. Your room faces the pool," he said, putting my suitcase on the bed and drawing back the drapes like a bellhop. He rolled open the sliding glass door, tugged at the erratic screen lurching on a stubborn track . . . "Son of a bitch!" . . . stepped over the aluminum rails onto the patio, then steered and banged the door closed from the outside.

"We can talk through the screen while you're unpacking. I got to lie down. I'm exhausted from opening doors."

He stretched out on a green-webbed lounge chair. "Don't let the tennis shorts fool you. I spend my time in inactive retirement. Lizarding it out. The only exercise I get is snatching at lady-flies."

His reptilian self-portrait was incongruous with his goatlike appearance, but as he reached for his sunglasses, I noticed his eyes. Narrowed by the push of swollen pockets underneath and the downward pressure of puffy lids, they lay idle. Waiting.

I opened the small top drawer of a white dresser. Serving as a liner, cut up and pasted to the bottom—a decoupage of *Playboy* crotches.

Backing up to my suitcase, I quickly turned around and unzipped it. I covered the ladies with my panties and watched my face in the mirror as a blush traveled my neck, then faded out at my ears, surprised that I could react to anything but my own knotted grief.

The day after Michael died, Seymour called me from Palm Springs. He had read the obituary in the morning paper.

"I want you to know how concerned I am about you. Libby and I think it would be good for you to spend some time here. It might make you feel better."

In drawer two, I found what drawer one was waiting for and folded my shorts and socks over it, then hung up the rest of my clothes in a regular closet.

"Libby calls it the Harem Room," Seymour offered.

Thematically consistent, I thought, noting the Indian cloth stapled to the walls, tasseled hangings, pictures of Seymour in caftans, togas, jellabas and a grass skirt—mementos from trips to India, Greece, Morocco, and Fiji. The rest of the house is normal, southwestern sandscape colors, contemporary furnishings, abstract paintings from Seymour's Beverly Hills office with inspirational sayings underneath and a nine-foot Polynesian fertility god in the living room with jeweled eyes and an enormous erection. A gift from a grateful patient.

A sigh shivered in my throat. What was I doing here?

Seymour and Libby (the woman he's lived with for twelve years) have a primary relationship. Libby has a meaningful secondary relationship with Claire when Claire is not seeing Marge, a gynecologist, who is her primary. Simply put, Seymour has Libby, Libby has Claire, Claire has Dr. Marge but basically—Seymour has Seymour.

I just came for the weekend.

When Libby isn't in P.S. (Palm Springs), she's with Claire in N.V. (Napa Valley)—Seymour abbreviates everything because he likes to save energy. They have a vineyard and are building a house. Seymour thought it would be a good idea because Libby likes to do that sort of thing—decorate, pick grapes—and Seymour just likes to stay horizontal, with either a book or a lady. So, when Seymour retired and needed a tax shelter, he introduced Claire (who was in therapy with Seymour) to Libby. They hit it off immediately and he bought them a winery, which is where they are now and why I got to see Seymour again after all these years.

I had finished unpacking, joined him outside and lit a cigarette.

"Why did you retire, Seymour?"

"Everybody's so fucked up. I got tired."

"Don't you miss helping people?"

"Not when they're depressed. I tell you, therapy could be done one weekend a year. I might start inviting patients from Fri to Sun, charge them five thou and if they listened to me they'd get it together. I'd guarantee it. But they'd have to do exactly what I said. . . . You want to go in the hot tub?"

"Are you going to charge me?"

"Don't be silly . . . that's a nice dress. Aren't you hot in it?"

"It's not a hot dress."

"Yes, it is. . . ." And Seymour slipped from his shorts and padded to the hot tub.

I plunged into my handbag, found a cigarette and put it to my mouth, crushing the one that was already there.

"Seymour's nuts!" I remembered Michael laughing when he said it and then added, "But he's sane about one thing. He told you to marry me."

Leaning his head against the edge of the tub, Seymour sighed. The jet streams whooshed around him, his gray beard bobbing on top of the bubbles. "Come sit on the deck and talk to me in my good ear."

I never know what to say to a naked psychologist.

He extended his wet hand upward, toward a fruit tree that formed a bower over the Jacuzzi, reached for a low branch and snapped off a swollen orange, then released the catapult. The fruit in the palm of his hand, he urged me closer. I tossed the cigarettes in an ashtray and sat on the wooden slats of the platform. He peeled the orange—no, tangerine!—and handed me a section. It was tangy sweet and the warm juice spilled over my lower lip. He smiled. I chewed as he hummed "Tangerine," preparing each segment for me, stringing the membranes, cupping the rind as I deposited the pits.

Thirteen years ago, Michael was playing a psychiatrist in a Movie of the Week and the leading actress was having a breakdown—on and off camera. So, Seymour, her therapist, would come to the studio at seven A.M. She lay on the couch, in the set of the analyst's office, sobbing, which was perfect for the part, except that she had rummaged in her attic of pain to the point of pathology and become so hysterical that she couldn't remember her lines. Seymour would sit in the brown leather chair behind her head, soothing her, "It's only a movie, darlin'," and as the gulps subsided, Michael coached her until she was able to *act* depressed.

But her nervous disorder became acute and she had to have a brain operation (on camera), which was how I got to meet Michael. I played a nurse—well, sort of a surgery stewardess. I was in the Operating Room and doctors whapped instruments into my hand.

Then I came out of O.R. and said to Dr. Jameson (Michael), "She's been moved to Recovery."

Michael said I was very good in the part. I don't know how he could tell. I wore a green mask. And I wasn't an actress. Someone I knew from New York was a TV production manager and when I moved to California he helped me get into Screen Extras Guild, which was perfect for me because I could never act alone. But that day, in an earlier crowd scene, the director spotted me and gave me a line.

I swallowed the last piece of tangerine.

"All gone," Seymour crooned as though he were talking to a child, indicating the peels and pits in his hand, placing them on the deck. . . . "Are you okay, Babe?"

"I was thinking of the time I met Michael—and you. . . . He invited me to a party at your house, when you were living in Beverly Hills. Remember? . . . I'll never forget. You answered the door, stared at both of us, raised your arms like the Oracle of Delphi and said, 'You two belong together!' . . . I was so embarrassed. It was our first date."

"Think of how much time I saved you." Seymour lifted a tear from my cheek with a dripping finger. "Michael was a loving, sweet man. I'll miss him. I should have made him a partner. He helped that actress more than I did. . . . Taught her to do a—what do you call it—an emotional memory that wouldn't make her bananas."

I trembled and hugged myself. I know about emotional memory, triggered by the tyranny of the senses. . . . "I walk through the house. If I touch an object from a place we've been, it feels as though I've had a concussion. . . . And cinnamon, when I open the kitchen cupboard, engulfs me. . . . I thought everything would be gray when he died, but driving here, the sun in the rearview mirror was siren red, and the windmills, you know, just outside of Beaumont—those generators, pieces of them floated up, zinc white against a cobalt sky. The world keeps banging its colors against me." . . . I told him that now, voices have a sharp, cutting edge, like cartoon characters. . . . Sometimes a face cancels out and I see only the slash of a lipstick smile. The blade of a butcher knife fades. I focus on the black handle.

Odd things meet in full light and hang, in deliberate discord, suspended as in a Miró painting.

Seymour placed his damp hand on mine. "You're in shock, Babe. That's why you feel disoriented."

"I have to cry . . . to go through grief."

Lifting himself out of the tub (I was about to turn my head), he quickly reached for a velour towel, and in deference to me, wrapped it around his waist, then invited me into his open arms. Gently, he rubbed my back. And I sobbed. Broken. Splintered. My head against his chest. . . . And kept on sobbing until I felt him shiver. I apologized but he told me to go ahead, as long as I needed, he was wrinkled anyway.

Grateful, but wet from his embrace, I snuffed back the last of my tears.

He took a corner of his towel and wiped the front of my dress. "How about my taking you out to dinner?"

I was afraid the towel was going to fall. "Seymour? Promise me you'll keep your shorts on?"

"I promise. Unless we have trouble getting a waiter."


*We sat in overstuffed Mexican* chairs. He dipped a chip in fiery salsa, then put the whole thing in his mouth without wincing.

"Have one," he urged, leaning toward me with the drippy hot stuff.

I shook my head, then reached for a taco, edged it into the sauce and bit down. I always suffer and I always do it. Flagging my tongue as the waiter set down our margaritas, I grabbed for mine but was unable to find any liquid in the congealed floe. Seymour offered me his lemony, uniced drink. I gulped down half of it as he reminded me again that I should not have ordered frozen strawberry.

"When was your last margarita?" His palm was on my thigh.

"When was yours?" I placed his hand back on the table.

"See, you're feeling better. You're making bad jokes."

The funny thing was that as soon as he said it, I believed him.

"This is what you should do . . ." he began his lecture, resting his head against the fake leather banquette. "Don't take Michael's pension from Screen Actors Guild in a lump sum. Interest rates are low now. Opt for monthly payments. They'll go up periodically . . . you're going to have a long life."

I told him that in the last television show Michael had done, he'd died. He played a funny gangster. After he was shot, a detective came and drew a chalk mark around his body.

"I saw him on that show with Carroll O'Connor." Seymour was still resting his head. "He was terrific. . . . Call AFTRA. I think when you work and die within the same calendar year, you're entitled to a death benefit."

He completed the organization of my finances on a cocktail napkin, borrowing a pen from the waiter, then took my napkin from under my glass and said as he wrote, "Here are five books I want you to read."

*The Human Encounter With Death*
*The Egyptian Heaven and Hell*
*Death, the Final Stage of Growth*
*Dying and Mystical Consciousness*
*Attitudes Toward Death and Dying*
*Among the Aymara Indians of Bolivia*

I lifted the napkin. "Those last two lines—is that one book or two?"

"And three weeks from now we'll go up to N.V. . . . visit Libby and Claire."

I was still staring at the list, poking the straw into the pink slush of the slowly melting margarita.

"One more thing," he said.

"What?" Finally, I was able to take a sip.

"You should have an affair."

Icy particles slugged up the straw. "What?"

"AN AFFAIR! I thought I was the one who was hard of hearing."

"With who?"

"With me."

My teeth froze. "What?"

"There you go again! AN AFFAIR! It's the best thing for grief."

"Seymour! I was your patient!"

"Once. You came to see me once. And I told you to marry Michael. I didn't even charge you." He flipped his eyebrows like Groucho Marx, twirled and tapped an imaginary cigar near his mouth, then snapped, "Just say the secret word!"

It was such a funny imitation that I thought I'd rupture myself laughing. And he joined me. I used to laugh that way with Michael, each new whoop sending the other off again, until we were ragged and limp, breathlessly begging for mercy.

Seymour handed me his handkerchief and I wiped my eyes. Thirteen years ago, I'd gone through a half box of his Kleenex. I had made that appointment with him because I was afraid to get married. . . . What if, after eight months, Michael changed his mind, like Bernie? . . . Maybe I was an imposter. Maybe I wasn't smart. Maybe— Seymour told me to quit that thinking. He assured me I was genuine. I was bright. I didn't need therapy. I was just basically baffled and would probably go through life that way, but not to worry, Michael loved me.

"Anyway," Seymour said as I gave him back the handkerchief, "what do you want with an old fart like me?"

"Oh, Seymour!" I reached across the table and stroked his fingers. "Don't say that. . . . It's just . . . I mean . . . Well, Libby. What about Libby?"

"Libby thinks it's a terrific idea. She's fond of you."

"Well . . . er. Don't we have to ask Claire and Dr. Marge?" When I'm nervous like that I play this game. A kind of sexual badminton. Pop a line. Pop back a feathered response.

"You don't have to decide right now." Seymour opened the menu.

He knew what I was doing.

"What do you say to chimichangas?" he asked.

He also knew what he was doing.

★ ★ ★

19

***Breakfast is ready.*** You've been in there an hour," Seymour called cheerily, punctuating the hour with a double rap on the bathroom door.

I'd taken a shower and was sitting on the edge of the tub wrapped in a towel, repeating his definition of grief: "A battering ram of self-punishment."

"I'll be right out. I'm going to take a shower." I reached over and turned on the faucets, then sat on the closed lid of the toilet seat. I wanted to go over what happened last night.

The light from the hall framing him, Seymour stood in the doorway of my bedroom, tying his robe. I'd been crying in my sleep. He moved toward the side of the bed, knelt down and my arms went around his neck. He patted my back, quieting the convulsive sounds . . . promising that tomorrow he'd take me downtown to see the tourists, buy me a hot fudge sundae. He invited me into his bed. It was king-size and he would hold me. I told him I couldn't handle that. He did his Groucho imitation again. "You don't have to handle anything—just sleep!"

He got up, rubbing his knees, and said he would put on his pajamas and I was welcome to join him under his covers anytime.

I watched him leave the room. If I could be that child again. If only I could be held, become that compressed, I could reach the vanishing point and be out of pain.

Hugging my pillow, I padded across the hall, then climbed into his bed and curled against him; the pillow, a cushion between my head and his shoulder . . . sandalwood cologne . . . the softness of his beard.

In the dark. Only a slice of moonlight between the blinds. His hand circled my stomach. I tugged at the hem of my creeping cotton nightie. He murmured that I looked skinny and he wanted to check if I'd been eating . . . round and round my stomach until there was a collar of fabric at my hips. His fingers traveled the outside of my thigh toward the center of my legs. I shivered and placed my hand on his, ashamed that I was wet and aching. "I can't. I can't."

Seymour sighed, smoothed down my nightie and folded his hands on top of the sheet. "Well, I guess I'll just catch me a line of Z's."

"What's Z's?" I knew what it meant but I wanted him to stay awake. Talk to me.

"Z Z Z Z's—like sleeping in comic books." And he rolled over and burrowed in his pillow, zeeing on contact.

I listened to the purr of his breathing and whispered to the ceiling, "Don't send me away."

One night, my hand was on Michael's stomach. Six months before he died, his abdomen had become distended and there were painful nodules from his waist to his groin. I was trying to soothe him. He shuddered, turned on his side and asked me to leave him alone. "I cannot make love to you, ever again," he wept.

"It doesn't matter to me!" I cried.

He slammed his fist against the bed frame. "Don't lie to me!"

I pleaded with him. "I just want to be near you. Don't send me away!"

So shattering was the withdrawal of my comfort, I could not hear *his* anguish. Two weeks later, he said I could touch him.

Seymour knocked. I jumped. "I'm not scrambling eggs twice," he hollered.

I turned off the faucets. At the mirror, I cleared my steamy reflection with a wipe of my hand and combed my hair. But the cloudy image returned. It would not go away unless I opened the door. I put on a soft summer robe and headed for the kitchen.

Seymour stood facing me, bare legs and chest, with a half apron tied around his waist. "Sleep well, darlin'?"

He turned to the stove. The tails of the apron flapped below the crack of his naked buns.

"Seymour!"

"I always dress for breakfast."

He had set the table. Place mats and napkins matched the design on his apron. A barnyard scene. Chickens, ducks and geese ran amok while a farmer with a fierce expression chased them with a pitchfork. In the center of the table: a Chinese porcelain jar, its lid curving like a wilted stem.

He brought two red candles to the table, placed them on each side of the jar, then served me perfectly scrambled eggs and hot rolls.

He kept refilling my coffee cup and apologized because he was out of orange juice.

He bustled around the kitchen like a short hermaphrodite.

"This is really good, Seymour."

He sat down and read the morning paper. I finished my eggs and started to clear the table.

He looked up. "Where are you going?"

"I'll do the dishes."

"Sit down. Just stay there."

I was at the sink. "That's all right. I'll do them."

He punched the newspaper. "I said, sit down! Stop being locked into a traditional role."

"I just wanted to help," I yelped.

"I don't want anyone doing my dishes—I'm a very controlling person!"

It was our first fight. Not really a fight. He told me what was wrong with me and I begged understanding from a naked man wearing an apron.

"Come on, don't cry. . . . You want to see Rhonda?"

Every time I cried he tried to distract me. Now I was a five-year-old whose tears could be assuaged by a new toy or adventure.

"Who's Rhonda?"

"Rhonda. You remember Rhonda. The patient of mine who died?"

"What about her?"

Winding his voice like Ed McMahon introducing Johnny Carson, he lifted the lid of the Chinese jar.

"Heeeeeere's Rhonda!"

He put his index finger in the jar. Ash and a sliver of bone shard adhered as he withdrew it. Pointing it in the air, he wiggled and jiggled it, forties' style, truckin' and chanting, then whirled himself in a circle, singing:

"DEM BONES, DEM BONES, DEM DRIED BONES . . .
NOW HEAR DE WORD O' DE LORD!"

His apron flew up. So did my breakfast.

The man is certifiable. I retched over the toilet seat.

"You got to have a sense of humor about death." He stood at the door.

He was always standing at the door. This time he was handing me a glass of water.

"Seymour, I'm going to throw up again."

"No, you're not."

He was right. I didn't. The man controlled my involuntary actions.

*It was noon, Saturday.* I lay on my back staring at the ceiling. I'd been here less than twenty-four hours, eaten my first cucamanga—what was that thing on my plate last night? . . . Chichimanga? No. Chimichanga. Almost had an affair. Sat down to breakfast with an urn as a centerpiece and threw up. . . . What's next?

The silver specks on the stucco ceiling winked back.

"Have you ever smoked dope?"

He stood in the doorway.

"I think I should go home, Seymour."

"You just got here. Besides, Libby and Claire grew some good grass last summer. It'll settle your stomach."

"The one and only time I had marijuana, I ate everything that wasn't nailed down."

"Forget that. C'mon to my house . . ." And he beckoned me down the hall to his room.

He patted the empty space next to him on the king-size bed.

"Before you get in, flip the stereo on. No. Keep that station. The Chicago Symphony of the Air should be coming on."

Simultaneously, the announcer's voice came through the speakers: "Welcome to Symphony Hall in Chicago . . ."

Seymour had not looked at his watch. He was on his own clock radio.

He lit a miniature clay pipe and passed it to me. Surrounding the bowl were raised carvings of bearded faces. For Tom Thumb it would have been a Meerschaum.

"Take a deep breath, hold it, then swallow."

I gagged.

"You're an ace cigarette smoker, how come you can't do that? Come on, Babe, try again."

"I can't"—(through a paroxysm of coughing)—"It's burning."

"You've never smoked pot and you're how old?"

"Thirty-eight," I lied.

"You're forty-two. Why do you lie?"

"I thought I'd be too old for you."

"You're a good kid but you've seen too many Doris Day movies."

"I can't help it. Aside from smoking, I'm a healthy romantic."

The phone rang. He picked it up.

"Hi, honey, how're you doing?"

I wondered who he was calling honey. I was always darlin' or Babe.

"Nothing much. . . . No . . . she's lying right here next to me."

He petted my thigh.

"No, not yet. Well, I gave her breakfast and she threw up. I'll take her for a walk later."

He was either talking about a puppy or me.

And telling it to Libby, I realized. I wrapped my robe tighter around me, feeling she could see me through the phone.

The tone of his voice changed. He seemed agitated.

"Don't ask me to do that. . . . I told you why. . . . Because we've never gotten along. . . ."

Who could he be talking about?

"You know they hate me. Every time I pass one of them, they shrivel."

He covered the mouthpiece and turned to me.

"Babe, will you water the plants in the living room?"

I nodded, dumbly.

Relieved, he continued. "Don't worry. She'll water them."

He gave my thigh a thank-you pat, then said to Libby: "Well, have a good time. I will too. . . . Oh . . . and tell Claire—that's great grass. . . . Bye, honey."

He hung up. "Where were we? . . . Oh yeah. . . . Romantic love."

And to prove that he was still connected to our conversation, he placed his right hand on his breast, gazed heavenward (arching his back), his mouth pouting like a sad swain, and fainted backwards from his sitting position on the bed.

"Ah yes," he said like W. C. Fields. "Twelfth-century romantic love . . . aaaah yes . . . I was around when it was invented. I wasn't crazy about it then."

It wasn't as funny as Groucho, but I laughed.

Spent from his performance, he reached for the pipe, following the slow exhalation of smoke with a worldly sigh.

A prelude to his philosophical dissertation.

"Grief is a Western trip."

I waited, not knowing whether to put on my "Please continue" expression or an "Is that all there is?" look.

With the patient sufferance of a fifth grade teacher he began to elaborate.

"Grief is a Western trip," he repeated, savoring his quintessential phrase—the distillation of all his thinking. "In other cultures, death is celebrated. Certain tribes—it's on the cocktail napkin—feel death is a great achievement. That's what all that dancin' is about. . . . I can't wait to die. That's why I like to come a lot. The French call it Le Petit Mort—The Little Death. Orgasm is the closest thing to dying."

"Maybe I should see a psychiatrist."

I didn't say it to hurt his feelings. I felt rooted. Stupid. Slugged with the pain of Michael's death.

"I'll tell you what you should do. Throw out everything you and Mike had together. Furniture, paintings, objects, photographs. . . . Don't keep anything."

"You kept Rhonda."

"That's different," he said. "I didn't keep her stuff. . . . Look, I'll make a deal with you. Spend the next six months with me. Give me your grief and I'll give you a pain-free guarantee."

In my house, *The Widow's Alphabetical Workbook* is on the desk. I skipped *Managing Money* and went on to *Masturbation*. The phone rings and the answering machine announces condolences. I stare at it, a scotch in my hand. My voice thick from lack of use. My vision blurs. Absence is ruthless.

"And my tears?" I ask. "What will I do with my tears?"

"I take them." He pointed to the pouches under his eyes. "I collect them."

"Did you ever lose anyone you loved?"

"My brother committed suicide. . . . I had a girlfriend—died in a car crash. I was twenty."

"Did you cry, mourn, grieve?"

"No. Never."

And he waved his hand in front of his face, dismissing the smoke and the discussion.

The Palm Springs sun slanted through the glass doors. Tomorrow is Sunday. I'll be on the freeway. A hundred and twenty miles of concrete.

His pipe went out. He reached for the matches, tearing off two. They fired together in a sudden spurt.

"You'll see," Michael once said. "Someone will love you as much as I do."

Seymour took a puff of his relit pipe, put it aside and turned to me. "All this talk about death is making me hot."

I unknotted the belt of my seersucker robe and pulled it through the loops.

The music stopped, followed by applause and the announcer's voice, "Ladies and gentlemen, you have just heard live from Symphony Hall in Chicago a performance of *The Mephisto Waltz*."

# T H R E E

*Seymour, there is something unreal* about our association. On Sundays . . . and it's a good thing I visit you only alternate week- ends . . . but when I do . . . even though I've had a very nice time these past few months—"

I could hear Seymour's whistling breath in my ear, waiting for me to get on with it, but I've always found it difficult to be decisive and sensitive at the same time. Especially on the phone.

"Anyway, Seymour. What it comes down to is this, every time I leave Palm Springs, I start to cry as soon as I hit Riverside."

Seymour sighed. "So take the Pomona Freeway. You'll by- pass it."

"I can't bypass myself. . . . I'm going to New York—for two weeks. I have to find out who I am."

"In Manhattan? In March? Don't kid me. You're going there to perfect the past."

"No, I'm not!"

My au revoir was definitive but tearful. I didn't tell him New York was Roberta's idea because I felt guilty changing mentors in mid grief.

Roberta is a widow, a year wiser than me. Her husband, Arthur, was Michael's East Coast agent. I'd never met Roberta. When Michael died, she telephoned. We talked long into the night. And after that, at least once a week.

Arthur always arrived in L.A. alone, but each time Michael and I had dinner with him, he was accompanied by a new discovery (all of them gorgeous) he had just signed.

"I think I'm his only male client," Michael would whisper as Arthur and his date entered the restaurant.

"Certainly explains why I never met Roberta," I'd buzz back, thinking how sad it was for her.

When Roberta and I became phone friends, she admitted that she used to be sad. "But not anymore!" Three months after Arthur died, she had a face-lift, a condo and a job. "I shop," Roberta announced, ". . . for actresses on a soap opera. I'm a liaison between 'One Life to Live' and Saks." She sounded like a model widow. "You've got to get back in the world."

"I visit Seymour," I said.

"Seymour is not in the world. He isn't married and Libby knows all about you two. Unless an affair is surreptitious, it's weird."

I never thought of it that way. Roberta warned me that widows go through a crazy lady period, but said she'd show me how to avoid it when I got to New York.

So, after I spoke to Seymour, I called the playwright because Roberta said I should reconnect with old friends.

Twenty-one years ago (Bernie and I were divorced), I met Patrick Sheehy at the opening night of his Off-Broadway play, a drama about an emotionally repressed Irish family (his) disguised as "the Shanahans." The audience was indifferent. But last year he won an Oscar for an original screenplay. It had the same family, only they were in orbit and their last name was Org. Sheehy was interviewed in *People* magazine. If I hadn't gone to the dentist that week I'd never have seen the article. Married and divorced twice, he never moved from his Greenwich Village apartment.

Chelsea 3-0758. Of course, I remember it. A time when a phone number had character . . . a time we embraced and he confided he was inaccessible. "However," he murmured, "you are the only woman who has touched my soul's dark night." Actually, it was three nights. I never heard from him again.

I punched the phone buttons. I was sweating. It was ringing. Maybe I should have asked Roberta? No. After all, once you've touched someone . . .

"Hello." A man's voice.

"Uh. Yes. Hello. . . . Is this Patrick Sheehy?"

"Yes."

I had planned the hello and my dialogue in his arms at the baggage claim at Kennedy Airport—but nothing in between. "Yes . . . well . . . not too long ago, twenty, twenty-one years or so—we were . . . we were friendly and well my husband died and I'll be in New York Tuesday and thought you'd be interested in uh in uh—"

"Who is this?"

A loonlike laugh warbled in my throat. "How silly! . . . My friend Seymour calls me Babe, so I guess my name went out of my mind."

He kept hooting "Who?" even after I'd told him who. Then I reeled out reminiscences and descriptions: "Five-four? Do you still have your brick fireplace? Strawberry blonde? . . . We used to have cappuccino with . . . Freckles? . . . on Mercy Street—I mean Mercer Street—"

A breath away from "The soul's dark night" he stopped me, choosing his words carefully, as though I were standing on a ledge and he was talking to a potential jumper: "Try to relax. Don't take this personally. I have no idea who you are."

"Yes. Well . . ." I wanted to laugh a feathery trill only the loon escaped. "If you're ever in L.A. . . ."

"Never," he said. "But have a good day."

Then I pitched myself off the building, covering my head on

the way down, crying out to Michael: "I didn't mention *your* name! I never said you were married to me!"

It would have hurt Michael's career.


*I walk right by Saint* Patrick's Cathedral. I have no plans to make a visit. I don't want to talk to anyone named Patrick. . . . I've just gone past the second bronze door when coming at me, through the crowd, is a chin-whiskered hag dressed in a costume from Albania. She hands me a note and croaks: "Don't read this until you're inside!" I follow instructions. One. Because I've been walking the city for hours and need to sit down. Two. I can't face Roberta—not after last night. And three and foremost. You don't mess with Albanians.

Up the steps . . . enter . . . genuflect (my father is Catholic) . . . sink into a pew and open the note. . . . It turns out a Gypsy has put a curse on me—just my luck—but if I call a 976 number the hex will be lifted. I pray and then head uptown.

I need $2.50 in quarters to ward off the prophecy. They won't give you change in New York unless you buy something. I'm in a liquor store. They don't sell scarves.

Clutching a pint of scotch in a brown paper bag, I make the call from a graffiti-scratched phone shell and then cut across Central Park on my way to the west side. What a relief! The recording said all omens are off.

Even after what happened at last night's party, I can enjoy New York. Maybe move here. Get a job. . . . It was snowing earlier but it stopped and it's warm now. I look for a dry bench. There isn't any. Except one. With a bag lady on it. As I approach, she reaches into a pushcart of tumbling rags and clothes and spreads the wooden slats alongside her with a pair of trapdoor flannel pajamas, inviting me to share the space. We introduce ourselves.

It's nice to sit, relax, make a friend. Her name is Aurelia.

"Everyone's got a story." Aurelia's voice is veiled. Thick with intrigue. "What's yours?"

Crumpling the paper bag at the neck of the bottle, I take a swig of scotch. Then Aurelia (about my age, I guess) tosses the curls of her outrageous Dolly Parton wig and unscrews the top of a silver thermos. I pour her a drink. She holds the cup daintily, fingers poking through a digitless glove.

I try to describe the events of last night but I keep flashing back to the story of Patrick and I interrupt my narrative with: "Michael never rejected me. He just died."

All through my saga, Aurelia taps at a wristwatch without any time hands, then yawns. "Put it in a nutshell!"

Slowly sipping her scotch, Aurelia tells me that the French authorities have stolen her uterus and stashed it in a numbered account in a Swiss bank. As soon as she can locate her welfare checks, she's off to Zurich—with a stopover in Honolulu.

My problems are pale. I give her a dollar, the rest of the scotch (there's a third left) and we promise to meet again. . . . Next time, I'll tell her about my elves. She'd understand. I walk away buoyant . . . less self-absorbed. I'm going to help other people. And when I get to Sixty-fifth Street and Central Park West, I have my chance.

It's early afternoon but the sky suddenly goes black. Pellets of rain, or something—who knows—are starting to fall.

An old lady bashes at a bus with her umbrella. It slaps us with slush as she waits to board and I'm about to cross the street. The bus doors open and the driver, a big beefy woman, orders the passengers to move to the rear. No one budges. The old lady asks if I would goose her up the step. I close my umbrella and press at her backside, but I can't pack her in. The driver stands and yells: "If you don't shove to de rear, I ain't movin' this motherfuckin' bus!" . . . Car horns honk. It's hailing on my head. Bus people heckle me: "Give it some balls!" . . . "Hey! Yo! Heave ho!" . . . The old lady turns, looks around for another pusher and flips me off with "She can't do it right!"

It's an allegorical synthesis of my life.

I apologize, back away, open my umbrella—a shield against sleet and sarcasm—only I'm trampled by a herd of pedestrians and tangled in overlapping spikes and ribs. Antlers locked in combat. . . . The losing moose retreats.

On the southeast corner, behind a garbage can, I unbutton my raincoat and feel my breasts. In case I was mugged in the crunch.

Roberta showed me how to disperse my assets. I pat my body. Bills in bra? Check. Gibraltar Visa still in pouch belt slung on stomach? Yes. Tokens and change clinking in skirt pocket? Uh huh.

"Look how lucky you are," I mumble as I amble. "Your handbag has never been lighter—'cause there's nothing in it. . . . The previous downpour has become merely drizzle and you're physically intact"—I raise my eyes in gratitude—except for two broken ribs above my head poking through shredded blue nylon. Oh God! Roberta's umbrella! I'll have to buy her a new one. I look for a store, but when I get to Fifty-ninth Street, I hear Michael say, "Look up!"

There it is. The Mutual of Omaha Building near Columbus Circle flashing its dotted sign: 72 degrees. Low 30s this evening. "New York has four seasons and they're all in the same day." I smile remembering his remark and the sun comes out. I flap the pile-lined raincoat, cooling myself, and then stuff Roberta's bilious-blue already collapsed umbrella into its sheath. I puncture the nylon. And try to reshape my smile.

Michael always took charge of umbrellas. He'd hold an oversized black one between us and my arm would go under and around his elbow. When the shower was almost over, he would toss the polished walnut handle into the air, grab it with his other hand, snap back the spring, and as the folds cascaded down, hitch the umbrella over his shoulder. Humming at the rain with his vaudeville cane.

What's the matter with me? I need to figure out what went wrong at the party. But I'm uncomfortable living in a past as recent as last night. And I can't hang out in the present, so I hover over the past perfect. A nomad. Nowhere to pitch my tense. . . . What about the future? No good. The future is not what it used to be. . . . Maybe I'll never replay the story of Roberta. . . . Is it a smoking gun—like the elves? Or perhaps this fragmentation is an early sign of insanity.

A crack of thunder. Whoosh of wind. A sudden deluge . . . Have to run for it. . . . Where? A delicatessen diagonally across Columbus Circle. It's a big intersection . . . angles and islands . . . can't figure out which WALK or DON'T WALK is for me. As I race across the street (I don't have boots and my shoes are sloshing) a taxi driver gives me the finger after his cab almost clips me. I make it . . . under the awning of Sid's Deli . . . lean against the steamy window . . . stare at a wall of rain. New York has a different kind of loneliness. You're very busy while you're experiencing it.

"Try to be cheerful," Roberta had instructed me. On the way to her friend Ellen's party.

Now the smells of toasted corn muffins and pickles hang in the open doorway. I'm a mess but I decide to go in.

A man is behind the slanted glass counter. Sid. His name is stenciled in red on his shirt.

"Excuse me," I say. "Do you have a bathroom?"

Sid saws at a corned beef on a wooden board. "Only for customers!"

"I'm gonna be a customer in a minute!" I snap back. Well, I didn't snap back that fast because I was fascinated by his resemblance to a rhinoceros, including the hornlike wart on the tip of his nose.

In the ladies' room (that's a euphemism), I dry my hair on a paper towel, pee standing up, wash my hands under an exploding faucet and (the dispenser's empty) dry them with toilet paper. But there's good news. No mirror. I can't see what I look like.

I come out of the bathroom. Sid is lancing a tongue. He doesn't walk over when I sit at the counter so I call out to him: "May I please have a knockwurst on a kaiser roll."

"Don't order that," Michael used to say.

"I love it."

"I know you do but an hour later you get a stomachache."

"I promise I won't." I'm twirling a small glass ladle poking through the slotted lid of an old-fashioned mustard jar.

"What else?" Sid blares, taking a fat frank out of the case and grilling it.

There's no one in the place and we're shouting at each other.

"A side of half-sour pickles, potato salad and a Heineken's."

Michael groans.

I lift up the jar and knock it on the counter. "I don't have to listen to you anymore!"

"You talkin' to me?" It's Sid's voice.

My hand is still on the jar and the lid is clattering. I know when I mumble to Michael, but to be unaware I was hollering at him—and in a public place!—that's losing it!

Sid puts the food in front of me, and I guess because he feels sorry I'm deranged, growls softly: "This'll do you good."

The aroma fills me with the joy of being half Jewish. I open the poppy seed roll. Smear mustard on the charred rod. Pick up the kaiser. Bite the dangling end of the dog. . . . It's the best wurst I've ever had!

I can concentrate now.

Yesterday morning, six A.M., I arrived in New York on the red-eye. Exhausted. I didn't want to go to a party but Roberta said it was all arranged and since I'm staying with her, I had to go.

So last night, we were in the elevator on our way up to Ellen and Marvin's Madison Avenue penthouse. Roberta was instructing me: "Widows are asked to lunch. Widowers are invited to dinner. I tell everyone I'm a divorcee. . . . Divorcees are more fun."

The elevator guy nodded in agreement. Roberta didn't notice. She was still talking: "There's always a single woman that married friends are anxious to match up with an available man. However, there are single widows, redundant as that may be, but they won't do. Too much sadness around the dinner table."

"You want me to lie?" I said, softly, into her ear. I hoped it was her ear. I couldn't find it because her black velvet hair was plastered to her head and hanging from this skull-like cap was a thick hank of hair on each side swooping like a *C* onto each cheek.

"To hide the lift marks," she had said, ". . . and I don't have to have my ears tagged. It kills two birds with one stone."

I didn't like Roberta in person. Twenty minutes after I met her, she was killing birds.

"Do you want me to lie?" I repeated.

"Not necessarily. . . . Just don't volunteer." Roberta untied the belt of her mink coat as the elevator slowed. "We also do it for the men. . . ."

The elevator guy took a long time opening the door. Obviously, he wanted to hear and maybe see the rest of Roberta.

She obliged him by opening the lapels of her coat and continuing: "A man can compete with an ex-husband who's a son of a bitch, but not an idealized image of the departed."

There was so much to learn.

On the sixty-fifth floor, the door reluctantly closing behind us, Roberta opened her mink all the way, exposing cleavage. Maybe she thought Henry and Gerald, the invited eligibles she had told me about, were patrolling the corridor.

"Roberta?"

"What?"

"Are there going to be any other widows at the party?"

"Yes. Marsha or Sally. They're friends of Ellen. One of them actually is divorced. I'm not sure which. . . . C'mon, let's go."

"Just a minute. Does that mean Henry and Gerald each get a widow and a half and split the divorcee, or do four women quarter Gerald and Henry?"

Roberta was not amused. She tapped me on the shoulder— "Don't slouch"—then linked her arm in mine and walked me down the hall.

What a thing to say! Anyone would appear slouched next to Roberta. She's five-ten! And . . . and cleavage is imprecise. Her chest is skeletal. You can't tell the breasts from the bones! I wanted to run but we were standing in front of 65F, Roberta buzzing the bell with a French-manicured nail. I looked down at my fingers. Not French but filed. And I was wearing a very nice raincoat except Roberta had pinned a pile lining inside because it was so frigging cold last night. My dress is pretty; with soft mauve and pink flowers. Michael loved it. Only it's chiffon. I don't own any winter clothes like Roberta's black wool sheath and there was no time to buy anything because I had slept most of the day.

Ellen, an arctic blonde with a blunt-cut chin bob, opened the door and leaned towards Roberta. I gazed up at the wire sculptures. Two Giacometti's kissing each other's air.

"And this must be . . ." Ellen looked down.

"A Munchkin." I was thinking it and it came out.

The two women gave each other a "What is she talking about" glance. All right, so they never read the Oz books. But not to have seen the picture?

Roberta formally introduced me as Babe, having picked it up from my Seymour stories. I used to like my real name but she preferred Babe. "It's youthful. Breezy."

After Roberta admired Ellen's chamois suede floor-length skirt and silk leotard, she said: "I wanted you two to meet and also take Babe to a party, so here we are killing two—"

"Thank you for inviting me." I was one sleeve out of my raincoat and I was so nervous. Ellen had spotted the lining. Wait'll she sees my dress. I'll be as dead as Roberta's birds.

Ellen reached for a hanger. "I'm sorry you lost your husband." She whispered it to me. Very low and fast. However, the subtext was clear. Condolences are meant to be left at the coatrack.

As we followed Ellen into the living room, I nudged Roberta. "I hate that phrase 'lost your husband.' It sounds as though I misplaced him at Bloomingdale's."

Roberta gave me a poke.

I clenched my teeth in the memory of a smile. It's a new world and I stared at it as Ellen announced the cast. Starring above the title: Henry and Gerald seated center in the middle of the couch. Their first glance transposed me into nonphysical. And then their faces were hidden by two fashion victims flanking them. Sally, with a leathery, red-ginger Dutch Boy hairdo, was thigh-close to Gerald, the upper part of her body grazing his jacket. And one-eyed Marsha, semiblind from her lopsided nut-wheat wedge cut, heaved over Henry. Sally and Marsha gave me a wave. Was it a hello? No. Probably, good-bye. I was the only woman in the room with big hair. Marvin, Ellen's husband, was behind the bar. He walked over to us. "What are you drinking, ladies?" He sounded exhausted. Maybe because he was as thin as Ellen. But *his* posture was terrible.

"Oh, the usual," Roberta chirped, making tracks for the ottoman opposite the coffee table and seating herself across from the couch group.

I got into trouble because I said, "I'll have the usual, too," and it took all of Marvin's energy to remind me that we'd just met and he had no idea what my usual might be.

Marvin loped to the bar. I followed him; over delicately embroidered rugs, past Louis XV commodes, rococo lamps and figurines . . . originals or reproductions? I didn't know but I said, "This is like a room at the Met."

He turned, slid his glasses down over his ski nose, slicked back his sparse hair and shrugged. That was it. And when he was behind the bar and I asked for double scotch neat, spritzer on the side, all he said was: "Ramlosa or Pellegrino?" Marvin poured, then joined his guests and Ellen went into the kitchen.

There I was, a drink in each hand, not knowing where to sit. Marvin had taken the empty side chair at the far end of the coffee table. I walked over to the marble fireplace. And from that angle I could see what Henry and Gerald looked like. Henry Kissinger and Gerald Ford. It was one of those (in this case, two) amazing coincidences. Except the couch pair were in their early fifties and wore three-pleated pants and floppy Armani-type jackets.

Roberta slanted her torso across the coffee table, talking at the same time as Sally and Marsha. The men were submerged as three pairs of nibbling lips sucked up plankton.

On the other side of the fireplace was a small chair with curved, slender arms and a tapestry cushioned back. I moved towards it. My bottom was just shy of hitting the seat when Ellen burst in: "DON'T SIT! IT'S AN ANTIQUE!"

I pitched myself forward and ran—I don't know where—with bent knees in a Groucho crouch, clutching the drinks.

I had their attention.

When Ellen screamed, Roberta had spun around. Now, with her back to everyone else, she snarled at me. I've never seen anything like it. One side of her lip lifted so high it hit her nostril. And it didn't even affect her speech as she said, "Why don't you join us?" and she shifted on the ottoman, making a space for me.

I studied the cover of *Smithsonian* and prayed for the decomposition of my flesh. And I helped it rot faster by stopping at the bar and refilling my scotch before I sat down.

Chatty Sally related a story about Harold, her ex, whom she managed to catch in a cabana in Cabo San Lucas with a blonde and now the son of a bitch is really paying for it.

Marsha laughed too loudly. I had noticed a dark circle under her one eye. Was she the hidden widow?

I was so close to Sally and Marsha I had the chance to scrutinize them but I couldn't lift either of my eyes. So I listened, putting aside humiliation and focusing on the mystery. Fortunately, the two women did all the talking. They pulverized Roberta. Henry and Gerald never spoke because they were too busy being entertained. Concave Marvin was holding up the mantelpiece and guarding the chair. Ellen strolled back and forth from the kitchen to the dining table fiddling with fluted napkins, three glasses, seven forks and two plates at each setting. And no food. I could see that because I didn't have to raise my head to look sideways. Not a mini Bonbel or a Wheat Thin in sight. Nothing on the coffee table except *Architectural Digest* and the *Smithsonian* I was staring at.

Sally and Marsha overlapped, discussing their jobs. No clue, yet. Their children—all of whom were college geniuses . . . Sally or Marsha? Marsha or Sally? If only *one* harbored a dark secret, why were they both dressed in black?

In Act One of Chekhov's *The Sea Gull,* Medvedenko asks Masha, "Why do you always wear black?"

Masha answers: "I am in mourning for my life."

"Babe, what do you do in California?" It was a man's voice. "Huh?"

Roberta, my interpreter, repeated the question.

I heard it, Roberta, only I'm not looking up because I'm stupefied that someone is actually speaking to me and I'm not sure if it's a setup. Does the person *really* want to know or is it one of those "What percentage of your intellect have you lost living in L.A. and how do you spend your weekends besides surfing" kinds of questions.

I could feel it. Seven people waiting. All thirteen eyes on me.

There comes a time when, as Michael would say, you gotta get the bastards. . . . You see, Roberta, I do not canonize my husband.

Slowly, I took a sip of scotch and straightened my spine. "Who asked me that?"

Gerald raised a finger.

"Well, Gerald . . . thank you for inquiring. I'm an eclipse photographer."

"Whaaaat?" It was a chorus.

"Solar. Not lunar."

"For heaven's sake!" Gerald was gaga.

"That's incredible!" Henry was floored.

Marvin managed to make it from the mantelpiece. "Tell us about it!"

I smiled sweetly. "Does anyone know the principle of ecliptic limit or understand astrophotography?"

"Nooo," said the male chorus.

Good, I thought. I had included the women in my question, but Ellen had taken root in mid-stroll. Sally and Marsha's awe had worn off and they twitched with jealousy. Roberta's jaw was still in space.

Another sip of scotch. "The obscuration, or the cutting off of some or all of the light from one celestial body by another . . ." Years ago, I'd written a parallel poem utilizing images of an eclipse. As I spoke, I pulled phrases from my left-hand column and what I didn't remember, I improvised. ". . . is a phenomenon that I view through an XG876 telephoto lens. My optic nerve fibers calculate the angularity from the nodes of the moon's orbit. Of course, there are variables. Appulse, occulation, totality . . . am I going too fast?"

"A little," said Henry, rocking with fascination.

"Excuse me." Ellen had recovered during my opening remarks, gone back to the kitchen, and was now standing next to Marvin trying to get his attention. She held a gleaming, round brass tray and on it, a beautiful presentation of smoked oysters bedded on toast points.

"Let me demonstrate the camera's tracking process . . ." I was starving, but you don't eat in the middle of an aria with a captive audience thrilling to the notes of a solar progression.

"Everyone's so engrossed," Ellen hissed, leaning towards Marvin, "I thought we'd have our first course at the coffee table."

Marvin shushed her and he gave me a wink. And Ellen gave him a look and then tiptoed behind the circle of guests with the tray.

What a night! In an astral voice, I murmured, "Imagine my left hand is the rising moon, preparing to cross over the earth's lifting right hand . . ." Everyone was breathless as my arms ascended like a ballerina's. Then, I changed the lyrical rhythm, rapidly soaring the firmament: "Velocity of shutter speed! One must shoot the penumbra at the instant"—I thrust my hands in space—a shiny disk over my head—who shrieked as

The moon hit the sun and the sky rained oysters.

Ellen crumpled to the floor: "MY AUBUSSON RUG!"

Would it have been any better on a Bigelow?

They were everywhere! Two, cemented on Sally's forehead. Six, clinging to Gerald's crotch. Marvin had a new tiepin. Nothing on me because I was the batter. The list goes on. Slapped like leeches, oysters adhered to the wall, dripping brown juice. Only on Ellen's suede skirt they hung like tassels.

There is no way to facilitate your own death on short notice. Maybe I'll travel. Japan. Israel.

Why was my offer to pay for the dry cleaning unacceptable? Because antique Aubusson rugs fall apart in the process.

There's more. During the cleanup, everyone treated me with tight-lipped outrage. When Ellen tossed the wilted salad, it got better. They ignored me. Then, over the crack of a burnt roll, Henry asked: "Why are you visiting New York in such foul weather?"

"I had to leave. Grief moved in." No one understood me. They thought I'd taken in a boarder with that surname.

I explained that anthropomorphically speaking, I had; and chose a big word so they wouldn't know how smashed I was.

Roberta's snarl was too late. As were the tournedos, overcooked and served at 11:45 P.M. By then, it didn't matter. I'd had 107 scotches, which launched me into a description of grief as a tatterdemalion thick with disease, hiding in corners, smacking me with silence. "If I speak, he mimics me, drowning me down in bouncing echos. He scatters sun motes in space. Tilts pictures I must adjust. Presses pillows into remembered shapes, knowing it will remind me."

I certainly put a pall on that party.

Marvin had to help me from the table. I didn't tell anyone, but I saw an oyster dangling from a ceramic cherub. On a little stand, far from where the action had been. Near the hallway.

I put on my raincoat and slurred my nine hundredth apology to Ellen. Sally was reaching for her imitation lynx and touched my shoulder. I thought she was steadying me. "When you talked about grief," she whispered, "I knew you were a widow, too."

"It's nice to meet you, Sally." And we left our secrets at the coatrack.

Roberta didn't say a word to me in the elevator. When we got to the street and I was concentrating on breathing, she asked: "Do you keep a diary?"

"What? . . . No. After Michael died I stopped writing in my journal."

"*That*," she said, "would seem to be the place for poetic despair."


*I have the worst stomachache* of my life.

It's seven P.M. The deli is crowded. I pay the check, say goodbye to Sid and on my way out (I hadn't noticed it before because it was behind the open door) I see a peculiar plant. A five-foot-notched-leaf-beanstalk, its tendrils clutching a scruffy bark, tied with a dilapidated red satin bow, sprinkled with glitter. . . . I got a plant like that once. Two days after Michael died . . . with a note on a plastic pitchfork sunk in the soil. "Best wishes. We'll call you when you get squared away. Love, Sondra and Charles." . . . People are weird. Either they're terrified of grief or they think it's comparable to a deli opening.

I hurry to the theater district, stopping at the Footlight Cafe to visit with Tommy, the owner who doubles as bartender.

"On the house," he says, handing me a scotch sour, expressing his sadness about Michael's death. Real condolences. And I feel better.

Several seasons ago, Michael had co-starred in a hit play that ran next door at the Golden Theater. We'd have dinner at the Footlight after the show. Michael's doctors tried to discourage him from taking the job. Too strenuous. Michael agreed, paraphrasing the theater quote: "Dying is easy. Comedy is tough." His portrayal of a befuddled musician was endearing. The audience loved him and for eight performances a week he was not in pain.

Fifteen minutes before curtain time I stand in front of the theater, then merge with the crowd into the humid, smoky lobby.

"Center door please. Have your tickets ready."

I bump against matted fur coats (it's still raining) as women supported by men wobble on one foot, changing from boots to evening shoes. And I'm in line, pushed toward the center door.

The man stationed at the stub box holds out his right hand. I shake it instead of giving him a ticket. "Hi, Jack. I'll just stand in the back of the house and watch Michael's last scene."

"Ticket, please."

"But I'm here practically every night . . . Michael's wife. Remember? . . . I always stand in the back."

"You'll have to step outside, ma'am."

I'm on the sidewalk. Shaking. Uncertain. Have I been in the lobby? . . . A moment ago? Years before? Or will I go there in the minutes to come?

# F O U R

*Seymour, I'm going to Jerusalem* in July."

"You really know how to pick your travel seasons."

"I met this wonderful man on the plane coming back to L.A. He asked me to join him in Israel. His name is Hjalmar."

"Elmer?"

"Hjalmar! . . . Ychh . . . Ychallmurr. . . . He's Swedish."

"What happened in New York?"

"New York was depressing."

"What do you think Swedes are? They're always shooting themselves in the third act."

"That's Norwegian—Ibsen."

"Whatever. Highest suicide rate. They off themselves in the winter. I once had a Swedish patient. He went back to Stockholm for Christmas and plugged himself in the middle of his smorgasbord—left the longest damned note. . . . What does Elmer do when he's not in torment?"

"He's a philosopher. He's not tormented."

"Some philosopher!"

"He's not like that. You should hear him say *Jag alskar dig'*— It's 'I love you' in Swedish."

"That's what he does for a living—goes around saying 'I love you' in Swedish?"

"He hardly ever says it! Existentially, no one has ever been able to define love; that's why he only says it to me."

"Then how can he make a living?"

"Seymour, I'm going to hang up if you don't stop. . . . He's an expert on the Messiah."

"Is there a market for that?"

"Good-bye, Seymour. I've got a lot to do. He's coming Thursday."

"Thursday. The Messiah's coming Thursday? I thought I'd have to wait at least another hundred years. Will he hit Palm Springs first?"

"Seymour—and this is the last time I'm going to humor you— Hjalmar is a professor at Falgersund University. He is now in San Diego attending a seminar on religious phenomenology where he's giving a paper entitled 'Ontology of a Messiah' and then he's coming to Los Angeles on Thursday . . . Seymour?"

"I'm not saying a word."

"We spent three extraordinary days together. He says we have a spiritual, sexual and intellectual relationship."

"How long has he been married?"

"Twenty years. But he's in the process of getting a divorce."

"Ohhhhh, Babe!"


*I was able to get* the last seat at an excursion rate on EL AL'S JETAWAY GETAWAY. FIFTEEN MYSTICAL MAGICAL DAYS IN THE MIDDLE EAST. I called Falgersund.

A series of spaceship beeps orbited our voices overseas.

"Hallo. Hello."

"Hjalmar, can you talk?"

I heard his low, lilting purr: *"Ni har fatt fel nummer"*; and he hung up.

An hour later my phone rang. "Will you accept an overseas collect call from Hjalmar—"

"Oh God! Oh yes! Oh, operator!"

"I was so sorry for the signal. I daresay, you understood. . . . I yust had to wait until Pia was not in the hoos."

"Oh, Hjalmar!" I sobbed.

"Yah, not to worry. . . . Together soon we will be."

"I joined a tour. I don't have to stay with them but the airfare is cheaper that way. They booked me into a single at the Ramada Inn in Tel Aviv. I told them I need a double, so there's an additional charge . . . seventy-five dollars a night. . . . I'll put it on my American Express card and you can reimburse me for your share of the room."

"What was that word?"

"What word?"

"Re-embers?"

"Oh, reimburse. It means pay me back."

"Ah. Yah."

"So . . . I arrive July eighth. Ben Gurion Airport. Flight Ten. Six P.M. Tel Aviv time. . . . Hjalmar . . . *Jag alskar—*"

He interrupted in an urgent, muffled stammer: "Pia yust now come back in hoos. I must hang . . ."—an overlapping of Swedish in the background. His voice surfaced. The words were unrecognizable but his shaky tone of pretense carried a universal ring: "I'm in the middle of a business call, dear." Swedish lyrics to an old Yankee song.


*I wanted to smoke, drink,* be on the aisle near the lavatories, toward the back, preferably alone. My friends who drove me to the airport suggested that the only seat that could make me happy would be the toilet.

Twenty-seven Hasidim, bouncing sidelocks below broad-brimmed hats, congregated at the tail end of the 747; swayed, and mumbled evening prayers, as white fringe flapped against long frock coats. As I passed them on my way to the bathroom, they averted their eyes, and several of them flicked their wrists at me, indicating an unsaid *"Feh!"* How could I be part of Israel? We were hardly airborne and already I was an infidel over my own country.

I did get an aisle seat in a row of three, next to Harry and Ethel Rosen. After my public shunning, I scrunched my foam pillow and tried to sleep off the humiliation. The rising and falling inflection of devotion from the rear of the airplane moved in rhythm with my memory. Hjalmar's religious medal floated above me. We made love like dancers, his crucifix clanking against my teeth. He descended in slow motion from a grande jeté, and in that moment, as Hjalmar was down-coming from flight, Ethel became a merciless biographer.

"So, you're married?"

"Huh?"

"That's not a wedding ring?"

"Yes. It is. But I'm not married anymore."

"When I got divorced from my first husband, I sold my ring. Didn't I, Harry?"

Harry was snoring. "Harry!" Ethel poked him. "Change seats with me so I don't have to talk over you."

With a springboard push and an "Alley-oop" two tubby circus tumblers rolled over each other and exchanged sagging cushions.

"I'm Ethel Rosen and . . ." She gestured with her ringed thumb. "That was Harry." He had fallen asleep on impact. "It says on the brochure there's going to be a Kosher cocktail party at the Ramada Inn. Maybe you'll meet a nice man. Have you been dating since your divorce?"

"I'm not divorced."

"Oh. Well. Then maybe you shouldn't sell your ring. You might get back together."

"No. We won't. I mean we can't."

"So, how long have you been separated."

"We're not separated. I mean we are. . . . My husband died."

"Cancer?"

"Yes."

Ethel sighed and put her hand on my shoulder. "You want a plum?"

"No. No thanks." The trolley came down the aisle. "I think I'll get a drink." I reached for my wallet.

"Harry!" Ethel pushed him with one hand and flagged down my wallet with the other. "Nonsense. It's our treat. Harry!" she hollered. "Give me seven-fifty."

Ethel sucked on the swizzle stick. "So you have to go on, you know."

"I'm trying."

"Corporation lawyers are good. Businessmen with a chain of stores—like Harry. . . . Doctors are terrible—and whatever you do, stay away from analysts. Professionally, you're better off calling a talk show."

"I already did."

She reached for my hand. "So don't worry about the past. It'll be here soon enough."

I wanted to tell her about Hjalmar, but I figured she knew. Besides, she had started to write postcards.

Harry woke up. "For God's sake, Ethel, who are you writing to? We're not even there yet."

There was a five-hour layover in London instead of the expected three. Some of the passengers had elected to break our hermetically sealed security and pass through the restricted holding area into the main portion of Heathrow Airport. It meant we would have to be checked and double-checked before reboarding for Tel Aviv.

"It's worth it! It's worth it!" Ethel was the first one out of the paddock, her voice urging Harry and me on, as we panted behind her into the duty-free shop. She vacuumed the store, charging seven bottles of Paco Rabanne, four Cardin scarves and a Gucci purse.

Harry and I sniffed cigars.

"C'mere you two. Look how much money I saved."

I bought a box of Coronas and a bottle of Chivas Regal for Hjalmar.

We celebrated our London shopping spree at the airport bar. After a round of four drinks, Ethel and Harry decided to adopt me. Before I could consent to the adoption papers, I felt I should confess. I was not worthy. I was not a nice person. I was fooling around with a married man. "I want you to know I'm meeting a ma—"

Ethel cut me off before the next syllable. "Ixnay. Ixnay, don't tell Harry," she said in a low voice without moving her lips.

"—ma . . . mahvelous man." I managed to scoop up to another vowel sound. Harry beamed. We all agreed the wedding would take place in their house.

"Announcing the departure of Flight Ten for Tel Aviv. Please have your immigration cards ready." The loudspeaker repeated the information in Hebrew, Arabic, French, Aramaic, Phoenician and Ladino.

Men and women formed separate queues in front of what looked like two brown-curtained voting booths.

I stood weaving in line, hiccupping from the martinis.

Two Israeli soldiers, rifles down, standing guard, whispered and watched me.

"Next."

The curtain opened and whipped closed behind me. Addressing me: a female Yemenite halfback in pants uniform, sporting shoulder holster and gun. "Who are you meeting in Israel?"

"A friend." I gave her my white card.

She passed her hand over my breasts, round and down my back, then brushed my skirt, halving it down my thighs. "Nationality and name?"

"Mine or his?" I'll answer anything from anyone in uniform, but it was hard to concentrate while she was doing that.

"His," she growled. "I already have yours." Having had me, she began to write on my card, then moved behind a small table. A gooseneck lamp illuminated her name tag as she sat: Rivka Bialik.

I needed water. I couldn't breathe. There was just room enough for Rivka, me and the table.

She waited for me to respond.

"Hjalmar Krogstrom." It seemed redundant to add "Swedish."

"Married?"

"Him or me?"

"Him!" She sucked up the last bit of air.

"I'm sorry, I've forgotten the question." I felt the top of my body roll and begin to pitch forward. . . . I was an RAF flyer shot down over Heidelberg but I wouldn't break under interrogation.

"Married." Rivka sneered. It was no longer a question.

I steadied myself at a forty-five-degree angle. It was the best I could do. . . . "Yes, he is." I had decided to brazen it out. "But he's in the process of getting a divorce—"

"What are his political affiliations?"

"He's a . . . I mean we're just friends—though on several occasions we—I think both of us would like a more meaningful relationship eventually. . . ."

Rivka's hand traveled to her shoulder holster and rested on the hilt of her gun. She was going to shoot me if I didn't stop talking and start talking.

"He's a . . ." There was a heater somewhere in the tiny cubicle. "He's a Messianist."

"Is that a branch of the PLO or any part of the Arab Federation?"

"Oh God, no! . . . It's a very small movement. . . . He's a writer and—" That was it. It was all over. Hjalmar would be arrested, Pia would find out about us, they'd tell my mother and I would be shot.

"It's a religious philosophy!" She wouldn't listen.

"Religious and political activists. Are you a writer also?"

"No. . . . I mean, I've sold a few poems. . . . Don't you know who the Messiah is?"

Rivka made a move toward the curtain. The SS would take over now.

I tried to stop her. In a final vainglorious gesture I clutched at the brown curtain, tearing it loose from its shower hooks, crumpling it to me like an embattled flag, and managed, on the way down, to utter the immortal cry: "The Messiah is Jewish!"


*Where am I?" I promised* myself if I ever fainted that would be the first thing I'd say. Somewhere, from someplace long ago, I thought I heard Harry laughing. Driblets of water from a cold compress plopped on my lower lip.

"You're on a plane." It was Ethel.

My lips were frozen. My mouth tasted like felt. I couldn't feel my teeth and I was afraid to ask. With my index finger I pushed a drop of water onto my tongue. "Am I being deported?"

It was Harry's laughter. "We're on our way to Israel."

My finger traveled my forehead under the washcloth.

"Don't look!" Ethel warned.

"Don't look at what? Don't look at what!"

"You hit your head on Rivka's gooseneck lamp."

My finger shot towards her, my thumb flicked up and I threatened her gunlike until she reached in her purse and handed me a small pocket mirror.

"Oh my God! It's a goose egg!"

"It's not that bad. You're looking in the magnifying side."

"I'm going to be sick!"

"Harry! Get the bag!"

Harry popped apart the paper sack with the instructions in English, Hebrew and Arabic. I threw up in three languages.

En route to the bathroom, I passed the Hasidim, rocking devotedly, and I prayed for their prayers.

I slid the bolt into place. The overhead light fluttered. I'll face myself slowly, I thought. And there it was. The final photograph. I had turned chartreuse. I could see the bump on my head bellying out. In three minutes, four at the most, it would burst, blasting my brains into noodles and sponges.

"Our prayers could not save her," the old Rabbi would say. "God took her somewhere over Israel, straddling an El Al toilet."

I washed my face, cracked open the bathroom door and waited for the devotions to end. The pious men had returned to their seats. I was still alive. As I walked down the aisle I said *"Toda,"* which is thank you in Hebrew, to one of them. His eyes stayed focused on the contents of his lunch box and he said something in Yiddish to his sandwich.

I sank back into my seat. My palms began to sweat. . . . Where was I going? What was I doing? Who was this Hjalmar? How would it end? . . . If I wasn't going to die, at least I could make myself insane. . . . Talk to me, Ethel, I silently screamed (she was busy addressing postcards). . . . Forget it, Ethel, I'll work it out myself. . . .

You sit next to a man on a plane. He turns to you and says . . . "From Sweden I am here. With udder scholars I make a conference." . . . What was so interesting about that? Just because he's a foreigner. Just because he speaks English backwards. . . . Never mind what he said. What did you think when you first saw him? . . . I can't remember. Well, what does he look like? Uhhh. Black hair. I never saw a Swede with black hair. Lots of it. Curly. . . . Six feet, five inches. Much too tall for me. I could tell that sitting next to him. Blue eyes, aquiline nose, broad shoulders. He probably skis. He looks like one of those skiers on "ABC's Wide World of Sports." They wave their wool hats and grin at the camera. I definitely remember not being crazy about him. SO WHAT WAS IT? . . . He said, "And you?" . . . He said, "And you?"! That's why you're flying to Israel, spending all this money to be with a man you hardly know, a man you only spent two weekends with in Los Angeles—because he said, "And you?"—are you fruitcakey? . . . He wanted me to introduce myself to him, after he told me he's a Vingåker (a Swede with black hair). He seemed so interested in me; that's why he said . . .

"And you?"

And I said, "Huh?" I was reading a book.

So then he said, "I think you are a pretty sad lady."

"I hope there's a comma somewhere in there."

"I am so sorry. I mean pretty *and* sad. But you are nice to make a yoke of it." And he smiled. A fanfare of teeth. Absolutely the most beautiful smile I had ever seen. And that was it—or the beginning of it. We talked nonstop. I told him about my life and Michael and Seymour and when he said he was writing a book on Yesus and that he was going to interview Yews in Yerusalem, I helped him with his J's. I remember my head swinging in rhythm to his undulating, elongated vowel sounds. Towards the end of the flight he leaned very close, his blue velour shirt brushing against my shoulder. "Is it possible for me?" he asked, meaning much more than his J's. I looked up, floated on his dipthongs, mesmerized by his teeth. . . . I felt better. At least now I understood why I was going to Israel.

Ethel turned to me. "I knew you'd figure it out."

"Ladies and gentlemen, fasten your—"

"Seat belts, girls, seat belts." Harry at the window continued . . . "We're landing!"

"Just in time. I finished my postcards."

"I see the lights."

"Where are the mosques?"

"My ears are popping."

"Here's gum."

"Why can't I see the stars the Wise Men saw?"

I started to cry.

And all the Orthodox Jews, who believe so devoutly in God, applauded the El Al pilot.

We trundled off the plane. A cordon of Israeli guards surveyed us. Shopping bag immigrants shuffling slowly forward in line. And again we waited. Displaced persons from department stores. Name? Joseph Magnin. Country of origin? K mart.

Behind the barricades, at the baggage claim, hundreds of people; shoving, shouting to us in a confusion of foreign tongues as we tugged at zippers and tumbled over wheeled suitcases.

I saw him. His head, framed by his upstretched arms, bobbed up and down. In his hands a large crayoned sign: SHALOM BABE.

"That's him, Ethel. That's him!"

She clutched at Harry. "Oh my God is he gorgeous!"

And then—three feet off the ground—he held me. In the air, I introduced Harry and Ethel. With promises of "We'll see you at the hotel," Hjalmar carried my luggage to a taxi—when he wasn't picking me up and hugging me.

I have always believed in romance. The warm wind of Tel Aviv whipped through the cab as Hjalmar held my face in his hands, kissing my lips, nose, eyes. "What have you on your forehead? I do not remember such a lump."

"A prayer book fell on me."

"Ohhh, Babe."

"Hjalmar, don't call me Babe."

"But it is so American. Humphrey Bogart says this."

"I know."

"I daresay, you did not like my sign?"

"Shalom is nice. I'm just not crazy about Babe."

He held up the fat fuchsia letters waiting for my full retraction. "Tell me about Tel Aviv."

As he spoke, he traced his fingers around the Crayola letters; a wistful five-year-old, disappointed that I had not been more enthusiastic about his coloring effort. "Here we are on Dizengoff Street. The city is a mixture of villas and slums and was established in 1909. But in order to understand Tel Aviv, we must first look to the old walled city just south of here, Yaffa—"

"That's Jaffa, Hjalmar."

"Yah, Yaffa."

I shouldn't have corrected him. I'd already spoiled one moment. I pressed out a wrinkle in the cardboard, patted the sign and took his hand. "Hjalmar, call me Babe."

I was dreaming my life. Hjalmar had arrived two days before and changed our room reservation to a suite overlooking the Mediterranean. Yellow roses everywhere. Room service: a supper of herring, cream cheese, bagels, lox, cucumbers, red onions, Manischewitz blackberry wine. The sea below, the Stage Delicatessen on the terrace table, painted against a backdrop of sky and violet sunset, waited for me. Memory had arranged itself.

I did everything at once; ate, showered, unpacked, ran back and forth on the terrace; squawking like a sandpiper at the white cliffs of the Mediterranean; interspersed with hugs, "How happy I am," "Me too"—the continuation of the archaeological beginnings of Tel Aviv—". . . so that tomorrow you will have a background for our sightseeing. Come, sit next to me. . . . Some seven thousand years ago, neolithic man was living close to the banks of the Yarkon River. We know this from primitive kitchens and human bones dug up near Sderot Nordau. During the time of the Patriarchs, Yaffa was occupied by the Hyskos, but in the fifteenth century B.C. the Egyptians seized the city. You know how this was done? The troops were hidden in baskets and smuggled into Yaffa. Yust imagine what life was like then!"

He had spent several summers in Israel researching his book. "Pia has been here once only. She is not interested in history or my work."

I was interested. I didn't want to let him down, but my head hurt and he was only up to the Byzantine Empire. "Darling, could you finish this while I lie down?" Actually, I wanted to say, I have a headache; let's make love.

I undressed, snuggled beneath the muslin sheets, and Hjalmar took off his shoes and sat next to me on top of the bedcovers, fully clothed. Something was wrong. I knew it. There were too many yellow roses in the room. He put his head in his hands and sighed. I was right.

Long pause.

"I must tell you . . ."

Oh boy, here it comes.

"I must tell you, my cook is not working."

"I'm sorry, I didn't quite get that."

"For two months, my cook not work properly."

"Maybe you're not paying her enough." I was fighting jet lag, passion and a throbbing skull. It was an inopportune time to discuss his domestic help.

"I'm talking about my cook!" He leapt to his feet and gesticulated wildly in the general area south of his waist. "Don't you understand?" Grabbing the SHALOM BABE sign, he turned it over to the blank side and with a turquoise Crayola wrote K U K, and then, in a bizarre show-and-tell, while repeating "Cook, cook, cook!" he underlined the letters and pointed directly to his penis.

"Waaait a minute!" I felt like the fat one in Abbott and Costello. "You meant to say cock!"

"I did not! I know the difference. My cock has nothing to do with my cook! In Swedish"—he was lettering again—"*C O K is a cook!*"

"Well, in English, a cock is a cock and a cook is a cook!—no matter how much you pay her!" I was really getting mad.

"Forgive me for being so upset. I forget you don't speak Swedish."

"I took French. Anyway, what's the matter with it?" I was never going to use that word again.

"My cock, cook, whatever in hell you call it, has a hook."

"You mean when it's erect, it's bent?"

He turned away from me and nodded.

"Sometimes that happens. Years ago, I knew a playwright who had it. It goes away."

"It does?"

"Uh huh."

"But it looks yust like a crooked finger."

"That's not so bad."

Long pause.

"Maybe I try it again."

"Sure."

He turned towards me, grinned and put his Crayolas back in the box.


*Tel Aviv looks like a* city that stopped in the 1950s. Parts of it remind me of Brooklyn. I don't know where to look first. The Carmel Open Air Market—vendors shouting and singing their wares. The Yemenite Quarter with Oriental restaurants under canopies of pinks and purples; ginger, curry, cilantro—spices so pungent I can taste the smell. We walk the city and Hjalmar holds my hand, pumping it rhythmically, the way you squeeze a bulb when you take a blood pressure. I like it. A counterpoint to my gasps of discovery. Museum Haaretz has museums inside museums and includes: excavations of Israelite and Philistine cities, religious and secular art, glass from the Bronze Age to the Islamic period, and documentary exhibits on the origin and history of the Hebrew alphabet. At Bible House, early editions, maps and manuscripts chronicle God's promise to return to Zion. But it was Mohammed's dream to build Jerusalem's Golden Mosque, a journey through seven heavens, into the presence of Allah. "Here and here"—Hjalmar traces a portion of a map—"in this Christian homeland—holy madness."

Skillfully, my guide blends past and present, and at the end of the long morning, I begin to understand how divisive and complex is the situation on the West Bank. Outside Bet Ben Gurion, the former home of Israel's first prime minister, four soldiers—three of them women—salute and exchange guard duty as Hjalmar quotes Ben Gurion: "To be a realist in the Middle East, you have to believe in miracles."

And then Hjalmar asks, "Did Yesus arrive in a politically exigent climate and is now the time for another saviour?"

I'm in love with this man.

*We were finishing lunch at* an Arab restaurant and Hjalmar laughed softly as he watched me croon over the last flakes of Baklava.

"Yah . . . Babe. . . . Yah, there is so much to do . . . and so little time and kronor."

"Kronor?"

"Money! Money!" He rubbed his fingers under his black curls, shampooing his head in distress. "I am in love with you and wish to take care of you, but I daresay, I have only a scholar's earnings."

"That's all right," I said, signing, then shredding the carbon tissue on my Visa charge. "Americans are born with unlimited credit."

"No! It is not right!" He was working up a vigorous lather. "Here, I want you to take this," his voice low, through his clenched teeth, as the waiter approached, picked up the paid check and left.

Hjalmar unfolded a wad of funny-colored money and spread it on the table. "This will take care of more than my half."

I don't know much about kronor. I know *nothing* about kronor. I was so touched by his pride that I didn't want to ask if the money was for his share of the trip or for lunch. Instead, I pointed to the portraits on the bills; the nineteenth-century queen with the braided hair and the fierce Viking, and inquired about them.

*During the five days we* spent in Tel Aviv, Hjalmar developed his theories; I carried a notebook and soon became his Boswell.

"I daresay, Babe, I am speaking at times like a bad translation of a foreign play."

I fixed his syntax.

"If only I could interview Rabbi Isaacson. So helpful to me he could be—sorry—he'd be so helpful."

I also taught him to use contractions.

Rabbi Isaacson was the head of Central Synagogue in Jerusalem, a theologian and historian. Hjalmar had tried every possible way to see him, letters of introduction, phone calls to his secretary promising a brief meeting, but the Rabbi was too busy.

On the broad steps of the Habimah Theater, we sat. Two disconsolate schoolchildren, the long summer ahead and no plans.

"What will we do about our book, Babe?"

Suddenly it was our book, our theory. Boswell had been elevated to co-author. And then, that light bulb flash—that's what I loved about him. He made me feel indispensable. I was important to someone again. Light bulb! Light bulb. . . . Well, if I was going to be co-author of a philosophical, sociological study on the phenomenological aspects of religion—I'd better figure out how to get this book written and what to wear on "The Tonight Show" when I'm interviewed. I glanced at a blow-up photograph of a bearded Israeli actor outside the box office. Tonight: Chaim Lebedek in *The Dybbuk*.

"I know him," I mused.

"You know this actor?"

"Uh huh."

"How do you know him?"

"I met him with Michael . . . a few years ago at a seminar on world theater."

"Do you know Robert Redford?"

"No. But I know someone who does. . . . Waaait a minute. . . ." I was sounding like Abbott or Costello again. "Maybe Chaim knows someone who knows the Rabbi." I left a note for Chaim backstage.

That night, Hjalmar and I were Chaim's guests at the Habimah and the next week in Jerusalem Hjalmar would have his interview. There are three million Jews in Israel and they are all related. Chaim's nephew is married to the daughter of Rabbi Isaacson's half brother.


*My friend Betsy gave me* very good advice before I left. Never ever ever, she stressed, ask a married man "So what's gonna be?" . . . They need to be needed, but not by the needy.

I had been sitting in front of the dressing table at the hotel, putting on my makeup, Hjalmar watching with an expression of determined curiosity to see how women go from drab to dazzling. I played with my pots and brushes; picked up my eyelash curler and clamped it over my lid. He gasped: "Are you replacing your eyeball?" When I explained it curls lashes, he borrowed it. The long hairs swept up, he stared at himself in delight: "You give me so much yoy!" We tickled each other and fell on the bed. And that's when it happened. It's too involved to go into now except to say I have elves. They live on a shelf in my brain and wait until I'm happy (that's why I seldom mention them) and then they strike. I was caught off guard, in the middle of a giggle, and they made me say, "So what's it gonna be, Hjalmar?"

It was out, uttered, unretractable. Maybe he didn't hear it. Maybe he's deaf in one ear, like Seymour.

He had heard. "Tomorrow we leave for Yerusalem. One week more we have. Then I to Sweden, you to Los Angeles. Next month, Pia and I are no more married. I find an apartment and you come to Falgersund. You are a gift to me. I will not let you go."

As the black window shade of fear lifted, the elves cringed and I sobbed in the light. "You are like a Messiah to me."

"Shhh," he soothed. "You must not say that. Remember Matthew?"

"Matthew who?"

"False prophets and false Christs will appear and promise great miracles."

"Oh, that Matthew." I snuffled back the tears and tried to figure out how to tell Betsy without hurting her feelings.


*Hjalmar drove; one hand on* the wheel, the other on my thigh. Wizened olive trees hugged pebbled hills. Two unescorted camels nuzzling each other started to cross the road, stopped, made a left turn in front of the car, and slowly led us, heralding our arrival through the gates of Jerusalem; their rear ends trumpeting gifts of welcome.

Behind stone walls in the Arab section is El Zahir, a former sultan's home, now a hotel. All the rooms surround a garden bursting with intoxicating flowers. Red turban buttercups, Persian cyclamen, Nazareth iris. Riotous crimson bougainvillea climb trellises in praise of Allah. . . .

*Outside the courtyard is a minaret*
*the sound of the Muezzin's call*
*moves the air in a minor key*

*I walk toward the old city*
*like the moment before a dive*
*my breath doubles skips in my throat*

*Cross-legged on a crate a watchful Turk*
*sipping smoke from a bubble of rosewater*
*hatches his own chickens*

*An Arab with a sheep on a leash*
*waits for me to return his grin*
*then pops open his toothless mouth*

*Two Orthodox Jews seeing me*
*shift their eyes to the sidewalk*
*black hats nodding dismissal*

*And two little boys behind them*
*hands low against their backs*
*join in solemn disapproval*

### KAROOMPH    SCRUNCH

*A bus with its motor exposed*
*is permanently coupled with a '68 Ford.*
*The Israeli busdriver in shorts and a Kippa*
*and the Arab in business suit and Kefiya*
*are being forcibly restrained by their seconds.*
*They will either kill each other*
*or be here when I return.*

A metaphor? . . . I scribbled some notes for a poem.
"Babe, what are you writing? I have not said anything?"

★  ★  ★

*Friday is the holy day* for Muslims. At the mosque, thousands of Arabs prostrated themselves in prayer. Saturday, we went to synagogue in Mea She'arim, the Orthodox section of Jerusalem; and Sunday, to four masses in three churches, then walked the Via Dolorosa, following the Stations of the Cross.

Monday I collapsed from religious exhaustion.

"You rest this morning. I go now for my interview with Rabbi Isaacson. At three o'clock we meet. Mount of Olives, near the foot of the cemetery."

"I'm ready."

He laughed.

"I mean I'm ready for the interview. . . . I thought I was going with you."

"But it will be so scientific. You will be bored."

Betsy would say, "Don't press it."

"He's my Rabbi too," I muttered, but Hjalmar was out the door.

It was the first time in twelve days we were apart. I sipped some Turkish coffee and chewed on the saturated sugar cube.

Seymour . . . Seymour would have a lot of questions—and answers for me. What do you know about this Elmer? I couldn't tell him he borrows my eyelash curler and hot rollers—he'd say he was gay, which he definitely isn't, because his cook straightened out and was working two shifts . . .

Why was I dialing the overseas operator?

. . . or about the time we walked along the beach and Hjalmar wore a bikini smaller than mine. Men gaped at him and women snarled at me.

Why was a phone ringing?

Why was I talking to Seymour? . . . "It's just that everyone in Sweden is so gorgeous, you have to keep up. He's a dedicated scholar, but no one takes him seriously."

"Maybe it's his bathing suit."

"He needs me in his work—most of the time."

"Get your own job."

"He's spiritual."

"Sure, when it suits him. . . . Elmer's the type who would write a book on Atheism and pray to God it'll be a best-seller."

"I AM MOVING TO SWEDEN!" I proclaimed over the oceans.

"Are you crazy? They're all cryogenic."

"What?"

"It doesn't matter. You'll be too frozen to notice."

There was no point in discussing it further.

*I walked on cobblestones through* crowded lanes of the old city, Bedouin women, tanned and wild-eyed like Gypsies, sabras, soldiers, tourists, Arabs with heavy-laden donkeys, beggars. . . . At the Wailing Wall, the limestone blocks wept from the morning dew, the air thick with the force of souls that had preceded me. Tiny scraps of paper pressed into crevices, written prayers of thousands of worshipers; lamentations for the destruction of the temple, for the dead, for the dying, for the Holocaust, for themselves . . . "For Michael," I wrote on a slip of paper, and wedged it between two mortarless stones.

Hjalmar was waiting for me, seated against an olive tree, flipping pages in his spiral notebook. "Your Rabbi is not so scientific," he said without looking up. "Most of what he says is folklore, quotations from the Talmud . . . but I know he was impressed with my theories. He yust kept his eyes on the ceiling—"

"What did he say?"

"At this time he cannot write a foreword to my book."

"You must be disappointed."

"Not at all. He will be an interesting footnote."

A tear dropped down from under my sunglasses. Hjalmar looked up. "Babe, you are crying."

"It's nothing. Crying is my hobby. . . . I guess I feel bad for you—for our book."

"But I never am sad. Aggravated . . . frustrated sometimes . . ."

That was true. I never saw him depressed. What I had here was one happy Swede. Seymour was wrong.

Hjalmar took my hand and we began our ascent. "Now you see, this is why I bring you here. Here epitomizes what Yerusalem is to three faiths. In the distance"—he gestured in a huge arc encompassing the slope of the mountain—"is the Garden of Gethsemane"—then pointed to the horizon—"the Mosque of El Aksa, and here on this slope, the holiest Yewish graveyard in the world, where for centuries Yews have bought plots because this is where the Messiah will walk through the Golden Gate, face the mount and on Yudgment Day, raise the souls of the dead. . . . So you see," he continued as we trudged over tablets, around tombstones, markers, crypts; rocks backsliding under our feet, "life is not so much a question of how much evidence we have but how much faith."

Why did I have the feeling that was a quote from the Rabbi?

"And if you look yust to the left you can see—"

"Ethel!"

"Ethel?"

"Ethel."

Ethel was lying on a stone catafalque; her pocketbook, a pillow under her head. Harry, a vertical footstone, keening, grieving over his breathing wife.

"My God, what happened?" I took out a Wash'n Dri and patted her perspiring face as Hjalmar held her wrist, checking her pulse.

Harry wiped his eyes with the tail of his seersucker shirt. "We were up there . . . we left the tour"—he pointed and blew his nose—"at the Basilisk of Agony—"

"Basilica," Hjalmar corrected.

". . . Ethel wanted to come down to the cemetery because her cousin Bertie's Uncle Max is buried here. Ethel promised to look him up. I said, 'How are you gonna find him—the tombstones are in Hebrew.' "

Ethel moaned. I wet her lips and she raised her head slightly. "He bought the plot through the B'nai Brith, they must have a section here." Her head fell back on her pocketbook.

"It's so hot . . . she sat on a grave . . . I told her we only had a ten-minute rest stop . . . maybe it's sunstroke."

"I will go get the tour bus and bring it down here." Hjalmar weaved through the burial ground and up the dirt road.

Ethel's left eye opened and seemed to follow Hjalmar's path until he was out of view. "I . . . have to . . . talk." The words pushed forward, urgent, yet effortful. Cradling our arms behind her, Harry and I supported her back as she leaned against me, her weight heavy, unilateral. From her throat, a gurgle, more like a rattle and then: "Maha gella tell cha kro nor you . . ."

"What is that?" Harry cried.

I was frightened and he saw it.

Words tumbled, distorted, fragmented . . . "Ram chay tell kro kro you nor . . ."

Don't die, Ethel!

The left side of her face drooped. Suddenly there was no more sound. She stared straight at me and gripped my hand. Still breathing, her mouth slack, she sat transfixed as Harry and I rocked her.


*All hospital corridors have that* same antiseptic trace. What is it called? . . . Ethyl? . . . Ethanol, I remembered as Hjalmar and I paced the hall with Harry, our shoes clicking against the tile.

The doctor came out of Ethel's room and caught up with us. "It's a stroke," he said, his hand on Harry's shoulder. "Her speech is affected but she can gain that back . . . and some impairment in her hands. It's a mild stroke. She'll recover."

"No stroke is mild." Harry waved his hand. "Our plane leaves the day after tomorrow. If it's mild she can be on it."

"No. No. She should stay here in hospital."

"Can I see her?"

"In a few hours. She's sleeping now."

The doctor reassured Harry again and the three of us shook his hand. We took the elevator downstairs to the synagogue and looked up at the magnificent Chagall window.

"She'll be all right, Harry. She really will."

"Hadassah is a fine hospital," Hjalmar added. "It was built by the Women's Zionist Organization in—"

"Why would she talk like that?" Harry continued his questions.

"It's a form of aphasia. Sometimes at the onset of a stroke, speech becomes garbled. . . ." Hjalmar knew everything.

I had the feeling Ethel wanted to tell me something.

*It was noon. Our last* day.

"I can't swallow anything."

"Yust try. You haven't had any breakfast. I have finished my packing and you have not started. The boy will be here for our luggage at twelve-thirty and we have to go to the bank. I must get sheckels for kronor."

"What?"

"I owe you money. We have to pay the bill."

"You gave me kronor."

"That was for Tel Aviv."

"I'll use my traveler's checks."

"You will have a service charge and lose money. Dollars and kronor to sheckels. Always pay the hotel bill in the currency of the country."

I improvised frantically as though I could hold him forever with an entertainment.

". . . And there's a high fly ball. Marks is under it. Francs is caught between first and second and it's a triple play—Drachma to Sheckels to Kronor and Pesetas is out on third."

"You are crazy," Hjalmar said, laughing.

It was no joke. I was falling apart. "I have to pack. I have to call Harry at the hospital. I have to go to the bathroom. I'll never see you again. I want to die." One thing about me—I'm not needy.

"Yust sign your name at the bottom of the traveler's checks, fill in the Bank of Israel and I will go and bring you sheckels."

I made a pitiful attempt to say something flip but nothing would come out. I sat there signing and crying. Twice I wrote "Babe" for my first name.

"I meet you in the lobby. One o'clock sharp." He blew me a kiss.

We still had time. Hjalmar had scheduled everything, ordered a taxi. The drive to Tel Aviv and Ben Gurion Airport would take an hour. His plane left at four, mine at six. We would check in early and then have time to sit quietly in the airport lounge.

I petted his suitcase. I wanted to crawl in. Instead, I made a slingshot with the elastic SAS tag. Flight Thirty-seven. Assad knocked; fourteen years old and smiling with an open mouth, proudly showing me his new gold tooth. I reached inside my wallet to tip him. The kronor! In the rush, we'd both forgotten it. Maybe they'll change it at the desk. If he's upset, I'll make up the difference. I gave Assad an American dollar. He nodded. "You have a nice trip." I wasn't sure if it was a question or statement but I said "Yes" and thanked him as he took the bags.

Zombielike I touched every object in the room, stared at each corner, the garden outside our window and then called Harry. Ethel was better, although her speech hadn't returned. "I'll miss you on the flight back, but we'll see each other in California." I promised I would drive to Costa Mesa to visit them.

Well, good-bye, room. Goodbye, Jerusalem.

I waited in the lobby, organized my handbag, checked my ticket, walked back and forth to the courtyard . . . one-thirty. . . . There must be a line at the bank. No. I know. He's buying me a present. I wished I had put a note in his suitcase. No. Pia might see it. What if I write something funny, noncommittal? I had an idea. I took a hotel postcard from the front desk and wrote: "My Compliments to the Cook."

I walked over to Assad, standing at the far corner near several suitcases. "Assad, I need to put something in the suitcase." He pointed to mine.

"No, the other one."

"Not here."

"What?"

"Not here. Gentleman come back and take."

"What gentleman?"

"Your gentleman. He give me this." Assad dug in his pocket and pulled out a colored paper bill. Ten kronor. "He say this is more then one dollar."

I backed away from him. Don't do anything. Don't say anything. You don't know anything yet. . . . But I do know. It was too painful for him to say good-bye at the airport . . . the traveler's checks! He's left a note for me at the desk with the traveler's checks.

"Excuse me. Did a . . . my uh . . . Did Dr. Krogstrom leave anything for me? Room twelve."

"No."

"Some traveler's checks?"

"No. But you can check with the cashier." He pinged the silver bell.

"Yes um . . . we're checking out. Room twelve. Did Dr. Krogstrom . . . leave anything for me?" I licked my lips. There was no saliva in my mouth.

"No. But I have your bill ready."

I gave her my Visa card. "Let me ask you something." I took out the kronor. "How much is this worth?"

She counted them. "That's two hundred and thirty kronor. I'll have to look it up." She thumbed through some index cards. "In sheckels or dollars?"

"Dollars." I rubbed my tongue with my fingers.

"At today's exchange rate: twenty-six dollars and forty-three cents."

"The bank. Where is the Bank of Israel?"

"Just here at the corner."

I ran. My chest ached and I held it. We had passed it every day. Why didn't I notice? I pulled at the oblong brass handles. They didn't move. No one was in the bank. A fan spun lazily on the ceiling. I tugged again. An elderly Hasid stopped to watch me. He won't help me. You people never talk to me.

"Ken I help you?"

"The bank. Is the bank closed?"

He tried the door and shrugged. "Ven de door is shut—de bank is closed."

Just what I needed. Talmudic reasoning. "What does the sign say?"

He shrugged again. "Closed!"

"What else?"

"Open eight to twelve-thirty, four to seven . . . twelve-thirty to four—Closed."

"Every day?"

"Every day. And on Shabbos it's closed alltogedder."

My lips began to move as I talked to myself in silence. I thought of Ethel. This is what a stroke feels like. I leaned against the building. The old man watched me. . . . Why would he do this? . . . The checks. The money. . . . It was all right. The bank wouldn't give him the money, not if they were made out to the Bank of Israel. . . . No! I hadn't! . . . Only one of them. I had signed my name at the bottom of all of them and then Hjalmar had told me to finish packing. He said he would fill in the middle for me. I had countersigned thirty one-hundred-dollar American Express traveler's checks and he took the packet with the reference numbers. . . . I must have stood there a long time. I didn't even realize tears were running down my face.

The Hasid stroked his beard. "Are you vaiting for someone?"

"Karl Malden."

There was one more thing to do. I still had time. It was ten after two. I could make it to the airport. To SAS. Meet him. There had to be an explanation. . . . No. I'll call. Leave a message for him at the check-in counter . . . give him a chance. I was sweating. Nauseous. At the hotel I asked them to connect me with SAS. I picked up the lobby phone. "I'd like to leave a message for a passenger who is leaving on the four P.M. flight for Stockholm."

"Flight number?"

"Thirty-seven."

"Flight number thirty-seven leaves at two P.M."

"Has it left yet?"

"All SAS flights leave at scheduled departure time."

Assad brought me a cup of murky coffee. There was really nothing more to figure out. It was quite simple.

That July in Jerusalem, the Messiah came and went—with three thousand dollars in cash and traveler's checks.

# F I V E

*. . . and Ethel tried to warn* me, but she had a stroke. She's psychic." I had delivered a forty-five-minute monologue and suddenly wondered if Seymour had fallen asleep, the phone on the pillow, next to him. "Are you there? You haven't said anything?"

"It could be worse."

"How could it be worse?"

"It could have happened to me."

"I can't talk to you."

"You just did."

"I am having a breakdown! I need a psychiatrist."

"You need a course in international banking."

"Seymour, I have no more energy for snappy repartee. I've lost three thousand dollars and my self-esteem. . . . I'm filled with self-pity, I'm writing lousy poetry, Roberta never wants to see me again, Hjalmar left me. . . . I don't know what I did wrong."

"Why did you take so much money with you?"

"BECAUSE I KNEW I WAS GOING TO BE RIPPED OFF!"

"Now you're talking."

"What?"

"Quit being so lame. You knew it all along. You're like a dangling plug . . . you're so anxious to be coupled, you'll plug in anywhere. You galvanize these defective connections and when the relationship shorts out—you scream for an electrician."

"That's what I have? Faulty wiring?"

"Stop playing the needy little girl. I'm saying you knew it all along. Roberta is a narcissist. Elmer is a sociopath—"

"And what are you?"

"I'm retired."

"Maybe I'm punishing myself for Michael's death by picking nonavailable men. . . . I'm still grieving for him."

Seymour exhaled. "You just saved yourself a fortune."

"I'll believe it when a psychiatrist puts it in writing."

"Not if they're psychoanalysts. When they're not pissing away your money obscuring the obvious, they backpedal into your unconscious, reducing every emotion to infantile aggression and sexuality. You'll be fifty-three when you get to the anal stage. . . . Anybody who ever had a mother is permanently traumatized and if you had the misfortune to be toilet-trained you're really in deep shit. . . . No more Ma and Pa! You'll have to call your parents archaic superego introjects. You want to live like that? . . . Psychoanalysts are all marginally socialized, self-absorbed elitists. They had offices in my building when I was in practice. I'd see them in the elevator with their beards and abstractions . . . you say hello and they stare at the down button—can't look you in the eye . . . and they drive those goddamned brown Mercedes. . . . Freud was a nuisance. All right. . . . Stop crying. I'll send you to someone."

"Who?"

"Zita. She's a friend of mine. A psychologist . . . won't charge you an arm and a leg. I'll call her and tell her you're coming."

"What are you going to say about me?"

"You don't trust your instincts."

★ ★ ★

*My relationship with Seymour had* changed. Actually, he changed it. One day he told me that unless I stopped being such a love junky, we would have to cool it. I was too emotional and exhausting for him. If occasionally I wanted to sleep with him, he'd make himself available—but only occasionally because he really didn't have the strength for an exclusive affair. He would still continue to be my adviser and I was welcome to call anytime and think of him as Uncle Seymour.

But that wasn't the only reason. I think it was the $10,000 he had to give me.

Toward the end of that first weekend marathon in Palm Springs, Seymour began to nag me about my smoking. "Listen," he said, "if you give up smoking this minute, after you exhale that very puff, I will give you ten thousand dollars six months from today." Now, he knew that I could use $10,000, but he also knew that I was an addictive personality, so he gambled on the premise that he'd never have to pay off. He figured if I cheated, I certainly wouldn't smoke around him and in the interim I'd be cutting down. The son of a bitch was wrong. I did it! I stopped completely. Ten or twelve times during the year, he drove to L.A. unannounced, rang my doorbell, ran through the house, sniffing in each room, foraging in cupboards and demanding a handbag, breath and refrigerator check. He simply couldn't believe it. On April 27, monitoring his heartbeat with one hand and holding a pen in the other, he wrote out the check.

So, now I had $7,000 left from the original $10,000—$3,000 went to the Swedish hit man. I would pay for my analysis with cigarette money.

I made an appointment with Zita.

*In the meantime, my friend* Marlene urged me to see Dr. Philip Wumbsley Smythe. Marlene is a marriage and family counselor who is getting her Ph.D. in psychoanalysis—as soon as she finishes her dissertation. For a while she thought her thesis would be

"Penis Envy in Pregnant Women" but after her third baby she decided she didn't want to think about that anymore so she changed it to "Bilingual Toilet Training: Observations and Significance."

Marlene has been in analysis thirteen years, nine with Wumbsley—or Wumbsley-Smythe, as she sometimes calls him—four times a week. "The difference is"—she fingered the edge of her margarita—"in psychoanalysis you learn how your mind works; therapy, if it's successful, though it rarely is, may change your behavior temporarily but essentially it's like putting a Band-Aid on a major wound."

"When my first marriage broke up, I went to a wonderful woman. A psychologist. She was a great help."

"See what I mean? It didn't stick."

"That was twenty years ago. Life goes on." I have never won an argument with Marlene.

She licked the salt from her finger. "Psychology is like lumpfish to caviar. Mr. Blackwell to Oscar de la Renta, a calliope to a pipe organ—she was on a roll—a Buick to a Mercedes." (Marlene owns a Mercedes and I guess she forgot, or she wouldn't have said it; I drive a Buick.) "Therapists practice from a metaphysical grab bag. They're preachers and cheerleaders. They'll harangue you about life scripts, regurgitating their half-digested knowledge of Freud and Melanie Klein . . . and if that doesn't work, they'll send you to be pummeled, wired, soaked; or worse, insulted . . . and they dress terribly—so if you want God and other masturbatory cures, go see the psychologist Seymour recommended; but a year with Wumbsley-Smythe . . ." She rolled her eyes upward, transcending the mirrored ceiling tiles of the Beverly Hills bar that fractured our images, and indicated with outstretched hands that P. W. Smythe was some kind of conduit to infinite understanding.

Both Marlene and Seymour were absolute and immutable. It must be wonderful to be that assured. . . . Maybe one day I'll write a self-help book, *I'm Learning to Be More Assertive, If It's All Right With You.* . . . I decided to interview Zita and Smythe and make my own decision.

★ ★ ★

**Dr. Philip Wumbsley Smythe is** English and has spaces between his upper four front teeth, which protrude slightly and taper to narrow points at the biting edge. As I sat across his desk, I was grateful he didn't ask what I was thinking because I had the persistent image he could eat an apple through a tennis racket. He's fairly nice looking when he keeps his teeth to himself. About sixty, tall, dark gray hair with two broad skunk-white stripes starting at the temples and wrapping back. In his blue, pin-striped suit, four-in-hand tie, vest with watch fob and chain, and his mouth closed, he reminded me of a male mannequin in the window of a men's clothier on Saville Row.

"You were ahsking," he said, in his British nasal song, "how far back one goes? . . . Nothing in our behavior is arbitrary, haphazard or meaningless." He rubbed a pencil lengthwise between his fingers. "Birth, infancy, early childhood provide the clues to our neurosis, sexuality and pathological behavior. In psychoanalysis the only true evidence is in the secret mansions of memory."

"Marlene told me your work is primarily with borderline patients. . . . She's an analyst in training so I guess she's the exception." Why did I say that? I thought. . . . "I guess I said that because I was wondering if I was borderline enough for you to take me." I was so nervous I called him Dr. Smith.

"Smythe," he corrected me. "As in blithe. . . . Would you care to . . ." He tapped the eraser lightly on his desk and then gestured to *it. It* stood away from the wall, loosed from its moorings; a nineteenth-century divan, free-floating in the midst of art deco. ("He bought it at an auction in Sotheby's," Marlene had confided.)

There it was. The hypnagogic ship that would carry me back to Ol' Vienna.

I lay on the mummy-brown, woolly-covered couch with tortured, bowed legs, a lace doily underneath my head, and fiddled with my skirt as he sat behind me; the headrest, slightly damp from the previous passenger and musty. I thought I caught a whiff of Georgio perfume, then it vanished, as garlic, I'm sure it was garlic, took over and then back to musty.

I smelled the silence.

Neither of us spoke. I turned on my right shoulder and pivoted my head around to look at him. Nothing. I realized that with lesser effort I could stay on my back, arch my neck and view his face upside down. Still nothing.

What I was hoping for, and I knew it was ridiculous to expect, was: Places please. Curtain going up.

Somehow I began and at various times during my broken recital, I heard from behind me, "Hmm hm. Hmmm hm. Hmm hm"; except when I asked him if he believed in death, he said, "Go on."

"I . . . my . . . died . . . cancer. . . . I don't know who I am . . . miss him so much . . . died . . . poetry . . . Palm Springs . . . Israel . . . three thousand dollars in cash and traveler's checks . . . Strange men in my life . . . Do you believe in death? . . . I've been trying to remember . . . What was I saying? . . ."

I shuffled through rumpled memoirs written on the loose-leaf pages of my mind. It was my life and I'd lost my place.

"You were ahsking"—he repeated verbatim the sentence before my lapse—"was it Lou or Bud Costello?"

"Did I say that?" . . . Papers flapped out of sprockets. My ring binder was busted. . . . "Oh yes, the fat one in Abbott and Costello . . . What's his name? Do you know?"

"You want to know if the fat man is Abbott or Costello?"

"Yes, I'd like to know that."

"And you want me to tell you?"

"If you could . . . it's been driving me buggy."

"And when I tell you, you will not feel buggy?"

"I'd feel relieved."

"And you want me to relieve you?"

"Well, not exactly . . . I . . . I . . . I just would have an answer to my question."

"You want me to answer the question?"

He didn't know.

Tears that hung on my ears like pendants plopped through the holes in the doily as a new surge washed over my face. I had used all his Kleenex, and he had to get up from his chair and supply a fresh box from a cupboard and set it on the little side table next to me. "I'm sorry I'm using so many tissues."

"Eck-chew-ally [actually] is it the tissues or something else absorbing you? . . . Do you realize how amused you look?"

"You just made a pun. I like puns."

"Did I? . . . Ahh yes. . . . So I did."

I swiveled my head around and he was smiling, his lips covering his teeth. He looked at me kindly, turned his palms upward with a light, lifting motion as though raising me from my crypt and murmured, "To be continued."

I was relieved. The wool tufts from the couch had poked through the doily, invading my ear canals, and I had to scratch the dampened, stray hairs with my index fingers.


*I liked Zita. She thought* I was well enough to sit up.

I sank into a poofy-cushioned wicker chair. Zita wore a caftan, the colors of a Tequila Sunrise. The office was filled with plants, flowers, baskets and floor pillows. She had a small yellow watering can, the kind I had once seen in my illustrated poetry book, *A Child's Garden of Verses,* and during our initial greetings, "Mary, Mary, quite contrary" saturated a begonia and then sat in a chair opposite me. "So how is the Pharaoh of Palm Springs?"

"Seymour? . . . Seymour is Seymour."

"He's a Theomaniac," she said.

"I thought you were friends."

"We are. The two aren't mutually incompatible."

"We had sort of an affair," I confessed. "It's over now but we talk to each other on the phone."

"You should have come to me first."

The session went very well. It was animated and chatty. We talked a great deal about Seymour. She referred to him as Bwana, Khan (Kahn *is* his last name) or the Dalai Lama. But when I told her about a particular incident, she called him "Shmuck."

She was funny about names and didn't have a last one. Just Zita, Ph.D. . . . something about needing to live without familial attachments. It seemed cavalier to me. I mean, it was all right for a manicure shop—Nails by Zita—but what about driver's license, Social

Security, bankbooks? I wanted to ask but felt it was too personal; besides she was telling me something even more astounding.

Zita was born dead.

At birth, the cord had been cut, she had been slapped several times, cleared of mucus, given mouth-to-mouth resuscitation, but there were no vital signs. Her grandmother, attending as midwife, wrapped the baby in a blanket and put her in a warm oven for about seven minutes, until Zita howled that she was *bien cuit* (done to perfection).

Zita explained she had gone beyond the theory of classical analysis and disagreed that a therapist remain neutral. "It perpetuates the childlike state in the patient; the analyst becoming the all-knowing, nongiving, parental figure. . . . I share my pain, my evolution, my life experience. . . ." She winked at me.

*I had had insights in* both sessions. Smythe made me aware that dealing with despair is a backward journey on the road ahead to feeling good. Zita made me feel good, and isn't a nice, forward journey a pragmatic way to avoid roads that lead to backward, despairing thinking?

The next five days I alternated between knife-edged anxiety and narcotized depression. I needed help fast.

I took out a yellow pad and wrote on it.

| **Smythe** | **Zita** |
|---|---|
| | |

*Charges*

| Smythe | Zita |
|---|---|
| $80 per session | $45 a session |
| billing once a month | check after each visit |

*Completion*

| Smythe | Zita |
|---|---|
| 4 times a week—4 years | 4 times a week—1 year |
| 2 times a week—8 years | 2 times a week—18 months |

|  Smythe  |  Zita  |
|----------|--------|

### Convenience

| Beverly Hills—less gas | Tarzana—farther, more gas but less per session |

### Cancellations

| three days in advance | 24 hours |

### Calling

| through service | home phone—anytime |

### Cathexis

| fatherly image—conveys sense of worry about me | motherly image—conveys sense of enjoying me |

### Concerns

| afraid he'll bite me | afraid she'll crush me (Zita is fat) |

### Credentials

| MBBAS, FRC, DPM British Psychoanalytic Institute | MSW, LCSW, PH.D. U.C. Berkeley |
| Supervising Psychiatrist—Blackpool for the Criminally Insane | *Residency*—Camarillo *Staff*—Channel 11 TV |
| *Associate Professor*— Psychiatric Division, Our Mother of Miracles, San Pedro, CA | *Ecstasy Seminars* 1981–83, Esalen, Santa Cruz 'Channeling, Crystals and Color Analysis' |

| Smythe | Zita |
| --- | --- |
| *Author*—"Counter-Transference in the Treatment of a Case of Pathological Masturbation" | *Author*—New Wave recordings on cassette: "Sin, Fear and Guilt Removal" LX457839 |
| *Co-Author*—"Kleinian or Kohutian Modalities? Pre-Genital Inquiries" | "Psychic Self-Defense—Practicing Inner Karate" BR256309 |
| *Articles*—"Die Schrecklich Kopfschmerzen," *Summary of a Letter to Sigmund Freud by Elsa Geisteskrank in Vienna Quarterly* February 23, 1908 | *Articles*—"Weight Loss Thru Rebirthing," a personal account, *Ms.* Magazine, October 1982 |

It was a difficult choice but I finally made a decision. I would go four times a week: two to each of them.

Monday 10:00 A.M., Thursday 12 noon—Zita.

Tuesday 8:10 A.M., Friday 12:10 P.M.—Smythe.

With input from two analysts, treatment would be more comprehensive, $7,000 would go further (Zita being $35 less per session) and I wouldn't be hurting Seymour's or Marlene's feelings. Two shrinks could "transform neurotic misery into common unhappiness"* a lot faster.

*I sat outside Zita's office* on a six-foot, yellow, cracked Naugahyde couch that faced two doors. ZITA and LONNY LEVANO shared

PH.D.        PH.D.

a narrow waiting room, a sterile contrast to the Hawaiian lanai in-

---

*Sigmund Freud.

side. It was 9:45, Monday morning. There were no magazines. I was thumbing through the high points of my despair when the hall door opened slightly, as though a breeze had pushed it, and a slim young man entered on a cupful of air. He sat on the couch next to me, leaving a polite distance between us, and crossed his right leg over his left, then double wrapped the top one around the supporting ankle. His arms intertwined in imitation of his lower half. Neither of us spoke in those first few seconds and then simultaneously: "Hello/ Hi." We rumbled our little laughs in unison.

He stared at his doctor's door. "I love your boots."

"Oh thanks," I said, and picked at a nick on the imitation black snakeskin.

"Where did you get them?"

"On sale at Bullock's."

"I never find anything there."

"This was Bullock's in Palm Springs."

"Well, no wonder. . . . What's your name?"

"They call me Babe but I'm working on changing it."

"Babe is nice. Zita only has one name."

"I know."

He didn't introduce himself and I didn't ask. Maybe he was having trouble with *his* name.

We sat in silence. He looked at his watch. "I see Lonny three times a week. Monday at ten, Thursday at noon and Friday at eleven. Sometimes we have lunch."

"That's nice."

"Have you had lunch with Zita yet?"

"No . . . not yet."

He seemed to strain for a new topic. I tried to help him out. "How come there are no plants or magazines here?"

"They get swiped," he said, and nodded gratefully. . . . "So Zita took the plants inside. Lonny has the magazines. Sometimes they use each other's offices. . . . Zita has more floor space for the Sensoriums but Lonny's bathtub is bigger for Rebirthing. . . . They're very good friends. . . . They take each other's phone messages."

"That's nice."

From inside Dr. Levano's office, footsteps. The slim young man unknotted himself, bounced off the couch, and expelled a tentative giggle as Dr. Levano escorted a plump, motherly type, dabbing her eyes, to the hall door.

"Don't worry, Mrs. Silberstein," Dr. Levano called after her. "He'll be fine."

The no-named young man introduced us. "Lonny, this is Babe. She's new."

The good-looking doctor walked over to the couch and gave me a reassuring double handshake.

They moved inside and Lonny turned back, "Great boots," he said, and closed the door behind them.

*I suppose I should start* with my childhood." I began talking the moment I saw Zita, overlapping her hello to me and her good-bye to a stringy-haired young woman, shielding her face in her hands, seemingly warding off news photographers. It was the second session and already I was panicked about time and money running out. What followed was a nonstop rat-a-tat-tat monologue, the kind usually reserved for conversations with myself.

"I used to think I was monozygotic—developed from a single fertilized ovum. I had a twin but I lost him or her somewhere. My mother said I was an only child but I never believed her. Other than that, I was happy. I mean they were crazy about me. They bought me this great sled at Christmas. I guess you could call it my 'Rosebud.' There was this hill that the kids called 'Suicide Hill'; I was the only girl who ever went down it. . . . I had buck teeth, freckles. . . . I'm very conscious of people's teeth. . . . I was a tomboy, but I really wanted to be cute like Melinda. One day, in the fifth grade, Steven Benson handed me a Valentine. He asked me to give it to Melinda. When Hjalmar said good-bye—well, that's a euphemism—I felt like Steven Benson had kicked me in the gut. . . . My head once got stuck in an iron grill. I was looking through a basement window. I got my head in but couldn't get it out. The fire department came with a hacksaw. . . . I was married to this criminal lawyer—Bernie the Attorney—he sent me to Chihuahua, Mexico, for a divorce. . . . I used to read my poetry in coffeehouses in Greenwich Village. Sometimes I danced to the verses. . . . Do you think I'm afraid of success? . . . When I was thirty I met Michael. I grew up. We were married for twelve years. He died of cancer. It's almost a year now. I love him."

"What strikes me," Zita said, leaning back in her chair, "is your childhood . . ."

"Yes?" I leaned forward expectantly.

"You were lucky. My mother was an alcoholic and my father was an asshole."

I cringed. I never called anyone an asshole in my life. It hadn't occurred to me a person could be known by his parts.

Zita mistook my cringe for empathy. "I've transmuted the experience. I've dissolved the negative images of my past. We really are the summation of our subpersonality units. On the physical level, I'm thirty-eight, crimpy brown hair, about five-foot-one; my face is heart-shape, my body pearlike, I weigh a hundred and forty-seven pounds and when I sit, my feet don't always reach the floor, but on the intrapsychic level, I re-experience myself and my affirmation changes your conscious conceptualization of me."

"How do you do that?"

"I visualize yellow."

"Is this therapy? I mean, how do I get rid of the pain?"

"That is the golden road." She clapped her hands together in delight and the cheeks of her heart-shaped face puffed in and out causing the point of her little chin to elevate and recede.

Zita was blissed out.


*I was afraid I'd fall* asleep on Wumbsley's couch. It was 8:10 A.M. Tuesday, too early to think. And my head was spinning from Monday's session with Zita. "Do you want to hear about my childhood?"

"Whatever you feel you want to tell me."

". . . got a letter from my mother yesterday."

"Why don't you explore your feelings about it."

"It's better if I read it . . . unless, maybe . . . you want to read it."

"I'd rahther you read it."

*Darling,*

> *Daddy and I are looking forward to our first trip to Europe. God forbid, the plane goes down we want you to have this information. The key to the safe-deposit box is in the metal chest next to where I keep the good silver in the hall closet behind the wicker basket. If anything happens to us, go immediately to the bank and take out the contents of the box. At the bank, where it says: "Is this person or persons to your knowledge deceased?"—write no!*

> *I just opened another account and under separate cover I'm sending you a set of serrated steak knives I thought you could use.*

> *Our will states that Daddy and I are to be cremated but Daddy still isn't sure. You see, the advantage of cremation is that you won't have to worry about perpetual care as that can add up. You remember how overgrown Grandma was when we went to visit her at Slumberland.*

> *If, God forbid, the plane goes down and Daddy and I pass on together, our old friend, Mr. Berkowitz—the lawyer—will explain everything to you; unless, God forbid, Mr. B. goes first.*

> *Try to remember to see a dermatologist about that bump on your forehead. You said you got it in Israel and it should have gone away by now. Those things have a way of spreading into some Latin name that sounds simply awful.*

> *Should we crash or catch on fire, you may have forgotten that one key opens two locks but in the reverse position on the front door.*

*We're looking forward to a lovely trip, if God forbid,*
*nothing happens in Europe.*

> *Love,*
> *Your mother*

"My mother is an anxious woman."

"Is that how you interpret it?"

"You got anything else?" My ears were filling with wool again. I was very irritable.

"I'm experiencing that remark as hostile."

"I'm sorry. I didn't mean to be rude. I just . . . Oh God . . . I don't know."

"I think you do. You feel deprived of your mother's breast, the infantile guilt of nursing is seen as damaging to her. The guilt turns to rage, is internalized, then displaced towards me with the hostility you express as I witness your aggression against dependency."

I felt terrible. "What'll I do? I can't call a seventy-two-year-old woman and apologize for the hole in her breast. . . . They're on their way to Europe. I want them to have a nice time. . . . Could I tell her when she comes back?"

*In the sessions that followed,* Smythe shoveled under the topsoil, unearthed every fragment and filtered the fossils through his psychoanalytic sieve. Zita cheerfully scolded that if I continued to dig in graveyards all I'd come up with is bones. After three months of analysis I was metaphorically cuckoo.

And I never mentioned my elves. One. What was the point? I was feeling so lousy they weren't bothering me. And two. Zita and Smythe might think I was crazy.

On the weekends I cried. Marlene wanted to fix me up with a physics professor at U.C.L.A. but told me to check with Wumbsley to see if I was well enough to date. . . . To date or not to date. That is the question. The only thing that gave me solace was reading Shakespeare. I tried Freud and Jung but I just felt worse. Everything they wrote about, I had. . . . Michael was right: "Whatever you want to know—look in Shakespeare."

I wanted to talk about Michael. His life, our time together, his illness, his death—but I felt pushed from the subject, caught between Smythe's "then" and Zita's "now." What was missing was the middle. Michael was the heart of my life and I had a vague notion that the clues lay constricted as a blood vessel and would burst out web-like, connecting past to present only if the center was pierced.

Why did I stay in analysis? Because a person has to have something to hang his head on. Smythe has Freud. Marlene has Smythe. Seymour has Seymour. Zita has whatever the hell it is. My neighbor collects bees and puts them in a jar.

And Zita said I had to be Rebirthed.

"Zita, I'm not sure I want to be reborn. Once was enough."

And Smythe wanted a dream.

And a dream was a prerequisite for Rebirthing.

I had failed them both.

Every night I got into bed early, wild-eyed, rigid, begging for sleep, a pad and pencil on the night table next to me, and waited. Zita suggested ginseng tea, which I laced with scotch. Then I tried warm milk. I studied the reindeer shapes on the empty glasses. Michael used to say herring gives you nightmares, so I forked a jar of Vita down. Nauseous and dreamless I tossed.

Finally. Finally. On a night before my session with Smythe—a winner!

There are two of me, joined by the feet, at a right angle, on the face of the Grand Central clock. Reaching. My twin bodies, the timepiece hands, reading three A.M. Motorized, we tick the hours. Then, one of me becomes Charlie Chaplin . . . climbs in back of the clock . . . tries to stop it. But I'm caught between sprockets and gears, sliding through cogged wheels while the other me turns into Harold Lloyd and hangs from the minute hand. The sweep/second is racing. I have to say good-bye. Track five or nine? Remember? You must! ALL ABOARD. Railroad time. Daylight savings. Eastern Standard. Not pacific. Not specific. "Please! Please!" I'm screaming. A black conductor stands on the floor of the terminal, calls up to me, "Sorry, Babe. You've done missed everything. Let go the clock."

Wumbsley sighed through his nostrils and exhaled the magic dust of psychognosis:

"Here we can see the infantile rage of your own impotence. You are longing for the train; the penis, of course, withheld from you by the formidable conductor who calls you Babe, or Baby, as a father would. You see yourself as passive, prone, glued to the clock as in your sessions with me. In a sense, I, too, am the conductor. I am denying you, as your father did, our penes—"

"What?" It sounded like flowers. . . . "Peonies?"

"Plural of penis. Penes or penises, if you will."

"Okay. I'm sorry. Go on."

Then he told me that three o'clock (the number three) represents the testicles and male organ and the ticking of the clock was my throbbing clitoris.

Oh, God!

I changed the subject. "And Chaplin, who is Chaplin?"

"Chaplin," he mused . . . "is the needy tramp."

"That's me! That fits!"


*Z*ita, how many penises are in my dream?"

"None."

I leaned back in relief.

"That's the problem," she continued.

I was done for.

"You mean I want my father's penis?" I couldn't tell her I wanted Smythe's.

"No. You want your own."

I was sobbing so profusely during her diagnosis that we had to stop several times to allow me to recover. It seems that similar dreams appear in neurotics and Aborigines.

"It's true," she consoled me, "we all have an androgynous nature, but yours points to your male counterpart strongly. The numbers, three, five, nine, are all odd, masculine numbers. You feel in a

84

sense you're an oddball. You can't get on the train. You can't be powerful. The symbols in your dream point to leaving behind the female self and the longing to identify with the train. . . . In our previous talks you've often mentioned that you thought you were a twin—"

"I was lonely for a brother or sister. . . ."

"There are too many clues to be disregarded. . . . There it is, the negative tape, some sense you have that you should have been a boy."

"And the black conductor?" I managed weakly.

"Soul transit."

"Soul transit?"

"You are yearning to be reborn again. A new you. A new identity. . . . Submergence. Emergence. A celebration!"

She handed me a Xerox sheet entitled "Rebirthing: Apparatus and Information." "The water is ninety-nine degrees, the temperature of amniotic fluid—you'll love it. I'm so excited for you."

The hour was up. I moved toward the door. "Why did I turn into Harold Lloyd?" I asked, getting my last minute's worth.

"Harold and Lloyd are both men's names."

I looked at her, balefully, hoping she would restore my lost feminity, but she made two pat-a-cake claps with her hands as though to reaffirm her insight.

Driving home it occurred to me that if numbers meant something in dreams, instead of viewing them as odd or even, what if I added them—three, five and nine equal seventeen. Michael died on the seventeenth of September. A year and two weeks ago. And I could not bear to go to the cemetery. . . . And Chaplin? Well, Charlie and I were flattened, squashed like in *Modern Times*. I had always felt like Charlie inside: down at the heels, tottering, pixilated. I lived on a bias. There was something funny in despair. Way back it stayed. Filed away. Maybe I'd find it one day. . . . But why did I turn into Harold Lloyd? . . . Who's to say what a dream means? Isn't the dreamer the only one who really knows?

I headed south along the avenue that borders a line of narrow streets in my neighborhood. All with first names. Agnes Way. Robin

Place. Willy Lane. Last month, the city planning commission passed a law. Due to traffic congestion, all the side streets are now one-way. It's such a nuisance. I have to make a left at the block *before* mine and go around. I keep reminding myself. Turn into Harold—then Lloyd.

*I was breathing through my* snorkel when the phone rang. I forgot I had my nose clips on. . . . "Huddo."

"Is that you?" It was Marlene. "You sound like you have a cold."

The rubber strap was tangled in my hair. "I hab my node clips on."

"Why?"

"I'm pracdiding for my Rebirding." The prongs boomeranged against my nostrils.

"What?"

"Hode on a thecond." The rubber snapped from my scalp.

"How's it going with Wumbsley-Smythe?" She hadn't understood me. I was safe.

"Not good. I think it started in utero."

"Until you understand the depressive position of your denial—"

I couldn't stand her anymore. . . . "All I hear about is my pregenital orgies. I'm a monster—"

"Did you say Rebirthing?"

"What's the difference? If I have to go back to the womb, Zita'll get me there faster."

"Who's Zita?"

Now I wanted her to hear. "Zita of Tarzana. A psychologist I'm going to!"

Her silence made me shiver. . . . Finally and deliberately she said, "Are you crazy?"

"Yes!" . . . Then I panicked. "Don't tell Smythe."

She hung up.

*The yellow vinyl sweated from* the October heat as I sat on the couch and waited; my snorkel, a periscope, surfacing from my handbag. I didn't hear any water running. I wanted my bath. I wanted to go back to the womb. . . . How would I be able to hear what my father said when I emerged? In those days, husbands weren't allowed in the delivery room. I WANT MY BATH. . . . What if the doctor said, "It's a girl," and my mother moaned, "No way!" and then they told my father while he was pacing the hall and he said, "Forget that!" What would I do. I'd kill myself. I'd have to start wearing jockey shorts. . . . And my high heels? What would I do with all my shoes? My sexy lavender sandals?

It was twelve noon. Zita was late. My friend wasn't there and I missed him. I hoped he wasn't sick. We tried to get to our appointments early so we could visit. Sometimes we'd bring each other coffee in Styrofoam cups. . . . Where was Zita? . . . Everyone was late for my birthday.

Dr. Levano's door opened and there was Lonny and my friend. My friend looked perplexed. "Where were you yesterday?"

"Yesterday was Wednesday."

"Yesterday was Thursday," Dr. Levano offered helpfully.

"Then today must be Friday," I concluded as ice wambled in my stomach. Smythe! Smythe! "I have to be in Beverly Hills in ten minutes. Could I use your phone? . . . And I have to apologize to Zita. Is she with anyone now? I was supposed to be reborn yesterday but I thought it was today . . ." I pointed to my snorkel.

They both looked genuinely concerned for me. My friend put his arm around me to quiet my shaking as the doctor said, "I think Zita is on the phone but you can leave her a note and use the other line in my office. . . . We're going out to lunch, so just close the door behind you when you leave."

I found a notepad on Dr. Levano's desk, looked up Smythe's number in my address book as I depressed one of the tile buttons near the base of the phone. A little red light winked at me. No dial tone. Instead I heard . . . Marlene was right. I was crazy. . . . I heard Smythe's voice. I hadn't even punched the numbers and I heard Smythe's voice: "I'm expecting her in ten minutes, Doctor, if I can call you that."

"This is highly unethical." It was Zita. "I won't respond to your remark."

Wumbsley's tone was lofty and arched. "We are dealing with an immature ego in a hypermanic state with perverse erotic transferences. Are you aware of that?"

Zita spoke with a mouthful of persimmon. "What we're dealing with is gender confusion and if there are any erotic transferences, they're yours, may I add."

"No wonder she's resistant. You've been damned damaging."

"Bullshit!" Zita said. "If you hadn't been polluting her with your negative mental mass we'd have released the old tapes sooner."

"Don't you dare ventilate your rubbish on me . . . reversing your messiness, talking to me like a W.C. I'm not your toilet!"

Their voices escalated and overlapped. I could hear Zita in stereo; through the phone and through two closed doors.

"She puts her index fingers in her ears every session," Smythe shouted. "Doesn't that mean anything to you? The woman is overtly suicidal and floridly sexual."

"You're the source of your own reality," Zita sputtered. "She doesn't put her fingers in her ears in my office!"

The phone was in my left hand. With my right, I grabbed the snorkel from my bag and smacked it on the desk. Then I heard my voice. I think it was mine. It came from the floor of oceans. It rolled and belched and spewed: "NOW HEAR THIS. NOW HEAR THIS. ZITA, YOU'RE A LUNATIC! SMYTHE, YOU'RE AN ASSHOLE!"

Airless hum. . . . *Click. Click. Click. Shuffle. Scuffle. Slam.* Ran.

*Recipe for Curing Madness:*

*Collect any item blown by the wind before it reaches the ground and mix it with the seeds of the Mufata tree, the roots of the Mupatamhora tree and a little of the patient's urine. Tie*

88

*them together in a bundle and hang from a branch of any tree. Leave it there for two days. Take the patient and two groundnuts to the tree. Ask the patient to sit under the tree and close his eyes; then cut the string of the bundle so it drops down on the madman's head. Immediately afterward, throw the two groundnuts onto his head and order him to return home.*

—Treatment of psychiatric disorders in southern Rhodesia as practiced by the Nganga of the Shona tribe.*

---

*★Magic, Faith and Healing* by Kiev

## S I X

*The exhilaration of having called* Zita a lunatic and Smythe an asshole wore off in about a week. At first it was absolutely heady. Giddy with power, I promised myself as I stood in line at the supermarket that if the checker continued to pack my groceries in a paper bag, after I'd requested ecological plastic, I'd scream, "Recycle, asshole!" If anyone took my parking space as I waited patiently to back up, I'd ream their front end, crunching and swearing, "Lunatic asshole! Asshole lunatic!" . . . But I couldn't do it. Everyone was nice to me.

There is something so lonely about not having anything to fix. And there was no one to call. Seymour was in China, my parents were in Europe, Marlene wasn't speaking to me and Betsy was with a married man in Lake Tahoe.

I had spoken to Seymour briefly, while he was in the middle of packing, and revealed that I was also seeing a psychoanalyst but he wasn't any better than Zita. I thought he'd be pleased. He hung up on me, too.

Three weeks later, on the same day, I received two photos. One was of Seymour, wearing a Ghengis Khan hat and leaning against the Great Wall of China. He had attached a note: "In words of Chinese Philosopher, Charlie Chan: 'When faced with obvious— look elsewhere!' " . . . The other was a photo postcard taken in front of Buckingham Palace. My parents were posing with their arms around each other and grinning at a busbied British toy soldier in his kiosk. On the back my mother had written: "Look how I'm smiling even through my hip is killing me."

*I drove to the cemetery,* winding up a narrow dirt road past shingled houses, framed by floppy green/gray trees. October. Back east the leaves would be changing. In Los Angeles you can never tell what month it is unless you know what month it is. . . . What was that saying? Basically there are only three choices. Life, death or Los Angeles . . .

Michael had chosen the cemetery—"You'll like it—a celestial golf course"—selected the plot and drawn a map which I still had, marking the freeway exit, an arrow indicating the correct direction at a four-way stop sign, the fork in the road and a shortcut to the back of the cemetery where I could park the car on a lane just outside a break in the fence nearest the gravesite. "If you come in this way, you bypass those pillars welcoming you through the Gates of Heaven . . . and you can't miss me—I'll be right there. . . ." He pointed as we walked toward a Monterey cypress, its top matted, flattened and plunging in opposition to its trunk. Michael nodded at the tree and shook his head. "She had a rough time at the hair-dresser." I swallowed and managed a short hum of laughter. In his anthropomorphic world, a lamp was a fat pest, pansies were thirsty orphans, trees waited on the unemployment line. . . . Objects were never what they were supposed to be. . . . I would never see anything again without viewing it through his eyes.

"What's that?" I noticed two numbered and lettered round disks in the ground.

"Spools two-fifty-six A and B. It's cheaper if you buy two plots. You can be in B if you want to, but if you get married again, sell it—you might want to be buried with your next husband, only try to get me someone compatible."

He took out a plastic pill bottle from his jacket pocket, pressing and twisting the cap with the heel of his palm. "Do me a favor, will you. When we get back to town, go to the druggist and have him change the bottle. Tell him a grown man is dying of cancer, there are no children around and to change the goddamned top."

"I'll do it." I handed him his Percocet. He noted the time in a small spiral notebook as I unscrewed the thermos top and poured him some lemonade.

Taking a sip, Michael said, "I've picked out the coffin. There's only one problem. I want a plain pine casket. They only have a few left and they need them for immediate customers. I couldn't promise the funeral director when I was going to die and there's a price change September fifteenth. I left a deposit—the papers are on my desk—don't let them sell you anything else. Not teak, not ebony, not walnut. Pine. Okay? Pine. It's the best. And no brass handles."

"Did he think it was weird?"

"Who?"

"The man who sold you the box?" I couldn't say "coffin."

"Mr. Moribund?"

"Who?"

"It sounds like that. Moriberg? . . . I have his card with the papers. . . . Moriarity? Maybe it's Moriarity . . . Mordant? . . . Murbidoo? . . . I'll think of it in a minute."

Muttering names and sounds beginning with *M,* he lay on his back on the grass, extending his arms to me. I curled into him, my head searching for that soft pad below his shoulder, now hollow and bone-edged. I looked at him helplessly and he answered with my favorite impression, narrowing the corners of his eyes and pulling downward on his lips, imitating the woebegone gaze of a bassett hound. "C'mere," he said. "We'll find you another place." And he lifted me higher, fitting the side of my face against the roundness of his cheek. He kissed the corner of my mouth. "I think I want my head this way. . . . Uh huh . . . I want my head this way." He looked up through the cluster of dark green needles. "The tree will be my headboard."

"Just stop it, Michael. Stop repeating everything. You always say the same thing four different ways. You do it all the time. It's a lousy habit. It makes people feel stupid."

"That's because nobody listens. You ever notice how no one listens anymore?"

"I listen."

"I know you do." He stroked my hair.

About three hundred yards from us, two gravediggers leaned on the tops of their shovels and waited, one of them ditching a cigarette as three cars, led by a hearse, snaked down the circular road from the mortuary and parked at the edge of the curb nearest the gravesite. Double doors at the back end of the hearse opened as two attendants efficiently slid a coffin onto a gurney, rolling it up the grassy incline. A woman, veiled, supported by a younger woman, emerged from the second car and joined the others as they waited to follow behind the casket.

I tugged at Michael's sleeve. "We shouldn't be lying here."

"Why not? It's paid for."

He compromised and we sat up, leaning against the tree, looking down at the funeral scene. Gathering a lacy bundle of fallen evergreen, he tested the sharp tips. "Did I ever tell you that Chekhov story?"

"Which one?"

"About the young acting student who goes to the cemetery to pay his respects to the famous actor Mushkin?"

"No. Tell me."

"Well," he began in a rumbling purr. . . . "Wellll . . . the young actor makes this pilgrimage to the cemetery. It's an old graveyard, terribly neglected . . . broken headstones, rocks, branches, debris. . . . Anyway, he finally finds the grave—"

"How?"

"How?"

"How does he find it if everything's covered?"

"He has a map, you see, just like the one I gave you, fixing the location."

"Okay. Go on."

"Well . . . he clears away the pile of leaves so he can read the inscription but the engraving is scarred and cracked and two of the letters have disintegrated. . . . The epitaph now reads: 'Here lies the --forgettable Mushkin.' Time had erased the 'un.' "

Michael closed his eyes, sucked air through his tightened lips, steering his breath downward to the center of his pain. He gripped my hand. "There are so many parts I never got to play."

Thirty seconds pulsed in his throat.

I knew he meant Ibsen and Chekhov and Shakespeare. "I wasn't put on this earth to do 'Baretta,' " he once said. Passionate about the theater, uncanny in his sense of truth; and chameleon, he could create the psychological and physical reality of another human being—"Wrap yourself in the circumstances. . . . Talk and listen with the illusion of the first time. . . . Acting is life chosen." For thirty years he worked on Broadway, in films, television, though he was convinced after each job that he'd never get another one. When we walked down the street he had the finger-snapping recognition of the public: "Aren't you . . . ?" *Click. Click.* . . . "Aren't you . . . Glenn Ford?" Michael would mumble and ask me, "Are you disappointed I'm not as famous as Burt Lancaster?"

"No. If you were, I'd get you mixed up with Kirk Douglas."

Aging is essential to the artist.

In the distance, charcoal figures moved against the watercolor landscape, forming a semicircle as the words of the Mourner's Kaddish, *Yisgahdal, v'yiskahdash sh'may rahboh,* fractured the sunlight.

He opened his eyes. Moist and darkened with pain, they had changed from clear blue to midnight blue. "Don't do that," he said.

"Do what?"

"Hold your breath."

"I wasn't holding my breath."

"You do it all the time. Whenever I have pain you hold your breath."

I looked at the inscriptions on the stone plaques next to our

spools: IN LOVING MEMORY: MARTIN FEINMAN 1917–1972. BERTHA
FEINMAN 1918–1974. She died two years after her husband, I
thought. . . . "What do you want on yours?" . . . I had said it as
though I was offering him a choice of salad dressings. He smiled. It
had been a long battle between us and now he smiled because he had
won. I had surrendered to his pragmatism. My belief in miracles was
painful to him. But he had not won. Not yet . . . "What do you want
on yours?" I repeated.

"Surprise me."


*I cleared away the grass* clippings, the brownish pine needles
and traced my fingers over his name, the dates and "Thy sweet love
remembered." The third *e* in "remembered" was not supposed to
have been there. When I ordered the stone I had written it out and
specifically told the engraver, "Rememb'red has a contraction instead of an *e*. It's from the sonnet." I stood there reciting as the old
chiseler clacked and hammered.

> *For thy sweet love rememb'red such wealth brings*
> *That then I scorn to change my state with kings.*

Nobody listens anymore. . . . You were right, Michael. And
since you died people talk differently, too. *Psychobabble*. A man
wrote a book called *Psychobabble*. It's a foreign country now. You
need a dictionary to get around. Remember when we used to speak
English? . . . I called someone an asshole last week . . . and another
one a lunatic. They both had licenses. You would have been proud
of me. I think I'm getting better. . . . But I didn't say the three magic
words. You told me whenever I got mad to put "In my opinion" up
front. It takes the edge off. In my opinion you're an asshole? I don't
know. It just doesn't sound right. . . . What do you think?

There was no response. I sorted through scraps of past events
trying to patch the present. I couldn't piece together any dialogue
for him.

Once I had lunch with Milton Berle. He kept file cards with
subject headings. Music, popular. "It's always the same joke," he

said. "All you have to do is update the name of the group. Instead of Dickey Do and the Don'ts—it's the Grateful Dead."

"What's the joke, Mr. Berle?"

"Call me Milton. What joke?"

"I forget. Do you want a bagel?"

Memory is not negotiable.


*That August day, as we* sat under the cypress tree watching the stand-ins mark the shape of our own funeral, which would take place six weeks later, I hit him.

He was holding my hand, cradled in his palm, gently pressing down my fingers, separating one from the other as he counted out his thoughts. "I used to worry about losing my hair." Dark brown and silver tossed softly as he shook his head. "Every morning I'd wake up and look at my hair. It was always there. Even with chemotherapy, I never lost it. I wasted so much time. . . . A solar eclipse is coming. It should be spectacular. But don't look directly at the sun." He tucked in the middle finger. "There are worse things than cancer. You could go through life aimlessly. . . . I'd like you to give the eulogy—"

"I don't want to talk about—"

"Listen to me. I want the burial private but if there's some kind of memorial service in town, I want you to speak. It'll be a good experience for you. I want you to thank my friends for enriching my life. We never told anyone I had cancer, they'll be shocked and I want you to say good-bye to them for me. And try to find a place with adequate parking." He touched the tip of my pinky and I backed away in a crouch, fists clenched, pounding the air, my voice rattling, "I don't want any more instructions."

"What did I say? All I said was: 'After I die you'll be so busy looking for meaning in all this—you'll forget to eat lunch.' "

"No more instructions!"

He got to his feet. "You want to hit me? Go ahead." Turning his arms and fists inward, he positioned himself in the stance of an old sepia print of John L. Sullivan. He circled me. "I weigh two pounds less than you. Come on. Take advantage of a skinny person."

"One hundred and twenty-two! We weigh the same. One hundred and twenty-two," I shouted, raging at the horror of his sixty-pound weight loss.

"Not since this morning!" he boomed.

The semicircle of mourners turned and faced us. One woman opened her mouth in the silent scream of the Munch painting.

"Let's go!" He inched toward me, jutting out his chin, tapping at his jaw. "Right here! Fight. It'll be good for you!"

Still in a crouch my fists swayed and sunk to the grass like an orangutan I had once seen in the zoo when its mate was taken away, crying in a closed-throated lament, "Wooo wooo wooo." I looked up at his gaunt six-foot, two-inch frame. "You're too tall. I can't reach you!"

"Wrong again. I'm five-eleven. Cancer made me shorter. Knock my head off and we'll be even!"

"I can't!"

"Don't you dare give up. Ever! Don't you dare!"

A fat man, sweating in his dark gray suit, puffed up the incline. "Stop that, this minute! There's a funeral going on here!"

Michael shot him a glance. From my squatting position I threw a limp punch brushing Michael's pant leg.

"Not like that. Have some guts. Get up and deck me."

The man hopped back on one foot and coughed into his handkerchief. "I'm calling the police!"

"Get Moriarity. He knows me!" Michael called after him as he toddled back to the group.

I flailed with open hands to push him away rather than hit him. "Please . . . Please . . . Please. Stop rehearsing my grief!"

"I'm rehearsing my own. I want you to stand on your feet. For Chrissake, I don't know who's protecting who. . . . For four years you've been a kitchen paramedic. . . . We're not connected anymore! Stop breathing for me! It's over! Finished! . . . We have to separate!"

"What is this? A divorce?" I rocked down on my knees.

"Yes!"

He offered his arm to help me up, then suddenly drew it back. I knew he could have lifted me with one hand if he had wanted to.

He watched me weave to an upright position, brush my knees and skirt and wipe my tears with a dirty, grassy palm; then shook his head and said softly, "You are making it impossible for me to die."

I hit him.

*The grass was spiny this* time of year. Brittle from the late summer heat, the sprinklers on the grounds had not saturated the roots, softening the new undergrowth. . . . That's how you tell it's October in Los Angeles. . . . I wondered if they would shave the lawn and plant winter grass. . . . There was no one around to ask. It was Saturday and the Jewish section was closed but I had come in the back way. I tucked Michael's worn map into my purse, spread my fringed shawl, sat down and poured some lemonade from the same thermos into its blue plastic cup. The liquid sissed and seeped through a hairline crack.

All the objects of our life together were wearing out. My car, parked by the fence, lay like a dispirited dog. The chassis had sunk and the mechanic said the tensile shaft had separated from the kranz-nurshem causing the differential between the snavver frats and the front end bushings.

"Does that mean it won't go?" It's the only thing I ever ask. That, and when they give me the bill: "How come it's so much?" . . . and they start the damn thing over. "We had to adjust the solon-oid on the coaxial . . ." Michael would have known what to do. . . . There's a course given for women at U.C.L.A. extension: Powder Puff Mechanics. Maybe I'd take it.

Dark shadow from the cypress tree formed an oblong bed. Four o'clock. I prodded my handbag into a pillow. Maybe I'd take a nap. Since I stopped going to analysts I'd begun to dream again. A mile or so up the road, the mortuary blurred in the steamy waves of the muted afternoon. I turned on my stomach, shimmied deeper into the ground, my hand covering the granite grooves of his name. . . . A car stopping? No. The cemetery's closed. Maybe in the other section . . . Methodists die. Presbyterians die . . . White sound . . . My mother was calling me: "Uncle Michael is here." He was my favorite uncle, always hiding wonderful secrets in his pockets.

Standing in a living room, handsome in his tuxedo was *my* Michael. But I was only seven. Hugging, tugging at my braids, "When you grow up, I will take you to China. Would you like that?" From his pocket, a black lacquer box with gold leaf Chinese characters. I clung to his coat. "No. Take me now." My head jerked and twitched on my handbag . . . something was pulling . . . who was pulling? . . . "No. No."

"Shut up and give it to me!"

In the blink between awakening and awareness, I rolled onto my side, my arms surrounding my handbag, scooping up my thermos. Hands and something black flashed in front of my face. In that instant of automatic defense, clutching the thermos, I banged away at them. The hands drew back and I tumbled and lurched to my feet.

Facing me, a man—no, a boy—in rumpled clothes, shaking a gun at me. He shot a quick look over his shoulder, lost his balance, steadied himself, seeming to force his eyelids open. He waved the gun at my bag. "Put that down and back off."

Nothing moved in me. Holding the thermos against my heart, wearing my floppy leather bag like a bulletproof vest, I gaped at the cable thin body and doughy face, ten feet from me. The flaccid lips moved. "You hear me?" He pitched his voice and the gun higher.

A click of alertness. One thought. I did not want to die. God knows it was convenient. I was standing over my own grave. "I've got about thirty dollars."

"Shit!"

What else could I say? Don't shoot, I'll write a check?

"I'm gonna count to three. . . . One!"

That druggie isn't going to take my money. Not in front of Mike. . . . Don't be stupid—he'll shoot you. He looks crazy enough to shoot me anyway. . . . Use your head.

"Two!"

My mother had given me a hand-held Sonic Screamer and a vial of Rape Repellent, but they were in the bottom drawer with my socks.

"Three!"/"I'm putting it down!"

I bent over as I placed the bag on the ground. He took a step toward me, the gun lowered, tracking me. . . . Use your head! What?

How! . . . LITERALLY! In that millisecond I remembered Sukarno's brother. Michael and I had met an actor in Europe who was married to Sukarno's daughter. She told us that when Sukarno was elected president of Indonesia, her enraged uncle ran headlong into a brick wall, bashing his brains out.

In that same crouch, over the same graves, that day when I would not fight for myself, in three strides of a racing start, thermos against my heart, I propelled myself forward, slamming my head into his midsection.

*Ping! Thwump!*

Spilling over him, I rammed the cup handle into his eye, jabbing, smashing, pounding for the dear life that since Mike's death I wasn't sure I wanted. I grabbed the gun near his splayed fingers, scuttled backwards on my knees, violently shaking, hanging on in a double-hand grip, screaming, "You try anything and I'll blow your fucking head off."

There is no original gun dialogue.

He scrubbed at his eye, held his groin, writhing like a desert rat, pleading with runny eyes, "Babe. Hey, Babe!"

"You call me Babe and you've bought it, Buster."

Thank God for movies. I knew what to say. But I didn't know what to do. Guns are heavier than they look in films. Gangsters lift, twirl and flip them like pencils. Steel isn't cold. It's clammy and greasy and the nozzle or whatever the hell it's called kept slipping downward and I was afraid it would go off, splintering my kneecap. Blood was running down my forearm. My shoulder was frozen, locked in its socket. He was getting up. I felt nauseous. His eyes shifted to the dirt road. . . . I followed his look. Was he going to make a run for it? Parked near my sagging Buick was a shiny red Ford, the dealer sticker still on the side window. "Is that yours?"

"Yeah."

The bastard had a new car. I wanted to vaporize him. I aimed the gun at his head.

"So, I stole it. Take it easy!"

What should I do? I couldn't drive and take him with me to a police station.

He jerked his body to the right, taking a step, testing to see if I really would shoot. Something was happening to me. I was terrified but there was also a bubbling inside me, blipping with manic intensity. In an antic parody, with comedic nutsiness as though I were entertaining Michael, I flourished the gun, croaked in a Broderick Crawford voice, "The victim strikes again!" and shot at his toe. He hopped and whimpered, "Okay! Okay!"

Ordering him to keep his hands on top of his head, I walked behind him up the circular road to the mortuary. There was a chapel and offices inside that served both sections of the cemetery, but what if no one was there? . . . He turned and tried to talk to me. I kept saying, "Shut up! Eyes front!" If I could just act like I had guts, pretend I was tough . . . Rivulets of blood covered my slacks. Pain ripped down my arm. I couldn't see the wound in my shoulder. Spurts of livid red popped through the shredded cotton of my shirt-sleeve. My arm joint was on fire. . . . That ping and then that thump sound? Of course! When I ran toward him, he fired, and the bullet, deflected by the thermos against my heart, pinged, skipped and was lodged now in my shoulder. . . . The bullet ricocheted. . . . Dithering with laughter, I repeated it aloud. I couldn't believe it. "The bullet ricocheted." For years I'd tried to use that phrase as a metaphor in my poetry. It never fit. Now it would be the title of a new work. I was sobbing. You were right, Michael, if you don't give up, if you can just live long enough.

A black car, speeding down from the mortuary, skidded to a stop. Two men bolted from the back, grabbing my prisoner. The man driving ducked from under the window visor, reading FUNERAL DIRECTOR, and raced toward me.

"Mr. Moriarity? . . . The bullet ricocheted. . . ." I collapsed in his arms. Cemeteries are violent places.

# S E V E N

*What the hell are you* doing in the hospital?" It was Seymour.

"The bullet ricocheted. . . ."

"What?"

I told him everything. . . . "Are you coming to visit me?"

"I never visit anyone in a hospital. That's how you get sick."

"I have a torn deltoid muscle—not hepatitis."

My mother took the tray from the nurse and placed it on the swivel table over my bed, motioning for me to hang up.

"I have to eat lunch. My mother's cutting my meat."

"You're forty-two years old and she still cuts your meat?"

"Forty-three, now. Anyway, my left arm's in a sling and besides, she likes to do it. Hang on while I chew."

I've never seen a happier mother. She bustled and hummed, menu-planned with the dietitian, arranged flowers; in two days made thirty-seven trips to the nurses' station, took notes on a clipboard when the doctor came, answered the phone "It's Betsy, dear," and before she handed me the receiver, always said "We're coming along just beautifully." It was my dad who concerned me. He sat in a chair, across the room, dabbing at his eyes and shaking his head. My mother, who was convinced each Sunday of her life that everyone she loved wouldn't make it to Thursday, behaved remarkably in the face of actual disaster; but my darling father, after years of waving away wars, recession and nuclear radiation with a flick of his wrist and a malapropism—"It'll all be over in one full swap"—was falling apart. "Your mother was right," he kept sighing, "I should have started worrying sooner."

Seymour waited. I swallowed and asked, "How was China?"

"China is China."

"That's it?"

"That's it."

"You know, Seymour, I'm not going to be cynical ever again. There's so much more in life to experience."

"Come on. . . . Since Mike died, you've been conned by a Messianic Swede, analyzed in tandem and mugged by a druggie. There's nothing left."

"I haven't had a job."

"That's true. But I warn you—you won't like it. . . . Why don't you write a book?"

"I have nothing to say. I'm a poet. . . . I mean I have nothing to say in prose."

"Haiku is not a big seller. Don't you know that? A publisher would sooner see a burglar in his office than a poet. At least he'd collect on the insurance."

"You left yourself out."

"When?"

"When you listed my adventures."

"Oh. . . . Okay. I'll be in your book—if you make me good-looking and print my phone number . . . sandy hair, blue eyes, cheek mole—"

"I can't do that. That's Robert Redford."

"Then I'm not going to be in your book."

"Seymour, my ice cream's melting—"

"And when you write your novel, compose it like a Tsimmis."

"Huh?"

"Yiddish for a stewed dish of dried fruits and veggies. . . . Cook your book with the wrinkled sadness of prunes, the laughing ears of apricots, sexy peaches atop limp, overcooked carrots, bracelets of bitter apples and the lumpy mellowness of a sweet potato. That's what life is."

I didn't know whether to laugh or take notes. "Are you being satirical or serious?"

"It's the same thing."

That's what's so aggravating about Seymour. Aside from an overly generous metaphor and insisting he could be Robert Redford—he's right about everything.

Betsy bounced into the room, looking gorgeous and overheated in a red fox jacket, white mohair beret over auburn curls and suede thigh-high boots. ". . . present from Murray," she murmured in my ear, flipping the side panel and kissing me. "Guess what?" She hugged my parents and dramatically presented each of us with a newspaper. "Our girl made the *Valley News*. Front page. Lower right. WIDOW FOILS MUGGER OVER HUSBAND'S GRAVE!"

There it was, in black and white, with a picture of me, head flopped to one side, hanging off a stretcher in the emergency room.

"Doesn't she look good with her hair that way?" my mother asked Betsy. "You should always wear a side part, dear. . . . Larry, what do you think?"

Dad got up from his chair, walked over to me and kissed my forehead. "Honey, can I take your bullet for a while?" He clinked the lead pellet, given to me by the doctor, in the dish on my bedside table.

"Sure."

"Where are you going, Larry?" Rose (my mother) looked up from her paper as Dad buttoned his sweater.

"Out."

My mother, who always said "Out is not an answer," this time smiled and replied, "Go. It'll be good for you."

I read the story with the removed curiosity conditioned by morning newspaper muggings, until I got to my assailant's name.

"Edward Zerba," I said aloud. "I wonder what's going to happen to Ed Zerba?"

Betsy threw her hands in the air and chuckled. "That reminds me of a joke."

"What joke?"

"Can I tell it in front of your mother?"

"Probably not." Knowing Betsy and my mother.

Rose got up, taking her copy of the paper to the door. "Never mind. You girls visit. I'll show this to the nurses."

Betsy moved to the edge of my bed, laughing as she began. "These two women are on a safari in Africa and in the middle of the night, while they're sleeping, a gorilla with an enormous hard-on sneaks into their tent, grabs one of them and takes her out into the jungle. For hours, he shoves her around, fucks her every which way, knocks her out and leaves her unconscious. The next morning, finding her gone, her hysterical friend gets a search party and finally they find her—still unconscious—and rush her by helicopter to a hospital in Nairobi. . . . For three days, she's lying in bed, moaning, incoherent. Finally, she comes to and her friend tearfully asks, 'What happened?'" Betsy lay back on the foot of my bed groaning her lines. "'In the middle of the night this gorilla took me and he slapped me, screwed me, smacked me, fucked me again.' 'Oh, my God,' the other woman says, 'that's terrible. How do you feel?'" Betsy wailed, "'How should I feel? He doesn't write. He doesn't call.'"

Wiping her eyes, Betsy recovered as I looked at her blankly. "I don't get it. How can a gorilla write?"

"You don't get it, sweetheart, because you're the woman in the joke."

My feelings were hurt but I wasn't sure why.

She looked at my glum face. "It's a jungle out there—wild animals . . ." She petted the fox. "And you expect them to behave like human beings. Human beings don't behave like human beings. Except for Murray . . ." She flapped the side of the coat, cooling herself. "And this was a trade-off."

"You're right. Michael always protected me. But I'm not going to be a victim anymore. I told that to Ed."

"You have the victim's perpetual excuses and expectations."

She kissed my cheek. "You've got to be your own parent, lover and provider."

Easy for you to say, I thought—when you're wearing Murray's coat.

Moving to the door, she turned and waved theatrically as if from the deck of the QE2. "Take care of yourself," she called to me on the wharf.

"Want to go with me on a safari sometime?" Why was I shouting up at her?

"Only if you toughen up."

"Oh, yeah!" I challenged, pointing to the newspaper. "What was that all about?"

"Adrenaline!" And she was off, leaving behind a nest of fox hairs.

A few hours later, when my dad came back I announced: "Tomorrow, I'd like you both to go back to Arizona. I want to take care of myself."

My mother started to cry. "How are you going to cut your meat?" Dad put a restraining hand on her shoulder.

"Ma, I'm forty-three years old. I'll order something else."

From inside his pocket, my father took out a tiny white box with a green bow on top.

"Isn't that nice," Rose sniffed. "Daddy didn't know we were leaving and he bought you a present."

My father always made a little speech before he gave me a present and Mom would say, "That's lovely, dear, why didn't you write it on a card?"

"Honey"—he cleared his throat—"it'll be nick and tuck from now on—but you'll make it!"

Inside was my bullet, a loop soldered to the blunt end, and threaded through it a twenty-four-carat gold chain.

*. . . healing nicely.*" *The doctor removed* the sling and checked under the bandage. "You know you lost a lot of blood—eat some liver." I made a face. He made one back. "Take it easy for two weeks. You'll be fine."

Home.

The cabdriver carried my baskets of flowers to the front porch, setting them down while I paid him. He wished me luck.

Waiting for me, dead center on the welcome mat, was another Deli Dracula plant. Probably from Sondra and Charles. I didn't even look at the card.

Last year, when I had come home from the memorial service, the front porch was dense with bouquets, blooming funeral wreaths, tubs of azaleas and floral sprays on wooden easels, although I had expressed Mike's wishes: In lieu of flowers, please make a contribution to the charity or medical research fund of your choice. "They might like something better than cancer," he suggested. . . . Nobody listened. . . . Afraid to go in the house, I had sat on the steps at the edge of the flower float, reading notes of religious affirmation, silver sympathy cards rhyming *sorrow* with *tomorrow* and handwritten letters, many beautiful and tender, sharing specific memories of Michael, but others rife with euphemism. . . . Passed over. Passed on. Passed away. One woman was shocked to hear of my husband's demise. . . . If death is so unspeakable, how could Michael have gone to his reward?

Now, buried again under a stack of mail; this time, letters from insurance companies, medical reimbursement forms, I sat on the steps, thumbing open the envelopes. . . . During his illness, Michael insisted on doing all the paperwork. He had taken care of everything.

"Don't worry," he said. "It never ends."

He was right. Why do they still need death certificates in triplicate? . . . How can a deceased have an incorrect Social Security number? . . . Enclosed are your payment plan options for death benefit. An oxymoron if I ever heard one.

In laborious idleness, thinking of oxymorons, I stared down the street, delaying the empty house (thunderous silence). But I needed a drink (sweet sorrow), so I got up and walked to the door where that bile-green plant stood and read the note. It *was* from Sondra. "Heard you were in the hospital. When you get squared away, let's do lunch."

And that's when I got pissed. Really pissed. I grabbed the sucker by the stalk, ripped the roots from the earth (I didn't even save the basket), then tossed the overgrown wort into the garbage can in the driveway—beating the tendrils with the lid of the can, growling at the fronds: "I DON'T *DO* LUNCH, SONDRA! AND I KNOW WHY YOU'RE NOT INVITING ME TO DINNER!"

I stomped up the steps—I was sick of all the sadness—unlocked the door—dropped my suitcase with a thud. . . . "I'll make my own dinner!" My voice bounced in the hallway. "I'll repair my shoulder and my ruptured life. I'll get a job. A new car. . . ." No more running away! No more embalming myself in a bottle of scotch or staving off loneliness with those teenagers—Hjalmar and Seymour. I'm tired of being an adolescent widow! . . . I faced the living room. I'll learn to like living in it, alone.

And I am never ever going to allow any man to live rent-free in my head!

The next day, I bought three books: *This Time I'm Really in Love—A Woman's Candid Confession of an Affair With Herself; I Don't Need a Man to Tell Me Who I Am—The Autobiography of the First Woman President of the Boxing Commission,* and *A La King—Fit for a Queen, the Solo Gourmet Cook Book.* After five long nights (they were big books) the theme was the same and stated endlessly: Love the you in you, only then can you give it away. You're worth it! Go for it!

In the first century, before there were singles bars at the marina, Rabbi Hillel said it better: "If I am not for myself, who is for me? And if I am only for myself, what am I? And if not now—when?" . . . I would worry about "And if I am only for myself" later. The now was important. I had to figure out something else to eat. I was beginning to O.D. on canned tuna.

There must be other things that go between two slices of bread. My mother made wonderful sandwiches when I was in grade school. Kids would pay fifty cents for my lunch. Pot roast with raisins, chicken with chutney and walnuts, salmon mousse sandwiches, cold roast duck and apple slices. . . . By the time I graduated it was up to $1.75. Actually I was a pretty good cook, but I hated doing it for myself. Oops! What was I saying? I took out *Fit for a Queen* and decided to start cooking that night. I used every pot.

"No kitchen for you! Out into the dining room! Spread that

tablecloth, light those candles, expensive flowers, excellent wine, put frilly paper panties on the ends of your lamp chop—remember, you're worth it!"

I looked at my splendid creation . . . the Broccoli Au Gratin in its Lilliputian casserole, steaming next to one grape leaf stuffed with pilaf, two tiny pink, can-can bloomers on the cross-legged chops . . . while the wine breathed and I waited for my dinner plate to heat and the salad fork to chill. I was just about to open the silverware drawer and take out a place setting when the doorbell rang. Somebody was coming for dinner, only I didn't know. Like in those dream plays. I wafted to the door in my caftan and makeup. It was Judith from my poetry group. Judith, of the long brown hair and liquid eyes, who wrote poems with lines like: "Swollen memory of him inside me, and the breast of the dove is the Prince of Capadecia."

"Oh, my God! I'm sorry, you're expecting company."

"No, I'm not," I said.

She looked at the dinner table with its blazing candelabra and then at me with the disdain reserved for not only obvious liars but inept ones.

"Honestly, I swear . . ." I pursued. "I do this every night for myself." That was a lie.

"I just came to return *I Don't Need a Man,* et cetera." Judith is thirty-nine and has never been married. "I should have called first."

"Judith, I am tired of rattling my tin cup for love! I'm learning to treat myself. It's all in the cookbook. I'll lend it to you."

"I'll go in a second. Wow! Those are expensive flowers. Is he rich? Famous? Why didn't you tell me about him? I thought we were friends. He's married—that's why you didn't tell me."

"Judith, stay here. Eat with me. You'll see—no one will show up."

"I already ate."

"Then stay."

"Not if you're having company." And she gave me one of those "Aren't you a little devil" winks. Suddenly her eyes misted and she sighed, holding my image. "You've never looked lovelier."

The vegetables were excellent but the chops were a little

tough. I kept apologizing to the gentleman caller seated in the empty chair across the table.

Delicious as it was, it was a lot of work. I went back to tuna and two days later broke out in a rash. I had to get my strength back before I started looking for a job and that meant I had to find a way to eat. . . . What's the matter with me? I'd go out to dinner. And not with a friend. Alone. That was part of the discipline. And a nice place. I got all dressed up and headed for Beverly Hills. I figured if I went early—five-thirty—the restaurant wouldn't be crowded and I'd be less self-conscious . . . and even if it was crowded—so what? The days had passed when a woman eating alone was considered a loser or a hooker.

Francoise looked nice. FRENCH/HUNGARIAN/AMERICAINE INTERNATIONALE CUISINE, the awning read.

"Good evening, madame." The maître d' bowed. "Do you have a reservation?"

"No. I'm sorry."

"One moment please." He checked his book methodically while I practiced poise. Hip to the left. Hip to the right. What was he doing? There was no one in the place. I was getting snow-blind—from the tablecloths.

"How many in your party?"

"One," I gulped meekly.

"Ah, we're in luck." He finally looked up. "I think we can seat you." And then, in a voice that rattled the napkined glasses, he proclaimed, "ONE! DINNER FOR *ONE!* RIGHT THIS WAY."

He seated me near the swinging doors of the kitchen, scooping up the second place setting as though I would contaminate it, and handed me a leather-bound, tasseled menu. I read the whole history of the California migratory birds, with drawings, before I got to the food on page seven and a waiter showed.

"Would madame care for a cocktail?"

I hated his smirky grin. "Double scotch. Neat. Spritzer on the side."

He bowed, came back with my drink, a roll and a plate of butter curls. "Has madame decided?"

"I'm only on page twelve," I answered, pleasantly snotty. "Just up to the salads."

He pushed the escarole and endive with mustard dressing, $8.50, and the *plat du jour*—not on the menu.

I had just bitten into my roll, when—when three violined restaurant Gypsies, replicates of the Ritz Brothers, banged through the kitchen doors, tucking their dickeys into flamenco jackets and adjusting their waist sashes. They leered, winked and goggled at me, stood sideways in size places, five inches, five years apart—65-70-75. The shortest and youngest, end right, had a front tooth missing. They hoisted their fiddles, white dinner napkins between shoulder and chin, and with a nod and a plaintive, unisoned "Oy," they cued themselves. Swaying their bows and torsos, they gazed at me, mournfully, soulfully, while the toothless one sang the refrain, lento, longingly.

*"PLAY GYPSY PLAY*
*PLAY MY LOVED ONE A RHAPSODY*
*PLAY ON THE STRINGS OF MY HEART."*

The roll stayed half in, half out of my mouth. With each phrase they took a step closer, surrounding the table. I didn't know where to put my look. I went from ceiling to butter, to wall, to violin necks. I tried to smile but my lips wouldn't move. I'd forgotten there was a roll there. The violins cried, kvetched in sorrowful falsetto, melting my heart. . . . "PLAY MY LOVED ONE A RHAPSODY." After World War II, the Communists banned Gypsy music. Decadent sentimentality . . . "PLAY ON THE STRINGS OF MY HEART" . . . I chewed slowly. The hardness of the roll and the music stuck in my throat. I couldn't escape romance. It's a law of the universe. If you can't have it—you shove it on someone else. The bastards won't let me live! A tear fell on the escarole as the waiter set it down. The Gypsies smiled pityingly, with closed crimped mouths. Ah yes, they silently said: We too have loved and lost. My tears seemed to inspire more passionate playing. Maybe I'd become a Communist. The strings were aching, breaking as the waiter thrust a pepper mill the size of a baseball bat in front of my face. "PLAY GYPSY PLAY" . . . I remembered what Mike had said: "The lousiest restaurants have the biggest pepper mills."

I was dissolved. The two end Gypsies were wet-eyed. ZIP! ZIP! Downstrokes of the bows sliced near the butter. *Plink plank plunk* of the pizzicato. *Click clack cluck* of their tongues. Tempo change. Wild czardas. My stomach was jumping. Vivace. I salted the salad furiously. My fork flew in and out of my mouth, escarole dangling and splashing. Sawing, squealing, skirling like bagpipes, the music and my hands went berserk. I shoved in the salad, buttered the rest of the roll, crammed it in. I jerked and twitched in my silent movie as the strings babbled and giggled, then champed like a cavalry troop. I didn't chew. I didn't swallow. I didn't have time. With a flamboyant finish and a Russian "Hey!" bows sweeping the air, they bowed, mopped their foreheads and sat down at a table across the room. The waiter brought them coffee while I ate some noodle and veal goop. They sipped silently, their eyes over the rims of their cups, watching me.

The minute I swallowed the last bite, they were back, with "Golden Earrings." I gave them three dollars. I thought they'd go away. They nodded and played "Fascination." This time I gave them five. They did a medley. Why did I stay? I usually don't know the answer to that question. This time I did. The waiter wouldn't bring the check. Finally. Finally. Spent with emotion, lips strained from smiling, my stomach burbling with indigestion, I paid the bill. $42.56.

May wild dogs eat my heart on the night of a wet moon (authentic Romanian curse) if I have exaggerated this evening one little bit.

## E I G H T

*It took two days to* get rid of the Gypsies in my soul. I did not call Seymour. How could I tell him I'd been bedeviled by a Zigeuner?

I phoned an employment agency to set up an appointment for the following week.

"Hello. I'd like to inquire about a job interview. My name is—"

"Can you type?"

"Yes, but—"

"Come in this afternoon."

"I . . . uh . . . can't today. I've got this gunshot wound."

"I beg your pardon."

"I have to lay low for another week." Why did I say that?

"I'm sorry. We're not a temporary agency." She hung up.

What did I expect? Of course she'd hang up. They want a secretary, not a gunslinger at the OK Corral.

I couldn't type. I mean I could if I looked at the keys. It never made sense to me. Why put letters out of sequence? *A* to *J* should be on the first row, then the rest of the alphabet in descending order, left to right on the second and third. It would come out perfectly.

I made a list of the other things I couldn't do. It was overwhelming. I had no practical skills to support myself.

Due to a traumatic incident, which I can't even talk about, I never graduated college, quitting in the second half of my senior year. I'd have to start all over again as a freshman in January at forty-three and a half. The administration building at C.C.N.Y. burned down twenty-one years ago (arson)—that was another trauma—and my records are not available. It doesn't seem fair. Even as we speak, thousands of doctors and lawyers are practicing in New York with charred credits, but they'd already graduated.

I'd be forty-seven and a half, orthopedic shoes drag-stepping to "Pomp and Circumstance," gray curls bouncing under my mortarboard, before I could enter law or med school.

I drew a line down the center of a yellow legal pad and wrote.

| Law School—3 years | Med School—4 years |
|---|---|
| Bar Exam—1 to 3 yrs, depending how many times it took me to pass | Internship—2 |
| | Residency—2 |
| Find a firm to hire me as a Junior—7 yrs | Medical speciality— say, brain surgery— 6 years |

Adding it up, I'd be a lawyer at fifty-four or a doctor at sixty-two. I could either open an office or apply for an early retirement.

Judith kept urging me to go back to school. "What's the difference. You'll be fifty-four anyway."

"Or sixty-two and a half!" I hollered into the phone, waving the yellow pad in front of the mouthpiece.

"You have a negative outlook."

You ever notice that a person who tells you to develop a more positive attitude is likely to be someone who never had the problem?

"You can get clep," she persisted.

"What?"

"C.L.E.P. Credit for Life Experience. A school in the Bay Area gives fifty semester units towards a degree in philosophy to any student who has experienced cosmic insights induced by psychedelic drugs during the sixties."

I ripped up the paper. "I can't wait eleven to twenty years to make a living and it's too late for me to take LSD 102."

Besides I was overlooking an important factor. I didn't like medicine or law. I certainly wasn't going to be a psychologist. All my divorced friends were majoring in that. . . . Actually, I wouldn't mind if I could have a talk show.

What else could I do? . . . Films? TV? . . . No. You can't make a comeback as an extra. Anyway, I had let my union dues lapse.

When I was living in New York, before I was married to Bernie, I was a lifeguard in a synagogue. A Reformed Temple in Queens had a swimming pool on the first floor. I'm still pretty athletic but how would that look on a résumé? . . . Bizarre.

In those days I cared about making just enough money to live in a four-flight walk-up in Greenwich Village so I could write poetry and dance to the verses. All I needed were the existential necessities. A table, a chair and a lot of pain. I belonged to a modern dance group. We gave concerts once a year. The rest of the time we rehearsed and mended our tights. . . . Oh, I forgot. I taught dance to teenagers. . . . Why not do that again? . . . No. They're all grown up now and go to aerobics classes. That athletic I'm not.

"Judith, I'm not being negative. I'm scared. I have the pension from Mike's unions but it's small, and enough savings to last another year if I'm careful. Every time I go to the bank I feel little. Michael's giving me my allowance. I never felt that way when he was alive. If I let him continue to support me, I'll never be separate from him. I can't think about a career. I need a job and I'm not sure I'm capable . . . and I . . . uh . . . can't stay in the house anymore. I walk from room to room with my hands behind my back like I'm a museum guard."

"I'm sorry, I didn't realize. . . . You want to go to the new mall with me and have lunch?"

"There's a new mall? Where?"

"Beverly Center . . . Bullock's . . . Broadway. . . . One hundred and seventy-five stores!"

I sensed a faint, familiar flush. "I haven't been in a department store since Mike died."

"You mean it's over a year since you've been shopping? How is that possible?" She spoke with the fervent tones of a holy admonition: If I forget thee O Jerusalem . . . "I could never be away that long—no matter what!"

"Judith! You just gave me an idea. I'm going! But this time, not to buy—to sell! Besides I need panty hose. . . . We'll have lunch another time."

*I got in the car* and drove to a mall the size of Cleveland. Unable to reach the red button that ejected the time ticket and lifted the wooden barrier, I sidled to the edge of the car seat, opened the door, thrust half my body outside, my left foot on the pavement, my right slipping off the brake as the hood nosed into the gate (cracking it slightly) and I skateboarded up the ramp to the Broadway.

MARK YOUR TICKET. YOU ARE PARKED ON GREEN.
3975 B
THE WILLIAM H. HARRISON MEMORIAL LEVEL.

I gave the nice young salesgirl/person a $10.00 bill for $6.75 panty hose while I inquired where the personnel office was.

"Excuse me." She flinched, biting her lip and fanning herself with the bill. "You're the first person that's given me cash. I'm not sure how to do this."

She tried but the cash register (only they're not called cash registers anymore because they don't take cash) went gaga. It buzzed, beeped, dinged, rocked on its base. Paper tongued out at us, winding itself inward and dropping in a fat curl at our feet. Frantically, she pressed the buttons: "I'm a college graduate and I can't learn this!"

The machine flashed its lights.

I put my arm around her. "Maybe if we wait long enough, an

American flag will pop out." I was thinking of one of those Rube Goldberg inventions.

She didn't get it. The floor manager, a snippy fellow in his thirties, appeared. He didn't get it either. No wonder. My allusions were even older than I was.

I wandered through the store deeply discouraged. I belonged to that generational blob of forty-to-fifty-year-old, reference-borrowing fence sitters of two worlds. Born between Debbie Reynolds and Debby Boone, too young for Geritol and too old for Yuppies . . . can't even follow the plots of current sci-fi pics, I mumbled to myself. The next time I go to the movies, I'll have to rent a nine-year-old to explain it to me. In my day we never had films like that. Oh, yeah. One. About a fly that ate the world.

I caught a glimpse of myself in a three-way mirror. A disaster in triplicate. I needed new clothes but I wasn't sure what I was supposed to look like.

Actually, I had two looks. When I wore my clinging silver knit, backcombed my strawberry-blond hair into pouffy pillows on each side of my head, erased the freckles and fringed my eyelashes with lots of mascara, I was often mistaken for a band singer. But without makeup, like now, stick bangs and a ponytail, plaid cotton shirt and wrap skirt, I was a housewife in Orlando, Florida, doing a hidden camera commercial for All-Temp-a-Cheer. . . . In the imaginative extremes, I was alternately compared to Betty Grable or Cissy Spacek . . . see what I mean?

EXCUSE OUR MESS. WE ARE REMODELING FOR A
BRIGHTER AND BETTER YOU.

"Pardon me," I asked a seventyish gray panther saleslady/person. "Where can I find clothes for me?"

"Threads are on three and five."

"Thanks. That's a new one." I sighed and moved on.

Punk rock music. Videotapes of green-haired models in layered, fringed shmatas. Spiral displays of limp, neon-colored fabrics that wrap around your body somehow. . . . What happened to blouses and skirts while I was gone? . . . Where were the dresses? I

117

mean regular dresses, with buttons, sleeves and a belt? . . . Jettisoned? . . . And suits? Were suits pensioned off? . . . The store was making me dizzy. I wanted to lie down. Maybe I could find the employees' lounge where the floor manager had sent the panty hose salesgirl—damn—person on his/her/its extended break.

I used to love the mesmerizing eternities spent shopping.

"Michael," I would call excitedly as he waited patiently outside, putting down his book and helping me with my packages, "there was the most incredible sale!"

"Go back," he'd tease. "Save me some more money."

Now I was feeling lost and frightened in a department store. I want my Michael!

With four free, pinky-sized samples of designer-signed male intoxicants, I rode the elevator to the garage. The pretty lass with artificial violets in her hair and basket had sample-sprayed me on the way out. "You'll like it," she chirped. "A light fragrance developed by Marsilupu, for the working woman in love." Convinced that I was both, she handed me several.

"Thanks. What's it called?"

"Matinee." And she gave me a cunning giggle and wink.

Pressed against the backs of strangers, I suddenly panicked. I hadn't marked my parking ticket. "Excuse me . . . I er . . . I don't know what floor to get off."

"Oh, they've made it easy now," a little old lady offered. "Each level is named for a president. I'm on Millard Fillmore. Orange."

"Where does it say that?" I gulped, desperately searching the panel board for a color-coordinated president.

"It doesn't. . . . Just colors. Try blue. That's Calvin Coolidge."

"There is no Coolidge level," a helpful chap volunteered.

It was a matter of seconds. I would either go crazy or be crushed to death.

An eleven-year-old with glasses, standing next to her mother: "We're getting off at Warren Harding."

"No, that's not it . . . but I think it begins with an *H.*" I clutched at engrams. . . . "Herbert Hoover . . . Alexander Hamilton . . ."

"Alexander Hamilton was not a president." The kid gave me a look of exhausted pity.

It was humiliating. Everyone in the elevator stared.

"Maybe it's Harrison?" she hinted snidely.

"That's it! Harrison!"

"Which one? William or Benjamin? Yellow or green? Green or yellow?" she piped through pursed lips.

"I don't know." I tried to stop shaking. "But when I was your age I knew who William Blake was."

"So do I." And a little pink tongue flicked out at me.


*It took an hour to* find the car but I decided, driving east, the hazy sun dipping in my rearview mirror, that I would not be upset; I would get a job, no matter what. I was not too old or stupid. This was a great country. That's what all those presidents stood for. The other night on television, Miss Texas in the Miss America contest affirmed it. When she was removed from the isolation booth, in answer to Bob Barker's question: "What would you tell the world about the United States?" Miss Texas drawled, "Ah would tell the world that America is the land of opportun*ists.*" The judges, favoring her beauty, overlooked the slip of her tongue and crowned her. As she took her tearful walk down the aisle, I thanked her for the hopeful malapropism that was now my credo. No matter what your age or color, a person could make something of him/herself. . . . I was a winner and I whistled with confidence . . . five-fifteen. Dusk. Oh, my God! What have I done! . . . The committee would be in session. Too late. They were shouting and scrambling to their seats.

It's time for me to talk about them.

This committee is not your standard suit-and-tie business affair. No Sir. It's comprised of crepuscular creatures that live in my head and rouse themselves twice daily. If I aggravate them, they call a meeting, which is why I try never to have a positive thought at dawn and to be done with pridefulness before dusk, resuming during the day or at night when it's safe.

About three inches high, they resemble those carved wooden figures, circa 1920, that waddle on pin legs when pushed—only they're not cute. They're the ugliest elves you've ever seen, with wrinkled faces, tattered teensy clothes and rotten teeth exuding halitosis. They crowd in my cranium, all six of them, sitting on a shelf in my brain, swinging fat little legs, laughing uproariously as they punch and fall over each other sideways. They hoot, jabber, slobber, fart or pull at tufts of blue hair in exaggerated boredom when I assert myself or show any signs of self-esteem. As I stand in the purple circle of the witness ring, I'm taunted with cruel limericks and obscene gestures. They hate me. The only time they leave me alone is when I'm depressed or we're all asleep. Even then, I'm aware of their niggling presence, but the force of their crinkum crankum shenanigans explodes during the creepy, crawly hours.

If Ed the mugger had attacked me two hours later, I would not have been able to overtake him.

When the world is at sixes and sevens, literally and depending on the seasons and where I am in the universe, it is best if I am not depressed to at least remain quiet and neutral.

Once they caught me unaware, feeling terrific on a New York–to–Los Angeles flight. They double-backed on me as we flew through two twilight zones.

Michael was the only one who knew about the committee. "Why do you give them magical powers?"

"I don't. They take it."

"Well, get rid of them."

"I can't. Anyway, it's something you learn to live with—like diabetes."

Twice, he betrayed my trust.

We were having cocktails with some friends— Oh, I forgot to mention, one of the reasons those buggers are so rowdy is that they have wet brains. They're alcoholic and booze escalates their insanity. Anyway, this man came over to where Mike and I were standing and he gave me an extravagant compliment. Michael looked at my beaming face, then at his watch and said, "Don't tell her that now, wait fifteen minutes."

The perplexed fellow shook his head. "I don't understand."

"She's got Gnomes syndrome," Mike whispered in a spooky voice.

I didn't speak to him for three days.

The second time was about six years ago. We were in Hawaii. He was doing a film and urged me to go down to the beach before dawn and watch the sun come up.

"I'll go but I won't look. I'm too happy."

"Fer Chrissake! I promise nothing will happen."

He held me with one hand as the other traced the horizon's first brush of light. We made love on the sand and he purred in my ear, "If anyone's watching, I'll tell them I'm Burt Lancaster."

The next day we went back to California. On the plane he had a high fever and fainted in the Los Angeles airport. It was the beginning of cancer.

So, there I was. At a stoplight, shaking both fists in the air, ready to have it out. "Okay, you murderous bastards, come on down," I said aloud. The driver in the next lane turned his gaze from me, obviously embarrassed by my madness.

"I did accomplish something. A collection of my poetry is in print."

One of the elves hooted, cupping his mouth. "It's not in print—it's in mimeograph!"

"It was done on rag paper—that's very expensive." I tried to impress them. "The publisher bound it in simulated leather, like a chapbook, with velvet ribbon. . . . During Shakespeare's time, chapbooks were very popular. Vendors would hawk them in the marketplace."

"She's got sixteenth-century credits," the smartass imp on the end shouted while two in the middle laughed so hard they fell off the shelf and had to be hoisted up.

The gnome who'd been elected chairman banged the thumbnail-sized gavel. Sometimes I thought he was on my side but he only quieted the rabble in order to hear what I was saying so they could piss on me again.

"I was published in magazines. *Cadences. Aurora. Transcendental Incidental* . . ."

A chorus of mock "Oooohs" and then raspberries.

". . . and *Field and Stream* bought one of my early nature poems."

"Nature! Nature!" One elf grabbed his partner and dry humped him.

They were getting to me but I was not going to cry. "I did do something else well. I was a wonderful wife. I helped Mike with his career."

Three of them stood on the shelf, heads together like the restaurant Gypsies, and played imaginary violins.

"You never had a baby!" a high-pitched voice rang out.

I lowered my head. There was silence for a long time. "I've explained that to you," I began softly, unable to look up at them. "When Michael's cancer was diagnosed I was thirty-six. The uh . . . radiation after the operation gave him an almost five-year reprieve. It affected the sperm count but we still tried . . . and then both our biological clocks ran out."

I should have quit then. Not another word. I was saddened and they stirred restlessly. We all had what we wanted.

A gnawing discomfort inside me. This time there was more to say. "You know," I began hesitantly, "Michael was proud of my poetry. He always said, 'Your soul doesn't know how much money it makes.' It's true I never had a child but that doesn't make me a failure any more than *having* children makes you a failure."

The tribunal scratched their heads, puzzled.

"There are things I know about. I just haven't put them together so I can get paid for it. . . . But my life is not over yet!"

That did it. The limerick writer, second from the left, stood up and recited in a histrionic pose:

*There once was a marriage so good,*
*now gone, so in sad widowhood*
*she stands on her head*
*'cause since he's been dead*
*she's a Yokel—a Babe in the wood.*

The light was fading. I would make one more plea before dark. I could not bear another twilight in chains. I rubbed away a tear and then like Joan of Arc facing her cold-blooded inquisitors, I raised my right arm with renewed strength.

"You may be right. I only saw who I was through Michael's eyes and when he died he took me with him. But he never wanted me that way. He does not need my passionate grief or my immolation to prove our heroic love. I must forget who we were so I can remember myself. And if I can celebrate who I am, he will be closer to me. And if I laugh as I mourn, I can love him more. The legacy he has left me is . . . is . . ."

## NINE

*Exhausted from last night's battle* with the elves, disgusted from trying on outfits, I confronted Judith, who sat on the edge of my bed next to a pile of clothes. "What's the matter with this?"

My hair was center-parted, slicked down over my ears and tightly knotted into a bun. I had on a mid-calf skirt, black stockings, black shoes strapped and buckled at the instep, and a high-necked blouse sealed at the throat by a cameo.

Judith searched for the right words. "It's . . . Gothic."

She was right. I looked like Margaret—of Margaret and Simon. "I'm trying to look sedate. I have an interview tomorrow."

Judith, from my poetry group, works part-time for the Rand Corporation. In a think tank. She can wear anything she wants. Her style is blankety itchy woven things from South American countries and her lank brown hair is waist-length. . . . But she's a very good poet.

The doorbell.

I was expecting Betsy—a better dresser.

In tailored slacks, Ralph Lauren polo, Betsy breezed in, sunglasses propped on her head. Carrying an armful of plastic-covered clothes, she sank on the bed next to Judith.

"This week has been hell!" She kicked off her Ferragamo shoes. "Donald's away and I need a dick! I'm so horny I made myself come five times last night. . . . But it's lonely doing it to my self. . . . I end up paying for my own dinner."

I shot her a look. That is not the way to talk in front of Judith, who is not only a Rhodes scholar but a classical Greek one and doesn't believe in "doing it to herself." Judith has had one romance in her life, in 1976, on the island of Crete with an exiled, impotent, Croatian revolutionary with whom she still corresponds.

I love my girlfriends. After Michael died they were there for me. Holding me. Betsy trying to make me laugh and Judith reading me her poetry. I have only one problem with them. They can't stand each other. Sibling rivalry for my affection. I'm sure Betsy says those things to titillate Judith.

"So what do you think?" I said, steering the conversation back to me and turning full circle, modeling my costume.

Betsy eyed me. "It's weird. You look like Olivia de Havilland in *Jane Eyre*."

"*Jane Eyre* is a novel by Charlotte Brontë," Judith stated flatly. "Not a flick."

"*Jane Eyre* was also a movie," I refereed. "Betsy's thinking of *The Heiress*." I unloosed my bun.

Betsy stood her ground. "I never saw that."

"*I* did," Judith came back, "with Joan Fontaine by William James."

I unclasped my cameo. "You've got it backwards. Joan played Jane and Olivia played in *The Heiress*, taken from the novel *Washington Square* by Henry James, not William—they were brothers." Judith is strong on Sophocles but shaky on English lit. "Before it was a film, it was a play and adapted for the stage by . . . I can't think now—Michael would know. . . ." Anyway, why weren't we talking about my problems.

They sat there miffed and I tried to appease them. "Besides, it's practically the same thing—they're sisters." It was a mistake to tell them because they didn't believe me. If Michael had said it, they would have listened.

I had begun to depend on the nurturance of women, the sisterhood I'd always heard about but never needed when Michael was alive. But now, standing in front of the mirror in my prim costume as they insisted that Olivia and Joan didn't look like sisters—I wanted to throw them both out.

"Anyway, women in the job market don't dress that way," Betsy, who never did anything, advised me. "They wear soft wool suits with silk blouses, strategically unbuttoned so when they lean over the desk the boss gets a flash of boob. . . . Here . . . I picked these up for you at Saks." She uncovered three lovely outfits. "Don't worry about paying me back. I charged them to Donald."

"I can't do that."

"All right. When you get a job, you can write me a check."

I undressed, then slipped into a silk blouse and tried on a beige linen suit. It was gorgeous.

". . . and chains. They wear chains." Judith reached into her bag, handing me ropes of filigree gold.

"Not anymore—pearls are back," Betsy countered.

And then Judith told me my hair was too long and Betsy said: "How can you say that to her when yours is practically down to your tush?"

I started to shake with indecision. How will I ever know who I am when my two best friends can't agree on anything?

*Victor, my hairdresser, took the* rollers out and brushed my short hair off my face. Kissing my cheek, peering over my shoulder, adoring his creation, my nonlover love instructed me to close my eyes. He ruffled his fingers through my hair, placing waves, pulling at wisps, and then whispered in my ear, "Open Sesame!"

"Tah dah!" he sang.

"Oooooh," I crooned, blinking at the mirror, thrilled with my new image.

"Here, do this." Victor shook his head vigorously.

I imitated him as he applauded. "That's it! . . . The new you! . . . Just toss it, baby—toss it! . . . Wait! Stop! One more thing." He reached into his purse, took his sunglasses out, propped them on top of my head and belted in his musical comedy voice: "Yes Sir. That's my babe-eee now!"

$Sitting$ $across$ $the$ $desk$ $from$ Mrs. Kieps at Careers Are for Kieps—I rubbed my chain-held bullet for luck as she studied my résumé.

You'd choose Mrs. Kieps for the cover of *Lear* magazine. The caption: FIFTY-FIVE-ISH AND FABULOUS. The copy: "Elegant figure, unashamedly gray hair, her pretty face laughs at its unretouched wrinkles."

She looked up at me for a moment, then back at the résumé. What was taking so long? Maybe I'm too young.

At the suggestion of Judith and Betsy, I was thirty-six, graduated with a degree in English lit at Radcliffe (although we argued as Judith retyped several versions whether Wellesley, Holyoke or Vassar wouldn't be more prestigious), had been a feature writer for the now defunct *Honolulu Express* and on moving back to the mainland, after my divorce, was a script analyst for Victor Harlan Productions (my hairdresser, who said he'd cover for me).

"Do you have any sample articles from the *Express*?" Mrs. Kieps asked softly.

"Huh?"

"The features you wrote."

"Uh . . . uh. No. They were burned in the fire of 'seventy-nine."

"I'm sorry to hear that."

"Yes. . . . Big fire. It happened when the volcano erupted. I was on Molokai when it came. My life's work . . . letters, photographs . . . everything. Up in smoke."

127

"That's a terrible tragedy."

She seemed like a nice woman. I felt sorry she believed me. Especially when she asked where I had lived in Hawaii and I said "Elm Street," hoping there were Elms in Hawaii. . . . Why did I let Judith and Betsy talk me into this? I can't get away with it. I took a breath and plunged in.

"Mrs. Kieps. I need a job. I'm not thirty-six, the only thing I know about Hawaii is the Kahala Hilton and I never went to Radcliffe."

"I know."

"How?"

"You wrote Holyoke on your résumé." She leaned across the desk and asked sympathetically, "Do you have any special skills?"

I couldn't think. She was so understanding I started to cry.

"None?" she prodded, handing me a tissue.

"Pot roast. I make wonderful pot roast." We both laughed and I blew my nose.

Mrs. Kieps smiled wanly as she offered me another Kleenex. "You're a widow, aren't you?"

The woman was amazing. "Does it show?" I tried to shrug it off as though it were a cape.

"I understand. I am too."

Mrs. Kieps opened Careers Are for Kieps—An Employment Agency for Women six years after her husband died. Her primary goal is placing older women who wish to re-enter the work force after facing divorce, death or the empty nest. "We've found most women aren't aware of the lifetime of talents they can bring to bear in the job market. . . . That's why I recommend our testing service. The employers we represent regard it highly."

"Test? What kind of test?" I shivered even though the room was warm.

"Kimble Diagnostic Skills Inventory and Academic Profile. . . . My sister, Mrs. Kimble, also a widow, administers the test and for a nominal fee . . ."

Right then and there, at that very moment, I should have stopped her, but she was talking fast, smiling at me, patting my hand and using phrases like "viable career options, computer-matched concrete data of motivational aptitudes evidenced by broad-based knowledge" and I was getting dizzy. I was about to inquire what the fee was when she asked what I considered my accomplishments. I of course said, "Poetry," then remembered I'd once helped Michael panel the garage, I could use a buzz saw and was quite good at Origami—all sorts of things I'd forgotten. . . .

"Now you're getting the idea."

While she was phoning for an appointment, I planned my strategy. She hadn't asked me for any money. I didn't sign anything. If I didn't like the test, I'd walk out, and if I took it and passed, she'd issue a search and placement for me. . . . Don't all agencies charge a fee? I figured I had nothing to lose.

"We're in luck!" Mrs. Kieps gave me a delighted grin as she hung up. "Mrs. Kimble has an opening now."

"Now? Now!" The silk blouse went clammy under my armpits and Betsy's suit began to pucker. "Don't I have to study for it?"

"How can you bone up on forty years of knowledge?" she soothed, robbing me of three.

Then, with another reassuring pat—"My sister, Louise, is on the same floor"—the chic and personable Mrs. Kieps escorted me down the hall.

They didn't look like sisters. I could tell that a hundred yards away. Louise Kimble was waiting for us outside her office. A brown helmet hairdo framed her pinched face of sixty-odd years. Owlish glasses dangling a chain bridged the pencil-thin nose. A print rayon dress with uneven hemline hung from an arthritic spine that rounded into a right shoulder hump; and supporting her, piano legs encased in brown laced shoes.

If you moved her hump to the left, she was none other than my fourth grade teacher, Miss Claxon.

Walking forward, I tottered backwards.

Every thirty-five years, a clone of your fourth, fifth or sixth grade teacher reproduces itself. I could only pray that God's grace had protected Mrs. Kimble from the transmigration of Miss Claxon's evil soul.

Everyone who ever had Miss Claxon hated her (but not as much as I did), and not because of her deformity. We could never understand whether God gave her a hump because she was so mean or she had the hump first and then she got mean. All the kids in my class would imitate her—only mine was the best impression.

As I stood in front of Mrs. Kimble, I started to shrink, my knees bending in slow motion. Mrs. Kieps held on to my arm—introduced us—and I heard: "What's the matter with you, dear?" Rattling through Mrs. Kimble's lips, the Dybbuk spoke! It was Claxon!

I wanted to say I'm sorry for what I did to you—but I just kept sinking and gaping.

There was a discussion between the sisters as to whether my test should be postponed or a short rest might revivify me. I did not participate as they steered me to a couch inside the office. I was thinking of Mrs. Bright, our sixth grade teacher. She had a wooden leg but we never, ever made fun of her. Not even a "thump thump" joke. We adored her.

Mrs. Kimble came toward me with a cup of water. In my anxiety, I grabbed it, crushing the paper pleats. Water puddled to the floor—as it had, then. Claxon/Kimble gave me a look of contempt as I wiped up the spill with a tissue from my bag and stammered: "I have this thing about tests." Sometimes you have to speak up.

Warbling a laugh, Mrs. Kieps assured me I'd be fine and instructed her sister to set up the carpentry bench. "You did say you can use a buzz saw?" I nodded dumbly as she pointed at a bulletin board above the couch and reminded me that in addition to desk jobs, unisex placements as carpenters, burner mechanics—a world of possibilities—were available.

They left me. Kieps down the hall, Kimble through a door across the room marked PRIVATE—a dark glass recessed in the top. Was it a two-way mirror? Was I going to be watched as I took the test?

My head flopped back against the frame of the bulletin board. A blue three-by-five card wafted into my lap. "Border Patrol Agent. Some Spanish helpful. Use of a gun required" . . . I could do that. I fanned myself with the card. Who was I kidding? I would never kill anyone . . . except . . . except . . .

This is what Miss Claxon did to me. It was during a math test and I couldn't do one of the problems and I was getting frightened and I had to go to the bathroom but she wouldn't let me. Instead, she made me stand at my desk, then picked up my math paper and shook it near my face. "What's the matter with you, dear? Are you stupid?" . . . My face got really hot. I squeezed my thighs together. . . . Suddenly the principal stuck his head in the door and said he wanted to speak to Miss Claxon. While she was in the hallway, I hunched one shoulder and recited a poem I'd made up about her. Not only because I hated her but because I didn't want anyone to see the trickle that was puddling the floor. I stopped peeing and reciting the second she came back into the room, but the kids were laughing and my best lines were the two at the end that rhymed, so I said them under my breath as she ordered me, in a voice of ripping cardboard, into the wardrobe with the hooks, leaving the sliding doors open, only a crack.

That day, as I sat on the floor of the October closet, until five when she let me out, next to smelly galoshes under steamy wool jackets, I plotted with my elves, stirring in the early fall twilight, her death.

It came the next day.

The principal told us she had had a heart attack but I knew I had killed her.

I begged my mother to take me out of school—"I know enough!"—but she said, "A person should be smarter than a Chihuahua!"

I couldn't tell her I was afraid I'd kill again.

The door banged open. Peering at me through her owl lenses, Mrs. Kimble announced it was time.

In past tense I had waited. In present terror I entered the room.

Nine by twelve. Cell-gray walls broken only by the dark pane of glass in the door that was closed behind me.

A small chair and desk with a test notebook and pencil on top. And next to them, a plastic wedge marked "A."

Against the long wall, a wooden table with assorted tools, drills, sheet metal, pipes, bricks and a bucket of cement. Exhibit "B."

I sat down at "A," held my breath and opened the exam. Spelling? I let the air out. I'm a very good speller. . . . A page of synonyms, antonyms—ridiculously simple. I almost cried with relief. What had I been afraid of?

## LITERATURE

Who was the author of *Washington Square*?
   a) Washington Irving
   b) Henry Irving
   c) Henry James
   d) William James
   e) Jesse James

Wait till I tell Judith! . . . This test was for morons. At the rate I was going, I could have any job I wanted . . .

## HISTORY

I was beginning to believe that everything in life happens for a reason because when I turned the page and read—

Which of the following was never a United States president?
   1. Franklin Pierce
   2. Gerald Ford
   3. James Knox Polk
   4. Alexander Hamilton
   5. Calvin Coolidge

—who'd have thought I'd ever be grateful to that kid in the elevator.
   I was almost at the end of part one! I glanced at the bottom of the page:

Given: All men are moral. Express a conclusion.

. . . Not necessarily. I mulled it over as I searched in my hand-bag for the small spiral pad I always carry—they hadn't provided any writing paper. . . . Morals are like learning to play the violin. It takes years before one becomes a virtuoso. I looked back at the test paper. I have to start wearing glasses. It wasn't *moral*. It was *mortal*. My virtuoso line wouldn't work. . . . Well, I know something about man and mortality, so I wrote an eight-mini-page philosophical dissertation with religious overtones, stating that man is indeed mortal but also noncorporeal; likening the soul to the Lord's Candle (Book of Proverbs) and concluding that those who make a distinction between the soul and the body have neither. . . . Maybe I'll become a Rabbi.

As I tore the pages loose from the spiral pad, trimming the ragged paper flakes, a black shadow filled the desk. I spun around as the hoarse whisper—"Can't you take directions?"—shattered my concentration. . . . That's probably the worst thing you can say to anyone. Mrs. K. stood there, frozen with disgust. "Where does it say, essay?"

I traced my fingernail along the bottom of the test notebook and recited in my "Please tell me I'm not stupid" voice, "Given. All men are mortal. Express a conclusion."

"There is no period after 'conclusion,'" she rasped.

I touched the black dot. It moved. I'd been done in by a fly dropping.

"Turn the page! Turn the page!" Her left arm flapped below her hump.

I couldn't do it. I was too weak.

Maliciously she delayed the revelation and repeated: "Given: All men are mortal. Express a conclusion [*then* flipped the page] that logically follows from the given statement.

    a) All mortals are men.
    b) If X is a mortal, then X is a man.
    c) If X is not a mortal, then X is not a man.
    d) If X is not a man, then X is not a mortal.
    e) Some mortals are not men."

I bleated like a stricken goat. Even if I'd read it right, I couldn't have done it.

I had to go to the bathroom but I was too humiliated to ask.

She gestured toward the carpentry bench with a look that suggested I might have better luck with my hands than I was having with my brains. And she banged the door on her way out.

I still hadn't finished part two of the written test, but I walked over to the wooden table and read the instruction sheet. . . . This is what I had to do. Number 1. Chamfer the edge of a cement curb. Huh? Ohhh. I get it. I'm supposed to pick a tool and chamfer. Maybe I use the brick as a curb? No. Because later on in Number 3, I had to cement the bricks and channel a one-inch pipe through them and there were only two bricks on the table. I hadn't lied. I could do some carpentry, but Mike was always with me. We loved to build things together. . . . Well, what's the use of dwelling on that. I wanted to yell at the glass: Gimme another brick, but I didn't because then Mrs. Kimble would find out I don't know how to chamfer. This time I was determined not to fail at something I couldn't do in the first place.

I dug in the bucket, feeling encouraged that I had recognized a trowel and slopped cement between the bricks, squooshing them together so they'd harden faster. *Plop!* On my skirt! I reached for a roll of paper towels provided for clean up and I managed to get most of the cement off but the fuzz from the toweling clung to my skirt and tufts of paper stuck to my fingertips. No water. . . . Well, I'll go back to "A" while my bricks set. I placed them next to the bucket at the edge of the table, turned and *splunk!* Wet, grainy gray mud oozed down the backs of my calves. Don't faint. Don't cry. One day you will think this is funny. Laughter will distance you from pain, I kept repeating as I sobbed, craning my neck and wiping my legs. Thank God the shoes were my own and as far as I could see there was no cement on the back of my skirt. It was all on the floor, moving like the Nile.

Pulling what was left of myself together, I sat down at the desk and with flypaper fingers turned to the next section of the test.

*Aaargh!* My reaction to what I saw can best be described by symptoms. My mouth ruffled with foam. I stiff-armed the desk. My head fell down, guillotined from its base, while the rest of me twitched like a decapitated chicken:

If a train leaves Poughkeepsie, New York, at 9 A.M. and travels to West Palm Beach, Florida, averaging 86 miles an hour, with the exception of New York City to Washington, D.C., when the speed is increased to 120 miles an hour, and another train leaves West Palm Beach, Florida, for Poughkeepsie, New York, at 10 A.M. traveling 78 miles per hour, making a stop in Orlando for 25 minutes, and the distance from Poughkeepsie to West Palm Beach is 1,418 miles—what time will they serve lunch?

There it was! That train that put me 'round the bend for thirty-five years.

It starts in Poughkeepsie when you're in the fourth grade and it only goes to Chicago. Then, when you get to high school it makes a stop in Schenectady and by the time you're in college, the mileage has improved and it meets another train from Fresno. And now this! But you can be sure of one thing. No matter how old you get—the fucker still leaves from Poughkeepsie!

That's why Miss Claxon put me in the closet. That's why I quit college, because when I went to C.C.N.Y.—during the Bronze Age—math was required to graduate. I failed it four times.

I was an imbecile.

Mrs. Kimble came to collect me.

In the part of the brain that still perceives reality before the ether of delirium vaporizes it, I heard Mrs. Kimble moaning something about a maintenance man as a fat rivulet of cement seeped under her feet and she frantically scraped it from her shoes like you know what.

I was an imbecile and a klutz.

I think she was screaming but it sounded far away and muted: "You're going to pay for this!"

So will you, Miss Claxon, I silently said.

She walked over to my desk—her nose as skinny as ever. I stared right through her owl lenses. And said aloud: "P.S. 154!"

She blinked.

But I knew this time it wouldn't work. I'd be lucky if I could give her indigestion.

Gone was the alchemy of childhood that could kill the Claxons. Gone was Michael who protected me from the Kimbles. It didn't matter I was screwed by two widows. THERE IS NO SIS-TERHOOD! . . . It didn't matter that Mrs. Kimble was demanding $500 plus $100 for damages. . . . I wasn't going to pay it. . . . The world is filled with Claxons and Kimbles—out to get you, to show you up for what you're not. They moved the refrigerator! Exposing the shameful, matted, mucky dust balls of my mind that lay hidden for years, unvacuumed, while I pretended if no one saw it, it wasn't there. That's what matters!

The elves were right. I couldn't cope.

I got up and slowly walked out of the room, trying to maintain my izzat (which means personal dignity). It's difficult to do when a chair is cemented to your ass.

*Dear God!* What next?

# E L E V E N

*I followed the remains of* my white Buick, hoisted like a polar bear, dragging from the butcher hook of a tow truck as I sat in a taxi, clutching my forehead, keening.

Sam Hartoonian (the cabbie) commiserated. "It happens, lady. It happens."

"But it's only twelve years old!" I wailed.

"Built-in obsolescence. Buy a foreign car!"

"Which one?"

"An Ichikawa."

"Okay."

Sam honked at the tow truck. Pissed, the service guy pulled over and climbed out.

"You talk to him," I told Sam, intimidated by the mechanic's string of "Cheesuses" as he strode towards us.

"She'd like to look at an Ichikawa."

"Lissen, Babe. I've been driving your wreck around for four hours . . . I got other calls. Already we been to three Buick places and now you want to go to Ichikawa! . . . Cheesus!"

"I'm making a decision. But first I have to go to the bathroom and use a telephone." I tried to keep my voice level but the indicator of anxiety kept jumping into the high-frequency zone. I ran across the street to a gas station and placed a collect call.

"Seymour, I gotta talk fast. I got a cab, a tow truck and my Buick hanging from it, waiting outside. You think I should buy an Ichikawa? Sam says it's good."

"What the hell is an Ichikawa?"

"A Korean car."

"Forget it. One tug on the fender and the whole body unravels. . . . Who's Sam?"

"The cabdriver."

"What happened to your Buick? . . . Wait a minute. . . . Before you begin, let me lie down."

"It collapsed. Two days after my aptitude test. But I'm not paying them. . . . They have my skirt . . . they wouldn't let me take the chair . . . I had to go home in my slip. . . . Hurry, Seymour! The meter's ticking. . . . So what do you think?"

"I'm glad I'm lying down."

I read from my spiral notes three repair estimates ranging from $900 to $2,250. "Buick will give me fifteen hundred on a trade-in or buy it outright for a hundred and eighty. The tow truck charges five bucks a mile. . . . I'm in El Monte, thirty-two miles from L.A. The cab fare on the meter is sixty-seven fifty. If I keep driving around maybe I could get another seventy-five dollars for the Buick—so I can pay the tow truck and the cab

or

I could have the tow truck and the cab take me to Torrance, where Ichikawa is . . . maybe they'll take my Buick but Sam says probably not because of the contempt generally held by the manufacturers of foreign cars in regard to General Motors. An Ichikawa is nine thousand plus tax and license. I could pay for it in cash but that would wipe out my savings

or

I could buy it on time but that would cost more

or

lease a car by the week and take it off my income tax—but I'm not working so it's not deductible . . ."

Somewhere in there I knew I was hysterical. "So what should I do? Seymour, say something!"

"Take a bus!"

"What?"

Seymour framed each work with exaggerated patience. "Save your money. Get a job. You don't buy a car driving around in a cab, following a tow truck with your Buick dangling from it."

"A bus!"

"After you hang up, sell the clunker to the first person you see. Take whatever they'll give you."

"A bus!"

"Then buy *Consumer Reports* and see what they have to say about Ichikawa."

"A bus!"

Dear God! Has it come to this?


*Three days later, I got* on my first Los Angeles bus. It cost a dollar. I didn't know it then but it was the best bus I ever took.

This is what happened.

I walked down the aisle and a man with an ingratiating smile stood up and gestured to the empty seat next to him—nearest the window. "I'm getting off at Wilshire and Bundy. If you're going farther, I won't have to disturb you."

"Thank you." I slid past him and sat down. "This is my first bus . . . I mean my first bus in Los Angeles."

"How do you like it so far?" he asked.

"I don't know," I said. "I just got on."

He pressed the frame of his glasses down on his nose and peered at me over the top of them with that look of bemusement that older men sometimes have for younger women. "It's nice. You can read the paper . . . talk to people."

"Well, I can't talk too much. I have to prepare for an interview." That was true. I was on my way to another employment agency but also I was unsure of bus decorum. I mean you sit next to someone and you want to be friendly but not too chummy.

I had read about the intimacy of strangers on trains that lapped the moonlit tracks crossing the Alps; rubbing foggy windows to summon vendors on steamy platforms, sharing secrets that had stayed in your pockets for years while you drank licorice coffee with crunchy sugar cubes on the Orient Express—not on a Number 99 RTD two-sectioned accordion bus between Crenshaw and Cloverfield that backfired at every intersection.

So why was I telling him about the Claxons and the Kimbles and my beloved Buick lying somewhere in an automotive necropolis? Maybe because *his* car was being tortured on a rack downtown and he said he'd rather have a tooth extracted than take his Volvo in for service, and when we passed the museum on Wilshire he told me about his early days at the Art Students League in New York in the 1950s and sighed and wished he could afford to spend all his time painting.

Jonathan. His name was Jonathan and he's an art director at Rubicon and Associates. "That's what I do," he said. "But it's not what I am."

I liked talking to him. We weren't flirting with each other. I didn't go all squirrelly inside—like I usually do—getting emotionally attached to men I pass on the freeway. It was just nice.

When I told him I was a poet, he didn't change his seat. Most normies are terrified you'll read them a poem and if you do they immediately get flustered because they assume they're not going to understand it so they fix their faces into dopey smirks of reverence and then they get back at you by reciting *Trees*. . . . No one listens anymore. And poets are worse. They audition you with the pinched concentration of the elite, excising every other image and reworking your title.

Jonathan didn't do any of these things. His arms folded, slouching his long frame forward, his angular face intent, he listened as I recited one villanelle, a double sestina and two satiric narratives. Several times he let out a long "Mmmmm" and licked his lower lip as though he were tasting delicious caramel sauce.

When I finished he said, "You're a wonderful poet," and a lady in front of us, hugging three May Co. shopping bags, without turning around, added: "She certainly is."

Flushed, shaken by the appreciation, I looked out the window. How wonderful to hear that again. So why did I feel like I was going to cry? Michael was the last person to have said that. . . . I miss someone believing in me. . . . Are there painful analgesics?

I tried to toss off my embarrassment. "Maybe I can get a gig playing buses?"

"Have you thought of advertising?"

"You mean take out an ad? My friend Seymour says 'Poetry is a small market.' I don't think I'd have any customers."

He laughed. "No. I mean as a copywriter."

"You know . . . I don't know exactly what a copywriter does." I can always tell when I trust someone. I'm never afraid of showing them what an idiot I am. . . . "I mean is a copywriter someone who copies other people's writing or does it have something to do with patents—like copyrights?"

We were nearing Bundy so he had to talk quickly. There was an opening at Rubicon and Associates for a Junior copywriter. If I could get my poetry to him, he would talk to Whitey, the creative director of the agency, about me.

"But I've never written any ads."

"But you have imagination. Besides, we've been interviewing people all week and you're right—they copy other people's writing. I can't promise anything but I think you should take a crack at it. And don't worry. Whitey'll give you some products to write sample ads for."

"You mean a test? Another test?" My heart started to pound.

"Trust me," he said. We exchanged phone numbers and then this stranger, this perfect stranger, adjusted his tie, buttoned his jacket, retrieved his attaché case and as he got off the bus, turned and gave me a V for Victory sign.

# T W E L V E

YOU HAVE JUST CROSSED THE RUBICON.

The polished steel letters were suspended, backlit in ice blue, above the office. Below, huge glass double doors windowed the reception area.

There's a new world inside—black carpeting, floating futuristic furniture . . . a chrome-framed silvery leather bench—and on it, two mini-skirted models (total length of legs—six kilometers) . . . a stunning receptionist behind a drawerless Plexiglas desk. He, the receptionist, looks like a print model for a men's cologne. The ad that shows the man in the foreground with one of those beautiful bench models panting in the background.

I pressed the clasp on my manila envelope of poems. Everyone's waiting for your Ronsardian odes. Stop holding your breath and take hold of the door handle. All you have to do is push. The door goes in and your breath goes out. Push. . . . Push.

"Excuse me. Are you going in?" A man's voice. In back of my ear.

The decision was made. A gray suit and Jacquard tie stepped in front of me and swung open the door, assuming I would enter.

I gulped a thank-you and studied the crisp suit and rumpled face of a harried man in his late thirties. After a while, it occurred to me that he might be an executive and couldn't spend the afternoon heralding my arrival. But I had solidified.

From inside the office, the receptionist greeted the gray-suited gentleman: "Hello, Mr. Rubicon."

Oh God! My doorman was the owner of the agency!

I managed to walk forward.

"May I help you?" the receptionist asked.

Mr. Rubicon crossed to the desk, picked up a pile of messages and then looked back at me before he went through the archway into the inner sanctum.

I still hadn't answered the receptionist's question.

"Uh . . . appointment . . . see . . . Whitey." I was talking like a Chinese person.

"You are . . . ?"

I couldn't seem to come up with the information. He tried to help me by referring to a list and reading three names. I wasn't any of them.

Finally, I thawed, told him who I was and he indicated a pouffy leather ottoman next to the towering silent models.

In my new "Betsy" suit, I sank down into it, trying to bolster myself up. . . . Look what you've accomplished. A door. A name. A seat. And you've been seen by the owner of the agency. Now, all you have to do is get the job.

Michael Michael Michael. I wish you were here to coach me. How do I play the role of a confident copywriter? How do I believe in imaginary circumstances? . . . When you talked about acting you said: Research the character's background. Be specific in the choice of behavior.

This past week, I've been reading books on advertising . . . subliminal techniques. All I can remember is that people buy things in plaid packages—like Scotch brand tape—because they associate

Scotland with frugality. I wear glasses, now, so I rehearse taking them off, chew on a temple tip of the tortoiseshell frames and I squint, pretending I'm pondering a layout.

The phone buzzed on the receptionist's desk.

"Whitey will see you now."

Oh, Michael! I'm living an actor's nightmare! The curtain is up and I don't know my lines!


*A white leather office. On* the wall, facing me, a large poster of a cracked eggshell and beneath it, Whitey. I sat across from him, the envelope of poems on my lap. He was so peculiar in his manner and looks that I forgot to be frightened.

The moment I walked in, he slid down in his chair, propped his legs on the desk and dipped his buttocks in the air, making a hammock of himself and talking nonstop.

"Jonathan says you're a good writer but you've never written any ads . . ."

White hair fluffed on his head like Johnson's surgical cotton.

"So what the hell am I supposed to do with a poet?"

His eyes were amber or pink and he had no eyebrows or eyelashes.

"We're bidding on a six-million-dollar account. Raymock and Campbell want to re-image their douche."

His face was an unlined moon.

"You've seen that commercial."

In his jeans, sweatshirt and jogging shoes, I couldn't tell if he was thirty-six or sixty.

"Two girls in a locker room telling each other about Pheno-rex—it's a lousy name and it's not a viable market anymore." He slapped his thighs in a dum de dum dum rhythm. "So, tell me, how the hell would *you* get women to pay six ninety-eight for vinegar and water?"

Take a chance, I thought. Be a character in this absurdist play. Slowly, I took off my glasses and chewed. Then, I cleared my throat: "Package it in plaid."

"I know that," Whitey shot back. "But we can't call a douche 'MacPherson'!"

What do I do now, Michael?

The phone rang. Whitey handed me a sheaf of papers. "Here, take a look at these psychographics. You know what psychographics are?" He pressed the button on the speaker phone and he and the caller talked for five minutes about market segments and compression messages.

I thumbed through the manuscript titled *Executive Study: Focus Group Profiles of Probable Douche Markets*. The top page of the report summarized the findings of an in-depth survey of women. Divided into four columns: Married, Single, Live-in Committed, Casual, it listed the percentages of women who had sex under the appropriate headings.

The body of the tract was an analysis of when they did it, where they did it, what age they did it, why they did it and even if they didn't do it, did they use a douche.

Whitey ended his call, then asked me, in a belligerent tone: "Any ideas on a sixty-second spot for Phenorex?"

The key to playing farce, Michael once said, is no matter how ridiculous the lines, you must always execute the dialogue with deadly seriousness . . .

Since I was both writer and actor, and I wasn't going to get this job anyway, I removed my glasses, chewed, tilted my head, squinted at the ceiling and after a long pause spoke.

"Get someone gorgeous. Put her on a horse. And shoot it through mist on the Scottish moors. And call it Mystique." Then I added with a flourish, "Because French is romantic!"

Everything happened very quickly after that. Whitey fell off his hammock and braced himself with his hands on the edge of the desk. "Don't move!" he ordered, leveling one finger at me, then he called Mr. Rubicon—on the speaker phone. They agreed my idea was a "great visual" . . . it would appeal to all women. Gorgeous for the aesthetic, horse for the athletic, mist for the douche—and in Scotland, where it's cheap . . .

I was rushed into an empty conference room with pads of

paper and sharpened pencils in a ceramic cup. *Now,* I was scared. I had to *write copy* based on my idea. . . . Before, I was playacting, with Michael coaching me. But this was real! I had to come up with something—on my own.

A secretary brought me coffee and the product report from a laboratory in Michigan. Whitey told me he wanted the copy to be scientific but not clinical. Then the secretary came back and said Whitey forgot to tell me it should be sensual but not sexual. Then over the intercom Whitey's voice filled the room: "Informative but not elliptical . . ."

"In other words," I tried to sound professional, "you want something vaguely specific."

"You got it!" He clicked off.

The secretary knocked and wanted to know if I needed a word processor.

God, if there is a God, I promise you I will give half my salary to charity if you help me get this job. . . . Moors . . . mist . . . water . . . clean . . . woman on a horse . . . breeze blowing her hair. . . . What does she look like? . . . How does she feel? Fresh? Fresh! . . . I GOT IT! . . . Oh, Michael, I got it!

And then I wrote:

*Woman announcer. Voiceover. Mellifluous, husky: "If you think I look fresh on the outside, imagine how I feel on the inside. Introducing Mystique. The new disposable. It's completely complete. And safe. Because it was invented by a woman doctor in Detroit. For him. For you. For the you in you."*


*Scotland was wonderful. Jonathan went.* Seven people from the agency—not Whitey, two client reps, key people from the production company, the model, and a crew of thirty hired from London joined us at the Holiday Inn in Aberdeen. I didn't see much of Scotland because I had been on the moors every day but I bought three mohair stoles for my mother, Betsy and Judith, a mohair robe for my father and a tam and Tartan for Seymour in the hotel gift shop.

The client loved the spot. The only problem we had on the shoot was the horse. Mr. MacTavish, our Scottish adviser, said, "Dinna ya know you can na gae no brume on the moors fer a fortnight." So special effects had to rig smoke pots upwind to create fog and the horse kept snorting. We lost a day waiting around the set until a dyna-fogger was rented from the British navy.


*T*wo *weeks before Christmas 1984,* I had been accepted into the agency.

"I got a job, Michael! I got a job!" I announced to every corner of the house.

Christmas holds special memories for me. When I was eight years old, our living room burned down. Usually, Christmas and Hanukkah are several weeks apart, but that year, Christmas came right in the middle of the Festival of Lights. My mother put the menorah too close to the tree. It was a religious conflagration and blew out the exterior wall of the house. The next morning, after the smoke cleared, my mother flopped on the sooty couch, not knowing where to begin as my father faced the fireplace, hanging his head on the mantel and I sat on the floor, salvaging my presents. Passersby stared into the blackened hole, gaping at the charred Christmas creche.

Michael would make me repeat the story every year.

Last Christmas, three months after Michael died, I was in Palm Springs and told it to Seymour. I started to cry. He told me to quit telling the story.

This year, I had no one to tell it to.

Jonathan called. "What are you doing Christmas Day?" he sang into the phone, improvising the lyric, imitating Andy Williams or someone like that.

"I'm trying to stay away from carolers," I said.

"Me, too. . . . How about escaping to Chinatown and eating a twelve-course dinner?"

148

"Don't you want to be with your family . . . friends?"

Long pause.

The silence indicated: It's insulting to assume the person who has just asked you has a gun to his head.

When I got the lesson, he stated he'd pick me up at seven.

*We sat in the corner,* at a red-clothed table in Chung Chow West under a green satin banner, sequined letters sparkling: HAPPY BIRTHDAY JESUS.

Jonathan pointed upward, shaking his head in mock resignation. "I can live with that."

"Me, too," I said.

Between succulent spareribs he delighted me with vignettes of everyone I was to meet in the agency. And munching on shrimp toast, we exchanged histories. He had guessed I was divorced. In the middle of rolling a moo shu pancake, he remarked that he'd just broken off a long relationship.

I fluffed my hair in the back, hoping the limp ends would turn up. He smiled at me. I had figured he was married. Grown children. He was about sixty and very good looking. Like Gregory Peck when he wasn't doing westerns.

He offered me a second helping of lemon chicken.

"I can't eat another thing." I sighed. "I'll become a cream puff."

"I already did," he said.

"Did what?" I asked.

"Turn into a cream puff."

"You didn't eat that much."

And he started to laugh and choke and hold his sides and the Chinese waiter stood by waiting to do a Heinrich, or whatever.

In certain areas my vocabulary is limited. I did not know "cream puff" meant gay.

Sipping water, he apologized because he thought I knew, and then I excused myself for fluffing my hair, because I didn't want him to think I was coming on to him, and explained that I liked him but I didn't have the squirls. It was a habit I'd acquired since I'd become single. Seymour was always saying: "Quit doing that with your hair." And then Jonathan was concerned that I not feel rejected . . . but he was crazy about me—and I assured him I felt the same way.

After that, I told him about the burnt living room and pretty soon it wasn't Christmas anymore. But it was. Because I had a new friend.


*My starting salary was $22,750.* When we returned from Scotland, Whitey assigned me to work on flashlight batteries and glycerine soap. I discovered if I rubbed the rim of an empty coffee cup with Binaca and poured scotch into the cup, it facilitated my acting and writing. I'd rock back and forth in my molded plastic chair and compose rumps and patches of prose . . . much easier than a villanelle. . . . There was no stopping me. Since I was convinced I'd be fired any day—my spirit was free. After two months, I was a copywriter minus the junior.

A month later, I had scored a new account for Rubicon. A car. A Greek car.

We were a mid-sized agency (our chances were slim) but Pseudopopolus Motors loved our presentation. I told Jonathan my idea and he created a charming story board for a TV commercial. It shows: A frazzled woman, riding in a taxicab, with the meter ticking, following a hulking American car (something like a Buick) suspended from a tow truck.

"Unique and original," Whitey raved.

The voiceover announces: "Isn't it time to own a Cronus?"

I also named the car. During our conferences, Creon, Medea and Oedipus were considered. Electra (already taken). Jonathan jokingly suggested we call it Mercouri—"At your Lincoln Mercouri dealers." Heather, a twenty-eight-year-old hot shot copywriter who last year won the Golden Cookie Award for her fudge-nut biscuit, toe-tapping in its little chocolate shoes, TV spot, came up with Charon. "It's euphonious—like a chariot."

They all agreed and were about to propose it to Pseudopopolos. . . . Well, all my years of delving into *Bullfinch's Mythology* in search of poetic metaphor saved the agency from embarrassment.

"Charon [yes, I was chewing on my eyeglasses] . . . Charon was the name of the boatman who ferried dead souls across the river Acheron, in Hades. But Cronus, father of Jupiter and Juno, was a titan who reigned supreme."

It became the hottest selling new subcompact import.

I was given a $5,000 raise and moved to the fifth floor with an office next to Jonathan (Rubicon has only six floors).

I was leapfrogging the corporate ladder.

Jonathan took me to dinner to celebrate.

"This time it's my turn to treat," I said, fanning my new credit cards like a gin rummy hand. "Pick one." I giggled.

His elegant fingers reached across the table, selecting the gold card. "I'll let you this time, but promise to stop thanking me, buying me ties and making me fudge-nut brownies."

"But if I die tomorrow, I'll owe you so much. It won't come out even."

"It's not supposed to." He gave a double rap on the table.

Another lesson from Jonathan.

Apart from teaching me the mechanics of advertising—"Less is more!" he would say as we leaned over the slanted easel, laying out copy and design—he gave me the courage to trust my instincts.

I'd say these things to Whitey, off the top of my head, and he'd yell: "Don't move, Babe!" and a new campaign would be launched.

Like Dunkfurth Scotch. First of all, it wasn't made in (here we go again) Scotland, but in Louisiana, and it wasn't selling, especially to women.

Since liquor ads are prohibited on TV and radio (wine and beer are permissible) there is only print, billboard and marketing to increase sales.

Whitey summed up his strategy statement as twelve of us sat around the conference table. Holding up a *New Yorker* cartoon, he pointed to the drawing of a grim-faced bartender assailing a cocktail waitress with "White wine! White wine! Doesn't anyone drink anymore?"

I spoke. A serious error. Comments are always made in order of seniority. It didn't matter. Everyone except Whitey and Jonathan hated me anyway. A whispering huddle would form into a silent semicircle every time I approached the water cooler. Heather hated me the most. She sat next to Whitey, the left side of her mouth dipping into a curve of contempt.

I held up the amber fifth of Dunkfurth with its horsy brownish yellow label.

"This bottle looks like the one Ray Milland stashed in the chandelier."

Only Jonathan laughed. Naturally. It turned out Whitey *was* thirty-six and everyone else in the agency was twelve.

"Occasionally, I drink scotch," I continued . . . ("occasionally" was to be the first of my corporate lies) . . . "And I hate these ugly bottles. I mean, men have those hip flasks, sailor-type things; why not package a two-shot size for women."

I anticipated Heather's disclaimer that it would not be appreciably different from miniature airplane samplers by adding that it would be "somewhere between a cruet and a flacon"—I flavored the words with my Simone Signoret accent—"but smaller than those dimpled jeroboams that hang around the house long after the holiday spirit is gone. . . . Good scotch should reside in a heart-shaped, swan-etched, Lalique perfume–type bottle with a crystal stopper. . . . Women will notice it on the shelves. It'll pull them out of their supermarket trance. It can be reused on a lady's dressing table for witch hazel or perhaps more Dunkfurth. . . . And this time don't talk about Scotland. No one cares about vats or proofs"—I spelled them with my visionary gaze—"It's made in Louisiana. Why not call it . . ." I waited until everyone leaned forward. I was learning to work a room. "Why not call it Shreveport! . . . A woman . . . at the rail of a riverboat . . . Scarlet O'Hara dress. But no Rhett. And this is important. Not even a promise of him. . . . The copy should reflect an elegant two-shot female who can cruise through life without Rhett. . . . What we're selling is emotional security."

"Don't move, Babe!"

It was a good thing Whitey said that. I was feeling woozy. I wasn't sure whether it was the three J&Bs I had for lunch or the whirring discomfort that I was not combating alcoholism in women by offering them smaller doses but selling them a balm for loneliness disguised in designer decanters.

*Benjamin, or Benny as he* likes to be called, is a perky, curly-haired, fifty-five-year-old with a Henny Youngman delivery.

On our first date, dinner at the Bistro in Beverly Hills, he handed the maître d' five dollars and said: "Get me a table near a waiter!" The son and heir to Sleigman Distilleries, the makers of Dunkfurth (now Shreveport), Ben started sending me flowers after I had made my presentation at the client meeting. A bouquet arrived at my house or my office every day for a month. He has more jewelry than Betsy. Filigree gold chains glistened in the candlelight. Four of his fingers on one hand are ringed and a giant scarab clutches and sprawls on the pinky of the other hand. He wears two watches. A dress one on the right wrist and a huge thing that looked like a chronometer on the left.

He leaned across the table. "Would you like a Piaget watch?" And he winked.

At first I thought it was a tic but he does it voluntarily—to punctuate the end of his sentences.

I sipped my daiquiri. "No thank you. I still have seven cases of Shreveport."

He toasted me with his champagne glass. "You deserve it, sweetheart."

At least Ben didn't call me Babe.

On our second date, I mentioned how exhausting advertising was. The next morning, tucked into the floral display—a supply of speed and Valium. I tried it for two weeks but I kept dozing off at work and at night I'd clean my house in twenty-seven minutes. Ben said I got them mixed up and what I needed was a long relaxing day on his sailboat.

"You loved it the last time." Wink. Wink.

"I did?"—and then quickly repeated "I did" without the question mark in my voice because I had no memory of ever being on his boat.

There is a sailboat. In a dream. Michael is standing on the deck. Martha's Vineyard. I can see him clearly, framed against a saturation of colors. I can hear his voice. And feel the spray. But the dream stopped months ago, when I began working at Rubicon. Every night, before I go to sleep, I keep hoping he'll reappear.

It was one of those crystal days at the marina. Ben was singing "I'd like to get you on a slow boat to China," and winking, as he unwrapped the mainsail cover and got his jib out, hanking it on to the forestay.

I sat on a life preserver, squinting at the sunlight behind him, trying to re-image Michael at the prow. Ben hooked the halyards to the sails. They flapped and rose, punched by the air.

"When are you going to sleep with me again?" he hollered over the boom.

"What do you mean again, Ben?"

I was able to recall what I ordered every time we went to dinner. And I remembered all his one-liners. But sleeping with him? How could that escape my notice?

"How was it, Ben?" I thought maybe I could ferret out some clues.

"What do you mean, how was it? Weren't you there?"

I covered rapidly. "I mean how was it for you?"

"Lousy. That's why I'm asking you again. . . . You made that joke about amyl nitrite and I lost my erection the next morning."

What morning? What erection? Emil Nitrate? What the hell was he talking about?

I got up, helped him clear the lines and we pushed off. I stared at him. "Wasn't Emil Nitrate that German actor in the old Von Stroheim films?"

"Stop saying that." He laughed. "Amyl not Emil . . . I pop them to get a rush."

He placed my trembling fingers on the knob of the tiller. His hand over mine, we shoved it to starboard and nosed out of the marina.

One thing was clear. Benny wasn't joking. That irretrievable gap had been my first blackout.

I looked out at the gray sea.

●

154

*Seymour! I know you're there!* Pick up the phone! . . . You never go out so why do you need a machine?"

His voice moaned the outgoing message as though he were speaking from a dead pharaoh's tomb—as if there are any other kind. . . . "Pick up the phone!" I yelled again after the beep. "I'm in jail!"

The receiver clattered on his end.

"Did you hear what I said?"

"I heard," he droned. "You need a keeper."

"It's not funny. I was arrested on a 502. Can you get me out?"

"I'm a retired psychologist—not a lawyer."

"Tell them I'm sick. Tell them I'm unstable."

"That'll get you back on the highway fast. . . . How much did you have to drink?"

"That's beside the point. The cop said I was weaving. But it wasn't me. I swear it wasn't. It was the steering wheel."

"You bought an Ichikawa?"

"A Cronus. . . . It's a Greek car—and I didn't buy it. The company gave it to me. It's our new account. . . . The agency loves me. The client loves me."

"So why didn't they give you a Mercedes?"


*When the arresting officer dismounted* from his motorcycle, his hardware clacking as he came towards me (all California cops look like Troy Donahue), I tried to lighten the mood.

"Evenin', ma'am." He tipped his helmet back with one finger. "Don't you know the speed limit is fifty-five miles an hour?"

"I know that, Officer, but I wasn't planning to be out that long—"

"May I see your license, please."

"License . . . uh . . . uh . . ." I reached into my handbag for my wallet. . . . Where the hell is it? Oh no! Oh no no no no. . . . Holding up the floppy purse, my head down into it like a feed bag, perspiration pouring from my eyebrows, I tried to explain that I had changed pocketbooks for my evening out. (I had met Benny in Malibu for dinner. We had Valium for dessert.)

"Please step out of the car, ma'am."

"You see, I have this steering wheel—"

Nobody listens.

He made me heel to toe it in my wobbly boots on Pacific Coast Highway, my arms flapping up and down like semaphores on a flight deck, signaling to a crippled F6 Hellcat, while he instructed me to find my nose and then made me recite the alphabet backwards (something I can't do even when I'm sober).

I never thought I'd be grateful that Michael didn't live to see this. . . . But if he had, none of it would have happened.

I started to sob. The bastard handcuffed me and called for reinforcements because I was obviously a slippery criminal.

It's so humiliating. You have to walk to the police car all hunched over, and they take your handbag, but it doesn't matter because how can you blow your nose with your hands clamped low behind your back. . . . And that's when it happened.

Mucus was oozing from my nostrils, my mascara felt like napalm and my lips were tight with fright and from trying to snuffle the snot back up. So, I turned, to reach with my fists into a side pocket for a Kleenex. As I swung—I don't know, maybe I did it too fast—the cop was right behind me and my knuckles banged into (Oh God I think it was his nuts). He made a "hlup" sound, jerked backwards, yanked down on my arms, and as my head came up to try to explain, it clipped him under the chin. He bunched the back of my jacket in his fist, picking me up by the scruff of the collar, and dragged me, yowling, as the police car pulled up. A Tab Hunter clone held the door while Ed "Kookie" Byrnes hustled me inside.

"You have the right to remain silent. If you give up the right to remain silent, anything you say can be used against you . . ."

What about hysterical? Do I have the right to remain hysterical? This wasn't any "Hill Street Blues." This was happening to me. I shivered sweat in the backseat cage.

When we got to jail (somewhere under a freeway off-ramp) I was booked on three counts. Driving under the influence—

"Of a broken steering wheel," I kept sobbing.

Driving without a license . . .

"I have one. It's just not with me."

And assaulting an Officer of the Peace.

I still didn't have a tissue.

I couldn't be released on my own recognizance because I didn't have any.

Tab and "Kookie" took me to a long bench, sat me down and attached my bracelets to one of the metal rings along the back. I waited, manacled next to a junkie in a fuchsia shirt.

"Hello." I felt that was enough to say under the circumstances.

His eyes narrowed. His head swayed. He formed fish lips, leaned toward me and crooned: "Strangers in the night . . . exchangin' glances. . . . Scubie doobie do . . ."

He looked too young to know that song.

From behind the waiting area, I heard a gate roll and slam and a policewoman/person came towards me, her fat legs and rear end trussed into khaki pants. She unclasped my cuffs and propelled me ahead of her, holding my jacket sleeve between her thumb and forefinger and generally treating me like I was a piece of shit.

Locking, unlocking, she took me through two wire cages. In the first cage, she stowed her gun in a little metal box, the size that Bank of America gives you when you open a minimum account.

The second cage door opened into a Spanish dungeon with cracked stucco walls and a vaulted ceiling. At the far end of the room, an open window sagged behind iron bars. In the center was a tall desk, surrounded by fencing, with a policewoman sitting on a high stool behind it.

I watched a seventeen-year-old girl in cut-offs and T-shirt slur her history; stretching on bare feet to plead with her inquisitor. That's the secret, I thought. That's how they break you. They make you short. And whenever I feel short, I get very frightened.

Then the fat cop took the young girl down a narrow corridor, out of sight. . . . Probably to the electric chair. . . . No. They don't terminate you that way in California. They gas you. My eyes darted to the far end of the room. That's it! That's how they do it! They make you stand in front of an open window and breathe in the freeway exhaust. You're brain dead in two minutes.

The cop in the cage studied my rap sheet, then reached for my handbag, which had been shunted like a football from officer to officer, dumped the contents, noted the items and sealed everything in a plastic baggie, minus $2 in change, of my own money, which she pushed towards me. I always keep that separate, in a little snap purse, in case I ever have to go to jail.

She gave me a ticket stub for the confiscated stuff.

In a hoarse voice I begged for my cigarettes. Bogart always had cigs in the slammer.

"No!" Her nostrils flared at the suggestion.

"Then, can I have a tissue?"

"No!" Finally, she relented and gave me one of her own. . . . Did she think I was going to hang myself by my Kleenex?

A Sergeant Grace Boniface came down the hallway putting on latex gloves. "Spread!" she said.

"Spread what? . . . I want to talk to my lawyer." I have no

lawyer. Well I do, but he's more like an accountant. He helped me with probate when Mike died. I don't think he does criminal work.

She frisked me. It was like going to Israel all over again; except Boniface took a flashlight and looked into my ears and mouth, and ordered me to loll my tongue around. "I'm in advertising," I gargled.

She didn't respond; instead took me to a bathroom, but didn't let me use it.

What she did—what she did then was so mortifying (even though she apologized before doing it)—

"Who the hell would put drugs up there?" I gasped.

"You'd be surprised at our clientele," Boniface quipped.

When she brought me back to the tall cage, the officer gave me a choice of a blood, breath or urine test.

Urine won by a landslide.

Outside the holding tank was a candy machine. I was so hungry, I bought a 3 Musketeers, Snickers, Butterfingers and Milk Duds. They were fifty cents apiece and I forgot to save any change for my phone calls. I gave Grace one-third of my Musketeers (Athos) and borrowed twenty cents. The operator kept the dimes even though I charged the call to Seymour on my AT&T credit card number, which luckily I had memorized. When I jiggled the hook, to report the loss, she told me she'd send stamps.

"I am calling from jail," I announced in the overly precise diction that I use when I'm dealing with bureaucratic idiocy. "I need the twenty cents now. I do not plan to be here long enough to receive mail. . . . I need to contact someone to bail me out."

"Please deposit twenty cents."

I exploded. "I have a credit card!"

"Number please."

Stricken by senility, the last three digits faded in a vaporous tail.

Grace yawned, leaning against the shell of the open phone booth.

It cost me Porthos but she came through with an additional twenty. I had learned the language of guards and convicts. If the candy held out, I could probably survive in prison for years.

Grace escorted me into the holding tank. . . . God knows how

159

long I'd be there. Jonathan wasn't in and I prayed he'd understand my thirty-second message: "In desperate need . . . under the Sepulveda off-ramp . . . jail. Bring money and tissues."

It was just after midnight and the jail cell looked like three A.M. Why was I surprised? . . . I had seen the movie. And this time Warner Bros. had sent the smell along with the film.

A tin-hooded ceiling bulb, suspended by a chain, swung shadows across six iron cots with gray plastic pads, now and then pausing to spill light, as in a Hopper painting, on two figures. The blond girl, whose pleading I had witnessed, sat on the edge of one of the beds, her head in her hands, whimpering. On the next cot, stretched on her back, breasts jutting ten inches from her chest, which was encased in a lime-green jersey top, a polka-dot wrap skirt clinging to the rest of the six-foot body, lay a mop-headed Medusa.

"Watcha got?" The lady in polka dots lifted a spiked, ruby-red fingernail and pointed to the candy bars clutched in my hand.

I recited my stash.

"Give her one!" She indicated the bleating blonde.

I approached the girl. I wasn't about to part with the rest of my Musketeer. "Would you like a Milk Dud?" I asked tentatively.

"Fuck off!"

I turned back to Wonder Woman. "I don't think she wants anything."

"Hey!" she yelled at the girl. "Take it! It's good for you." And then, as though apologizing for her, Polka Dots continued. "She's crashing."

I nodded and walked back to the girl. This time she held out her hand as I rattled the contents and spilled some into her palm. Then she took the box.

I was getting panicky. Athos and Porthos were gone. But I couldn't help myself, and popped Aramis into my mouth and huddled on a cot near the back of the cell. Here I was, locked in jail for the night, safer than I would be walking the streets, and I was terrified. What if—

"Dottie . . . my name's Dottie," the giantess called to me.

What if Dottie wanted my Snickers? I started to tremble. Maybe I was sobering up. . . . I stared at the bare gray walls. In the

160

corner, an open toilet, shielded by a partition on one side and a soggy roll of toilet paper on the floor. . . . Nothing to do, since I'd already gone. . . . The blond girl curled on her side into a fetal position and clasped the Milk Duds to her like an otter.

"What's your name?" Dottie demanded, toying with one of her springy black curls.

I shoved a large hunk of Snickers in my mouth, chomping the chocolate goo in my cheeks and hoping it would muffle the lie. "Bub."

"What?"

"Babu . . . Beb. . . . My nabe id Bab."

She gave up and went to the next question. "What do you do?"

Why do I let myself get pushed around? Just because a stranger asks you something personal, you don't necessarily owe them the truth.

"I'm in advertising."

She found that hilarious and her chest bounced for about half a minute. Then she turned on her stomach and lifted her chin in my direction. The beam from the overhead light slanted full on her face, and what I thought had been a smudge on the cheek turned out to be a tattoo of a blue-and-yellow butterfly. With large round eyes and a tilted nose, she was pretty and the shape of her face delicate, incongruous with the mountainous body.

I was dying to ask her about the butterfly. "What's so funny about being in advertising?" I said.

"Why don't you tell it like it is? . . . What do you call that when someone gives you a name for somethin' that's not so gross? . . . You? . . . Eu . . . euphoria?"

"Euphemism." I sighed.

"Shit!" the blond girl muttered in her stupor, covering her upstage ear with the Milk Duds.

"That's it!" Dottie exclaimed. . . . "I used to advertise. I was a walking billboard. I got busted tonight and I wasn't even selling."

"Huh?" I leaned forward, intrigued.

There's that moment before a story unfolds that I love, when the narrator takes that stroke of thought, that inrush of breath, framing the opening, as I wait suspended.

Dottie propped her chin in her hands. . . . "When you've been out there, drinkin' and usin' since you were sixteen—I'm thirty-five now—it leaves a hole in your résumé. . . . I never did get beat up, though. Every guy I knew was half my size." She gave me a knowing wink. "So you work alone, or what?"

I didn't want her to stop her story, so I answered quickly, "With a company."

"No kidding. You got steady clients, then? . . . I tried to get with that. . . . You know, go out on calls . . . but they never thought I was classy enough."

Now, it's not that I'm slow. But when you've had a night like I'd had, you're sitting in jail, the embalming fluid is slowly leaving your brain and there's a semicomatose waif on one cot, detoxing, and a tattooed Amazon on the other, it's understandable that I'd be a beat behind. . . . "I'm not a hooker," I apologized.

Dottie turned from me, rolled over, sat up and watched the girl on the cot, who was beginning to shiver. Untying her wraparound skirt, revealing panty hose and a violet bikini, she walked over to the blonde and covered her. "Let me have your jacket." Dottie pointed her polished finger at me, the same way she had instructed me to give up my candy.

Ashamed that I had not thought of it myself, I wriggled out of my jacket. I knew then that I was not a good person, palming the unfinished Snickers in my skirt pocket while I offered them my Butterfingers, which neither of them took. Thank God.

"Friggin' bastards," the girl moaned.

"I know. I know." Dottie sat next to her, tucked my jacket around the twitching shoulders and stroked her hair, saying almost to herself, "Detox is hell. I went through it over a year ago. They gave me Antabuse but I went out and drank anyway. I nearly died. Anyway, it takes what it takes. I've been sober eleven months now." She grinned and looked like a little girl who had just announced her birthday.

I stood in the middle of the cell, feeling awkward, not knowing which of the cots to sit on. Dottie motioned to the one nearest them. "I guess you've got some more drinkin' to do?"

"Well, tonight I had a little too much," I admitted.

162

"Don't check out before the miracle."

"Huh?"

"You see it's really okay that I'm here. I'm exactly where I'm supposed to be."

I could follow the words but I didn't know what she was talking about.

"It's the craziest thing." She slapped her thigh for emphasis. "After I got out of detox, I went to live in a halfway house. Six blocks from the corner I used to work on. I had a motel room on Hollywood Boulevard but they were kickin' me out. I mean this place had roaches that wore boxing gloves. . . . It's a good thing I got sober when I did. I wasn't makin' as much money as I used to. It's downhill after twenty-three."

"In every profession," I commiserated.

"Anyway, so this one night, about a year ago, I pick up this middle-age John. Very drunk. Very Kansas. And I take him back to my zoo and he can hardly get it up but anyway, my time is my time . . . so he unpeels me a fifty from this huge roll and starts to leave. . . . When I was twenty-two I used to have a guy give me a hundred and seventy-five . . . but like now, I'm desperate, so I do my little number and tell him how terrific he is and I give him a scotch and pop a Fiorinal from my candy chest into it. He passes out and I take six hundred from his wad—the guy was walkin' around with six hundred and twelve bucks! I leave him the twelve and stuff fifteen of my last singles I was down to back into his roll, so's he wouldn't notice. Then I get two girlfriends, one of them has a car, and we drop him on the sidewalk around the corner from Grauman's Chinese Theater because he goes there every March when he's in town and that's where I picked him up. And I'm prayin' that he'll wake up and not remember . . . so now it's like a year later and I've moved, and I'm clean and sober, I'm going' to A.A. and I'm workin' the steps and I got a job—don't ask, I'm a waitress—and sometimes I make less in a week than what I used to make in twenty minutes, but it's okay because I'm not insane and there's lots more I can do with my life. . . . So, it's a program of rigorous honesty, right? And you have to clear away the wreckage of your past and make amends to everyone you've hurt. . . . It took me a month just to finish the list. . . . So, I'm thinking about this guy and I've been savin' up to give him the six hundred back, minus my fifteen ones. . . . It took me like seven months. So now it's March again, and every night I'm walkin' up and down in front of Grauman's 'cause he's supposed to be there the first week, right? And the cops don't bug me because they know I'm cool. . . . And I see him! I can't believe it! And I go up to him and say, 'I got somethin' for you!' and he fuckin' freaks out and jumps into a cab and I jump into a taxi behind him and say: 'Follow that cab!' and I'm goin' nuts 'cause even though I got the fare, it's his money! . . . So we're followin' him forever—on the Hollywood Freeway, the Ventura, the San Diego, then the Santa Monica and finally he must have thought we lost him because he gets out in front of a restaurant on P.C.H. . . . And I nail him. I grab onto his jacket and I go, 'Take this,' and I open my purse and try to shove the money at him and he doesn't know what's goin' down and I'm holdin' him and shakin' him and the bills are fallin' on the ground and then there's a siren and red lights and two cops and finally this guy opens his mouth, screamin', 'She stole my money!' And the cabdrivers have split and I'm goin' 'Last year! Last year! I'm trying to give it back!' But the cops don't believe me—'cause they're not from Hollywood, and anyone who looks like I look doesn't give six hundred dollars back."

The young girl had fallen asleep. Dottie glanced down and stroked her hair.

I shook my head. "What's going to happen to you?"

She shrugged. "I'll have to do some time, but it's okay. . . . Funny, all those years on the streets, the most I ever spent in the can was overnight."

I reached across the cots and touched Dottie's other hand. She enfolded her fingers around mine. "Why do you have a butterfly on your cheek?" I asked.

"I always wanted to be special."

# F OUR TEEN

*I'm not going to any* goddamned A.A. meeting. I'm not an alcoholic!" Jonathan listened while I ranted into the phone. "Alcoholics have noses you can strike a match on. . . . The men all wear plaid slacks and the women walk around in curlers on Saturday nights. . . . Besides . . ." I plummeted into a morose tone. "How will I get there? I'm too drunk to drive. I'll have to call a cab to take me to Skid Row."

Jonathan waited until I'd run out of steam. Then he said, quietly, "You're not the same person I met six months ago."

"Well, that's what happens when you do time."

"It's not funny. I'll be over in fifteen minutes." He hung up.

I sat on the couch. On the coffee table I stacked five miniatures of Shreveport into a pyramid. Jonathan had remarked several times at work that my hands shook. As I gingerly placed the sixth tiny bottle, straddling it perfectly atop the two below, I decided to leave it there to show him. A testimony to my control. Instead, I went to the kitchen, took an orange, squinted at them from a distance of nine feet, and in perfect carnival aim, tumbled the bastards off the coffee table.

Jonathan was full of shit! I had not undergone a personality change . . . goddamned judge! Some choice! A ninety-day alcoholic program and a $390 fine or one hundred hours of community service or thirteen days in jail. I picked the first one but he lied. . . . When I went to pay the bailiff, the $390 was actually $664 because of surcharges, penalty assessments and defraying the cost of hiring the chemists to analyze my urine. . . . Well, I'll fix them! Once, when I had renewed my driver's license, I had promised my organs to whoever if I died in a car accident. Good! They can have my liver. I'll marinate it for them!

I tried to explain to the judge that my Cronus had a faulty steering wheel because of the cheap plastic shims on the ball joint between the tie rod and the steering arm and that's why I was weaving, and in the month between jail and the hearing, thousands of letters arrived at the dealerships—the car also fills up with blue smoke when you shift to third—everyone was suing everyone, the Cronus was being recalled. . . . The judge kept banging the gavel and said that had nothing to do with my alcohol intake.

Justice sucks!

And then last week! The same day as my sentencing! I was fired!

I went into the bathroom, washed my face and stared at the dripping reflection. Six months in the agency. Well, I never thought it was anything more than an accident. . . . Jonathan enjoyed my success. I couldn't live in it so I sublet it to him. Besides, if I had really accomplished something, I would have heard from the elves. I kept waiting for the exhilaration that the writer of "Where's the beef?" had chronicled in *Advertising Age*. It never came.

The doorbell rang, ending my drunkalogue. I dried most of my face but left the watery eyes. Jonathan would turn to mush when he saw me and I'd get out of the meeting.

The minute I opened the door, Jonathan told me the news. It was terrible. I'd been rehired.

"How could they do this to me?" I moaned. "I was looking forward to collecting unemployment."

Jonathan peered at me over the top of his glasses. "You know something? You've become as glib as your copy."

"You used to like me." I flirted with Jonathan, which never does any good. I keep forgetting he's gay.

"I know," he said, finally hugging me. "I created a sixty-second monster. . . . Come on. . . . Let's go." He picked up the bottles, found my purse and placed it in my hands.

"Wait a minute. Let me get a drink."

"I don't think it's a good idea to go to an A.A. meeting loaded. You won't get as much out of it." He took a comb out of my bag and tried to pull it through my matted bangs.

"Ouch!" I stood there, slumped, arms akimbo. "What kind of business is this—Ouch! You're hurting me!—works you so hard, burns you out and then to top it off has the gall to un-fire you. Why?"

"Because I'm the new creative director and unless you become completely catatonic—you're too valuable to me."

"You mean, Whitey Mouse is gone!" I gave a little jump and stumbled on the way down.

"Knock it off! Stop pretending you're drunker than you are— just because you don't want to go."

That was some smart Jonathan.

In the car, Jonathan told me about a new account that Rubicon had secured. Briard Books. A medium-size West Coast publishing house.

"Don't publishers promote their own books?"

"They have an in-house department," Jonathan explained, "but it's small. We can offer them a more comprehensive marketing strategy. . . . And they've got a hot new author. . . . If you promise to sober up, you can have this account. It's perfect for you. You'll be reading books, meeting with writers, editors . . ."

"No more douches?"

"Nope."

We pulled up in front of a church in West Hollywood.

"Relax," he said. "I have friends there." And then, with a reassuring pat on the shoulder: "You'll see. Everything's going to be okay."

Whenever anyone tells me that, I get a sinking feeling. It's akin to someone giving you driving directions and then adding, "You can't miss it!" I always do.

Jonathan refused to go in with me, promising to pick me up at ten. I took the deepest breath I ever took and followed the arrowed sign to the church basement.

The smoky room was crowded with men. Not one woman. Why hadn't anyone told me about A.A. before? I fluffed my hair and sat down in the back.

There was a young man at the podium. "Welcome to the Thursday meeting of Alcoholics Anonymous. My name is Pierre and I'm an alcoholic."

A rocketing burst of response shook my chair. "Hi, Pierre!"

When the debris settled, he continued. "Are there any other alcoholics present?"

All around me, hands shot up with the thrusting energy of a call to arms.

"Not to embarrass you, but in order to get to know you, is there anyone here in their first thirty days of sobriety? If so, please raise your hand."

Everything was still.

I felt a tug on my sleeve. In a stage whisper that would have carried to the second balcony of Radio City Music Hall, coming from a guy next to me, I heard: "You're in the right place."

I wanted both of us to die.

Seventy-five heads rotated. As my left arm limply raised itself, I pivoted from it, refusing to acknowledge that we were in the same company.

"Would you like to introduce yourself and tell us the name of your disease?" The heads turned to the speaker.

"Huh?"

The heads rolled back.

A guggling sound came from my throat. . . . Oh God! . . . "My name is . . ." What the hell was I going to do? What was it Dottie said? It's a program of rigorous honesty. . . . More guggles. Finally, from somewhere I found the courage to say, "Charlene." It wasn't *my* name, but I found the courage to say it! . . . And now that I was truly anonymous, I added hastily, "The judge made me come here, but I don't think I'm an alcoholic."

There were screams of laughter, you would have thought I was Rodney Dangerfield. The hilarity was topped by showers of "Hiya, Charlene!" "Charlene!" "You're in the right place, Charlene!"

I sklunked down in my seat. I wanted to be noticed—but not that way!

Pierre introduced Austin. A good-looking fellow. The raucous routine repeated itself.

Austin started off by saying that he used to bemoan the fact that nobody loved him. In mock self-pity he whined, "Why aren't I lovable? Why doesn't anyone love me?" . . . Everyone in the room chuckled and nodded their heads. When the noise subsided, he went on: "Until I realized that half the world lives in China, their last name is Wong, and they don't give a fuck about me." The audience fell apart. And I thought I was Rodney Dangerfield!

He talked about his childhood; how his father beat him and his mother died of chronic alcoholism and he ran away from home when he was eleven and began "drinkin' and usin'." He said it just the way Dottie did. And then he told how he discovered he was homosexual. He was living with this older man when he was fifteen. . . .

Waaait a minute! . . . Where was I? . . . I took a careful look at the men to the left and right of me. This was a gay A.A. meeting! I had been a beat behind. Again!

It wasn't all bad. Now that the probability of finding Mr. Right was removed, I found I could concentrate better.

I caught up with Austin as he was saying that this older man got sick, that he loved him very much and Austin nursed him through a long illness, but the man died. And Austin drank. One night he hurled a rock through a liquor store window. After he did time, he still drank and one night woke up in a freight car, in a train yard in Idaho. He had bottomed out. "I knew then that the only job I could possibly get was as a doorstop."

More laughter.

And then, as swiftly as the laughter had surged, it died down and the room became very quiet. I was startled to discover tears flooding my eyes. What he had said, almost throwing it away, was: "All I ever wanted in my life was to be held." I don't remember the rest of the talk. God. A.A. Friends . . . learning to be of value . . . I was watching the profiles of the men in my row—handkerchiefs lifted to their faces and the young man next to me, crying into his hands.

There was a coffee break before the next speaker. I walked out, to the churchyard patio, and tried to light a cigarette that trembled in my fingers. As I stood in the shadows, I had an impulse to merge with the group as they came out of the meeting and join in their animated conversations. I didn't. I went up the steps to the street. I had been moved by Austin's story of despair and recovery—and Dottie's. But apart from that, I had nothing in common with them. I heard voices behind me: "Charlene!" "Charlene!" I didn't turn around. They weren't calling to me.

# F I F T E E N

BRIARD BOOKS: Publicity Packet: Quetago

Rich in symbolism, intricately plotted; Eric Rothender takes the reader on a journey of five decades and gives us a searing look at war. Seen through the eyes of Mark Chalmers, a charismatic former news cameraman; Klaus Potofsky, the diabolical, former World War II double agent and now with the CIA; the Santiago family; the controversial Father Rosario; and his niece, Consuela, leader of the insurgents and presently in Juanelope Prison, we are drawn into the world of Gabrielita and Rodrigo, whose lives are inevitably changed.

Set in rural Quetago; Eric Rothender explores the topography of the soul.

★   ★   ★

*The manuscript of Quetago was* so heavy I had to separate the pages into sections, piling part of it on the couch and settling the other half on my thighs. It still felt like lead.

## CHAPTER ONE

*It is carnival time in Quetago. The eve of*
*Epiphany. And in the small village of*
*Xotchilatchikotchl, Gabrielita and Rodrigo are*
*herding their mules into the barn . . .*

Three A.M. Sunday morning.

"The question," Judith said, "is not how he did it, but why he did it?"

I didn't know if she was talking about the author or the protagonist.

We had been reading since Friday night (not aloud but to ourselves), alternating chapters (I had the odd numbers) and giving each other a short synopsis before we went on to the next.

Judith handed me the damp washcloth. I placed an ice cube inside and put it on my forehead. "Anyone who can survive nine hundred and seventeen pages has a right to commit suicide."

Now, Judith wasn't sure if I was referring to the author, the protagonist or myself. "The author isn't dead," I moaned. "I'm meeting with him Tuesday." I hefted my half of the manuscript and located the next-to-the-last chapter. Fifty-seven. "It's right here. . . . The minute Potofsky says it, Chalmers has no choice." I pointed to the line and read aloud: "When I hear the word 'culture,' I reach for my gun."

*I remember when bookstores were* musty, when the only sound was a bell that bounced as the door opened. I remember when a book was something you saved for. I was fourteen and went back to the shop three times to see if *The Complete Works of T. S. Eliot* was still there. I remember Michael surprising me with *The Poems of Robert Browning*. It didn't need a jacket. Let me imagine what Robert Browning looked like.

Judith and I had taken a break from our weekend marathon and gone to a bookstore in the mall. As we approached the windowless shop we thought we heard Joan Rivers's voice coming through a loudspeaker. It was Joan Rivers. On a cassette. Reading *The Never Before Published Letters of Wallace Simpson*. Piles of them on wire racks in high-tech colors . . . Jackie Collins dolls toddled towards us. You wind them up and they wiggle their little tushies. . . . A life-size cardboard cutout of Norman Mailer standing next to a basket of balls. If you can knock him off his pedestal, you get a free copy of *The Executioner*. . . . A rubber chicken with a pull string that snaps back and squawks, "Today, from the French Chef." . . . An exercycle—and on it, a Saturday afternoon author, pumping away, promoting his paperback. . . . And in the center of the store, stacks of an unfinished mystery novel, displayed around a miniature island, with teensy palm trees, sunk in a rubber raft. If you guess the ending, you win a trip to the Bermuda Triangle.

Judith kept gasping. I was nonplussed. We stood there, like those two middle-aged women in a *New Yorker* cartoon. The caption: "I don't suppose they have Emily Dickinson here."


*Florence Phister, editor in chief* of Briard Books, was definitely not thrilled with me. Whenever she glanced in my direction, she flicked off tiny incrustations of dried lipstick from the corners of her mouth.

Lester Heckenkamp, the publisher and president, never looked at me. A formidable man, with an imperious air, his small eyes focused on the top of his nose. He looked like—I warn you this is not a pleasant image—an eagle taking a shit on a mountaintop. (If it weren't for the vodka stingers before the meeting, I would never have thought such a thing.)

Eugene Vuillion, vice president in charge of marketing and promotion, wasn't there. I mean, he was, but I couldn't get a reading on him, until he spoke, with the precision of a metronome: "We expect *Quetago* to be the mega-book of the year. *Quetago* is more than a novel. It is an experience. Our research indicates consumers and merchandisers are ready for it. We are getting behind *Quetago* because we feel it is the answer to the nonbook." He stopped his recitation to ask me a rhetorical question: "You are familiar with the nonbook?" He lifted the copy of my budget breakdown. "We see here the usual items—X amounts for print, radio, TV, author's tours—but we are looking forward to a unique marketing approach. We are on the threshold of creating a brand-name book. We feel we can target a wide audience with a unanimity of factors." He nodded deferentially to Ms. Phister. "Florence?"

Ms. Phister aspirated her words as though we had entered the Cathedral at Chartres and she was our tour guide. "What we see here is a breakthrough book that is complex within its structured simplicity. It has the punch of Hemingway, without the mannered *tics*. And Rothender takes primal leaps of imagination usually found in Latin American writers, Fuentes, Vargas Llosa, et cetera, but rarely in American authors. . . . One can also find the tautness of Ludlum and the tension of LeCarré . . . in addition, and this is very exciting—notice the political timeliness. It mirrors our involvement with Nicaragua."

I had missed that connection. Maybe it was in the even-numbered chapters.

"So," she said in closing, "what Eugene is referring to is the concurrence factor." Florence gestured respectfully to Mr. Heckenkamp. "Lester, will you sum up?"

"We gave Rothender an advance of a hundred thousand."

In ladderlike ascension, they had made their opening remarks. It was my turn and I was in deep trouble. Eric Rothender was an important new writer. I doubted if Heckenkamp would want him winking from a T-shirt. But according to Eugene Vuillion, *Quetago* is a natural fruit cola, and Florence?—I don't know. How do you package a war? . . . Well, they wanted a promotional blitz. That's why they hired Rubicon—look what we did for Cronus.

It's rare that a publisher sets aside money for a TV commercial, but Briard was in trouble, so they decided to put most of their chips on one pile. *Quetago.*

I took the large art folder with the preliminary storyboard sketches, placed it on the table and opened it. . . . A montage of terrorist attacks, crops burning, bridges blowing up (we could use

TV news clips, I explained), dramatizations of love scenes between Gabrielita and Rodrigo, Gabrielita and Potofsky, Chalmers and Gabrielita. And over this, a narration, proclaiming *Quetago* as the novel of the decade. As I pointed to the copy over each frame, I suggested that the voice be an Orson Welles or Rod Serling soundalike.

I knew that the concept was derivative and the reception from Eugene Vuillion was lukewarm. He felt it lacked "clout."

My palms began to itch.

Florence approved the terrorist attacks but noted that it was indistinguishable from anywhere else in the world and how could we hint at Central America.

Something happens to me when I drink at lunch. My tongue gets heavy and rests on my lower lip. I forget to pull it back when I speak. I bit down and cried, "Cuidado!" I wailed through the pain, "Socorro! . . . Fuego! . . . Salga!"

Heckenkamp finally looked at me.

I reached for a glass of water, rushing to explain that we would dub Spanish cries throughout Welles's narration. They liked the idea but I suddenly felt uncomfortable. Winding down through the water a drop of blood turned into a pink swirl. There is something so moving about a cry for help—in any language, it seemed manipulative to use it for a television commercial.

Then Florence said something about the lack of political literacy in this country, especially in the area of international affairs. Eugene echoed that it could be used as a promotional tie. "Political fiction—an easy read." Lester added, "Rothender knows everything. We paid him a hundred thousand dollars."

All at once I got this absolutely wonderful idea—and I could cut the Spanish from the sound track. I found myself raising my hand. "Instead of a voiceover, why not have Rothender himself, in the foreground, narrate the commercial. . . . From the point of view that he was there, he saw it happen, and *Quetago* can deepen our understanding of the crises in Central America."

You would have thought I was . . . Francis Ford Coppola. Florence stared at me without rubbing her lips. Eugene murmured, "Good, good, good," and Heckenkamp saluted me by lifting his glass of water and asking if I were still going to use the Spanish.

According to his bio, Rothender had lived in Central America for many years. The fact that he had never been a news cameraman, nor was he a political analyst, didn't bother me. He'd be perfect on "Good Morning, America."

I elaborated: "Eric Rothender is not only Mark Chalmers— he's James Reston."

For the next three hours we tossed ideas and planned strategy. Rothender would be arriving from his home in Oregon tomorrow. Photo sessions were planned, press interviews . . . a gala signing in two months at Doubleday's flagship store in the Beverly Center Mall. . . . Oh God! . . . Eugene kept pressing for the Carson show. "Isn't the producer, Fred De Cordova, a Latin? He must be . . . Cordova is the monetary unit of Nicaragua."

"Cordo*ba!*" Florence corrected.

It was Eugene's turn to get the lipstick brush-off. . . . I remembered that Renato Sands, who sang the jingle for Cronus, was a friend of De Cordova. I'd make a sample tape of Eric and send it to Fred. . . . July 19 was the anniversary of the Triumph of the Revolution. If there was a party, we'd get Rothender there. And if there was no party, we'd make one—at Spago's.

By the time I left the meeting, I had promised that Eric Rothender would play Vegas.

## SIXTEEN

*Janice, who had become my* secretary since Whitey's dismissal, closed the door to my office and leaned against it. She crossed her wrists behind her, arched her back and shook her torso, as though she were tied to the mast of a pirate ship and twelve buccaneers had just had their way with her. "Eric Rothender's here!" she heaved and breathed.

Advertising was temporary for Janice. She was waiting for her big break in TV.

I was impatient with her theatrics. I'd been up all night reading the even-numbered chapters and I couldn't wait to meet Eric Rothender. Florence had been right.

Through the eyes of one anguished family, I experienced an earthquake, a bloody revolution, a proxy, counterrevolution, and heartbreaking scenes of poverty. It was Nicaragua. There were beautiful descriptions of an uninhabited wilderness of timbered plains and

177

rolling hills cut by rivers . . . (according to his bio—Eugene said that could be changed—Rothender, fifty-one, had worked as a forester in Oregon before joining a lumber company in Central America) . . . tender, sensory love scenes between Gabrielita and Mark Chalmers—in a climax forest. There is such a thing. I looked it up. It's when trees reach their ultimate balance due to perfect climatic conditions—something like that.

Judith definitely had read the best part and there was no way to relate it to me in a scenario. Of course, there was overlapping and weaving of plot, character and description in both the odd and even chapters, but mostly, I got Potofsky, encripted files and cameras that literally shoot you.

I had the weirdest sense that the novel was really two books.

"Janice. Ask him to come in."

Eric Rothender was dressed like the owner of a Christmas tree lot. Reddish brown hair lined the sides of a duck-billed cap that read "Keene's Hardware." I couldn't see his eyes, because the beak of the cap almost touched the rounded arch of his Mount Rushmore nose.

"Eric Rothender?" he suggested in a deep, throaty whisper.

"Right," I said. And after that I was stuck.

He motioned to a chair and moved slowly towards it, surveying my office. Six feet, three inches of nose and clothes.

I recovered a beat late. "Please sit down."

He settled himself, stretching his long, rumpled corduroys, tucked into some kind of galoshes, and folded his arms across a shirt of bright squares and a scrungy, padded nylon vest.

"So," I managed. And I was stuck again.

"Eric Rothender," he provided. And this time without the question mark.

If I said "Right" again, we'd be back where we started.

His mouth barely moved when he spoke. "Guess you're wondering about my clothes?"

"No no no." I flapped. "I like plaid."

With the tip of his finger, he edged his cap slightly upward and I could see his face. Tan. High cheekbones. Eyes crinkled at the corners . . . studying me. "I had to spray deer repellent." Medium pause. ". . . Doesn't hurt them."

"That's good." There was a time when I spoke in compound sentences, but I was spelled by him, caught in the jerky telegraphese of his Hemingway dialogue.

". . . Almost missed the plane."

"It's understandable."

Short pause.

". . . Airline lost my bags."

"That's terrible."

Silence.

Somebody would have to say something soon. The office closes at five.

He stopped staring at me and said, "Did you like my book?"

I was so grateful to him for reminding me why he was there (lately, I'd become easily distracted or I'd blank out in the middle of conversations). I answered enthusiastically, "You've written one helluva book! I mean *a* hell of a book."

I thought I detected a slight, closed-mouth smile. Then he asked in an offhand manner. "You want to have dinner?"

"Tonight?"

"That's when people eat dinner."

"Sure. Where?"

"Wherever I'm staying."

"Didn't Eugene make reservations for you?"

"Eugene is a peckerhead."

I buzzed Janice and told her to make a reservation at the Beverly Hills Hotel, dinner at the Polo Lounge at—"Eight o'clock?" He nodded—and to call—"What's the name of the airline?"

"United."

United and have his bags delivered.

We stood, simultaneously. I fidgeted and cleared my throat. "I know you have a meeting with Florence in the morning—on the final edit . . . so I've a . . . scheduled a photo session for the late afternoon . . . and er . . ." He was just standing there. Masculine. Mysterious. Looking down at me. I handed him a typed list of the month's activities. "Well, it's all there . . ." He wasn't making it easy for me.

As my voice trailed off, he took a step toward the door, balanced back on one foot and tipped his cap lower. Apparently sensing my discomfort, he mumbled in a gruff apology, ". . . Takes me a while to warm up to people."

I gave a nervous little laugh and thought, I better get him to the Carson show early.

He walked out without looking back. Reaching into my top desk drawer, I located my mini-scotch and was just about to unscrew the cap when the door opened and Rothender stood there. I don't think he saw, because I got it back in the drawer and slammed it hard.

"Your secretary said your name is Babe. . . . You got another one?"

I was so startled, I blurted out, "Not right now."

He left and I went for the scotch, savoring the first "bite," tracing the calming effect as it went down.

Don't say to yourself, There's something about him. What is that something? He's not really good-looking. Yes he is. No he's not. He's . . . he's impressive . . . unnerving, but at the same time I felt—WHAT? . . . safe with him. That's it! . . . He was the kind of man you could trust with your first name.


*When you knock on a* door, you expect the person who answers to have hair. It's amazing how shocking that can be. What Eric had was still reddish brown, but only two inches of it circling his bald head. And with that nose . . . Where have I seen that nose? I stared at it. "They told me at the desk your luggage is on its way up."

" 'Bout time," he said, and headed for the bathroom.

And the way he speaks. No adjectives. No nonsense.

I waited while he showered. The bellhop brought the bags and put them on the bed. I tipped him. He left.

Eric opened the bathroom door. He was naked—except for a towel wrapped around his waist. His body was gorgeous. Bronze skin. Natural muscles. He padded past me. Picked up a suitcase. . . . Of course! He was an American Indian—with a monk's haircut. I reached for the *Beverly Hills Hotel Guide* and tried to read it, upside down.

180

". . . Be ready in a second," he murmured, taking the bag into the dressing room area.

"That's fine." I waved one hand casually. "Don't body about me."

"What did you say?"

"Huh? Uh, nothing."

Eric called from the door, "You want to order a drink from room service?"

"No. Thanks. I don't drink." Actually, I had given up drinking—*at night*—because of my A.A. meetings.

He raised his voice over the splash of the faucet. "Can't hear you—running water."

See what I mean. Indian talk.

After the whooshing and patting sounds of aerosol lather and skin bracer, he said loudly, ". . . Shaved off my beard and mustache three days ago—grows kind of scruffy—figured I should look like a writer, not a bounty hunter."

Mistake. Eugene pictured Mark Chalmers as a cross between Tom Selleck and Castro.

"We were thinking more of an outdoor look." I was right in the middle of hollering that when he walked out in jeans and a white shirt. Is it possible to drown in a whiff of shaving lotion? I've got to get a grip on myself.

"It's too late now," he said, stroking the memory of his beard.

*I felt very clumsy at* dinner. I began by saying, "Well, Eric, if I may call you Eric, tell me about yourself."

He drank his water. "Don't like talking about myself."

Perfect for Phil Donahue.

He smiled imperceptibly. "Tell me about yourself."

I shrugged. It was such a complex subject. I didn't know where to start. I wanted him to like me.

We studied the menu.

"They have wonderful Coquille St. Jacques," I suggested.

He flipped the pages.

I tried again. "Tournedos Bordelaise?"

No response. . . . He's definitely an Indian.

"How does Veal Marsala sound to you?"

Guess what he said? "I don't eat white man's food!"

I tilted my head. "Are you an—"

He pitched his deep voice lower, anticipating the question. "Great-grandfather. Chinook."

I laughed but then I wasn't sure if I should have. He still kept that poker face and I didn't know if he was teasing me or not. I needed a drink. Remembering what I'd told him upstairs, I ordered a carafe of Chablis. Wine doesn't count. I had the Tournedos and he asked the waiter to bring him steamed veggies.

We ate in silence. Naturally, I wanted him to expand on the Chinooks, but since he didn't volunteer, I couldn't press it. Also, I heard on the radio, driving over, a talk show psychologist saying to a distressed female caller that men are overwhelmed by bright, professional women. "Leave your power at the office. Men love a woman who listens." Of course, all this is predicated on the fact that the man whom you're having the relationship with talks. . . . And I was waiting for the perfect time when I would bring up the subject of our innovative campaign. Eric Rothender as Mark Chalmers. After he had a drink. Or dessert. He didn't want either.

He pushed aside his half-eaten veggies and leaned forward. "In your office, you said that I'd written *one* helluva book."

I got very flustered. *"A* hell of a book."

"No. You meant exactly what you said." He pinned me with a steady look.

I knew he knew I knew. I can't get away with anything I think. Like upstairs—when I said, Don't body about me. It always comes out, sooner or later. I had no choice but to tell him what I suspected. Why I went into this long preamble, I don't know. Maybe it was just the relief of talking, or the wine. "Years ago, I knew this woman— Myra, who had six toes on each foot. She was always on the beach— Fire Island, this summer place—Bernie, my first husband and I rented a house there. All summer long, Bernie used to say, 'Whatever you do, don't mention Myra's toes.' So I didn't. And it was ridiculous for him to say that because why would I talk about her toes. . . . Then, one evening over the Labor Day weekend, Myra and her husband came to dinner and I was in the kitchen getting dessert and Myra wanted coffee so I shouted back, 'Myra, do you take cream and sugar with your toes?' "

Eric rocked back in his chair, laughing with such abandon and basso richness that everyone in the Polo Lounge turned to look. When he stopped, he wiped his eyes and people went back to their dinners. Then he started again and I laughed to keep him company. He had great teeth. When he recovered the second time, his eyes still sparkled but he said in a monotone: "Now that I can trust you, I'll tell you my secrets."

He *was* funny. No, he wasn't. Droll! I hadn't thought of that word in years. He had a droll sense of humor.

I leaned forward expectantly, waiting for him to continue. An agent and a screenwriter at the next table edged to their left. It was easy to figure out who they were because earlier I had overheard:

"Marty, sweetheart, they see it as a comedy."

"I don't want anyone pissing in my soup!"

"Take the money and run!"

Eric noticed them—"Not here"—and called for the waiter.

Studying the addition on the check, he seemed saddened. I reached for the bill, explaining that it was part of my job. He sighed. ". . . Doesn't matter who pays—it's still too much." He wasn't being funny, then.


*Upstairs, in his room, he* lay on the bed, hands under his head as though he were counting the acoustical tiles. "How did you figure it out? I thought I did it so well."

I sat on the chair near the window, overlooking the swimming pool. I wasn't completely honest. I didn't tell him about Judith and the odds and evens. "You did it well . . . but I think you wrote the book about the Santiago family first. . . . It's very moving. And then, as an afterthought, you put in Chalmers, Potofsky and the CIA. The writing seems"—I didn't want to say hokey—"different." Here's where I lied. "I re-read the *whole* book and the even-numbered chapters are the best."

He thought for a long time and turned on his side towards me, propping himself on one elbow. "In December of 1979, five months after the revolution, I finished the book. No one cared about a tiny country. No one knew much about it. Except Washington. They had plans for Nicaragua, but no one else was interested."

When Michael was alive, he would read the morning paper. As I placed the eggs and rolls in front of him, I'd glance at the headlines and put my arms around him. "Darling you tell me about it." The world was very far away. When he died, it vanished.

I told that to Eric, but not that way. My truth is highly decorative. "What is so difficult in regard to Nicaragua is that newspapers presuppose one knows what has happened previously. Even though I have some background—I've been trying to follow the situation [LIE!]—I find it exceedingly frustrating . . ."

He waited for my convoluted explanation to end. Or was it that? No. Not quite. When I finally stopped ploppling and looked directly at him and said, "I don't know anything about this. Please tell me," he nodded and gave a half smile of approval. He wanted me to be truthful.

Placing me geographically in Central America, Eric set the scene. Remembering he had a map of Nicaragua, he got up, took it out of the suitcase, and spread it between us. I pulled my chair closer and he sat back on the far side of the bed.

He demarcated the topography of the country into three major zones, then discussed the contrasts in terms of two major ethnic and political-economic sectors. Beginning with the history of the people—"Most Nicaraguans are Mestizo, a mix of European and Indian, and the culture follows the basic lines of its Ibero-European ancestry with Spanish influence prevailing"—he took me through the Somoza regime, the Sandinista-led government (my head was spinning), the plummeting third-world economy, the wrath of the Reagan administration (was it the excitement of learning something new, or the sweet way he'd sometimes stop and ask if he were going too fast. Yes, but I always shook my head, no), the discontent of the Nicaraguan bourgeois, the plight of the Campesinos, the attacks by the Contras (or the way my hand accidentally brushed his as I touched the map?), and then, integrating the conflicting machinations of the United States and Russia, he brought me up-to-date.

Whatever the reason, I was in a state of academic arousal.

I stood and stretched. I'd been hunched over the map for about an hour. "Why didn't you write the second book the way you just told it to me?" I asked, preparing to lead into the proposed TV commercial.

"Because we are a generation tired of politics . . . and I'm not a political writer. I can't make any sense out of what's happening. . . . Do you know that Reagan just ordered a total economic blockade of Nicaragua? All exports, imports, canceled. . . . We're strangling the country while we continue to have diplomatic relations with its government. . . . Oh, and you'll appreciate this. We select a Contra leader, create an image for him, and if it's not working we rearrange him."

I wondered who had the account.

It's a miracle when a man and woman connect. How can they, when there are at least three conversations going on at the same time? There was the one we were having with each other, re: Nicaragua. Then there was me with me . . . I have to talk to him about P.R. and I'm not making any headway. Why doesn't he make a pass at me? . . . "Because he's not interested." Who said that? Oh, my God! The elves were back! Of course. For the first time, since Michael died, I finally meet a special man. Someone I could really like . . . Michael had always urged me to read the newspaper. I should have listened. Is it too late to call room service and order wine? . . . And, there was him with him, which was an absolute mystery to me.

Quietly, as though he were summing up for himself, he said, "Nicaragua is a human tragedy, people caught in the crossfi—" He stumbled over the word, then stopped.

"Crossfire?" I repeated.

He clenched his back teeth and laid his head on the pillow. I heard him say "Yes" in a low voice and watched his inward turning mood of reverie.

The story was in that silence.

When he spoke again, his voice had a flat, self-deprecating edge to it. "I wrote a political entertainment."

185

Why was I protesting "No no no!" when that's exactly what we were selling?

"Don't lie for me! It's hokey. . . . I studied the formulas of all the best-sellers—wedged in all the junk I could think of. . . . What was it the guy downstairs said? 'Take the money and run'? . . . Well, as soon as this P.R. is over, I'm going back to Nicaragua."

I looked at him to see if he'd noticed the sharp intake of my breath. He hadn't. He was stroking his bald head, his face toward the window.

"Why?" I asked, as casually as I could manage. "Another book?"

"No, this is it . . . heard once, 'If you make people think they think they'll love you for it. But if you really make them think, they'll hate you.' I didn't do either."

Was I going to cry? . . . I barely followed the rest of what he said. When the Sandinistas forced the American Lumber Company out of Nicaragua, he stayed, demonstrating how housing can be built utilizing the country's resources, without importing materials . . . stone, adobe, Spanish clay tile, hardwood from the forest, reforestation . . . turned shacks into quality housing . . . destroyed by the Contras . . . one hundred American dollars can build a house . . .

Who was this Eric Rothender? A one-man Peace Corps? Why had he stayed? Why was he going back? Why didn't he ask me to go? . . . I'd live in a mud hut with him, until he built me a better one. I'd be barefoot and (I was too old to be pregnant) I'd fight the Contras. I'd go to Banana Republic and buy khaki clothes. Yes! I'd do all that and more for a man I wasn't even sure liked me. . . . I had to know. The problem is, I have never found a way to successfully feign indifference while asking a man, "Are you married? I mean . . . er . . . do you have family there?"

"No," he said curtly. I was obviously getting too personal.

The elves were right. He wasn't interested. I was mad at him. So, I launched into what Briard had in mind for Eric Rothender.

Inscrutable, he leaned against the headboard as I strode back and forth, pouring energy into the "sell." Stressing the correspondence of book sales relative to the persona of an author, I ended my enthusiastic pitch, hand sweeping the air, emblazoning an imaginary headline: MARK CHALMERS, WRITER, INTREPID TV CAMERAMAN, POLITICAL ANALYST . . .

Lips pressed, his head moved slowly to the left, then to the right. Was it a no or a neck stretch? On his third swing back, reaching the center, there was a plosive sound followed by an outburst of laughter comparable to the one in the restaurant. . . .

". . . Can't pretend to be Mark Chalmers. I am Mark Chalmers!"

"What?!"

The heels of his palms turned up, he glanced heavenward and nodded, as though some perfect retribution had befallen him. Between booming chortles, he explained that when he rewrote the novel—not wanting the publishers to remember his name or the book, he submitted it as *Quetago* and invented Eric Rothender. ". . . Never liked the name Chalmers, but it's perfect for that character."

I wanted to hug him. "Then you'll do it?"

"No!"

"But . . . but the TV commercial?"

"Change the copy."

". . . The press conference—the Carson show . . ." I gibbered. "What will you talk about?"

I should have known the answer. "The Pantasma Cooperative." He swung his legs over the edge of the bed. "Sorry."

In the words of Tennessee Williams: I do not have the charm of the defeated. But I tried. "Will you ever let me call you Mark?" It sounded so plaintive.

"When you get rid of 'Babe.' " He was serious.

All evening long, I'd been wearing my jacket, because the air-conditioning was on high. Underneath, I had this clingy blouse, and I wanted him to see what he'd miss if he went back to Nicaragua. So, when I got ready to leave, I took my jacket off. "It's getting warm in here, isn't it?" No reaction. . . . Holding both our reflections, I paused at the mirror and fiddled with some stray hairs—"Oh! I'm a wreck!"—and fixed my expression, waiting to playfully argue his next line, which was going to be: "No. You look great!" It never came.

187

At the door, shuffled, mumbled good-byes of "Tomorrow" "Four P.M." and then he touched me—for the first time. On the head. Patting the top, kid sister style. As I stood on the threshold, he said, "Don't drink anymore tonight."

*Why does loneliness feel so* much like terror? Inside the elevator—wet hand against the brass rail. Polished bronze door distorting my image. In beige suit, with gathered skirt and fashionably full jacket, I would die standing up. A descending mushroom, forced through eternity to look at myself. . . . How could he say that? I had only four glasses of wine at dinner—that's all! No one ever suspected I drank too much—except Jonathan. Did Eric see the shot I took in the office? Was that why he was cautious? . . . Well, what do you expect from an Indian? . . . I'd had a Valium to relax me before going to the hotel and some speed—just to get me started in the morning—but the problem was, I hadn't spaced everything right. I needed a drink.

The Valium wedged in my throat. You can't ask the Polo Lounge bartender for water, so I pointed to what the guy sitting next to me was having. The pill slid down with the first swallow of bourbon and soda.

There are those memorable moments of drinkin' and usin' when you get the exact proportion of booze and drugs—just right. And you're sailing! Why should I go home? I was afraid to be alone.

"Long day?" the guy on the bar stool asked. He looked vaguely familiar.

"Long and rough," I responded. Sure! He was either the agent or the writer who sat next to Eric and me at dinner.

I remembered that. The rest was fragmented. There were two other rounds. He paid. Finally I was going home and I needed energy to drive, so I took some speed. But I'm not sure if that was before he said that funny thing or after. "You know you're in trouble when your agent tells you to have a nice weekend—and it's only Tuesday." . . . He was the writer. When did I put my hand on his knee? Were we laughing downstairs or later when he asked me a riddle: "How do you say 'Fuck you' in Hollywood?"

"I give up."

"Trust me!"

That was hilarious. Was my jacket on or off? . . . He knew lots of funny stories. . . . There was that smell of shaving lotion. No. It wasn't the same as Eric's. This was cloying. Pearl buttons on my blouse, a nailhead between my breasts. Something snapped in my stomach. No. On my stomach. *Ping!* Giggles. A window was open. My legs were cold. "Cover me."

      *Ohhhhh   yes   whoops   wet   hard   stiff*
                        *nice   yes*

"Did you hear about the Polish actress in Hollywood who wanted to get ahead by sleeping with the screenwriter?"

    *Ha ha ha   choo choo choo   Ha ha ha   choo choo choo*


*Here comes that famous line.* "Where am I?" No answer. For a second I thought I was in Eric's room. No. This bedspread was puce. And I was under it. I lifted the heavy damask and looked down. . . . How was that possible? My blouse was on but no bra. Nothing else. Across the room, folded neatly on the arm of a chair— my clothes. . . . I felt my face. Checked the front of my body. There weren't any bruises. Easing myself to a sitting position, my buttocks were tacky and pulled against the bottom sheet. A bubble of vomit rose and blipped in my throat. It held until I hit the bathroom. The splashing was voluminous and I sank to my knees, hugging the bowl. Everything came up. I lost ideas in that toilet.

Then the terror. Not galloping. This time—knotted.

As hot as I could stand it, I stayed under the shower, scrubbing my hair with the wafers of hotel soap. When the steam cleared, I looked towards the bathroom mirror. There was a note taped to it. "Thanks. Check-out time, twelve noon."

I didn't go to work that morning. I didn't have to. Attached to the note was a $50 bill. . . . I didn't know whether to be pissed or pleased.

I wished I'd had Dottie's number.

# S E V E N T E E N

*When Michael was acting on* TV he'd hold up the original script printed on white bond paper and say, "I'm not studying this. I'll only have to relearn it." Instead, he rehearsed his aggravation. He knew that day and night, pages of rewrites, dropped or reversed scenes, deleted or added dialogue, even a name substitution, would arrive by messenger from the producer's office. And they came! In assorted colors. Green. Blue. Pink. Buff. And written at the top: "Fuchsia replaces orange." On a sixty-second commercial, no matter how many changes, the copies are always white. Which is a good thing. Because if our script was a *prime time show* about Nicaragua and it involved Eric—we'd run out of colors.

That's what I thought during the six-hour eleventh-hour production meeting on Wednesday. And why five of us, behind the camera—Lester Heckenkamp, Florence, Eugene, Jonathan and

I—sighed in unison on Thursday as Craig, the director, yelled, "Quiet everyone. . . . Marker!"

The clapboard lifted and snapped in front of the lens. Take 57.

"Roll rear screen projection and cue Rothender."

Standing in front of a screen, his back to us, Eric watches a newsreel film . . . helicopter view of an agricultural co-op. Semicircle of adobe houses on one side of the farming area. . . . The camera moves across the field of workers to a bank of trees. . . . Behind the trees, in a medium close shot, we see armed soldiers in camouflage fatigues holding AK-47 assault rifles. . . . Cutting back to the field of workers, we hear the sound of ratcheting bullets. People stagger, fall as they're hit. . . . At the left of the picture, a burst of gunfire. On the right, a cookhouse shack is torn apart. The camera pans left again. We are about to identify the type of weapon, when pulsating in front of it, the letter Q licked by fire appears, followed by *U,* until a blazing title is spelled across the width of the screen.

## Q U E T A G O
by
### ERIC ROTHENDER       *(bordered in flames)*

Eric turns . . . faces the television camera and speaks:

"My name is Eric Rothender. What you are seeing is real. It's happening now in—"

"Cut!" Craig hollered. He waited . . . clenched his teeth and said through them, "We've lost the smile!"

This time, Eric matched Craig's silence (outlasting him by a beat), then pointed to the screen. "See what's going on there? . . . You want me to be charming?"

Craig, a recent graduate of U.S.C. film school, was pissed because his first directing job was a commercial. "Take five everyone!" He glared at Eric. "Makeup, mop this person down and reset for flat frontal light. Can we do anything about that shine on his head? We've got a flare like a halo!"

The sound man lifted the boom from his shoulders as though it were a two-hundred-pound barbell. The camera operator slid from his perch so fast that his foot got caught in a cable. Craig strode towards us with an exaggerated I-give-up shrug. Eric walked off the set in the direction of the makeup table at the far end of the sound stage. I wanted to follow him but Eugene was whispering in my right ear, "Serious is different than glum," while Florence, in my left ear, retracted her earlier decision. "If he won't smile, let's go back to the beard." Lester, on his second Bromo-Seltzer, pounded his chest with his fist and burped. "BEARD!" Jonathan suggested we solve new problems.

We had given in to Eric. Solemn was appropriate. All we asked was that he be pleasant about it. He did try. On one take, lips pressed together, the corners of his mouth turned up as he attempted a half smile. But his expression read like someone suffering from heartburn.

Eric was angry. He hated his name in flames and the fiery *Quetago* covered the U.S.-made M-60 machine guns (in close-up) blasting destruction on the quiet agrarian village. He insisted they be in the clear but after the production meeting the burning title had been superimposed on the print.

I felt it wouldn't hurt his cause to be affable. However, I was the only one Eric wasn't furious with and I wanted to keep it that way, so I said, "Let's not push it." On the other hand, I had a job to do. "What if . . . at the top of the dialogue we ask him to say hello. That might soften his presence."

"Wonderful" was the consensus.

Naturally, I had to ask him.

Seated at the table in front of the lighted mirror, Eric was reading the *Los Angeles Times* as Hal, the makeup artist, sponged a heavy application of pancake base to the top of Eric's head.

The atmosphere on the set had been so tense that I thought it best to be professional. After an exchange of greetings, I got right to the point. "Eric, they think . . . they'd like you to consider . . . would you say hello—"

Eric lowered the paper. "No!"

"But it's such a small word." What do I do now?

"Let your head dry," Hal said to Eric. "I'll come back to powder." And he walked off.

Eric picked up the paper. I was about to go when his fingers gave a backhanded slap to an article in the middle of the page. "See this? . . . Show it to them."

Does he want me to read it first? Stand next to him while I read? Leave? . . . What? There was no way to know because when I took the paper from him he turned back to the mirror without saying anything.

Under an arc light, in an isolated area, I found a chair. It was terrible news. The House of Representatives and the Senate had voted in favor of funding the Contras for "nonlethal" aid, the House having reversed its April vote.

I crossed the set. Eric, his back to me, was still at the makeup table, staring ahead. A part of my image was in the mirror. I stopped. It was clear. Just because you agree with him it doesn't mean he needs you. I passed by him. He didn't call to me. I was beyond his reflection.

As I approached the group no one asked for a report. They read it in my shuffle. I held up the *Times*. "Have you seen this morning's paper?" No one had and they weren't interested. The director of photography had been in the middle of saying something when they paused to look at me. Well, they'll find out soon enough. When Eric gets to the third line in the script. If he ever does.

Then a gaffer joined us, indicating the amber gel he carried as witness to what he was about to tell us. "We've done everything. The guy still looks terrible."

That hurt me. I accepted Eric was difficult. Or precisely: loquacious about Nicaragua, laconic about everything else. Now, this! How is it possible that a man who causes my heart to melt whenever I look at him is not photogenic?

At seven A.M. Hal had applied a reddish blond mustache and beard to match the two-inch fringe bordering Eric's skull. Eric consented because at seven A.M. he hadn't seen the *Quetago* title, was in a fairly good mood and always wanted a beard. But he can't have one. Eric is one-quarter Chinook and can only grow sparse patches of chin and side whiskers (which explains why Indians have no hair on their chest). Jonathan, Eugene and I thought it looked great. Florence and Lester felt it was too fierce and since Rothender refused to be called Mark we had a new image to contend with. Eric the Red . . . fifty-seven takes of trimming and cutting until it was a final cut and by then Eric was so upset about the film he didn't want it.

Which brought us to this crisis. Negotiating a half smile from a bald and beardless man whose world was falling apart.

Craig said he had time to do only one more take and then we had to break or we'd be in meal penalty.

Film is rolling. Eric turns. No hello but a slow nod to the camera. It's intriguing. I like it and hold my breath.

"My name is Eric Rothender. What you are seeing is real. It's happening now in [pause] Nicaragua—"

"Cuuut!"

It was open warfare.

Heckenkamp went ballistic: "NOT NICARAGUA!"

Eric's voice boomed: "You're damned right I'll say it! It's insanity to call one hundred million dollars in aid humanitarian that in reality will be used to fund a country to fight against itself!"

Eugene got shrill: "You didn't name it in the novel. Why are you identifying it now?"

Heckenkamp plowed through the end of Eugene's line: "You'll lose every Reagan reader!"

"That's an oxymoron!" Eric shot back.

Somewhere in there a high-pitched screech, from Craig. "I can't work with amateurs!"

Florence stuttered: "We comp— . . . comp— . . . compromised. You're supposed to say 'Central America'!"

"*I* compromised! . . . Don't you people read the papers!" Eric overpowered us.

I moved in like the Red Cross, rushing to explain that the two Hispanic actors hired to play the four-line love scene from the book were born in Honduras. "They still have their accents!"

Then Jonathan blew up. "No one will think it's Sweden!"

"LUUUNCH!"

Eric stormed off to his dressing room.

Why did everyone look at me? Just because I doubled over, my head heading for my waist as I grabbed my stomach. I had terrible indigestion. On the way to the deli platter I reached into my bag, took out a bottle of Maalox and unscrewed the top. Everyone wanted one. What could I do? Tell them, Don't take it because I dumped the Maalox and replaced it with Quaaludes that Benny gave me for such an emergency? Thank God I had the presence of mind to suggest they swallow the tablets rather than chew. I was afraid the lack of mint would be a hint.

Between the potato salad and the pickles Craig gave us his editing expertise. Eric had paused before saying "Nicaragua." He could scissor it out, pan to the love scene as Eric said "Central America" (we had Eric's voice on a wild track when they were testing sound) and then cut back to the news footage.

Jonathan reminded him there wasn't enough film to cover the remaining dialogue. "You have to return to the end shot on Eric."

"And he won't have gotten any better-looking," Heckenkamp said.

I did not like Lester's remark so I countered with: "When Dick Cavett interviewed famous writers none of them matched my image. . . . Only Isaac Bashevis Singer looks like Isaac Bashevis Singer."

Eugene speared a bagel. "Well, it's all right for him . . . but if it wasn't for Roger Moore, 007 would look like Ian Fleming."

"He used to look like Sean Connery," Jonathan muttered.

"What's the difference?" Heckenkamp plopped Russian dressing on a slice of rye. "People have short memories. Sales were better when he was whoever he was."

Florence found that hilarious and began a series of staccato hiccups, or maybe her laughter had something to do with Lester's pulling apart his sandwich and complaining that the pastrami made his tongue buzz.

That's the thing about 'ludes. They work a lot faster than goofballs or bluebirds. Personally, I like the sensation of not having any bones in my body, but everyone has his or her particular reaction.

Craig mellowed out. He smeared mustard on top of his lox and cream cheese and kept grinning at me, his head cocked to one side.

I was fixing a plate to take to Eric. "I'll talk to him." And then I made a joke. "I'll try for Central America. If that doesn't work, I'll try Central Casting."

At that moment an adage I'd once heard came true. The biggest mistakes you make are the ones you never know you're making.

I watched Eugene part his lips to speak and then reflect on the fact that nothing came out. After a series of fish-mouthed attempts, he exclaimed, "That's it!" It was just like Whitey saying "Don't move!"

Through my toxic haze I gathered that they were going to call Screen Actors Guild and hire an unknown Paul Newman to not only film the commercial but do press interviews, talk shows—to become Eric Rothender. I couldn't believe they'd taken me seriously. I kept piling mounds of cole slaw on the plate. "What'll we do with Eric? Send him to the Justice Department's Witness Protection Program? Hide him in Wyoming? Give him a new identity? He won't do it!"

That's the other thing about 'ludes. You can still get upset but it feels like it's happening a year ago.

It didn't affect Lester that way. He punctuated the end of each sentence with the jab of a plastic fork. "He wants the book to sell— tell him he's shooting himself in the foot! He wants to save Nicaragua—he can't do shit *unless* it sells! Tell him to go back to Oregon! We'll send the money! When he's not in the woods he's in [thrusting and shouting in the direction of Eric's dressing room] CENTRAL AMERICA! Who ever saw him, anyway!"


*H*ow do you tell someone they don't exist?

I stood in the doorway of Eric's dressing room. His arms folded, long legs stretched on the cot, head against the wall, he looked like a sweet moose as he scanned my face.

"Is Burt Reynolds worried yet?"

I should have segued from his question into my opening remarks but as I handed him his lunch, he sighed. He was tired. It was a long sigh. I didn't want to give him bad news.

He swung his legs off the cot and patted the space next to him. I sat down. He shook his head. "We're at an impasse." It was such a sad shake. I certainly didn't want to give him bad news all at once. It's like the old story about your mother falling off the roof. You get the mother up there gradually. And you try to relax the listener, so it's not a shock.

"Eric, you know how some people say, 'Hollywood must stop mixing show business with politics!' Well, in this production, we can't get started."

He gave a little "grrr" of a laugh and kept his eyes on me for several moments. I didn't know if it was the 'ludes or his look but my heart was racing. In the past weeks there'd been an undercurrent of smoldering sexuality between us. Well, that was my interpretation. When I checked it out with Betsy, she said, "You'll know when he makes a pass at you."

That's why, when he offered me a forkful of cole slaw, I realized this was the sign Betsy meant. . . . I didn't want to give him bad news at all.

So, I swallowed the slaw and said (God forgive me), "Eric, I have a feeling they'll come around . . . to your way of thinking." And I rattled off some technical jargon describing how the lab could fix the film.

"Terrific!" he shouted as he hugged me, making me feel rotten and wonderful at the same time. "I bet that was your idea!"

"Sort of . . ." I suggested he take a few days off. I had to get him out of town because Heckenkamp was expecting me to tell them Eric had agreed.

Later, I'd give Eric the news. Gradually. The lab couldn't do it. The network wouldn't approve "Nicaragua." The camera has a way of photographing certain people . . . well, I'd figure it out.

Grabbing a towel, he vigorously rubbed the makeup off his face—"Think I'll go up to Oregon"—then paused and gave me a half smile. "Want to come?"

What could I say? I'm responsible for annihilating you, but don't let that deter you from asking me for the weekend.

## E I G H T E E N

*Why does love feel so* much like a seizure?

At the point where the North Umpqua and Little River meet head on, Eric parked the car.

He held the door open for me and shouted over the colliding rush of waters as the two tributaries crashed head-on and rose into foamy geysers. "... rare phenomenon."

My head was under the dash, changing from heels into rubber boots. "I hate flats. I always feel like I'm standing in a hole."

"We're not going in it." He stood there patiently. "We're just going to look at it."

I put my heels back on and tumbled out of the car, tripping over the mossy stones on the embankment, and slid into the arc of his outstretched arm.

That's when it felt like a seizure; watching the spindrifts of spray, surrounded by blue-green spires of Douglas fir and Jeffrey pine, as his sturdy arm circled my shoulder. I recognized the sensation. Impending happiness.

Try not to talk, I said to myself. But the elves were demanding I spill everything.

"Start by telling him if he doesn't ravish you by the rivers, you'll have a stroke. Follow that by explaining you're responsible for his being replaced and the reason Heckenkamp was stretched out on three chairs and Florence had a cold paper towel on her head was that you gave everyone Quaaludes and then told them it was muscle relaxer pills that the orthopedist had given you for your bad back and you transferred them to the more convenient Maalox bottle . . . and what about that guy you picked up at a bar—waking up in his hotel room with a sense of incomprehensible demoralization—deeply ashamed because you'd made fifty bucks without even knowing how. That'll get him. Be sure to stress you're completely off alcohol (almost) but take Valium for maintenance. And don't forget to mention you're a jailbird. . . . After such a catharsis he can't help but love you. You'll be sobbing and he'll pray for you. It'll be like Sadie Thompson and Reverend Davidson. You always get laid after absolution."

In a spasm of clarity, I realized my solutions were the problem and silently screamed at the elves.

". . . Never seen you quiet for so long," Eric murmured in my ear.

I smiled at him. "I often let my mind go blank."

A sudden crash and the waters spewed upward, arching over the rocky ledge. He drew me closer, protecting me from the crystal shower, wrapping me from the waist up in half of his windbreaker. I wanted to stay there forever, smelling his skin.

"Enough already!" piped an elf, and I turtled my head through his jacket and out the lapel.

He bent his head toward me. Our noses almost touched. I held my breath. Slowly, he said, "It's the dry season in Nicaragua. People get dysentery from drinking contaminated water. . . . Eighty percent of the population is without sewers and half of the illness is due to substandard sanitary conditions."

"Huh?"

"Think you can get that in a commercial?"

Astonished that he was not contemplating me, I managed a professional tone. "It would take a telethon. . . . Besides, how will that sell your book?"

"It'll make people aware. . . . When was the last time we thought about a Campesino on a co-op—what he wants for his life . . . standing five hundred yards from the house he's just built . . . watching it blow up? And what do we ask in this country? 'Why do we support the Contras covertly?' And the answer is: 'Because it's against the law to support them overtly!' Sixty seconds is a powerful tool."

"You're right," I acknowledged. "But I'm in advertising. We have to entertain."

"Why?"

"Sure, tell him," an elf niggled, ". . . that Friday before you left you selected a bearded Robert Redford type who is even now rehearsing the life of Eric Rothender/nee Mark Chalmers and that you lied to Florence, Lester, Eugene and Jonathan (what else is new) and said that Eric had agreed to the charade. That'll win him over!"

I have to trim my inner monologues. . . . Not that Eric's exactly swift of speech. Always taking a stroke of thought before he says anything and mulling my answers in his teeth. . . . "Why, what?" I asked, forgetting the question.

"Why do you feel you have to entertain?" It was not a reproof, but seemed two-edged, as though he knew the response would convey some truth about me.

I shrugged. Let him chew on that.

We drove on, the river on our right. Crinoline-skirted trees at the edge of the woods on our left dissolved into reflections of dappled strokes of moving light and color.

"Ohhh," I crooned, "Monet! . . . That's what he did . . . broke nature into little pieces and put it back together."

He stopped the car at a point where the river bellied out and the pulsating flow was dispersed and soothed into obedient ripples. "There it is," he said, as we climbed out of the car and he took my hand, "your canvas of shattered images. . . . Come on . . . want to show you something."

We crossed the road and walked into the woods as he named the giants. "Ponderosa pine. Noble fir. Western cedar." And then, standing under the pagoda branches between two trees, I followed his finger straight up as the trunks of "Western hemlock" converged into the sky like railroad tracks. My gasps turned into a wheeze.

"I was born in New York. We had a philodendron in the window. My mother kept it alive for ten months."

"Ten months is a weekend to a Douglas fir," he said with that somber grin whenever he was being droll.

I was a prosaic pygmy at the base of sky-shattering monoliths. All I could say was, "Wow! Wow!" I'll never make fun of Joyce Kilmer again.

Eric seemed to enjoy my exhilaration. "Didn't you ever go camping?"

"Once. I was a Girl Scout and our leader took us to Central Park. We sat on a bench and she lit a long wooden match and we toasted marshmallows stuck on twigs."

"That was it?"

"Oh no. We ate peanut butter sandwiches."

"Did you see any animals?"

He obviously didn't know Central Park, so I was not going to make a joke about muggers. "I fed the crusts to the squirrels."

"That's it?"

"Uh huh."

"Birds?"

"New York has pigeons! They fly but they're not serious about it."

Long beat. I could hear the scratch of his teeth. "Why is it, when you say something funny, I feel sad for you?"

"You mean, because I had a deprived childhood?"

"Not just that. Everything."

"It wasn't so bad. I had a Labrador retriever."

"They're great dogs."

This time, I paused. "He committed suicide."

Very long beat. "Dogs don't commit suicide."

"Inky did."

"How?"

"I'm not going to tell you."

"Why?"

"It's too sad."

I'd like to say that's when he took me, bursting with love and pity in the midst of this rhapsodic beauty. I'd like to say that, but it's not what happened. Instead, we went to a fish hatchery and watched fish climb ladders. I wanted to get a postcard and send one to Seymour and my mom and dad but there weren't any. No people, no postcards, no Cokes. Just salmon slithering up wooden slats.

In two hours I had learned that if you boil the stalks and leaves of a banana plant you can make a paint for outer walls, which is what they were doing on this co-op in Nicaragua, and that it's possible to develop an olfactory sense so keen you can smell elk and possum, which he modestly admitted he had, and that mosquitoes can tell when you ovulate. The deeper into the forest, the more talkative he became, though he never lost his laconic manner, and except for the mosquitos remark, which was the sexiest thing he said, I hadn't a clue how he felt about me. And yet, he was so dear, always taking my hand, watching lest I slip on something, showing me around . . . I finally figured it out. I was a cousin from Chicago.

About five miles from the hatchery, Eric slowed the car as we approached a . . .

"Covered bridge!" I cried out. "That's a covered bridge! . . . I've lived my whole life without seeing a covered bridge! . . . How will I remember this day without a postcard? Are we going across it?"

"On foot," he said, stopping the car.

I followed him to the trunk. "So how does the car get to the other side?"

"Stays here. Planks have rotted away. Better put your boots on."

"Why? I mean we're going on it . . . not under it." The river swirled below and I had a picture of myself swinging from the supports like what's his name in . . .

"It's not the River Kwai," he finished my thought. "It'll hold us but—" He swung my Val Pack that was wedged in the trunk onto the ground and looked at me with an incredulous expression. Oh God! I hadn't listened when he told me to pack light.

The reason Eric hadn't seen the suitcase before was that he left on Thursday and I had to be at that clandestine casting session Friday so I took a plane to Eugene on Saturday morning. His Jeep, which never breaks down, did, so he couldn't pick me up and asked me to rent a car at the airport and meet him at a garage in Glide, which is perfectly named because I passed it twice before I found it.

"It's on wheels. You can roll it." This was the helpful hint that I'd learned to say in four languages when porters would try to lift my suitcase and crumble under the weight.

"I can take it." He lowered his voice in a parody of a macho man, "But the bridge can't."

"Huh?"

"No. It's not dangerous . . . only problem is we've got a half-mile hike when we get to the other side."

"Well, can we wheel it across and I'll come down to the river when I need a few things?"

"If the elks aren't wearing them first."

"I don't want to hear about elks. I just want my stuff."

"Tell you what . . ." He took off his windbreaker and spread it on the ground. "Put whatever you want in here and I'll make you a knapsack. . . . You just need jeans."

"That's what I have . . . sort of. . . . I could leave my makeup if Elizabeth Arden has a branch up the road."

I unzipped the load and began sorting my supply lines. It was so embarrassing. I'm probably the only person on earth who still owns a push-up bra. He pointed to a pair of shorts and a T-shirt. I could leave the tiered black-and-white Mexican skirt and my Esmerelda off-the-shoulder blouse and my dancing sandals. I held up the four-pound sack of makeup. "My face is a blank canvas. I don't know who I am without makeup," I wailed.

Aiming his finger at the center of my chest, he said soothingly, "You're in there."

"Don't give me that E.T. philosophy." I was becoming anxious despite my joking. "Let me take my eyeliner! . . . Look, how much does mascara weigh," I bargained, holding up the wand. "I'll walk slow."

And so, divested of my stuff, my connection to me, and poling a knapsack, we crossed the bridge and began to trudge through the woods.

A few yards up the trail (that marked the edge of one hundred acres of his property given back to his Indian grandfather by the state)—"That's bigger than Staten Island!" I wowed and gasped again—Eric stopped in front of a slender tree enclosed in a mesh fence. "Hybrid . . . from Nicaragua. Everyone said, 'Won't make it here,' but look . . . doin' fine." He gave the leafy top a delicate brushing. "You see this spindly part? Represents a year's growth."

The way he caressed it, I didn't know whether to say how old is she, he, or it.

"Five years?" I guessed, estimating the height and dividing.

"On the nose!" He beamed and touched his own.

"I got to go back."

"What for?"

"My err . . . toothpaste." Actually, I had forgotten my diaphragm (I don't believe in pills) and now that I was sophisticated in dendrology, I figured there might be a chance.

"I have baking soda," he offered.

"It's not the same. I have this special kind . . . made a solemn promise to my dentist. He said I'm losing the war against plaque."

Eric was still studying the tree as I rejoined him.

Extending his hand to help me over the slippery places, through a corridor of rock, losing sight of the river that appeared again as a running brook which looped and huddled with mossy stones, and visiting briefly with a felled crocodile tree trunk— "That's Charlie!" he announced—we continued our climb.

"How does Pizza Hut deliver?" I panted.

"Don't need him. Make my own."

The foliage changed. The air, moist. "We're in a rain forest," he said quietly . . . low growing plants, intensely green in hauntingly beautiful light. . . . I could smell the earth. And then ahead of us— Oh my God! A fifty-foot waterfall, spilling over glistening rock and cascading into the mouth of the same brook which had widened into a natural oval pool. And to the right, where woods had been . . . a clearing and a log cabin.

It was breathtaking . . . enchanting? . . . I had no right to call myself a poet. But I couldn't think of anything else. I was busy crying.

Wiping my running mascara with Eric's red bandanna handkerchief, I thought . . . If I lived here . . . I would never drink or take a Valium. How could I? The nearest store is thirty-four miles.

Eric patted the side of the cabin, nut brown in the late afternoon sun, as though it were a handcrafted piece of furniture. "No nails."

"It's like a . . . huge wooden blanket chest." I stared at the roof, certain any minute the slanted lid would unhinge.

"Interlock system . . . logs are square-notched and fitted."

Following the pattern of his hand, I touched the smooth dovetailing and my astonished fingers realized it wasn't the ragged crate of my Abe Lincoln imagination. "Are you building these in Nicaragua?"

"Not practical . . . can't withstand an earthquake. We use their indigenous rock and adobe method, adding diagonal bracing in the walls and a perimeter tie beam so the roof won't collapse."

I loved the way he explained things I'd never understand.

"Am I getting too technical?"

"Not at all."

"Well, you'll see."

What would I see? A construction manual or was he inviting me to Nicaragua? . . . I wanted to ask but he was busy showing me around outside. . . . The outbuilding, outhouse, outdoor shower. I tugged at his sleeve, dying to go inside the toy box, but with a sly sense of drama, ever so slowly, like the teasing red ribbons of Christmas, he explained stump water and flumes . . . for God's sake!

Finally. Finally. With a *churk* of the door and a welcoming *yeee* from the hinges, I was under the lid.

My tongue flapped. No voice, again. Well, what do I need it for? Speech isn't one of the five senses.

It was a snuggery existing only in pipe dreams.

A rocker bowed to me as the breeze from the open door

pressed at its back and a slant of sun illuminated the riderless seat of—"Woven cattails," Eric said. Against one wall, a four-poster bed—"Cherry wood" with a "barn-raising" quilt, paled now but still goldenrod yellow, indigo blue and crimson the color of poke-berries . . . "Grandma's prized possession. It was registered in her estate list." In the center of the room, the multicolored cords of a braided rug—"Don't look too close . . . made it when I was stuck on a chapter." And on it, two ladder-back chairs at each side of a thick round table with stout legs which Eric said reminded him of two schoolmarms scolding a fat kid.

I decided if I touched everything, firmly, I could stay in the nineteenth century.

I walked to the bed and pressed my fingers on the mattress. It rustled, then softly crunched.

"I think it's got some corn shucks in it." Eric was leaning against the wall, arms folded, looking at me, and then, when he added, "It's comfortable," I thought I saw him blush.

I watched as he shifted his weight.

Oh, for a long muslin skirt and a poke-bonnet. Eric is already in costume . . . the house lights dim.

Places please for Act II.


BABE

(Center Stage as Curtain Rises)
I reckon this is the finest cabin I ever did see.

ERIC

Yes, ma'am.

BABE

And I know your grandma's lookin' down and mighty happy we're gonna be usin' her bed.

ERIC

Yes, ma'am.

BABE

We're married now, Eric. Ain't no need for you callin' me ma'am.

*Yessum . . . 'cept I don't know your name.*

*It don't make no never mind . . . jest as long as you love me.*

*I reckon I do.*

*And I love you, Eric. And I reckon I will until the day—of reckoning.*

"Are you all right?" Eric asked.

I had been so moved by my performance that my chest was heaving.

Crossing the room, my steps unsettled two logs in the fireplace. The top one rolled and thumped in the grate. A whiff of hickory. Tears.

I wiped my eyes on my shirtsleeve, my back to Eric, and rubbed his desk, a thick plank of cedar, whorled with knotholes . . . and on it, an old portable typewriter . . . books—mostly on Central America, but above the desk, on a shelf, between carved onyx bookends, were volumes of poetry. I touched Virgil's *Aeneid.*

"The only thing I go into town for is Wite-Out." Eric was standing behind me.

"You can use Clorox." I sniffed. "Once I didn't have any and I used Clorox."

Great! I finally speak and the first thing I talk about is bleach.

"I'd have to go into town for Clorox," he said logically, turning me around—catching two huge drops with his handkerchief as they met on my chin. Playfully, he wrung out the cloth. ". . . Going to have to put this out on the line."

"I'm sorry."

"Do you know why you're crying?"

"It's my hobby."

"Don't do that."

"What?"

"You can tell me what you're thinking."

"You'd run for your life."

"I'm not so sure. . . . Hungry?"

"Starved."

He opened the black belly of a little Buddha standing in the corner and lit a fire in its tummy, and then weighing a cooper kettle in his hand to see if there was enough water, he placed it on the burner. "I'll catch us a fish."

"What if you don't?"—which was the wrong thing to say to a man who fells trees, rigs up a washing tub with a plumber's helper for an agitator and braids rugs.

"Beans!" was the answer. He took down a fishing pole that was pegged to the wall, snapped open a tin box and removed some brightly colored—

"What are those?"

"Flies."

"Flies? They're too pretty to be called that."

—propped his Keene's Hardware hat low on his forehead, and then, holding on with one hand to the top of the door frame and bending slightly, he turned back to me, edging the cap up with one finger. "I'm glad you're here."

With the whoosh and whistle of the kettle the overture begins. In place for my opening number, ready to sing the title song from the new Broadway musical *Babe in the North Woods* (adapted from the earlier play), I pour tea. In this rock candy set, the curtain is going up on my life.

## NINETEEN

*Twice in my life, I* was stricken with extravagant joy. It had such a detonating effect on my psyche that it knocked the socks off the elves and took them hours to recover. The first time—when Michael and I walked a dawn beach in Hawaii and sunrise surfaced as a shout.

And then, earlier this evening. Eric and I were having dinner (grilled salmon with a sauce of mushrooms, shallots and lemon juice sprinkled with a little fresh basil—to die) when the sun, a cannonball of burnt orange, descending behind the waterfall, dropped to a hemisphere of throbbing red and published the night.

Delirious with metaphor, as trees became ink drawings, I thanked him and thanked him and thanked him until we were mountain cold.

That's why, when it happened, I was so frightened. We had gone inside and the cabin, our tiny planet, was warmed by its own sun—because I had learned to make fire. Holding the tongs and giggling as Eric coached me, I trembled suddenly and violently. My heart rate increased. It felt as though I had been infused with the nervous system of a race horse. And this time, it wasn't the elves.

"You don't by any chance—" I couldn't finish speaking. The tongs clanged to the floor. Eric's arms went around me.

"I'm here. It's all right. . . . Don't try to talk."

"I think I'm hyperven—"

"Don't talk! Breathe through your nose. Easy! That's right."

After several moments the shattering in my chest subsided and my breath returned to a measured flow. With a sigh of relief, I tried asking again, as nonchalantly as I could, "You don't by any chance have some wine?"

"No. I can give you some cranberry juice."

"No thanks. It's not important."

"Yes it is."

I hadn't had a drink since noon on the plane and the Valium mixed with a supply of other pills (my traveling M&Ms) was in a plastic vial, low in the pocket of my jeans. I could have gone outside to take one, but Eric was slowly rubbing my back.

"This help?"

"Lots."

Tension flowed away from my body. Seven silent circles. Then he said, "Would you like to tell me how your dog committed suicide?"

"Okay. But don't stop rubbing."

"Tell you what . . ." He braced his hands on my shoulders, looked at me carefully to make sure I was steady, then crossed the room and took two pillows from the bed and placed them in front of the fireplace. "Why don't you lie down . . . so you can see the fire."

I nestled my face into the plump softness and then turned to the empty pillow. He was standing there, watching me, again. I propped my head on my elbow and from that position, as my eyes lifted, I felt like I was following the trunk of a tree. "So, where will you be?"

"Hang on a minute. It's a long way down for me. Okay . . . here I am. . . . Go ahead." And his hand began to massage my back.

"Well, Inky had been very morose. For about two months he

210

was flat out, in front of the kitchen door. I'd say to him, 'You oughta go out more,' but he'd just lift his head and look at me as though the effort was too much for him. I had to practically drag him to the park just to do what he had to do. The vet couldn't find anything wrong with him, but I knew it was because he missed the cat. Silver. We had to put her to sleep."

"He died of a broken heart."

"No. He committed suicide. . . . I'd remind him how wonderful the world was—that there were all sorts of adventures waiting for him and he'd put his paw over his ear like he didn't want to hear it. . . . Well, we had one of those old stoves—the kind where you light a match to the burner as you turn on the gas. And there were these wobbly old knobs. My mother always complained about them. . . . Inky used to sit watching my mom cook, so he knew how the stove didn't work. Well, one day I was at school and my parents were out—my mother always kept the windows closed and locked, even when we were inside, because she was frightened of burglars. My father used to holler, 'There is no air in this house!' My mother was terrified of everything. She still is. Anyway, you can guess what happened. . . . Inky turned on all four jets and we found him asphyxiated . . . dead . . . when we came home."

Eric studied the fire, then turned to me. "Is that what you're doing?"

"What?"

"Trying to commit suicide?"

"Me! Of course not! . . . You can stop rubbing, I feel better."

"It doesn't correct the imbalance of loneliness."

"What doesn't?"

"Booze."

"Do you think I have a problem with drinking?"

"Do you?"

"I have a problem with living."

"When did your husband die?"

"A year and nine months ago. . . . Who told you?"

"Jonathan."

"What do you do when you're in pain?"

"Sit still and feel it . . . whatever it is. . . . The Sioux have a

211

prayer: Yesterday is ashes. Tomorrow is wood. Today the fire burns brightly. . . . Listen. Can you hear the music of the fire?"

"Not really. Not now."

"Sure you can. . . . *Crackle crack sizzle. Pop crickle hiss.*"

"You have to be brain-damaged to live in the present."

"It alters your perception."

"What does?"

"Alcohol."

"How do you know so much?"

"My father died of liver failure and my mother from watching him."

"I'm so sorry."

"Do you take anything else?"

"No. Not often. Sometimes. Occasionally. Once in a while."

"My dad hung on to a bottle of whiskey, while he was in convulsions, swearing he wasn't a drunk."

"It's the white man's fault. We should never have introduced the Indians to alcohol."

"Right. My father was half Chinook—but it's an equal-opportunity disease."

"Sometimes I feel . . . I don't know how to say it . . . that my life is close by but never quite there."

"You're like the waterfall."

"Because I cry?"

"No. Because two sides of you never see the sun."

"How do I light the shadows?"

"Stop sabotaging yourself."

"How?"

"Would it help if there were a man in your life—loving you?"

"It wouldn't hurt. . . . Sorry. It's the punch line of an old joke."

"You have some fantasy that you can recognize yourself through romance. I grab you . . . we make love . . . it fixes everything. It's not fair to you."

"I've had lots of unfairness in my life."

"That's not amusing."

"Look, Eric, I'm lying here with my stomach locked in my

throat, trying to find a little gaiety in all this. What's so terrible if I try to be funny?"

"Nothing. Except when you use it to humiliate yourself."

"Why would I do that?"

"So you can dramatize the pathetic . . . keep yourself little and stuck—because you're frightened. . . . There's a beautiful woman behind that waterfall. She's an adult, but you'd like her."

"Wow! I went to two shrinks and they never told me that. And I saw them both at the same time."

"That might have been the problem."

"I was also having a relationship—I hate that word—with my friend Seymour. He never said anything like that."

". . . Difficult to do when you're having an affair."

"There was a man from Sweden. I knew he was a turkey, but I stayed with him until he took my money. My friend Betsy said, 'You lost your husband, you didn't lose your mind!' . . . Do you think I hung on to humiliate myself?"

"Yes."

"It's not only men. After Michael died everything I tried turned to shit."

"Of course. You have to keep proving to yourself that you can't survive without him. That the world is out to get you."

"It is."

"Then it would have gotten you by now."

"That's funny."

"You're not even an authentic victim."

"That's a terrible thing to say."

"You're right."

"And the drinking keeps the illusion going?"

"Yes."

"I don't blame you for not wanting to get involved with me. After this talk, I'm not so thrilled with myself, either."

"It's late. You must be tired."

"No. I have to tell you something. Not only is this the longest conversation I've ever had, but it's different for another reason."

"Why is that?"

"Well, I'm a compulsive overthinker. Usually I have this convoluted brain work going on, before during and after I speak or the other person speaks. Tonight, I'm just talking and listening like a regular person. It goes much faster. . . . You see I live in my head."

"You can move."

"It never occurs to me."

I sat up and slid my hand into the pocket of my jeans and touched the round plastic pill holder. My thumbnail traced the ridges on the lid. . . . "Eric." I withdrew the bottle. "Eric. . . . You can have these. I won't take any more. . . . You can have them."

He shook his head. "Not for me. For yourself."

I threw the bottle in the fire and found myself saying the moment I thought it: "I'm looking forward to meeting that woman."

"Me, too," he said, and wrapped me in his arms.

A loud pop! The pills exploded in the flames and I heard the music of the fire.

## T W E N T Y

*The first one to say* I love you loses.

So why isn't he saying it back, instead of that long "Mmmm" as his hand caresses my thigh, then rests on my mons veneris, which I used to refer to as my mom's veneris until I realized that it belonged to me.

"Oh God, I love you"—in case he hadn't heard it. I want to grab the pillow and stuff it in my mouth but it's under my back.

"Shhhh," he murmurs, unzipping the fly on my jeans as I raise my hips and skittle out of the pant legs.

Over my silk panties his fingers trace the outline of the labia majora. It's always been a problem for me. Not the labia majora but substituting its generic name. That's why it was such a victory when I called Smythe an asshole. When push comes to shove I can use those words but I'm extremely uncomfortable. My mother's fault—again! She gave me (and I'll never forgive her because I didn't have

215

to sneak it) one of those illustrated technical books (black-and-white drawings) when I was eight. I memorized the geography of the sexes: labias majora and minora, the epididymes, seminal vesicles, inguinal canals, avaducts—and I studied the topography of men and women copulating. It was like watching slides of someone's trip to Madagascar. It's only interesting if you've been there.

My vulva throbs. I feel a swelling moisture in my Bartholin's glands. "Eric?"

"What?"

I tell him how intense is my libidinous desire and he rolls on his side, stares at me and says, not unkindly, "Shaddup!"

"I thought you want me to say things as they occur?"

"Not now."

He shakes his head, indicating *What am I to do with you?* and murmurs, "Dear heart." Does that mean I'm his heart's dear one, or is that his Indian name for me—Deer Heart? Like Bear Claw? . . . I better not ask. Moving closer, he sweeps the hair on the back of my neck to one side and nips me there with a gentle cat bite. I giggle softly, hold my arms straight up and scrunch my face. A child urging him to lift my sweater. The turtleneck reverses itself and he bags my face, gathering the wool folds and playfully bouncing the gunny sack with my head in it. He should take me now. Sightless. Voiceless. Inhaling mohair fuzz. From inside the executioner's hood, my stifled voice. "Let me out! I want to live!" He presses his face against my upholstered ear promising release if I do not talk. As the sweater slips off, I grin and ask, "Can I speak when I'm climaxing?"

"If you keep it simple." His look is serious. His tone, concerned. After our discussion I am still not being real. He brushes the hair from my forehead. "Why are you so frightened?"

"Be—. . . because," I stammer, ". . . after Michael died, every man I had sex with couldn't stay the night . . . I mean figuratively—sometimes literally." And then I add, "In the midst of coming, they were in the midst of going."

"Is that it, or are you afraid if I get close I'll make some other discoveries?"

I shrug and do not answer. Honesty is terrifying and I am fearful of this last purification rite. He will know how deceitful I am, that

I have deceived him and organized his replacement. How is that possible? Because there is a plumb line that plunges from my cerebral cortex into my genitals when they are activated, disgorging secrets. Or as Betsy succinctly puts it, "When his dick gets hard, my brain goes soft!"

"Haptics," Eric explains, responding to his own question.

"What's that?"

"Information that's perceived through a sense of touch."

"Haptics," I repeat, astonished and relieved there is a word that encompasses my bizarre thinking, although its exact meaning is probably closer to tactile rather than sexual data.

Eric leans closer. "Want to give it a try?"

I touch his cheek, stroke his face and tell him "Yes" with my fingertips. A whiff of shaving lotion as he cradles me in arms that promise safety. Our lips whisper to each other, politely meet and release, increase in tempo until his mouth envelops mine and our tongues search out corners, exchanging urgent messages. . . . Don't leave my mouth. I cannot breathe on my own. . . . And I am slain! A dead person! . . . In the English language there are very few words for kissing, but the Germans have about thirty, including one for the kiss to make up for all the kisses that have been missed. This kiss. An elixir so potent that it annihilates and revives me in the same moment. I shiver as his hand travels my neck and chest and his face brushes my ear. How wonderful it is to discover his bald head and I fall in love with the auburn fringe that encircles it. He traces the lace edging on my bra, unclasps the flimsy defense, reaches for the wisp of panties. I am about to get very real as he removes my highly stylized way of relating.

But not yet. Holding me with his eyes in a downward glance, he separates from me for a moment. I am not touching him. I cannot know what we are thinking. He stands . . . undresses with the grace of an athlete. His torso spirals as he tosses aside his shirt. Powerful carved arms. The broad smooth planes of his chest . . . unnotches his belt, shifts his weight, steps out of his jeans and shorts. The modeling of his stomach, hips, the long legs, an integration of bone and muscle. His body, chiseled, articulated . . . Harmonious . . . And what was Socrates' doctrine, that the visible world is but an imperfect reflection of the world of ideas? Not so. Not here. In the shadows of the flickering firelight, I see the realization of my erotic daydream. A priapic Greek god.

I am in the south wing of the Metropolitan Museum of Art, ground floor, Section K, five minutes to five. There is a sarcophagus I can hide behind (220–225 A.D., gift of Abdo Dabbas)—bordered by oak leaves, in relief, Eros awakens Psyche with an arrow. When the gates clang shut and the light fades on the wild boar, I will be here, with bearded Heracles, Hermes in his winged sandals, Diadumenos, tying a fillet around his head, Atlas and the golden apples and Zeus with his thunderbolt. And I will know that the gods decorously avoid shocking the tourists, but at closing time they become tumescent, proclaiming the glory that was really Greece. Even the headless Apollo.

My imagination is so archaic that fantasy should be spelled with a *ph* and yet it has marched, unaided by me towards the goal it has set itself, arriving finally in an Oregon cabin, 2,400 years later.

A helot, I kneel on a pillow as Eric, sprung from marble, returns to me. My arms slide down his back. Alabaster and silk. The guard isn't looking. I am touching the work of Praxiteles. I feel as though I am going to swoon. I cannot help myself and exhale the name "Adonis." He pulls me toward him, kisses my forehead as strands of hair play through his fingers and I hear his voice, not in Haptics but real, "Her ambrosial hair breathed forth the fragrance of the gods." And I melt into his mouth as his tongue curls the inside of my lips. I arch my spine, he lays me down, cushioning my head with one hand while the other sculpts my chin and throat. Now I am the one who is being created. His kisses follow his hand, celebrating every part of my body. I abandon myself to his radiant touch, breathe through every pore. . . . Don't leave my breast. I am only half formed. His fingers mold, press and caress me, his breath alternately light, then warm, then chilling me in its wake. I try to release a locked bubble of air. I cannot speak but I can moan. "Ahh. Ahhh. Ahhhh." I know I am too noisy. His hands tighten at each side of my waist as he forms my stomach with his lips, fusing me to him. With tensile strength my legs are framed, rubbed and contoured and my thighs are shaped with kisses. I grasp at his shoulders. I am not finished. Do not craft only what the eye can see. Inside I am formless wet clay. And his tongue, love's talent, parts the valves of the seashell, penetrates, cajoles, pushes harder and faster, implores me to emerge as I pulsate, eager, terrified, clinging to the ribs of the shell until with the beating of wings I spring free. Aphrodite, surging upward from the sea.

When it comes to sex, I'm basically Baroque.

He slides up my body, hugging me, his face pressed against my perspiration and tears. And in a husky whisper he says, "Aurora in her rosy chariot has already crossed mid-heaven in her course through the sky."

Again, I am stunned. "What? I thought we weren't supposed to talk."

"Just recitin' a little Virgil. . . . Aren't you Aurora?"

"No."

His brown eyes glint with flecks of gold and he smiles at me. "Then who are you?"

I do not answer because I know I am loved. I am not Aphrodite. Not the illusion of self but a real self. . . . Me. . . . I am not a dork. I will not end up in a trendy little nuthouse in Palm Springs, inventing myself. So long, the forlorn identity of a hapless child. Adios to a life of being pulled backwards through a knothole. Goodbye, better living through chemistry. . . . He takes my hand in his to touch his penis. I raise my hips and he enters me, slowly rhythmically. I will never speak again except with my body. I feel his erection against my pubic bone. My hands explore his back and buttocks. I am overcome with the wonder of him. I ache . . . want him so much. And as for gods, well, they are as close as our breath. There is such tenderness in his passion as he thrusts through every part of me. And then, delaying that fearful moment when he will lose himself as I have, just before, in a gasp of air, he cries, "But Phaeton, his auburn hair ablaze, is rolled headlong and falls in a long course through the air."

And I find myself saying, "Fuck me, fuck me. Oh, fuck me."

And so we trade sensibilities. . . . Except for the Brownings, most affairs cannot sustain two poets. . . . Who will scramble eggs in the morning?

## T WE N T Y - O N E

*How wonderful it is to* wake up instead of just "coming to." Sunlight . . . the smell of hickory lingering from the evening fire. . . . Coffee. And I had four and a half orgasms last night indistinguishable from epilepsy. Not counting the three in Grandma's bed earlier this morning. Eric did everything that Mark did to Gabrielita in Chapter Six. I wished there was a phone so I could call Seymour and let him know that romance is alive in the twentieth century. And Betsy. Wait'll I tell Betsy. And Judith.

"Mornin'." Eric smoothed the barn-raising quilt and sat on the edge of the bed, so handsome in his jeans and plaid shirt, offering me a steaming cup of coffee in a speckled blue mug. My hand trembled as I reached for it and I watched as though it were some curious oddity with a pulse of its own. I was sure he had noticed because he seemed so solicitous as he adjusted the pillows under my head and leaned forward to kiss my cheek. "Have we met?" he asked in a scruffy cartoon voice, "or shall I call you Has No Name?"

I stretched luxuriously. "I like Dear Heart. . . . Is it true an Indian child is named after the first thing a mother sees at the child's birth?"

He nodded. "Right. Nothing happened when Has No Name was born."

"Sounds like me."

"You made up for it." He clapped his hands. "Tell you what, first activity this morning, everybody gets to be called by their real first name."

I stroked the sleeve of his shirt. "Do you have an Indian name?"

Eric pointed to his nose and I giggled as he lifted and displayed his prominent profile, announcing "Otter Nose." "Come on," he said, tugging at the covers. "It's ten A.M." And he crossed the room to the potbellied stove.

"And the day?" I knew what day it was but I wanted to hear how he said "Sunday." Michael once told me every day was Sunday when we were together. I waited . . . Eric didn't say that. Instead he asked if I wanted Cream of Wheat. Men are like that after sex. Women need to cuddle and men have to stir the cereal. It's the law of something or other.

But my ego, like a monkey in a feeding frenzy, grabbing at scraps of reassurance, had to know. "Is there a Gabrielita?" Why did I say that? Had sunlight melted last night's resolve? I didn't want much. Just the promise that he would love me until shrimps learn to toe tap.

The wooden spoon halted in its swirling track. He was completely motionless, suspended in stop frame as he reached above him with his other hand to take a cereal bowl from the shelf. And then, with a short outrush of breath he dismissed the previous moment and turned toward me. "Eve asked Adam: 'Do you love me?' And Adam said, 'Who else?' "

I laughed, grateful for the joke though I wondered what he'd been thinking in his silence. Was he unearthing my subtext—or his?

His tone lightened and he banged the spoon on the pot. "Okay, campers. Breakfast outside. Then a two-mile hike, a swim under the waterfall . . . Oh, and I have an idea about the end of the commercial." I had to tell him! I will tell him—after breakfast. He tossed me my jeans and was out the door with the cereal bowls.

I swung my legs onto the floor. As I stood they buckled under me. I slid. A rag doll against the side of the bed. Legs spayed. Arms holding the edge of the mattress. Stunned, I hung in that stupid position. Naked. How long was it? Where had I been the moment before? I tried to focus on an object . . . the desk across the room, to ground myself but the sides softened and undulated. I shook my head. The blurred image resumed its solid shape. Weird, I thought and justified the clumsiness by reassuring myself that I hadn't been vertical for about ten hours.

Flushed and anxious, I wobbled to my feet, slipped into my jeans and patted the pocket. Where was the Valium? I stared at the smoldering fire and remembered. Couldn't I have saved a few before tossing them in what now seemed an excessive melodramatic gesture—something out of an Ibsen play, like Duse when she played Mrs. Alving in *Ghosts,* raising her fist, swearing to fight off the specter of the past. I took some deep breaths and the trembling in my chest subsided. I could make it without a drink or a pill. I had Eric. Mrs. Alving kept her word. I raised my fist. No good! Only in Ibsen. "The rest of us backslide," I mumbled, pulling on my sweater.

"You okay?" Eric called from outside.

"Sure!" I yelled.

And to prove I was, I skipped out of the cabin, past Eric, to the outhouse, sat on the lid, wiping my sweating forehead with wads of toilet paper as I peed and then washed my face and hands at the outdoor pump, playfully splashing as he watched, and bounded back towards him, praying I looked twelve instead of a demented aging sprite.

I sat next to him, breathing heavily. It was a crystal morning. The waterfall plunged liquid silver. The air, quiet. Warm.

He glanced at me as I took the first few mouthfuls of cereal. I felt like I was going to cry but somehow managed, "Eric, there's something we have to discuss."

He nodded. "Yes, there is."

"I feel terrible. I can't breathe unless I talk to you about it."

"I understand how you feel."

"You do?" Isn't he wonderful. He's going to forgive me without even knowing the details.

"C'mon," he said, after I indicated I couldn't eat any more. "Let's take a walk." He held my hand as we started up the path away from the cabin. A rivulet of water etched its way through a fractured rock as we stepped over it. He cleared his throat. "Whatever you're sensing is real. You know I'm going back to Nicaragua when we finish this commercial."

"Yes, that's what I want to talk to you—"

"I'd like you to listen," he interrupted. "I'm very fond of you and . . . uh . . . I want you to know why I have to go back."

I did not persist. I hoped what he was about to say might provide a clue to my approach but I also knew by his preface that something was to happen in the next moment. I paused, feeling the fuzzy bark of a tree and shivered as we left the clearing, climbing into the dense shade.

"I've had a wonderful time with you . . ." he continued.

Don't do that. Prefaces never soften the blow. Long before the specifics of the paragraph explode with meaning, I get it. The introductory line is the main hit. And even further back, in the stroke of breath he took before the opening sentence. As animals sense the onset of an earthquake, I trembled in the foreshock and asked, "It's Gabrielita, isn't it?"

The muscle in his right cheek jumped as I looked at him in profile. He seemed even taller this morning and I loved him very much.

He stroked the side of his face. "Manuela . . . I called her Gabrielita in the book."

The heel of a boot shattered my chest. I waited until I recovered, swallowed and said, "I see, Eric is Mark, Gabrielita is Manuela, Dear Heart is Babe," and then I tossed off an epigram worthy of

Noel Coward, "How confusing it is to be on a first-name alias with each other."

He ignored my remark, staring ahead, and then this bizarre thing occurred. As he spoke, this tune kept running through my head, underscoring everything he said—that Sondheim song, "Send In the Clowns."

"After the revolution . . .

*Isn't it rich?*
*Are we a pair?*

when the lumber company was thrown out by the Sandinistas, a group of us stayed on as private citizens . . ."

*Me here at last on the ground,*
*You in mid-air.*

It wasn't the elves. They only carry on when I'm feeling good. I was singing so I would not disintegrate. . . .

"Land was given back to the Campesinos. We felt we could help, show them how to build. . . . There was a family on the co-op—like the Santiagos in the book I'd started to write. They'd had eleven children. Four died in the revolution, three others before they were seven . . ."

*There ought to be clowns . . .*

I'd forgotten the lyrics, only fragments of phrases came through as the melody continued and we walked. Eric slightly ahead of me, still holding my hand.

"They were very proud of the children. All of them knew the alphabet before they died and they could sign their names. Manuela was teaching them to read. She saved labels from cartons, canned goods . . . anything. . . . When I met her she was twenty. I was astonished . . . thought she floated up from the pages I'd been writing . . ."

*Don't you love farce*

I stumbled over a dirt-covered root that burrowed like a snake under the path

*My fault I fear*

and I remembered her description in the book. Darkly beautiful.

224

Mysterious. And I was oafish and American. Well, she was old by now. Twenty-six at least.

*Losing my timing*
*so late in my career.*

"And so we began to build. Sixty families—thirty-four children without parents. By eighty-four we'd finished twenty houses and a schoolhouse. We made it through dry seasons, rains that cascade like horse piss, Contra snipings, insects, a clunker of a trunk, broken tools and a portable sawmill. . . . You know what the most amazing piece of equipment is? A wheelbarrow. . . . Want to talk politics—it's in the gravel and cement. It's in your back—it's in the fucking mud!"

His expression, tight with impatience, softened as he said, "When a Campesino hugs you, you know you've been hugged."

To the right of us, an old logging road cut through the forest. Felled trees. Stacked. Rotting. Splinters of wood cracked underfoot. Our fingers were intertwined but he had not looked at me since we'd begun our walk. I was grateful. Bruised by my own breath, I knew my face was contorted. . . . Where are the clowns?

"One night Manuela and I were in bed. I started to say something and she told me to light a match. 'Only the dead speak in the dark.' . . . The attack came at noon."

The tune stopped. Eric unlaced his fingers from mine and my hand froze, curved in remembered shape. He reached down, picked up a slim dead branch and snapped it in pieces as he told his story to the shadows in our path.

"We'd just finished the schoolhouse . . . the children were plastering the outer walls with a lime-salt mixture . . . a cow came by and started licking the plaster. The children were giggling and scolding the cow for eating the school. Manuela was on a ladder putting up the sun-dried terra-cotta roof tiles. I was in the sawmill—it's in the clearing in front of the mountains. . . . The schoolhouse is in the center of the compound and the meal hall to the right of it. She saw them before I heard them, coming down through the trees and signaled to the Campesinos in front of the meal hall. We all carried rifles—when we ate, when we planted. She got down off the ladder and quickly sent the children inside and then she ran . . . across the field to the sawmill to warn me. . . . I screamed, racing to the door. She stopped. Startled . . . her arms reaching for me as bullets from both sides ripped into her . . ."

The air was thin. We had climbed to a place above the waterfall. Against the sky, images of what he had told me, sharper than any newsreel film . . . I sobbed silently and the shaking brought me to my knees. "I have been thinking only of myself."

"We all do." He was several feet ahead, facing away from me.

"No. Not you. You think about other people . . ." My body went into a spasm. Fearful of another, I waited . . . tried to remember . . . what? A quote. Yes. From Heraclitus: "A man's character is his destiny."

"The past is my destiny." His voice drifted into the trees. "I have to go back."

"For her?" I asked. "You are not responsible."

He shook his head. "For both of us . . . the part of us that lives is always responsible."

As we spoke, pieces of me burst from the center of my chest, my brain raging for a drink, a pill. I could not stay there. Raw. Torn open.

I pressed at the earth. Eric turned and tried to help me as I pushed up but I broke away and ran. Choking on my dry throat, I licked my lips. I had no saliva . . . Valium! I ran and ran, racing toward the cabin, slipping and tripping. I fell as I opened the door. . . . Where are they? I crawled on soaking hands to the fire, keening over the pyre of ashes. Who has their fingernails under my skin? A dagger of light glanced off something shiny. There it is! The little plastic bottle! I pawed through the top layer of charred wood, scattering ebony lizards against the side of the smoke hole, wiping away sweat and tears so I could see it. There! Down near the grate. Teasing me—hiding under black smoke . . . What color is Valium? White. But it had changed into fractured red crystals and I grabbed for it, clutching the searing flakes in my cracking palm . . . A scream. Was it mine or his? I don't know . . . I felt myself being lifted. He carried me to the waterfall. He was holding me. But it wasn't me. And never would be.

# TWENTY-TWO

*In freezing fire*
*wax mannequins wilt*
*faces weep with whimsical horror*
*I run*
*fall thru moon craters*
*clutch at luminous blue gas*
*collide against bladders*

                                      *membranes*

                                                   *flesh*

*then crash*
*to the floor of a drained sea*

"Michael? Is Michael here?"
"Shhh."

"Who is here?"

"It's Eric. . . . I'm taking you to the hospital. . . . Open your eyes."

"Will Michael be there?"

"No."

"Did you fall with me?"

"Where?"

"Through the blue gas?"

"I'm going to put a blanket around you . . . carry you down the hill."

"Get away from me."

"I have to take you to the hospital."

"Am I a lunatic?"

"Open your eyes. Listen to me."

"Do you think I'm hard of seeing?"

"Don't struggle . . . I've put a wet bandage on your hand."

"It hurts."

"I know. Can you put your arms around my neck?"

"I'll be good. . . . Is it raining?"

"Yes."


*I remember that* . . . and floating through trees . . . clinging to the underside of leaves as nightmare sweats soak the blanket and rain splatters my drenched face.

My body is a roller coaster of whips and snaps rushing headlong into black-green mountains . . . roads slap up at me . . . branches lash my eyes . . . wipers slash at streams of water . . . and then, a siren wails in my throat. "Oh God! Get it away!"

Eric's hand restrains me. "What is it?"

It covers the windshield, clawing to get in . . . bulbous eyes hold me . . . its chartreuse underbelly seeps through the glass. With a swat of the flat tail it crashes in and leaps on me. I rip at scales of skin as it tears through the blanket and clutches at my sweater. Legs scuttle down my arm . . . dry rattles of terror. "Get it off! Get it off me!" . . . Teeth fused to the ridge of its jaw sink into my hand unraveling the gauze.

228

Eric is rocking me . . . a shivering limbless torso but the twitching will not stop. "Is it off? Is it off?"

"Yes, darling. Hang on. It's not far."

"What's happening to me?" . . . My arms are unhinged. I cannot touch him. He presses his face against mine and his cheek is wet with tears. I remember that.


*beep beep*        *beep beep*        *beep beep*

"Bed number two."

Dry mouth. I sit on the side of the middle bed watching an old man gurgle oxygen through a mask, as my palsied hands flap under my chin. He has kicked his covers off. But how did he do that? He has no legs. . . . A baby is crying. Where is the baby?

"Get some Silvadene for that burn!"

A shower curtain hung on a ceiling track conceals the bed on the other side.

I smell vomit.

I arch my neck, searching the dimpled fixture above me, terrified that the thing will explode through the casing.

Someone is holding my wrist. I wince in pain. "I'm Dr. Hailey." My gaze stays fixed overhead. "Can you hear me?"

Why is he shouting? I'm sick. I'm not a foreigner.

"Eric, what's going on here? Is she a diabetic? What?"

And Eric answers, "Booze and Valium."

"How long has she been in withdrawal?"

"About an hour."

My eyes continue to patrol the ceiling.

"Any convulsions?"

"No."

Goop is spread on my hand.

"So what's happening with the book?"

"Sold. Be out in the fall . . . Doc, is she going to be—"

"Second-degree burn, but she'll be fine—only you don't look so good. . . . Get yourself some coffee."

"I'm okay. What about the tremors?"

"She may stop on her own, but I'm going to load her pro-phylactically."

A woman's voice: "Doctor! The baby is seizing!"

"Be right there. . . . Kathy, see if you can get a history on her."

"Do you have insurance?"

Against what? I don't know if I am speaking my answers be-cause I am checking for cracks in the plaster. . . . Can anyone tell me if I have speeching?

"Date of birth?"

Eric's voice: "Her handbag's up at the cabin."

"How old are you?"

Go away, Eric. Go away and I will tell her.

"She's not responding. . . . Do you know if she's allergic to any medication?"

"I take everything." I think I heard myself say that.

"Kathy, I need you here."

I see rollers of the ceiling track curve and press against the wall and I look down at the bed to the right of me. . . . A baby . . . ten . . . eleven months old, naked, with tubes sucking and bubbling in every orifice.

"He's posturing, Doctor!"

"Oxygenate him fast or this kid's gonna transfer out! . . . Kathy! Where the hell is his mother? . . . Did the baby-sitter say he swal-lowed anything?"

"She doesn't know, but the paramedics found some ampheta-mines on the coffee table."

"Christ! Get an NG tube! Pump him!"

I get up and move to an empty space between two men in hospital greens. I can almost touch the baby. The doctor jumps. "What is she doing here?"

"Is the baby going to die?"

The baby's arms are stiff, turned in from the shoulders, palms up and out, and his legs, rigid and extended, vibrate in a locked position.

"We can't be sure what we're dealing with here. . . . It's like veterinary medicine. . . . Kathy, keep trying that mother!"

Kathy tells me I have to sit down. . . . Where is Eric?

Eric is in a little glass cubicle near the entrance, filling out forms.

"Eric, is the baby going to die?"

"They don't know. They're trying to save him. . . . Let's go back to the bed. They'll give you something in a minute."

And then—I'm not sure, but it felt like I'd been shot . . . I mean that startled moment when you become rock hard—and I am falling back and flatten like a snow angel against the frozen linoleum.

"Establish an IV . . . five milligrams of Valium!"

Just what I need.

"And hang a banana bag on her!"

*I'm soft now and everything* smells sweet and the ceiling is safe. I can lie here under white wool. They said I'm post ictal. . . . It feels nice.

"Eric, we don't have stat labs here. I can't do a thorough workup on her—sorry, what did you say her name was?"

"Babe."

"Babe? . . . She your girlfriend?"

"Friend."

"We've got a helicopter on the way for the baby. We'll life flight both of them to Eugene General."

I would like to cry, but I can't.

Eric is asking, "What do you think, Doc?"

"Well, we're lucky she had the seizure here. There's no loss of oxygen, but I'm concerned. She should have an electroencephalogram."

Eric! Ask him what that is, for God's sake! . . . Even if you don't love me.

I hear a whirlybird.

I'm put on a stretcher . . . rolled across the floor.

Kathy's voice: "Doctor . . . Mr. Alder . . . bed one. He's going to crump . . . pressure is sixty and dropping—no longer mentating—oxygen, forty."

"What's his code status?"

"He's a no code. And the family called again to confirm no heroic efforts."

"Well, make him comfortable and he'll dribble off the court."

A growling sound as I glide past the old man's bed.

Is that what's going to happen to the baby and me? Are we going to dribble off the court?

# T W E N T Y - T H R E E

*Between sheets of illusion* I lay. My body, managed by others who filled it, emptied it, plugged it, shlepped it through hollow cylinders and took pictures of it. I had found what I was looking for: a life-style that doesn't require my presence.

"You have a visitor."

Nuts.

"Open your eyes."

Everyone wants me to open my eyes. I've seen enough. Don't they know that reality is injurious to your health?

I waited until the visitor spoke but Nurse What's-her-name— probably Ratched—kept talking. "She's been like this for two days. No response. The doctor says she should be up and walking."

If it's my mother, I'll crump out. What if it's my father? N.G. My mother would be right behind him. . . . Maybe it's Eric. No. He was here, but he's not back yet. He's gone to the underworld to recover my soul. It takes a while. . . . Shhh. Be quiet! I'm trying to remember what he told me. A story . . . about Has No Name, who suffered a series of misfortunes and then became ill. The Indians believe that when bad stuff happens to you it's because your soul has been kidnapped and taken to the Land of the Dead—and if it's not brought back, you weaken and die. So Has No Name went to a Shaman who had the power to journey to the underworld in a magic boat—a spirit canoe—and fight with the ghosts and bring back my soul, I mean, Has No Name's soul . . .

Someone is touching my shoulder. Don't do that! Can't you see I'm invisible? I peered through a left eye slit. A gray beard zoomed in. Seymour!

"All right! Knock it off!" His beard whisked my cheek. "Enough already!"

A scraping whisper startled my throat. How long has it been since I've spoken? . . . I did not recognize the falsetto tone that came out of me. "Get rid of Nurse Ratched!"

"It's all right, Nurse. I'm a doctor. . . . You can leave us."

The sound of her padding feet receded and I gave Seymour a one-eyed stare. "You're not a regular doctor. You're a head mender."

"That's what's wrong with you."

I flipped my lid closed—"Thanks for visiting me, Seymour, but I have to take a nap"—and turned away from him, burrowing into the pillow. . . . I knew what he was going to say, though he put it in an interesting way. "You're terminally immature."

"Well, a lot happened since I've seen you." I extended my arm, fluttering my bandaged hand like *The Dying Swan*. It hurt.

"What else?"

"Life. I don't have the temperament for it."

"So, that's how you deal with it? Wake up every morning and take a sleeping pill? And booze and speed and God knows what else . . . commit psychic violence?"

"I dunno." I rolled over and faced him. He really looked very sweet and concerned. "Did you talk to the doctor?" I asked.

"Yes."

"What did he say about the electroencephalogram? Did I pass?"

"The brain wave pattern shows abnormal activity. You might have a seizure again."

"I see."

"They also gave you a CAT scan."

"And the results?"

"Diffuse cerebral atrophy. But with proper nutrition and no alcohol or drugs it can reverse itself."

"How long?"

"Sometimes in less than a year."

I assumed the attitude of a consulting specialist, nodding and detached, as I had done years before when the operating room doors opened and Michael's surgeon and I conferred with the floor.

"I see. That would explain the disconnected thoughts and my tendency to be bizarre."

"It's suggestive and consistent with the damage you've done to yourself."

"And blackouts . . . and memory loss."

"What do you expect after years of crapulence?" Seymour's tone shocked me out of my monotonous role.

"That's a great word. What does it mean?"

"Intemperance in drinking." Seymour leaned over, lifted a hank of hair that had fallen on my cheek and tucked it behind my ear.

I sighed. "I know it's bad news but the doctor should have told me personally."

"He did."

Well, there it was—smaller than the sponge I use to wash my car, this repository of experience and regret. Doesn't have the energy to turn on a light bulb but it can stop time and memory. . . . Maybe they can re-solder the synapses and while they're at it electrocute the elves. I haven't heard from the bastards in a while. Maybe they crisped out when the wires crossed. Well, it wouldn't be so bad, never having to feel anything again . . . to void out.

"What are you thinking?" Seymour asked.

"Nothing. I'm just watching my mind drift away and applauding its exit."

"I've told you, if you take care of yourself, you'll get better."

"Don't worry about me. All my life I've wanted to live in I.C.U."

"That's a terrific goal, ultimate dependency."

I continued my fugue of despondency. "Friends will come and tsk-tsk over my bed. 'She was a very nice lady but she lost her modules,' or maybe I'll move to Amherst and wear a shawl and a frozen braid and live in seclusion like Emily Dickinson and if a stranger talks to me I will answer in a breathless voice, 'I hardly know what to say, because I've lost my modules.' "

"Keep it up. You're on a roll."

I studied the four walls. "Seymour?"

"What?"

"How come I can still make these snappy comments?"

"Unfortunately, that's the part of your brain that didn't atrophy."

"Seymour? . . . I'm afraid to ask."

"What?"

"Where am I? I mean I know I'm in a hospital, but you're here so I don't know if I'm in Oregon or Palm Springs."

"Eugene, Oregon."

"Did you meet Eric?"

"He called me. Said you asked me to come."

"Anything else I've been doing that I should know about?" And then I started to cry. Lurching sobs traveled down my body and as I thrashed I pulled down the feed bag hanging from the pole, tangled with the plastic line and garroted myself trying to shield my face, yelping in pain as I bopped my forehead with my burned hand. Seymour untwisted me. I wailed that Eric didn't love me and neither would anyone else if I was mentally deficient and I wanted to die and Seymour said there are better ways of getting attention. And he held me, rocked me and promised that if I didn't pack it in I could become an adult and who knows, if I was lucky I might even achieve the summit. The quiet miracle of emotional maturity. . . . I would be autonomous, self-esteeming, secure, self-regulating, experiential, self-nurturing—everything I hated . . . and if I didn't off myself, two weeks from today I was invited to his birthday party in Palm Springs.

He held a tissue against my nose and made me blow into it. "How old will you be?" I sniffed.

"Sixty-nine."

"That's wonderful," I said, wiping my eyes.

"Depresses the shit outta me."

"Why?"

"I can't get laid anymore." He handed me another Kleenex.

"Why not?"

"By the time I get it up, it's too late to find anyone to do it with."

"There's more to life than getting laid," I said, propping myself up.

"What?"

"Whatever it is you just told me."

"I've already done that. I still can't get laid."

Nurse Ratched entered with a glass of orange juice. I finally saw what she looked like. And her name wasn't Ratched—it's Keister. Bulldog jaw. Bad legs. Seymour didn't seem to mind.

"Well, I see we're sitting up with our eyes wide open. Thank you, Doctor." She plumped the pillows and checked the IV.

Seymour gave her a charming smile. "My pleasure."

"Will you be visiting us for a while, Doctor?"

Seymour bared his teeth. "That depends. . . . How long is your shift?"

"Oh, I've got another two hours." Giggle. Giggle.

Forget it, Keister. He won't make it.

With dueling winks they flirted until she ran out of things to fix and left. I held the glass and tried to pull the orange juice through the straw, then grabbed at my throat in a panic. "Seymour! My sucking mechanism is gone!"

He quickly examined the accordion bend in the little tube. "Don't go crazy—the straw's broken."

"That makes two of us, Seymour."

We went limp with laughter and that's when Eric stood in the doorway. His expression, bitter as Maine gray winter, slammed against my chest. Puffs of laughter froze in the air.

He was holding a suitcase, which he left by the door, then walked to the foot of my bed. . . . Chinos, bush jacket (papers sticking out of the pockets), carry-on slung over one shoulder . . . I knew the flight he was taking was not domestic.

Seymour extended his hand. "I'm Dr. Kahn."

"Rothender," Eric said, perilously polite. "We spoke on the phone." He stared at me. I prayed. But God, with all his works of grandeur, has never been able to manage my one simple request. Undo the past.

"Why in hell didn't you tell me!" The thud of his bag hitting the floor punctuated the shout.

"I . . . I . . ." A landed fish gasping a series of I's. "I tried but—"

"But what?" he demanded, his voice escalating.

"Things kept happening."

"What do you think this is—an idiot comedy!"

Comedy. Comedy. The walls bounced in echo, as Seymour, half the size of Eric—Willie Nelson next to Paul Bunyan—sharply took charge. "Now just a minute. You hold it down! She's not well enough to handle—"

"Hard to believe with all that hilarity going on," Eric retorted.

I tapped my finger against my skull. "I'm brain damaged," I whispered, trying to be seductive and pathetic at the same time—then mortified at my cheap ploy.

Keister ran in. "This is a hospital! Sick people are trying to get well!"

Seymour smoothed the air with his hands, nodding to Keister that things were under control. Eric tightened his jaw and mumbled from inside his teeth, "My plane leaves in an hour. I want to talk to her."

"I can't allow you to—"

"It's all right, Seymour. I deserve it."

I didn't want what I deserved. I wanted God's mercy. But when you're that deep in your own end zone, divine assistance is out of the question.

Eric told Seymour that it wouldn't take long, that he should stay. Uncertain, Seymour glanced at me. "Yes, stay." One day, I thought, you can interpret the dissolution of my life. . . . I wish I had a comb. I must look like hell. . . .

Keister sniffed suspiciously as Seymour with a reassuring pat on the small of her back escorted her out, closed the door, then crossed the room, seating himself on the chair next to the bed.

Eric began, his throat tight, beads of perspiration shining on his bald head. "I called Jonathan . . . told him you were in the hospital with a bad burn—covered for you. He said, 'Not to worry, the commercial looked great.' 'What commercial?' I asked, feeling like a fool. 'Babe said you knew about it.' Lie number one. Then I called Heckenkamp—you told him I'd given my verbal agreement. Lie number two. Then you came up to the cabin—said the lab was working on the film. Third lie. . . . Any others I should know about?"

I tucked my hands under the sheet, they were shaking so. . . . "On the set that day . . . I put Quaaludes in a Maalox bottle. Everyone wanted one. I didn't tell them."

Seymour shook his head and whistled.

"We were all wacky. . . . I said they should call Screen Actors Guild . . . I didn't think they'd take me seriously."

Now both of them were shaking their heads as Eric continued. "Never heard of such an insane thing . . . you and those over-designed human beings telling me I don't exist . . . promote a book by getting a stand-in for the author!"

Seymour, who knows everything, said, "It's been done before."

"Not without my permission!" Eric snapped.

"Call your lawyer," Seymour suggested.

"Oh, I did that . . . been on the phone for two days. Their lawyers . . . mine." And then, Eric, his eyes burning, banged his fist on the bed frame. ". . . Thought you'd understand how important it is for people to know what was going on there. . . . How could you, when everything about you is a joke—your name—who you are . . . You run around in an adult costume, impersonating a woman, not giving a fuck about anyone or anything. No wonder you can't tell the truth. You don't have an authentic bone in your body!"

I pulled the sheet over my chin. I was afraid I'd throw up.

"Say something," Seymour urged.

I swallowed the blip in my throat. "He's right."

"Is that all there is to it? You feel that's an accurate judgment?"

Just the tip of the iceberg, I thought. Eric picked up his bag. I would never see him again. I would chart his life for years to come. And worse than his not loving me, I would always remember his disillusionment with me.

Seymour got up and took a step toward Eric. "Hold on. She's going to say something."

"What is there to say?" I managed weakly.

"Fight for yourself. Get angry. Say what you feel."

"I can't. It makes me sick."

"You'll be sicker if you don't. Stand up."

Not again. Men are always trying to get me to stand up and fight. Women are nicer. They tell you to relax. Take a nap.

Eric was at the door. "Please wait!" I put my rubber legs on the floor. He turned, his face solemn as the Indian penny, and I knew, because he had turned and would stay to hear, that a vapor of an idea I had about him was right.

I hung on to the IV pole with my good hand, my other gauzed paw dangling, throbbing at my side; in that stupid hospital gown, bare legs bowed in parentheses on a square of white tile, a breeze from somewhere blowing up the back . . . Statue of Wounded Greek Warrior with staff on a lit plinth. I was up, but I had my doubts about being adequate to the stance.

"Seymour," I gulped. "I read an article about creative fighting. I know you're supposed to say I feel such and such, instead of accusing the other person with you did thus and such, but I can't do it that way."

Seymour, settling back in the chair, arms folded, said impatiently, "Start any way you want to—but start!"

I began by pointing one pole-wrapped finger at Eric and taking such a deep breath that I almost fell over backwards. "You think you're so pure! You wrote a beautiful book but you didn't have the courage to hang in with it. You put in all that hokey stuff and then accuse us of trying to sell it as an entertainment when that's what you wrote. . . . You're ashamed of yourself. That's why you're so angry—"

"A little more volume," Seymour coached.

"And don't tell me about names—that's why you changed yours." I turned to Seymour. "Eric isn't his real name. It's Mark Chalmers. . . ."

Seymour silently acknowledged: Advantage, Babe.

"I know I did a terrible thing. But you were driving us crazy and we were making you miserable. I wanted everyone to be happy. It's not a documentary! It's a commercial! Even Ivory soap is only ninety-nine and forty-four one-hundredths percent pure! . . . And truth . . . well, you did the same thing. It's not that we don't tell the truth. We just orchestrate its timing."

Eric studied his shoes and mumbled, "What do you mean?"

"When you told me about Gabrielita . . ." I filled Seymour in: "Her real name is Manuela." Seymour looked confused. "I was devastated. Why hadn't you mentioned her *before* we made love? To get me in the sack? No. You told me afterwards to sabotage the relationship . . . because you were in love with me and it scared the hell out of you. . . . Every time you felt yourself getting close to me, I got a lecture on lath and plaster."

Eric wiped his forehead. "How do you know I was in love with you?"

"Virgil!" I announced.

"Virgil who?" Seymour asked.

"Virgil of *The Aeneid*."

"Oh, that Virgil." Seymour pondered.

"And I know I'm selfish, but I'd like to change. . . . If you had asked me, I would have gone to Nicaragua with you."

Eric raised his voice. "What is that? Some romantic hallucination?"

"No," I hollered with a spurt of energy, "because I—" There was a banging on the door and Keister was in, mad as hell. "—because I love you."

"How do you know that?" Seymour asked quietly.

"He listens to me." I looked at Eric. His head was down and I was grateful because tears were running down my face, but I was determined not to fall apart. "Michael used to say, 'Nobody listens,' but you do and that's the most extravagant gift you can give anyone," I yelled.

Keister sputtered, "Stop that. You'll make yourself sick."

"Quiet," Seymour shot back. "She's getting well!"

"And Adlai Stevenson said . . . I forgot what he said. Oh yeah, I remember. He said, 'What this country needs is a hearing aid'—but you hear me and care about me, that's why you stayed just now, only you won't admit it! . . . Manuela died but you'll keep her alive in order not to feel anything but pain. . . . You can't stay in love with a dead person."

"You are," Eric said.

I looked at Seymour. "Am I?" He gave a *Fiddler on the Roof* shrug.

"Well, maybe I am, but there's one difference. I don't think it's disloyal to love you, too. . . . You can edit me out of your life but when you go to heaven, God is going to ask you one question. It's in the Talmud. God asks, 'Did you accept all the love that was offered you on earth?' And you're going to have to say no!"

The IV pole was shaking. Keister sniffed. Seymour rubbed his beard. Eric stared at the floor. I got off my lit plinth.

Eric cleared his throat, fingered the strap on his shoulder bag and said, "Take care of yourself, Dear Heart," and left the room.

I wasn't crying anymore. I sat on the edge of my bed as Keister fixed the feed bag.

"I threw in everything I knew, Seymour."

"More important is what you threw away."

"What's that?" I asked.

"You threw away your training wheels."

# T W E N T Y - F O U R

*Palm Springs in July. . . .* One hundred and twenty degrees!—Who's gonna come to the party?"

"Everyone," Libby said, covering the mouthpiece while the caterer put her on hold. "Ask Seymour if he wants vegetable pâté or foie gras."

I padded down the hall to the bedroom. Seymour was horizontal gazing at the ceiling. "Vegetarian or foie gras—the caterer wants to know."

"Veggie." That was it. Not even a Babe, Honey or Darlin' . . . two days before his birthday. . . . Why was he so cryptic?

I walked back to the kitchen. "Veggies, Libby."

She anchored the phone on her shoulder. "Honey, could you run down to the party store? See if they have any purple-and-black streamers and there's a fabric shop on Palm Canyon. Get six yards of

243

black felt for the dining table and pick up three dozen maroon-and-black candles . . . twelve-inch tapers."

Weird, I thought.


*I covered the blistering steering* wheel with a towel and held two ice cubes wrapped in a Baggie against my forehead. Summer's poisonous gas had annihilated the residents. On Friday afternoon I was the only moving vehicle on the main drag. . . . It's a good place to have an obsession. Nothing to distract me. "Libby," I had sighed, "what'll I do. I can't stop thinking about Eric."

"Did you ask Seymour?"

"Uh huh."

"What did he say?"

"He told me I'm lucky to have an obsession. When I get up in the morning, I know what I'm going to do the rest of the day."

"Well, honey," Libby soothed in her wispy voice, "Seymour's got a lot on his mind."

"Is he obsessed?"

"Seymour? Never. He's focused."

"I see," I mumbled to myself, wondering why I was waiting at a four-way stop sign when the nearest car was in Phoenix. . . . Neurotics have obsessions. Normies have focus. . . . Eric. Eric. Eric. I replayed every frame of our time together, locking in the sprockets each millisecond, cranking the cutter's wheel back and forth:

> *Then he*      *but she*
> *or me*      *then we*
> drumming a maddening iambic monometer

> *Why cry I*
> *discover*
> *a lover*
> *then shove her?*
> broken occasionally by an anapest

*Alone*
*I drone*
*He's prone to phone*

*I'll call*
*and bawl*
*He'll fall*
*then crawl*
rivaling the insane trickery of Ravel's *Bolero*

*NO!*
   *I'll write*

                       *tonight*

   *and cite*                                *our fight*

   *as slight*                  *it might*                *ignite*

            *delight*                  *unite*

                       *despite*
                       *his fright*

   *I'm stricken*
   *I sicken*
   *I'm quicken*
   *to chicken*

                 *l*                   *i*
               *o*                   *f*
             *n*
               *e*                 *o*
               *l*                 *n*
                 *y*               *l*
                                      *y*

*I*

   *amplify*
   *vilify*
   *nullify*
   *clarify*
   *magnify*

*crucify*
*rectify*
*candify*

*AND*

*aggravate*
*cogitate*
*vitiate*
*vacillate*
*calculate*
*undulate*
*emigrate*
*liquidate*
*castigate*
*postulate*
*fornicate*

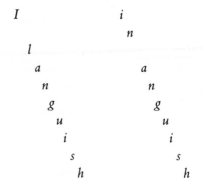

*I*            *i*
           *n*
   *l*
     *a*         *a*
    *n*        *n*
   *g*       *g*
  *u*      *u*
   *i*       *i*
    *s*        *s*
     *h*         *h*

*It's over*
*Rover*
*He's half seas over*

*I plan it*
*I'm granite*
*Oh can it!*

For the past twelve days I've been this way. The affair was only forty-eight hours. My obsession was longer than the relationship.

The fact that I was fired (this time, permanently) didn't bother me . . . and that I had about $2,000 left in the bank. . . . How was that possible? I must have spent my savings to supplement my salary. . . . It goes. It just goes. I have an addictive personality. I can take a year's supply of any product and consume it in two weeks. . . . When Seymour and I stopped in L.A. to pick up my mail, messages and car, I found a series of angry letters between Briard and Rubicon. My name was mentioned so they sent me copies. . . . My mother wanted to know what I've been doing lately. . . . My Cronus exploded for the second and last time, which coincided with the revocation of my driver's license, since I had not met the mandatory requirement of attending ninety A.A. meetings. . . . I did not tell Seymour or Libby because they wouldn't have let me take their Mercedes downtown and that's why I was being very careful and still waiting at the stop sign.

But there was good news. I was sober. I had not had a drink for twelve days or a pill (except for Valium, which was titrated and ordered by the doctor to be administered by Seymour three days after I left the hospital). . . . Pronounced harmless to the general public, I was discharged. Libby and Seymour fed me. I rested, read, and the only withdrawal symptom I noticed was that poetry salad tossing in the rhythm section of my brain.


*I'd been awake for three* hours when I realized something odd about me. It seemed as though a net of gray, which I'd been shrouded in, lifted. Maybe it was Seymour, hugging me at breakfast, saying we'd have a long talk later, or Libby offering to lend me her pink sari for the party. I was part of a family. . . . I hadn't thought about Eric all morning. . . . What was really peculiar, when the Zeitgeist depression evaporated, I was able to identify it. Isn't that terrific! . . . If it didn't return by noon, I would tell Seymour and Libby. I couldn't wait and grinned as I sat cross-legged on the floor in front of the coffee table, writing place cards for the party.

"What'll I do with Shirley MacLaine?" I asked, holding the fold of a card between my thumb and forefinger, flapping it, to dry the ink, trying to sound show biz casual.

"Put her next to Jack Nicholson," suggested Libby, arranging a centerpiece of dried flowers and miniature cacti on Table Five.

Seymour was horizontal, directing the proceedings from the couch that had been pushed against the wall, the Sunday paper on his lap. "No! They didn't get along on that film, *Terms of Endearment*."

I was aware Seymour knew famous people. Michael referred to him as "shrink to the stars," but until I saw the guest list I never realized he knew so many luminaries.

"Well, there's no other place!" Libby sounded exasperated.

"You can put her next to Nicholson," I mediated. "He won't even see her. He always wears dark glasses indoors."

Seymour denied that Shirley and Jack were ever in therapy with him. "Just friends," he said modestly. Seymour was never modest about anything. He was probably upholding his Hippocratic oath even in retirement.

Libby surveyed the room. "I can move Arthur Janov."

"Arthur Janov! The author of *The Primal Scream*!" I wished I had known that before, but Libby had done the *A* to *L* cards. It was too late now. In 1971 I had started Janov's book. There was no way I could finish it by five o'clock.

Seymour pointed to Table Three. "I want Arthur with the seven widows."

Seven widows. A wrench of empathy. "How are they doing?" I sighed.

"Great!" Seymour seemed surprised at my question. . . . "All ex-patients of mine. . . . Three are living with younger men and four went back to school and got their Ph.D.'s."

I stopped feeling sorry for them.

Eleven A.M. Sun blazed through the sliding glass doors. Ten (Abbey Rents) round tables for eight, draped in maroon and ringed by ebony chairs, paid obeisance to the rectangular dining room table, covered in black felt, which had been moved along the side wall with seating for seven on the unraised dais. In eye-blinking light, jet and purple candles in silver holders surrounded parched centerpieces. A Dali hallucination. *Black Mass in Sunlight*.

I liked Libby but she had unusual taste. She reminded me of my friend Cassandra, whose real name was Agnes. Twenty-five years ago, we studied modern dance together. Hank of long, dark hair, tied low in a ponytail. Modigliani face. No eyebrows. She shaved them. (Libby's were sparse.) Both women, inspirationally thin.

"Do you want her at the head table?" I asked, referring back to Shirley MacLaine.

"N. O." Seymour rattled the paper. "She'll read from her new book."

"Because I can sit with Jack Nicholson," I offered.

"No, again," Seymour said patiently. "You're at the head table with Libby."

"Who else?"

Libby leaned over my shoulder. "Dr. Wernicke and his wife." She pronounced it with a V and flipped the page of the guest list to point it out. "But it's spelled with a W—can you read my handwriting? . . . He's Seymour's psychiatrist."

I looked at Seymour. "You have a shrink? How old is he?"

"Otto? . . . Ninety-five."

"And he's coming?" I dipped my pen in the ink, shaking my head. "In this weather?"

"I keep telling you," Seymour said sharply. "It's dry heat."

"That's the kind that kills you," I mumbled.

Libby assured me that he was fine. Most of the guests had checked in Friday or early Saturday at the Racquet Club and Seymour had spoken with Otto earlier that morning. And his wife promised not to get him excited. She's thirty-six.

The crème de la crème . . . An analyst's analyst . . . I imagined Wernicke and Seymour together, vertiginous with enlightenment. . . . I stroked the first letter of the next name on the guest list, certain that people at the party would assume I was somebody since I was to be seated at la Sainte Table. "So, who else is sitting with us?" I asked.

"Khakja Baba Sukmawati."

"I don't think that will fit on a card, Seymour."

"Just write Baba." Libby chuckled. "Everyone calls him that . . . he's a Hindu mystic. Seymour met him in Ranchipur—and he's bringing his friend, Afifi, a Dervish."

Now, I'm not a big laugher, but if you want to put me away, just introduce me to an Indian. Not Eric's kind, but an Eastern one.

There's nothing funnier to me than that clipped dialect; the tone, pitched like a Theramin and boinging in the nostrils, as they nod their head yes when they mean no. "Once," I told Libby and Seymour, "I was in New York and went back to buy earrings from a Pakistani selling them on a street corner. . . . They were gone. 'I'm so disappointed,' I said. 'Don't you have any more?' " . . . I imitated the vendor's nasal quiver: "Oh heedless one! This item finished. This item no more!"

Seymour and Libby laughed and she added, "Then you'll be on the floor when you meet Baba."

I was nearing the end of the cards. A former president's girlfriend, also retired. A designer friend of Libby's (Libby was a textile designer before she quit—much too early—to live part-time with Seymour) and—Oh no!—Zita of Tarzana, the psychologist I had been to last year. "I didn't know Zita was going to be here. She'll Rebirth everyone."

"Not me," Seymour chortled. "But that's an idea. Put her next to Shirley. They'll both be on Planet Trancas before dessert."

Picking up the cards, Libby walked to the couch to show them to Seymour—"Aren't they lovely?"—then turned to me. "I didn't know you could do calligraphy."

"I can't really. Just capital letters."

"Why don't you say 'Thank you,' " Seymour bristled.

"I'm sorry. Did I forget to say thank-you for something?"

Seymour glared at me, putting down his paper. "When are you going to quit doing that? . . . Hello, I'm Babe. I'm sorry."

"I'm sor— I mean . . ." Why was he so testy with me? "I won't do it anymore. I'll use my real name."

"Stop erasing yourself!"

*Ding dong.*

My feelings were hurt but it was Libby that looked weepy, even though she gave me a "Don't let Seymour upset you" smile—and

*Ding dong.*

I bounded to the door—"I'll get it"—grateful for the interruption. . . . On the list of life's stresses, giving parties should come right after death and divorce. . . . It was the man from the liquor store with the tub of ice. It wasn't due until five but he said in half Spanish and English that if he took it back, it would melt on the way and they'd have to charge twice. Seymour barked instructions from the living room. "I ordered fresh ice, and that's what I want!" . . . He was an old man and it was a heavy tub. "Hold on a minute," I said, and ran down the hall to my room and came back with five dollars. Handing it to him, I apologized, "Dr. Kahn is sixty-nine today and he's nervous about it." He wiped the sweat from his forehead into his black hair, rubbed the side of his pants and shook my hand. "Feliz cumpleanos," he said, and promised to bring it back—no charge—later.

"Did you straighten it out?" Seymour asked as I walked into the living room, passing Libby, who was wandering around holding the urn with Rhonda's ashes, looking for a place to put it.

Seymour pointed to the coffee table and Libby set it down.

"Uh huh," I answered. "And he wished you a happy birthday." I wondered why Rhonda was being moved from the kitchen and if they'd want me to write a place card for the memento mori . . . "Oh, by the way, what does your horoscope say for today?"

"Astrology is a disease, not a science!" Seymour snapped.

"C'mon, it's fun!" I couldn't believe I was still feeling good, despite his crankiness. He reached for the paper but I got to it before him and searched the section. "Here it is . . . Moon Children. June 22 to July 21 . . . Isn't the sign called Cancer?" I mused, remembering my cocktail party astrology. "I guess they changed it. Who would want to be born under that sign?"

Seymour tugged at the paper, pulling it from me as my eyes flashed down the forecast with the corresponding Zodiac symbols next to the dates, and I remembered. "Wait a minute! Aren't you a goat? . . . The lady in the party store said that's Capricorn. If you were born today, you're Cancer the Crab. She said I mixed it up . . . all those C's." I walked over to Libby and whispered in her ear, "I always thought he was a goat but I bought him a paperweight with a crab on it."

"That's sweet," Libby said, averting her eyes.

"I don't know," I mumbled. "It's part of my brain damage . . . forgetting things. . . . I'm a fish. Libby's a scorpion. . . ."

I thought I detected a sheepish glance between them, but I

continued: "Didn't we go out to dinner once on Seymour's birthday? . . . In the winter? Sure. It was January, I think." And then, I stopped . . . absolutely still and leveled my gaze at Seymour. "What's going on here?"

Seymour got up from the couch, walked to the den, came back, and handed me an engraved invitation.

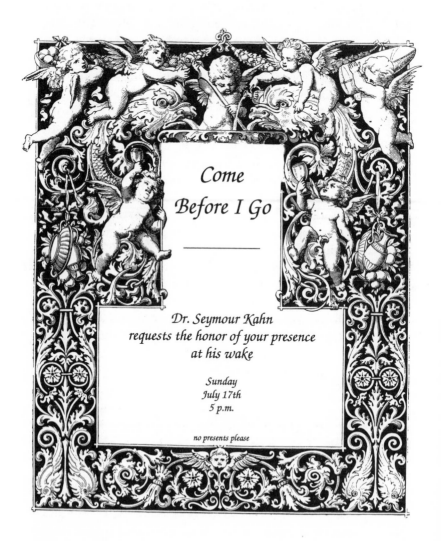

*Come Before I Go*

Dr. Seymour Kahn
requests the honor of your presence
at his wake

Sunday
July 17th
5 p.m.

*no presents please*

Headlong into rice paper. Whirling through borders of black, brushed scrolls. White sound. Then:

"This is not an unfriendly thing that I'm doing."

Ripped. Stripped of coherence. A jaw flaps aimlessly. Eyes blink at an invitation in my hand. How did it get there? . . . Am I passed out standing up? . . . Was there a moment before? . . . Shard of memory. Seymour went into the den . . . came back with this card . . . said he wanted to talk to me . . .

"This is not an unfriendly thing that I'm doing," Seymour repeated, his arm around my shoulders, a concrete block, leading me to a chair, seating me.

Libby held a glass of water to my lips.

"Babe, darlin'," Seymour continued, "I'm going to off myself."

My teeth chunked against the rim of the glass as I swooned forward from a sitting position. Seymour propped me up. I exhaled spurts of horrified laughter. "Is this a joke?"

He shook his head. "No."

"When?" I gasped.

"After the party."

"After the party," I restated. Benumbed.

Seymour lightened his tone. "Well, not before. I want to look 'em in the eye when they eulogize me. How else will I know if they're lying?"

Through a wind tunnel, voices; dense, delayed . . . Libby, stroking my hair. "Seymour, she's not moving. . . . You should have told her earlier."

"You've been watching her. . . . This morning was the first time she's been well enough to hear." He rubbed my frozen hands.

I twitched and dug my nails into his fist. "Oh God! That's it, isn't it? What you said to me in the hospital—about not being able to get it—" I couldn't finish. I didn't know how to say it in front of Libby.

"It's all right, honey." She made me take a sip of water. "I know about it."

Panting, tumbling over my words, fingers gripping up and down his arm, "That's why you're packing it in? . . . What are you missing? How long does sex take, for God's sake? Five, six, eight minutes at the most, with three, seven minutes tops for foreplay, twice a week—not even that—maybe once a month . . . you can have a penile implant—I read an article."

Seymour overlapped, "I wouldn't be able to go downtown in shorts."

"So, wear long pants!" I screamed. "Have it done when the weather gets cooler!"

"Babe, please," he said, freeing his arm, holding me as I trembled. "Listen! It's not only my dick. It's my cholesterol, my heart. . . . I've got a hearing aid in my glasses because I can't stand the damned thing in my ear, so I have to put on my glasses, which I don't need, except to read, in case someone might want to talk to me. . . . Old age is an outrage."

"Cholesterol? So what?" I was off again, selling indulgences. "You can buy Egg Beaters, Imo, Tofutti, String Cheese and—" I stopped. . . . "What's wrong with your heart?"

"I have a severe cardiomyopathy. It's a chronic heart condition which can cause my heart to suddenly go into a chaotic rhythm. . . . I can drop dead at any minute. I don't want to live under a loaded gun." He walked to the coffee table and unwrapped a sugarless candy. A hurricane whipped through my gut. His gray beard was silver fur through my tears. Libby handed me a tissue from her caftan and murmured, "Seymour needs to be in control," then moved to the couch.

I searched their faces. "Can't anything be done?"

"Not really." Seymour popped the lemon drop in his mouth. "Some experiments with an implantable defibrillator . . ." He rattled the cellophane in a shaking, closed fist, and tossed it onto the table, watching it bounce. "Better odds at Vegas."

"Drugs!" I urged, ever faithful to my tenet.

"If you want to live with blue skin, rashes, diarrhea, pulmonary fibrosis and—back to square one—impotency. I'm not into Gnostic suffering."

I whimpered like a little girl, tugging at the hem of the long T-shirt I was wearing. "But you feel well now?"

"I want to stay that way—that's why I'm heading for the cosmic mountain." He gave me a wink, as though that would cheer me up.

"My grandmother used to say, 'Better ten times sick than once dead,' and she'd give two little spits."

Seymour pointed his finger at me. "Don't handle my destiny."

What could I do? Libby was just sitting there, nodding in agreement. Where is she in all this? . . . And Seymour, answering everything flat out. He has a Ph.D. in philosophy. Why doesn't he say something in it? . . . Oh, please don't leave me. I blinked at the living room through my tears. As though a spotlight were playing on a whirling globe of mirrored chips, overhead, sequins of sun splashed on maroon tablecloths, glanced off black candles, and flickered around Rhonda's urn. . . . Don't leave me, bereft of understanding, with only an image of this sepulchral Disneyland. "Why? Why? Why?" I keened.

"What is the opposite of birth?" Seymour asked.

"Death," I blurted.

His face reflected an attitude of weary grandiosity. "That's what most people think, but it's wrong. Life has no opposite."

"Oh God Oh God Oh God. You're going to die and leave me with a conundrum?"

"After Michael died, I told you to read the *Upanishads, The Tibeten Book of the Dead,* and *The Bhagavad Gita—*"

"When you're grieving you don't have time for big books. Besides, if there is no death, why are all those Hindus so hysterical about coming back in any body they can get?"

Seymour sat on the couch next to Libby and sighed. "You know, we should have Xeroxed these questions and answers and included them in the invitations."

"Don't tell me there is no distinction between light and death!" I corrected myself. I had meant to say, life and death, but Seymour smiled and said I was right the first time. Then he told me he was tired of opening doors, parking his car . . . that the radiance of the finite world was over for him and he was looking forward to the ultimate detachment.

What more could I say? Quote some edifying cliché to a Nihilist lunatic? You bet. . . . "Think of your children!"

"I am. I'll be on my way to dropping dead and some yoyo might resuscitate me. . . . You know what a pain in the ass it is to have your kids hover over you in I.C.U.?"

"Honey," Libby finally spoke up, "we've been battling this out for months. The phone hasn't stopped ringing and Seymour's exhausted from explaining." She glanced at the newspaper next to her and read his horoscope. "You see, it says here 'Capricorn: Don't allow your emotions to rule your intellect. Avoid conflict. Stay around people who agree with you this evening.' " She handed him the paper and he threw it on the floor. "Seymour doesn't view death the way you do."

I clenched the sides of the chair, dizzy with disbelief. "And you accept it? . . . Why?"

She gave me a beatific smile. "I want him to be happy."

The woman is senile.

I rocked back and forth, pleading in three little bleats, "Think of me!"

"I did. I need the rest." He took his glasses off. He didn't want to hear—just wanted to sum up: "I vote for an across-the-board demotion of pain and terror. Death is the only physic. . . . I refuse to undergo what Michael went through."

I felt like hitting him. He put his glasses back on. It didn't matter, I hollered anyway. "Are you telling me that clinging to every moment of life is futile?"

"Who clung?" Seymour asked softly. "You or Mike?"

"Both of us!"

"Wrong! He wanted out. You made it impossible for him to die. You wouldn't let go. . . . You still can't."

My body was vibrating. Why wasn't someone putting their arms around me? . . . "In the h-hospital," I stammered, "you told me to fight for what I believe."

Seymour got up, took a chair from a round table and set it down in front of me with a thud. "What *you* believe—not what you think someone else should believe!"

Steadying my knees with my hands, I picked at a blue thread hanging from the edge of my shirt and yanked at it, unraveling the hem. "How do you know that—about Mike?" I asked, curling the crinkly strand into a tight ball, a trace of blue dye bleeding between my sweating fingers.

"He called me."

"When?"

"After the cancer was first diagnosed and then several times over the years."

"What did he say?"

Seymour swung his legs over the chair, straddled it, then seated himself, resting his arms on the back edge. "This is going to be a tough one for you. Michael was concerned about your re-entry into the world after his death. Not because of grief. If anything, grief would become your ally and alibi, because the truth is, you never entered the world in the first place, and he felt he was in collusion with you, as your parents had been. The price you pay for being adored—not loved—there's a difference, puts you in an emotional deep freeze. . . . You better get this because I haven't any time left and neither do you. . . . The terror is in claiming the real self. Alone. Unattached. . . . When you look in a mirror, what do you see?"

His question startled me. Why was he gnawing at my innards at a time like this? I was well now and if he was going to withdraw my comfort by killing myself (I did it again; I mean, killing himself) I'd fix him. I'd drink again. . . . "I hate mirrors," I said.

"I'm not surprised," Seymour continued. "When you look in a mirror it's as though the glass has been removed, and you wait for someone to step into the empty frame. Without their image reflecting you, your attention to reality loosens and you go crazy. . . . Michael wanted to end his life about a year after he found out he had cancer."

My heart was hurting. My legs were numb. "That's not true! He hung on, up to the last minute, hoping to find a cure."

Seymour shook his head. "He knew that wasn't possible. . . . There was something else that kept him alive."

*Ding dong.*

"His love for me!" I stood up, bracing myself on the arm of the chair, waiting for him to agree.

257

"No," he said. "Your dependency."

*Ding dong.* Seymour continued as the bell rang again. "He was a better man than I. I wouldn't pay that price."

Libby got up to answer the door but I was closer to it and ran, flinging it open as I turned back to the living room and shouted: "Committing suicide is against the law!"

Seymour walked toward me. "Attempting suicide is against the law. Committing it is beyond litigation."

The caterers from The Bountiful Feast stared at the three of us and balanced their trays.

## TWENTY-FIVE

*The ferryman arrives at midnight* with a tank of nitrous oxide. That's how he's going to do it . . . boosted into the astral plane like whipped cream. Puffed and fluffy. Laughing all the way.

Why did I stay?

"One favor," Seymour had asked. "Be with Libby tomorrow."

*The tribal rite begins.*

How would I get through the party without booze? . . . I'd been sober two weeks and I was so proud—high on my accomplishment. But now, I started to sweat. . . . What was that I'd heard at an A.A. meeting: "Think your way through a drink? . . . What will happen if you touch one drop of alcohol? You'll end up in the gutter, jail or a looney bin." They were right. A double scotch would not help my anguish. I needed a vat.

259

Reeking with depression, I gulped some sparkling water and tried to focus on the room.

It was impossible to distinguish Jack Nicholson because most of the men were wearing dark glasses. I heard several of them say, as I crossed the room, "Hey, what's happenin'." They had to ask "What's happenin' " because they were too stoned to know.

"Excuse me, can I get through here."

Seymour, resplendent in a long purple velvet robe, a gold medallion blazoning his eminence, had beckoned to me as he held court. He looked like King Lear and I whispered in his ear, as he put his arm around me, "Thou should'st not have been old, till thou had'st been wise." Acknowledging the fool's reproof, he raised his billowing sleeve and proclaimed, "Let copulation thrive!" and introduced me to a stunning woman in a beaded sheath . . . luminous eyes, peach skin, midnight hair caressing her shoulders and a voice that growled upward from her groin, saying, "I'm Danny." As though the group of us that surrounded her had shared centuries of secrets, she/he gave us his/her history: "There was no need for me to have it lopped off. I'm not a transsexual, I'm a transgenderist. My boobs are real . . . I've been taking hormones. . . . See." Danny squeezed the left one and I thought it was going to honk like Harpo Marx's horn, and then giving Seymour a kiss on the cheek she said, "But thanks to my darlin', I still have my prick."

When you hear things like that, it's a good idea to involve yourself in some physical activity so your mouth doesn't hang open, unattended. I dug for the lime slice in the bottom of my glass of Perrier and plastered it, green side out, against my teeth.

"Excuse me, can I get through here."

Forbidden by Seymour to mourn his presence, I detached myself, marking the shape of behavior as I hovered over fuzzy-edged cartoons arriving for the captions, then floating on.

"I don't see Ted anymore. Seymour told me to ask for something less religious than the missionary position."

A tray, spinning like a Frisbee, circled in front of me and I reached for a miniature piece of spinach quiche wondering what to do with it, as two men on either side of me, in jeans, pirate shirts and chains, talked over my head, their breath ruffling my hair:

"People hate me as soon as they meet me."

"Why is that?"

"Seymour says, 'It saves time.' "

"Excuse me, can I get through here."

The air-conditioning was on full blast but as I headed toward the bar, the skirt of my silk sari clung to my clammy thighs, encasing them in culottes. Forced to secrete myself behind two musk-coated women, I overheard:

"Bob's been in analysis seventeen years, four times a week. Seymour says, 'No one is that deep.' "

I tugged at my puckering legs as a bookish fellow took off his glasses and rubbed them in a handkerchief, pretending not to notice. He was standing at the edge of the bar, not talking to anyone, so I waited a few moments, ate my quiche, hoping he'd forget and then walked up to him. "It's very sticky in here."

"That's for sure," the much-too-young-for-me but sweet-looking man said.

Seymour had also forbidden me to challenge his decision by obtaining a quorum, but I had not sworn to bear my sorrow alone, and sighed. "I know we can't do anything, but I'm in such despair about Seymour."

"Seymour who?" he asked.

I stared into his eyes and touched his hand. Had grief rendered him witless or had mourning completed itself and Seymour was already fast forwarded into ephemera?

"Seymour," I said gently, "is our host who is going to die tonight."

He looked flustered. "Isn't this Peggy Burgess's party?"

"No it isn't."

"This isn't 621 Hot Springs Drive, Palm Desert?"

"No. It's 621 Desert Drive, Palm Springs."

He gave a nervous laugh and backed away from me, breaking the line at the bar with, "Pardon me, can I get through here."

No longer floating, now leaden with sorrow, drowning into the aphotic zone, iridescent fish flashed, then vanished as I sank. I had mourned two deaths before their time. My own ego lay incinerated but I would dispose of my ashes later. . . . I'd give Danny's left tit for a comforting conversation.

I searched out Khakja Baba Sukmawati, his walnut-stained and wrinkled face one-third the size of his turban. "Excuse me, Baba . . ." With flattened palms pressed into church-steeple fingers, he bowed to me. My voice broke: "I know there isn't much time left, but could you help me understand?"

Baba nodded, then lifted his head, eyes rolling back so all I could see was the whites, and intoned, "O impetuous one. If there is a worm on a rock, can he not feel the touch of an ant's foot?"

"Huh?"

And that was it, until Afifi, the Dervish, came over and gave him a poke, saying, *"Hahakalrashi zawapati!"* and Baba came to.

A tray of hors d'oeuvres was passed and Baba declined for Afifi, who spoke no English, telling the waiter, "O generous one. Bread and water to a Dervish is like yogurt to a donkey." Afifi, about twenty-five and toothless, grinned and just stood there in his gorgeous spangled bolero and red gauze skirt over pantaloons nipped at his ankles. Asceticism hadn't gone to his clothes.

"Excuse me, can I get through here."

One more try. I looked around for the oldest living man and found Dr. Wernicke propped against the air-conditioning vents talking to Shirley MacLaine. She's very pretty. She was in the middle of theorizing that the protocosmos is six-dimensional and at zero point of limit, existence in time does not embrace the radii of the mesocosmos—and there's some interest in a musical based on it.

The world was simpler when Michael was alive, I thought.

"Pardon me, Dr Wernicke. I'm finding it very difficult to accept this decision of Seymour's."

He answered in an accent as thick as strudel. "I vas saying eggzectly zat to Seymour zis morning. 'Seymour,' I told him, 'suicide iz at best only a temporary solution!' "

Libby, dinging a silver bell, announced that before we sat down to dinner, Afifi would dance for us. The sliding glass doors opened and Afifi stepped outside to the patio as we pressed together, watching him, wafted back for a moment by the sudden inrush of heat.

He lifted one leg, squatted on the other and raised his hands, imploring the stubborn sun hanging over the Aerial Tramway, with a yowling so ferocious and baleful that in another time must have been the call of a Brontosaurus. The coral sun shimmied as he howled and then he began to whirl, covering in dizzying pirouettes the circumference of the pool. With the whipping wind of an ice skater he eddied up and down—a footless, red corkscrew swirling above the cement. Again and again he wound himself round the patio, when suddenly in the pink wash of sunset, he passed through an unbroken pyracantha hedge and was gone.

Baba's voice was heard above the gasps. "O fortunate one. He has fragmented himself."

"He's out there somewhere." Seymour laughed. "Palm Springs is one huge patio."

Libby's bell tolled again, "The gazpacho's getting warm, everyone."


## Soup is slurped.

I am left of Seymour, on the dais, Otto Wernicke next to me, then Mrs. Wernicke.

Crispy dinner rolls crumble and flake on the black felt cloth.

To the right of Seymour is Libby, Baba—and Afifi, who hasn't shown up yet.

Snails clank on china, rolling in a nose-stabbing sauce.

"Ve are not eating," Dr. Wernicke observes, pluralizing me.

I want to throw up.

Every spring, slugs invaded our garden. Sometimes they'd crawl to the back door to look at me, snaking out their pointy-eared heads, drooling their foamy spittle. "Kill them!" I begged Michael. He wouldn't. "I'm not going to rob them of their season," he had said.

clatter chatter chortle

I stare at the guests like Alice at the party in my madder pink sari.

After the salmon mousse . . . what time is it? . . . after the salad, spoons clink against glasses.

Zita, hips like a farthingale, rises from her seat, faces the head table and includes me in her smile even though I had once called her a lunatic. It was a breakthrough for me, but I haven't done it since. . . . What about Eric? No. That was different. I was fighting for my life. I lost. So much for heroic stands. . . . Who knows, maybe one day I'll say, "In my opinion" and let someone have it.

Zita goes on for about ten minutes. "Seymour," she declares, "has reached the penultimate chapter, purging his negative masses . . . blessed with the percipience to surrender pejorative judgment . . . realizing entropically the exigency for ultimate rebirthing, thereby becoming the bellwether for us all."

It's so brilliant, I don't understand a word of it.

That's not accurate. The content makes no sense; however, I know the definition of all those recondite words, although I rarely use them in conversation. When I do, I apologize. It's like I want people to think I'm a dummy or something.

Applause. Applause.

Dr. Wernicke is supposed to speak but he's fallen asleep. Seymour says, "When I went to Otto for therapy, he'd nod off. I was furious when it happened. Otto told me, 'Come up with something interesting and I won't doze!' "

The laughter wakes Wernicke. "Absolutely true!" he snorts, and his head flops down to his chest.

What time is it? How long is a second? The party, clacking on the express train, rattles past me as I lurch back, listening on the local.

An old army buddy of Seymour's tells a story about the time they were stationed in Guam and Seymour was screwing this woman when he heard her husband come home, so Seymour bolted out the bedroom window and climbed up on the thatched roof and waited until it was safe rather than run into the clearing in daylight. Except it wasn't safe, because when Seymour started to get off, he fell through the roof and landed back in bed between the woman and her husband and Seymour spent the Battle of Midway in the hospital with a broken coccyx.

Big laugh.

How many times since Michael died had I fallen through the roof—flailing for the attention of someone I didn't even like?

Margery is the spokesperson for the seven widows. They owe

everything to Seymour . . . their Ph.D's, their sex lives, their children's sex lives . . .

The hyperbole rains like confetti and Seymour beams and guffaws under the colorful shower.

Maybe if Seymour had been my therapist instead of my friend I'd have gone back to school. Michael said I was capable of many things but any compliment sends me into my shuffle/shit dance. I wondered why I stayed married to my denial.

Seymour introduces Baba. They bow to each other with prayerful hands, acknowledging their reciprocal divinities. Baba boings through his nose: "An elephant and an ant spent together a night of love. The next morning the elephant died and the ant cried, 'Now I will have to spend the rest of my life digging a grave!' . . . O no, my friends. We must not be like the ant, for Seymour is the blissful one, passing from time to timelessness, from desire to desirelessness, from vehicle to vehiclelessness"—Afifi wasn't there to poke him and stop that infernal adenoidal ping—"from conscious to consciouslessness"—so Libby touches his hand and says softly, "Thank you, Baba," and he drones down—"from being to beinglessness . . ."

"Ten forty-five," I hear Libby whisper to Seymour and she signals to the caterer waiting at the kitchen door.

Shirley does not read a passage from her book but throws kisses to us all. "See you soon, Seymour," she says, and everyone gives her a standing ovation.

Lights are dimmed. Music. My stomach is marching to *The Galloping Comedians*. I cool my dry mouth with an ice cube. In the pop of flash bulbs, a fiery cake hisses and almost singes Seymour's beard. His purple sleeves ring the fire. A velvet backdrop to *Gotterdammerung*. . . . Blow, Seymour. Blow hard. Blow for all the unbirthdays to come. . . . A parade of snails, whirling Afifis and ants carrying shovels jiggle in candle smoke . . . a barker's pitch, "Hurry hurry hurry hurry. The main event is about to start!" . . . I see Hjalmar in a sandwich board of traveler's checks, waving to the crowd. And circling the arena, Smythe, laid out on his rolling couch—fat Zita on his lap. . . . Ed, the mugger, in prison stripes, drags his ball and chain. . . . "Getch yer popcorn, peanuts, cotton candy!" . . . A silver Cronus wheels in, stops, and tumbling out of its doors, Mrs. Kieps and Kimble in twinkling tutus, pink-eyed Whitey, Dottie in polka dots and the addict with the Milk Duds . . . Eric with a tree under his arm . . . "Hurry hurry hurry hurry!" and behind the car, my elves, all six of the motley bastards, carrying as pallbearers a gigantic bottle of scotch, with me embalmed inside. . . . Whose traveling road show is this? Who is dying here? Who is dead? . . . Seymour in the costume of an Indian merchant rides in on an elephant, a rare bird perched on his shoulder. I push back the haze with my hands, coughing my way through the ragged shadows, as the ringmaster (the buddy from Guam) introduces Seymour's final farewell.

"Ladies and gentlemen. Seymour is moving closer to the front of the chapel, and we are here tonight to pay homage to the nearly departed. I know I speak for all of us when I say—"

"SEYMOUR, IN MY OPINION, YOU'RE A SHMUCK!" And I am up, standing tall, and the music fades out and everyone gasps and sits. For in that Lourdes-like shout, I have tossed the crutch of my lifelong affliction. Disabled thinking.

My voice deepens, no longer lame, but vibrant with authority: "To call you bizarre or unconventional or eccentric is too kind. . . ."

Seymour stands, pulls at my arm, but Wernicke wakes up and says in a loud snap, "Sit down, Seymour! Maybe you'll learn somezink!"

Everything synthesizes, and with intoxicating logic, I continue: "What is in question here is not your right to this madness but your reason. You are the most outrageous narcissist I have ever known. Next to me."

Heads lean forward and dark glasses come off, except for one pair. Libby is glaring at me, but I'm not afraid—although I have to take a sip of water and clear my throat. Careful not to upstage myself, I angle my body, including the guests as I announce to Seymour, "You are so grandiose you can't even die like a normal person. . . . Skip aging? The maturation process? That's the one that takes guts! You taught me that. Remember? . . . You've lived your life through your dick—" More gasps. "And now you can't get laid. Tough. Whatever happened to golf? . . . You want to go from feeling good to feeling good and I go from feeling bad to feeling bad. I did it with booze. . . . You do it with sex." And then I turn to Wernicke because for a second I'm not sure. "Am I right about any of this, Doctor?"

"Abzolutely right!" Otto says. "Infantile eroticism."

Encouraged, I go on: "You see, I'm an alcoholic." Nobody applauds. It isn't a big deal in this crowd. "Life didn't go my way either, so I whipped myself into the dependent position and vanished like Afifi." Suddenly, Afifi staggers in the front door, panting, hanging on to the knob, blasting my metaphor. It's all right. I haven't lowered the big ones. I wait until he takes his seat and gulps down a pitcher of water. I can wait. The audience is in the palm of my hand.

I lean towards Seymour. "You have designed your farce as I have designed mine because neither of us can bear the pain. . . . If you create a circus around yourself, you become one. As soon as Michael died, I joined your circus and everyone else's and I have spent almost two years roving in tents. A flap-footed, pathetic, rejectable, nameless clown. I've played a very cruel joke on myself. And so have you. Only you've done it with more panache. But we've both taken center stage. You became a Theomaniac and now you're stuck with it and have to go out like one. I pretend I'm a piece of shit around whom the world revolves. It's still narcissism. Arrogant and depressive. The flip side of a fake self. . . . You know madmen make history so you're going to kill yourself like a madman, leaving us all 'oohing and aahing.' Go ahead. But don't lie about your motive. Don't try to convince us you're some wise old bird. You're not cheating death. You're cheating reality. Neither of us has ever been able to mourn our losses as adults. We've been too busy throwing that sparkle dust around."

Dr. Wernicke interrupts with an enthusiastic "Ya ya!" and then prods Seymour, whose head is in his hands. "Seymour, is she your patient?" Seymour doesn't answer.

"I'm nobody's patient now." There's a round of applause and I hold up one hand. "I haven't finished." I wish I could see Seymour's face but I can tell by his hair that he's listening. "You know that mirror you told me about? I gaze into it, waiting for someone to define me, while your image is reflected at twice its natural size. But if we knock out the mirror—put clear glass in the frame—it's a window, doesn't reflect anything. It looks out on the world. On a new day . . . You want to opt for transcendental vegetation—go ahead. Not me. I'm tired of taking myself out of life. . . . You see, I'm beginning to think that when Michael died he left me a gift. The promise of a lesson. A chance to become a more resilient, courageous human being. It was a precious gift and I wasted it. But his was genuine. Yours is bogus. So, I don't want your present because I won't learn anything from it, and if you give it to me, I'll return it first thing Monday morning. . . . Remember what Nietzsche said? . . . Ummm. I forget what he said."

"*Amor fati*," Seymour mumbles, his head still down.

"Right. *Amor fati*. The love of your fate. Whatever it is. Say yes to life . . . because under this big top, with all the laughter, there's also grief and confusion. If you don't affirm it, if you say no to it, you've missed the fucking challenge!" Nietzsche didn't say that last part. I did. And it makes me cry. I'm exhausted but I feel wonderful. Not fake wonderful. Real. I take a long look at the crowd, figuring my finish. . . . "Your books are terrific, Shirley, and maybe death *is* swell, but I can't think about that now because I'm only five years old. And Seymour shouldn't either because he's not even three. . . . Baba, thank you. I'm going to quit burying the elephant and I'll read *The Upanishads* and *The Tibetan Book of the Dead*. When the times comes, I'd like to accept death. It's not the American way but I'll try. The reason I didn't read them before was I was already dead but now that I'm going to live, I'll take a look at them. . . . Zita, I apologize for calling you a lunatic, but you really should beam down occasionally. . . . And Seymour. Oh, Seymour, I love you. I'm sorry that I talked about myself"—I lace my fingers together—"but it's all woven into the fretwork."

"On certain magical nights," Michael once said, "the actor and the audience confirm themselves." It feels delicious. I am in the center of the proscenium arch of my life. There is whistling and shouting and cheering and the guests are on their feet surging forward and someone yells, "Who are you?"

Seymour picks his head up, his face flushed. Tears bead on the pouches under his eyes. Two halves of a crystal bracelet. I don't know if he's going to hug me or hit me because his lips are pressed together so tightly the corners upturn in a smiling snarl. The crowd is going bananas. "Who are you?" Now it's a chorus. Seymour extends one hand as though he's going to present me, then lifts the other billowing sleeve, takes a faltering step forward and enfolds me in purple velvet. I cling to him, brushing my face with his beard, inhaling sandalwood. He keeps holding me. His upper body slumps against my chest. "It's okay," I murmur. "Everything's going to be okay." But he won't let me go. I think I should release him—give someone else a chance to be embraced. I loosen my arms. His head falls on my shoulder. I kiss his hair and whisper, "Aren't you going to introduce me?" He doesn't answer. Gently, I separate from him, lifting his chin with both my hands. His eyes stare past me and a blue tint washes his face as he slips through the open circle of my arms and folds into the floor.

# T WEN T Y - S I X

*An hour before his death,* I killed him."

"How long are you going to keep saying that?" Judith asked.

"All those Ph.D.s and there wasn't a doctor in the house. Except Wernicke. He tried to give Seymour CPR and passed out. Besides, it was too late. . . . An hour before his death, I killed him!"

Libby had forgiven me, but a month later I was still saying it. I showed Judith the check. "Twenty-five thousand dollars! What'll I do with this?"

"Start by depositing it," she suggested.

"The will stipulates it has to be used for a business. He knew I couldn't do anything."

I stopped myself. Seymour had forbidden me to think those thoughts. "I mean, why didn't he give me a hint?"

Judith shrugged. She was off to a poetry reading in Venice. I'd promised to go with her, but I just sat there, moldering in my robe, watching the cream cheese squoosh out the side of her Sunday bagel.

"I could publish our poetry," I sighed. "Let's see . . . thirty-two relatives between us, five friends each, at seven ninety-five a copy—that should offset the cost of the printing press, which we could buy used for three hundred thousand dollars."

She poured me a cup of coffee. "My family has my poems. I make copies of them and send a package every Christmas."

"That's nice," I said, stroking my finger along the bottom of the check as she held a paper napkin under my chin, catching a tear that was about to plop on Seymour's signature. "Got any grief poems, Judith?"

"A few. But they're nonspecific." She pulled out a pink flyer from the side of her handbag. "C'mon," she urged. "Get dressed. You know who's reading this afternoon?"

"Who?"

"Phyllis Walker. She's excellent. Kinetic. Vibrant . . . she's into rites of passage."

"Uh huh. Who else?"

"Geoff Metzger. Remember him from our workshop? Elegant images. A celebration of words." She rubbed my hand as though she were trying to get my circulation started. "You really should submit your work again. Whatever happened to those charming triolets of yours?"

"They're in a box with my dirges."

A cartoon light bulb did not go on over my head. It was more like a slow flame traveling a wire. "Let's go, Judith. I'm about to have an idea."

# TWENTY-SEVEN

*You've probably seen them or* you've bought them already. Doubleday, Pickwick, Crown, and Scribners in New York carry the line. We're on our second reorder in six months. They're not sold individually and you won't find them in stationery stores. We call it "Imprints," a collection of art and poetry, fifteen cards in each box. The face of the card is a signed, color reproduction of the work of a new artist and inside each card (the author's name above the title) a poem; not rhyming *sorrow* with *tomorrow,* not rhyming at all, never mentioning graduation, Father's Day, Christmas or death. . . . A poet's song voicing an emotional season. Generic greeting cards.

Our office is in Venice. We split the rent with a Falafel Quick Lunch. Mr. Mouslakhan is on the street side . . . tables are in front now, and we're behind his grill, a six-foot partition separating us. It couldn't go to the ceiling. Fire ordinance . . . smoke has to circulate. But it's wonderful.

272

We have four phone lines and a computer. Geoff's uncle (a printer) deferred full payment when he saw our presentation. Jonathan helped with the photography, overall design and packaging. I, of course, know about ad copy and promotion. . . . And I pay the artists and poets. In money. Plus a percentage.

I go to A.A. meetings. Guess what? I've met three people who have elves in their heads. And I'm trying to investigate my spiritual life. It's been a low-grade search. After all, I've spent years stockpiling an arsenal of compulsive behavior.

Yes, there are times I want a drink or a pill and my hands start to shake. The craving is less frequent now, but when it occurs, I call someone on the program and they listen and talk me through it.

It's been suggested that I develop a belief in a higher power. God? *God* is a word that flips me into a sentence. . . . Dottie, remember Dottie? I saw her at a meeting. She says, "It's God as you understand Him or Her. The group conscience. Nature. Something. Anything. . . . Pray to a bush."

So, at seven A.M. I'm out in my backyard, falling on my knees in front of a hibiscus, praying to be a better person. One morning—I couldn't believe it—and cried to Dottie on the phone, "My bush died!"

"Get a tree," she said. "They last longer."

I'm not honest. I still commit self-robbery. My poem is the only anonymous one in the collection. . . . What am I hanging on to? I'm sober. I make executive decisions. Michael would be so proud of me. And Seymour. Some nights, I call him and listen to the recording: "The number you have reached is no longer in service . . ." and I pretend he's saying, "You're doing great, Babe!" . . . I realize now that I was not responsible for his death, but I am definitely the architect of my own despair. One day, I will have to give up completely my attachment to suffering. When?

## TWENTY-EIGHT

## Den Shadows

*In slanted cellophane light,*
*street lamp's night eye,*

*a silhouette*
*wrapped in blue velour.*
*I roll your sleeves*
*three times over*
*lap the sash twice around*
*and still    the tied ends*
*dangle.*

*At the oak desk*
*I trace a splotch*
*where once you spilled*
*washable Waterman's blue/black ink.*

*The digital clock flips*

*A car passes*
*spotlight scatters*

        *this wooly room*
        *of biscuit and tan*
        *pillows from Spain*
        *posters with your name,*
        *flares at a theater mask*
        *changes its face*
        *from hollow to quizzical.*

*Where are you when I knock?*

        *tilted on this swivel chair?*
        *feet propped up? graceful smile*
        *as I pad in   a poem written*
        *between paper towels and Comet.*

*What does never mean?*

        *I answer my own questions*
        *spin your wheeled eraser*
        *wipe a leaf on a striped plant*
        *tug at a loop in the shag rug*

        *curator of a museum*
        *holding your image*
        *now absent from corners.*

*Next door   blinds are parted*
*Mr. McKenna watches me*
*as I study reindeer shapes*
*on my glass of hot milk*

*This morning he asked,*
*leaning on his cane*
*gnarled as his brogue:*
*"Will ya be cuttin' your roses back this year*
*Ya got to let them breathe   don'tcha know?"*

The walls are bare now. The room stripped of accessories. Only the desk and two chairs. If Bekins is on time, they'll be here at eight. I've found a place near the beach, closer to my office. Small. Funky. But

I can hear the ocean. And I'll double-hang the closets, so I have space for everything.

The street lamp just went off. It must be 6 A.M. . . . I'm still in Michael's robe. I've got to get dressed and finish packing his clothes.

Last night, afraid that I'd forget this room, I sat at his desk and wrote the poem.

Now, in front of the closet, I slide the left-hand panel open and instinctively take a step back, as I've done for almost two years. Jackets and suits on rounded hangers, angled in military precision. After he died, I never touched his "costumes" as he called them, but would view them, as though I were cordoned off by a bell rope.

Breaking through the invisible barrier, I reach for his ties on a rack at the back wall. Silk slips through my fingers. Paisley prints on English red. Taupe with a splash of laughing blue. Marching pin stripes, claret and navy. Ongoing. Separate. Fabric of a life. I carry an armful of ties to a Safeway carton.

Checking the pockets of his suits . . . lint, toothpicks, quarters. I leave them there and fold his clothes neatly into a box.

Then, I stop, to stroke the sleeve of a brown wool jacket he wore early that day, before the ambulance came. I remember he wanted to hang it up himself and I watched him as he gave the shoulder a reassuring pat. My hand travels down to the waist. Sheets of paper edge up under the flap, limp from time, folded to the size of the pocket. I carry it to the window, holding it like a prayer book, press back pages that fight to return to their original crease and shiver in the first light of day as I recognize Michael's handwriting.

> *My darling,*
>
> *Who knows when you will find this. It might be years—because you never throw anything away—or else you'll bury me in this jacket and I'll be stuck with my own letter, but I doubt that, since you will probably choose the black-and-white herringbone.*
>
> *I'd give this to you now, but I don't have the strength for another scene like we had in the cemetery, so I trust you will find it when you need to.*

*I'm worried about you. Worried that after I die, you'll
sit in the big chair near the window, with a tumbler of scotch,
listening to Charles Aznevour records and feeling sorry for
yourself. I'm afraid you will fail at everything—especially
success, because it will be a way of staying connected to me.*

*Remember Robert Anderson's play,* I Never Sang for
My Father, *and the line: "Death ends a life, but does not
end a relationship, which struggles on in the survivor's mind
towards some resolution which it, perhaps, never finds." . . . I
hope you have ended the struggle. What we had is over. You
will always love me. Let it rest now, in a quieter place.*

*Don't stop being curious. Don't knock yourself off. You
are going to have more than one life to live. Forgive yourself for
the lousy affairs you will have. It may not be love. Don't be
too grateful if a man brings you flowers. You're going to have
to learn to decorate your own garden. But if you meet a nice
fella—don't fuck it up. You won't be disloyal to me. . . .
Watch out for con men. I know I sound like your mother, but
I'm enclosing an article: "Widows Are Easy Prey." Don't be
mad. . . . Find work you believe in. Go back to your poetry. . . .
Drown your elves. Every time you activate them it keeps
you little and stuck. Relegate them to the far corners of the
lateral ventricles so any sound they make is muffled by the
sloshing.*

*And don't go running to shrinks. It's like trying to catch
a bird by pouring salt on its tail. There are only six people
who have the answer to the meaning of life and none of them
are psychoanalysts.*

*It's Sunday, September 14th. Will has just gone after
giving me a haircut and you're in the kitchen. The ambulance
is coming at 12:30. I know I have only a few more days.
Don't believe doctors—why do you think I got a haircut? I
didn't mean to shut you out, but while I have some lucid
moments, I want to write this.*

*I have a confession to make. I've read your journal. For
that, I apologize, but you've got it all wrong. I do not define
you. You see, love is not experienced coming toward you—*

277

*it is only felt going out, away from you, towards another. It was not my love for you that made you strong, but what you felt for me and for some reason you have made that insufficient. . . . You have enough courage for twenty people. Help someone else. . . . One last thing. I want you to sit down with your journal. What is it my mother always said, "The palest ink is better than the best memory." You told me you never reread it. Review it. Then, leave it.*

*I am past the fear now and feel a quiet sadness as though I were hearing a calliope from far off. Another town? Somewhere a carnival is going on. I regret I will not be around. I wanted to be half, and only half, of the charming old couple we would have become.*

*I think that love is an agreement to see the world in a certain way, and I will miss the comedy. The understanding we shared, that laughter is pain remembered.*

*The Rabbi will probably quote Solomon from the Book of Ecclesiastics: "For everything there is a season. . . . A time to mourn and a time to dance. . . . A time to be born and a time to die." . . . I hope you listen. It's time to dance.*

*I'm very tired now and have to stop writing. I embrace you and hold you close for the last time.*

*Michael*


*P.S. Why don't you visit Seymour? It'll be fun for you. Just take everything he says with that same grain of salt. I always thought he was a little nuts.*


*P.P.S. Toss this jacket. I never liked it.*


I stared at the pages trying not to cry. He was the only person I knew who wrote with a fountain pen. A Mont Blanc. I didn't want my tears to smear the ink.

Would I have listened if I had found his letter earlier? Would it have changed anything? . . . I knew what I had written in my journal. But I could not admit to Michael what I'd chosen to deny.

278

"There's nothing in that old notebook! I'm throwing it away!"

"Not yet," Michael said, leaning back in his swivel chair.

I lifted one of the boxes and dropped it in front of him. "Look! I'm moving! Doesn't that count?"

"No." He shook his head.

"You want it all, don't you? Death and resurrection—like some Indian rite of passage."

"Could be," he said.

I walked to the one carton in the hall marked "Toss" and unearthed my ragged journal that ended four days after his death. Trembling, I carried it to the den, sat in the big chair near the window and turned the loose-leaf papers to

*Sept. 6*

*Frightening morning. 5:30 a.m. Taking his Percocet, he drops the glass. His hand has developed a violent twist. Loss of motor control. Fingers wander absently to his brow, then plummet suddenly to nowhere, disembodied from his arm. 7 a.m. Trying to get through to him. "Cereal or eggs?" . . . Only a smiling owl stare. Sees me cry. "Don't be upset that you don't understand." Wraps a napkin around a box of straws. Wide-eyed he observes it. "What is the story of this?" I have lived through many changes with him but this is the most dramatic. This dissociation.*

*Later, he asks, "Am I still alive?"*

*"Yes."*

*"How do you know?" he demands.*

*"Because you are eating a tuna sandwich and I don't think they do that in heaven."*

*He smiles.*

*Jack stays with him, 9 to 11, so that I can go to the market, pharmacy.*

*When I come back, Jack is panicked. Mike was disconnected all that time.*

*"Has the cancer affected his mind?" Is it the beginning of metastasis to the brain? Dr. S. calls to see how he's doing.*

*Tough with me on the phone. "You are not going to save his life." I am saving my own.*

*Sept. 7*

*Mike and I on the couch. Falling over with laughter. He says he will never live to collect his social* _in_security.

*The morning is a battlefield between us. Falling to his knees in the shower. Trying to lift him. He's sinking; naked and soaking to the bathroom floor, begging for bed, crawling on his hands and knees. I'm following him—like trying to catch an indignant dog, shaking his hair after an unwanted bath. Clutching at him as he flops atop the covers, moaning. Trying to dry him, crying, "Please! Please! I don't know how to help you anymore!" The struggle to dress him. And we are both exhausted.*

*Friends come to visit. We sit on the patio. He is less vague now and comes out with succinct funny lines. Karl sits next to him. All energy, fighting for him. Mona, swallowing her tears. Carla and Barry, deeply silent. Mike seems lucid until they leave, then asks me, "Was Marlon Brando here?" . . . still the hand flicks out the contents of the glass. I support it with mine and he kisses me on the cheek like a child.*

*Sept. 8*

*Quiet morning. I do my chores, moving him from room to room with me so I can be with him. Like a child in a playpen. But I am not just keeping an eye on him. I need him there for me. Hoping he will turn his gaze outward, again. I need him. . . . He sits in a chair like the old men he always played so remarkably. He showed me how he worked on the part of a ninety-year-old man when he was rehearsing* The Chairs. *Now he has become that, lives it out. He is not acting now. I am stunned by the accuracy of what he once created. He knew it all along.*

*Sept. 9*

*4:30 a.m. He paddles in the kitchen. I sit with him,
watching him drink Perrier and count out his pills. "If they're
doing all these things for me—why am I dying?" I am
frightened. I sense he wants to talk about death as being closer
than we had anticipated. But if I give in, then who will be left
to fight? He answers for me. "Just a little while, let's play the
game, until you realize it can't be played anymore." And I
try—but it doesn't work. I cannot plan beyond the next hour.
And I begin to grieve for myself because I am terrified of taking
up my own life. I know that if I let him go, I will have to face
myself. And I have never—ever dealt with that. It is easier to
keep the illusion going—that I am fragile, that I will never
recover from his death, because I have never been able to
tolerate becoming an adult . . . I sob in his arms . . . I am the
trickster's trickster. It has nothing to do with him. He kisses
my hair. "I don't know what you're thinking . . . but I have
a feeling it's important."*

*He has enough energy to water the lawn and asks for
oatmeal with brown sugar. Small miracle. And he's been
laughing this morning. Aware of his spaciness he refers to an
article in* Newsweek *on teenage sex—"I thought it said
'Mexican sex.'"*

*Sept. 10*

*His dreams are horrific. Combinations of secret plots to
exterminate him. Sophisticated, coded spy messages. A book
where the names of those who will die is circulated, covertly.
Only aliases of the real names are listed. Bells, noisy demons,
clanging, ringing, coercing him to join them. He is trapped in
his fantasy. This so real nightmare. Chemotherapy.*

*Sept. 11*

*Writing in my journal—he comes toward me. 5:30
a.m. Light stinging his eyes as I sit in the kitchen. Bouncing
his body off the hall walls to the bathroom. He didn't want*

my help. *He looks like those pictures of Auschwitz.
Cancer—the visible enemy. It has taken everything from him.
Crippled him, haunted him, annihilated and humiliated him.*

*I run errands—run. Now I am the one who is
disconnected. Constantly forgetting what I'm in the store for.
Finding myself repeating phone numbers three times. I've
developed dyslexia. . . . He is less spacey today but so weak. I
have to help him off the toilet. Always our hands outstretched
toward each other. Who is helping who?*

*Sept. 12*

*We sit tonight holding hands and we talk about dying.
"What's out there?" he asks. I don't deny or argue anything
he wants to talk about now. I've begun to experience a quiet
acceptance. "I don't know," I answer. "Maybe it's
good—like all the times you took chances and it turned out
well." He nods. "You mean dying is like going to
California?"*

*Sept. 13*

*David and Nancy call and ask if they can come over.
They've just seen Michael's last film. David sits on the edge
of the bed, talking to Mike. He adores him. Nan and I walk
around the block. She tells me about a time when she almost
died and they pounded on her chest, resuscitating her. How
angry she was. "They brought me back to live in this garbage!
It was so damned beautiful when I died." As they leave,
David wiping his eyes, says to me, "Well, you seem to be
bearing up all right." I tell him this acceptance does not mean
an absence of hope. That I am learning to live in the "now,"
that I am past the rage and my own terror. He looks at me
like I'm stoned, stupid or brainwashed.*

*"Never mind," Michael tells me later. "You don't have
to convince everyone." . . . We lie in bed, stroking each other.
It is a time of soft remembrance. We have passed the fear.*

*Sept. 14*

Will, his barber, comes to the house. Mike sits up—like
a child at his first haircut, with a dazzled smile. And he is
wrapped in sheets—to catch the blood. He wanted an hour
alone in his den. No Percocet for two days. Seemed stronger
than in weeks. Got dressed. An hour or so later he
hemorrhaged. He wants this haircut, even though he knows
the ambulance is coming for him at 12:30. "I'm not bleeding
that bad." But he is. He wants the hospital. It is
overwhelming for us to handle. He apologizes because we had
chosen to die at home. . . . Two attendants move a stretcher
into the den and lift him onto it. He is all bones now.
Willing. Pliant. I am in shock in the front of the ambulance as
we drive to Cedars. On this bright sunny day, he is dying.
The attendant sips a soda pop as we drive—he is dying. The
intercom blasts as he is dying.

*Sept. 15*

Settling him into a super-deluxe room—the eighth floor,
usually reserved for senators and Arabs. No matter. Whatever
it costs. I can sleep on a cot, next to him. Dr. G. comes. Dr.
S. Dr. P. . . . all of them corroborate metastasis. . . . But
Mike seems comfortable here. His favorite nurses, remembering
him from his second operation. Shirley, who keeps saying
she'd rather see him on Broadway. Valerie, bringing him a toy
clown. . . . He eats a little more, sipping Ensure through a
straw. . . . I watch him, waiting for his shot of Demerol to
take effect. And we both sleep, praying he will not have
nightmares.

*Sept. 16*

3:30 p.m. No doctor has shown up. Only a woman
from patient relations—explains that deluxe rooms are
automatically charged $60 extra for the evening meal. Do I
want it changed to a standard menu? Michael tells her that

*it's not like going to the electric chair. When you're dying of
cancer you don't feel like ordering lobster tails for your last
supper. . . . Dr. A. finally arrives. I am angry because they are
staying away. There is nothing more for them to do? He puts
the question of "Code Blue" to me. "If Michael's heart
should fail, do you want us to save him—try to bring him
back—temporarily—only to have him die twice?" . . . We
were standing out in the hall. The tile floor floated up at
me. . . . Dr. A. put his arm around me, waiting for my answer.
"No. No." I walk back to the room and sit on Mike's bed.
He takes my hand. "I hope you told the doctor no. . . . It's
very hard to die between creamed spinach and Jell-O."*

*Wed. Sept. 17*

    *Pink sunrise. Crystal and rose. 6:30 a.m. Noticing the
change of shift. He had a bad night. Vomiting, moaning, not
too coherent. Said something about a bicycle. I held his hand,
kissed him and arranged a signal. If he could not answer he
would squeeze my hand. Once for yes. Twice for no. I went
out of the room for one or two five-minute intervals. Coffee. A
cigarette. 8:30 a.m. When I came back into the room I heard
a gurgling sound. Is there a machine on? No. A sudden
bubbling sound from his chest. Oxygen clips in his nose to ease
the breathing. A nurse, Lee, trying to suction the congestion
from his chest. Michael, fighting her violently. "No, darling,"
I tell him. "It's not a permanent tube—just to relieve you. I
promise you, Michael, no one will torture you anymore." His
words, clear. "Thank you, darling." . . . Dr. A. comes at 9.
Late. Apologizes to me. Thinks it will be two or three more
days. How did it happen so fast? Why? Pneumonia in his
lungs. . . . We sit quietly. The head nurse comes in. More
nurses. Blood pressure has dropped rapidly. They leave the
cuff, attached. They try to change his position but he wants to
stay on his back, not his side. "Leave him there," I tell them.
"I think he wants to talk and see." The head nurse tells me,*

*"No matter how prepared you are—you are never prepared. . . .
Talk loudly. The hearing is the last thing to go." I start a
dull, stunned litany: "I love you. I love you." He squeezes
my hand, once. Yes. . . . "We will always be together."
Rapidly, he presses my hand, twice. He does not want me to
say that. . . . "I've had a wonderful life with you." Yes.
"God will take care of us. I will have the courage to live my
life, without you." Yes. . . . "I bless you for the gifts you
have given me." . . . The nurses confer about a pain shot. He
squeezes my hand. No. He does not want to be drugged.
Shirley comes in, beyond professional concern, deeply caring. I
pull her outside the room. "Is it really happening now?" I
demand. It is really now. She nods in agreement. Suddenly,
no more bargaining for years, months, days. I want hours.
Minutes. I devise a way of taping the oxygen line to a
washcloth against his cheek. He seems to want to speak, but
the bar from the nose clip impedes his upper lip. He calls my
name. Loudly. Clearly. Crooning to each other. Alternately.
Together. I love you. I love you. A nurse comes in at one.
Checks her watch against the wall clock. He trembled.
Shivered. I put another blanket on him and he said, "No
touching! No touching!" but then, warmed, he reached for my
hand again. The bubbling sound, his struggle to breathe,
vanished—for ten minutes or was it five or two. I remember
his last breaths. Clear. Easy for him. Then, suddenly, his
eyes, which had been previously closed, popped open—wider
than I'd ever seen—and looked straight at me, enveloping
my face. Then two more deep, sighing breaths . . . and that
was all.*

*Sept. 18*

*Images from a filmstrip, flapping out of sync. . . .
Handing clothes to a Mr. Moriarity. From the mortuary. Had
I met him before? No. Mike had. What? Oh yes. Give him
the check Mike had made out. Top desk drawer. Just fill in*

*the date. . . . Stroking the black-and-white herringbone jacket.*
*Selecting a tie. Red. Putting his favorite poem of mine in the*
*left side pocket. It was not real. Mike was somewhere on*
*location, had forgotten something he needed—gray flannel*
*slacks—and this somber man would bring it to him. Shoes?*
*No. Shoes weren't necessary. Underwear and socks in a small*
*shopping bag. He took the clothes and the check and left in the*
*hearse that was parked outside.*

*Sept. 19, 3 p.m.*

*We didn't get lost. Mona and I in the car, talking about*
*Thomas Wolfe's short story* Only the Dead Know
Brooklyn. *I had arranged who went in what car, typed up*
*directions, included Mike's map to the cemetery. . . . We all*
*got there forty-five minutes early (Mike would have been*
*pleased) except Janet, Mike's cousin, who came stumbling up*
*the slope, clutching her car keys, late as usual.*

*Prayers in English and Hebrew. Each of us taking a*
*handful of earth, dusting the coffin, immediately followed by*
*the thwacking sounds as shovels of dirt covered the polished*
*pine box. Then, Janet, sinking to her knees, crying, "Oh*
*my God!" Michael had been buried with the keys to her*
*Cadillac.*

*Sept. 21*

*I sat in the chapel crowded with friends as the Rabbi*
*recited: "For everything there is a season, and a time for every*
*matter under the heaven . . ." and I wondered what I would*
*do Monday. Seymour had called. Maybe I'd visit him in*
*Palm Springs. Voices in the background. Friends, eulogizing*
*Michael. And then the Rabbi: "It is not easy for a Rabbi to*
*speak at a memorial service. It is harder for a friend. It must*
*still be harder for a wife. A man's death is felt by many*
*people, but the Talmud says: A man dies only unto his wife,*
*for it is her life that is most radically changed, and it is she,*

*who has the closest message to bring. And so, I would like to
present*

Tears wash the last word in the journal. I can't read my name,
can't stop sobbing. . . .

Michael is standing at the window, looking out.

I know he does not want to talk about his death.

Wrapping Michael's robe closer around me, I reach into the
pocket and dry my eyes with one of his handkerchiefs.

When my breath is quiet, I try to sum up a life of pretense. "I
was duped by my self-appointed dependence."

He turns. "That's a fancy way of putting it, but you're right."

"And you waited—for a sign that I would survive without you."

Michael studies me for a long time, as though there's something else I haven't understood, then asks: "Any idea what time
it is?"

"No. I packed the clock."

"The movers are here." As he says it, the doorbell rings.

"I'll be right back!" I run down the hall, past the living room
piled with boxes—suddenly, skid to a stop—realizing what I have
to do.

My handbag is on the entry table. I take out my wallet and
open the door.

Two men are on the front porch. Abbott and Costello. Bekins
has stitched "Bud" and "Lou" to their coveralls. I can finally tell
who is who.

"Bud," I say to the tall thin one. "There's been a change."

Lou, who's short and fat, looks up at Bud. "She's not moving?"

"Yes, I am. However, my attachments are not the world's
glue."

"Waaait a minute!" wails Lou and I laugh.

Bud interprets: "She's not taking her stuff, Lou."

"Oh, yeah! Well, what'll she sit on, Bud?"

I give my rear end a double pat and hand them each ten dollars.
Lou shrugs.

Bud tips his cap. "It's your life, Babe."

I want to get back to Michael, but I watch them go down the steps, waiting until they're almost in the truck.

Then, from the front porch, I shout to the early morning street, "Dorothy! My name is Dorothy!"

I race to the den.

Michael's gone.